Praise for

Sandy Hingston's novels

"Hingston strikes the perfect balance of history, modulated characters, and snappy dialogue that is what all romance should aspire to be—transporting."

—*Publishers Weekly*

"An altogether delightful love story! Sandy Hingston's words leap from the pages and wrap around your heart! A lovely romance sure to keep readers turning pages late into the night! Ms. Hingston has crafted quite a gem . . . most entertaining . . . beautifully written."

—*The Literary Times*

"The story line humorously centers on high society's strict rules. Sandy Hingston is heading to the top."

—Harriet Klausner

THE SUITOR

Sandy Hingston

BERKLEY BOOKS, NEW YORK

THE SUITOR

A Berkley Book / published by arrangement with
the author

PRINTING HISTORY
Berkley edition / July 2002

Copyright © 2002 by Mary Sandra Hingston.
Cover illustration by Leslie Peck.
Interior text design by Julie Rogers.

Visit our website at
www.penguinputnam.com

ISBN: 0-425-18543-5

BERKLEY®
Berkley Books are published by The Berkley Publishing Group,
a division of Penguin Putnam Inc.,
375 Hudson Street, New York, New York 10014.
BERKLEY and the "B" design
are trademarks belonging to Penguin Putnam Inc.

PRINTED IN THE UNITED STATES OF AMERICA

10 9 8 7 6 5 4 3 2 1

For Larry Stains,
still a true believer

The heart has its reasons,
of which reason knows nothing.

—BLAISE PASCAL

Prologue

Mrs. Treadwell's Academy for the Elevation of Young Ladies
Kent, England
June 1813

"Oh, Martha," Bessie Boggs said with a heartfelt sigh. "That is absolutely, utterly, the most beautiful wedding gown that I have ever seen."

"You truly like it? Does it suit me?" Martha Westin stood in front of the small mirror in their shared suite at Mrs. Treadwell's academy, leaning this way and that to try to catch a fuller glimpse of her reflection in the gown of creamy damascene.

"As feathers suit swans," Gwen Carstairs assured her, coming up behind Martha with the bridal headpiece in her hands.

"I can't believe how lucky you are," Bess said wistfully. "Why, you've only been here for three months, and you're already getting married! You make me feel quite hopeless as to my own prospects."

"Nonsense," Martha said stoutly. "You forget, Peter and I have known one another since we were children. It was always understood between our families that someday we'd wed."

"That doesn't mean he had to go through with it, though," Bess countered, watching as Gwen gingerly settled the tiara of seed pearls and peridots atop Martha's upswept chestnut curls. "Lord Fanning has turned out to be quite the catch."

Gwen shot Bess an amused glance. "So is our Martha, Bessie."

"Oh, I didn't mean it that way!" Bess flushed crimson. "Of course you are, Martha!"

But Martha was laughing. "Never mind, Bessie. Believe me, I am every bit as overawed as you." Her hands smoothed the lustrous fabric of the gown, and her gray eyes glistened. "I have loved him from forever. How I hope that I will make him happy!"

Bess swooned dramatically onto her bed. "I want to fall in love!"

"Peter has several very eligible cousins," Martha assured her. "You will have the opportunity to meet them at the wedding."

"With you in that gown, no one is likely to so much as glance at me."

"Ah, but I shall be taken!"

Bess brightened slightly. "So you will. Well, who knows? Miracles do happen, they say."

The door to the suite had opened as she spoke, and a tall, cool blonde stepped into the room. Bess, who had been about to say more, fell silent, and Martha's hands went rather nervously to her skirts once more.

"*Don't* tell me," the blonde drawled, looking Martha up and down, "*that* is what you're wearing for your wedding."

"Oh, do hush, Katherine," Gwen said sharply.

Bess spoke up then, too: "Why shouldn't she? It is a *lovely* gown!"

The blonde shrugged. "Well, she can please herself, of course, but . . ."

"What is wrong with it?" Martha asked uncertainly.

"Don't you listen to her, Martha! She is only out to spoil others' happiness—as usual," Gwen told her friend.

Katherine Devereaux arched her exquisite brows. "On the contrary! My only intention was to save her from embarrassment."

Martha blanched. "*What* embarrassment?"

"I merely meant the sleeves."

"What is wrong with the sleeves?" Martha demanded, her voice edging upward.

Negligently Katherine crossed to the wardrobe, taking off

her hat. "Never mind. I'm sure it's nothing anyone in Lord Fanning's set will notice."

"Lord Fanning's set?" Gwen said in astonishment. "Good heavens, Katherine, not even you could possibly find fault with Lord Fanning's set! He is the catch of the season!"

Katherine unclasped the necklace of very sizable pearls she was wearing and laid it in her jewel case. "Rather a grim reflection on the season."

"Why, you jealous thing!" Bess cried indignantly. "Just because Martha has made a match of it and you haven't—"

"You forget—I am a duke's daughter," Katherine noted. "There are rather fewer suitors in my elevated sphere."

"There aren't *any* suitors in your sphere," Gwen muttered, "so far as I can tell."

"Lord Fanning is an earl's son," Bess said triumphantly. "A *first* son, too, at that. And from a family with a long and distinguished pedigree."

"I suppose," Katherine replied, looking down her elegant nose at Bess, "it would seem long to *you.*"

Martha squared her small shoulders in their swath of ivory damascene. "Are you insulting Lord Fanning?"

Gwen laughed. "For heaven's sake, Martha, don't pay her any mind. Surely you've been around *Lady* Devereaux long enough to recognize that she never has a kind word for anyone."

But Martha didn't seem inclined to let the moment pass. Her cheekbones bore bright blazes of crimson, and her fingers clenched her skirts so tightly that her knuckles were white. "She may say what she pleases about me, but by God, I'll not stand by while she insults Peter!"

Bess hurried forward to give Martha a quick hug, her forehead creased in concern. "She meant nothing by it, did you, Katherine?" There was a pause. "*Did* you, Katherine?"

Katherine raised her head on her long, white neck. Her amazing golden ringlets gleamed in the late-afternoon sun that streamed through the windows; her azure eyes shone as well; and her mouth, a pouf like summer's last rosebud, formed a glorious smile. "I think Lord Fanning is the perfect match for you, Martha," she said. "After all, his great-great-great-grandmother is said to have been King James's second-favorite whore."

Bess drew her breath in sharply. "Jesus, Katherine!" Gwen said in genuine shock. And Martha rocked a little on her heels, as though she'd been struck.

"You'll excuse me now, I hope," Katherine said breezily, catching up the bag that held her needlework. She cast one last look at Martha's wedding gown. "Pity about those sleeves." And she swept toward the door.

"You." The stark word as Martha spoke it made even Katherine hesitate just a little, her slim fingers on the doorknob. "You hold yourself out to be so high and mighty."

"But I *am* high and mighty," Katherine said complacently. "I am the only child of the duke of Marne."

"And what about your mother?"

"My mother," Katherine retorted, "was also of impeccable pedigree. She was the heiress to the duke of Southerby."

"So she was," said Martha, her voice low and tight. "What do you imagine she would have made of the woman who succeeded her into your father's bed?"

"What's all this?" Bess asked curiously.

But Gwen, who had seen Katherine's blue eyes narrow in an altogether unaccustomed manner, said in caution: "Martha . . ."

"What? What of it? She has said wretched, wretched things about the man I love!"

"You had best mind your tongue," Katherine warned her.

"Why should I, when you never mind yours? You may say what you like about Peter's family, but you may be sure no one in his line ever stooped to marrying—"

"Who? What?" Bess demanded avidly.

But Gwen broke in: "Do you know, I think it's time for tea. Shall we go downstairs?"

"I would stop now," Katherine told Martha, "if I were you."

"But you're not me, are you? You only wish you were!"

"That," Katherine drawled, "is the most preposterous notion I have ever heard."

Martha, wild-eyed, turned to Gwen and Bess. "Did you never wonder why the great heiress to the duke of Marne is sequestered here at Mrs. Treadwell's instead of making her debut in London? After all, she's well past the age when ladies of *her set* usually come out."

"The question has crossed my mind," Bess admitted. "Every five minutes or so."

"How long, Katherine, do you reckon it will be before the furor dies down—before you'll be acceptable to society? How long has it been already—six years?"

"Since what?" Bess demanded.

"Martha, please," Gwen said again, but with an air of resignation.

"I don't need to stay here and listen to such folderol," Katherine snapped. "I could go to London anytime I choose! I may very well go tonight!"

"Who did her father marry?" Bess fairly screeched.

Martha finally unclenched her hands. "Surely, Bess, you have heard of Nanette O'Toole."

"Nanette O'Toole! Of course I have! I never had the honor of seeing her perform, but my father told me she was the most accomplished actress of her—" And then Bess's eyes went saucerwide. "Nanette O'Toole is your *mother,* Katherine?"

"My *stepmother!*" Katherine cried in fury. "My stepmother and nothing more!"

"But she's Irish!" Bess said, bewildered.

Gwen couldn't help it; she began to laugh. And then Martha joined in. "Irish is the least of it!" she said, giggling helplessly. "She'd had dozens of lovers—but they were all of the *topmost* echelon, weren't they, Katherine? All very grand . . . but none so rich as your poppa. He got himself taken in by a common fortune hunter, didn't he?"

Katherine had leveled a finger at the slight figure in bridal finery. "You'll be sorry you ever said that," she pronounced, so coldly that Gwen, at least, stopped laughing and shivered.

But Martha's merriment only increased; she doubled over, clutching herself, giddy.

"Why?" she managed to ask. "It is no more than the truth."

"Nanette O'Toole!" Bess marveled. "Lord, I would give anything to meet her!"

"Don't give up hope," Martha said through her giggles. "I'm sure the scandal will die down any day now, and she'll venture out into society."

"Martha, that's enough," Gwen said, sounding very sober. Katherine took a step toward Martha, and Gwen quickly moved between them. "Let it be a lesson to you, Katherine. Even the meekest dog will bite if you tease him enough."

But Katherine had recovered her composure; she shook her golden curls with insouciance. "It's of no import to me what she says about me," she announced coolly, calmly. "Little people always want to drag everyone down to their own level, don't they?"

"I should say your father did his own dragging—"

"Martha!" Gwen burst out. "No more!"

"She ought not to have said what she did about Peter!"

"No. She ought not have," Gwen said thoughtfully, as Katherine, silk skirts swishing, turned and left the suite, closing the door with a curt click. "But oh, Martha. I do hope you haven't gone too far."

One

Christiane, the countess d'Oliveri, rapped sharply on the box to catch the driver's attention. "Faster, please!" she shouted above the rattle of the carriage wheels. The driver's voice floated back to her on the wind:

"Can't get no more from this pair, mum."

"Then stop as soon as you can and change them! I *must* get to London immediately! It is a matter of—" Christiane's voice caught in her throat, like a sob. "Oh, God. Of life and death."

"Well, it always is, ain't it," old Stains, the driver, muttered, but he did crack the whip.

Christiane sat pressed hard against the seat, hands knotting and unknotting in her lap. In the two years since she and her childhood friend, Mrs. Evelyn Treadwell, had founded their academy for girls in the hope of liberating the fairer sex from the strictures society set on it, this was the worst crisis they'd faced. She would never forget the way the expression on Evelyn's round face this morning had changed from happy anticipation—"Do look, Christiane, it is a letter from dear Martha's mamma!"—to blood-drained shock: "Oh, God in heaven . . ." And the letter had fluttered from her hand.

Christiane had snatched it up, scanned it, and felt her heart stop. She'd blinked, looked again, certain she'd misread the missive, but the words Lady Violet Westin had set down in a hurried, crabbed scrawl utterly unlike her usual handsome penmanship remained unchanged.

"Why would she *do* such a thing?" Evelyn had wailed, reaching for her hartshorn.

Much as Christiane adored Evelyn, there were times when her tendency to go to pieces were most unhelpful. "Violet says something about a rumor," she'd noted briskly. "It's damnably hard to tell what she means, but it seems someone has impugned Martha's virtue—and that Lord Fanning took it enough to heart to question her about it."

"But to try to *kill* herself—" Evelyn was shaking. "Oh, Christiane, imagine the scandal! Poor Martha!"

"Take hold of yourself," Christiane told her sharply, ringing for the maid. "Clarisse, bring Miss Carstairs and Miss Boggs at once."

"Yes, ma'am." The maid bobbed a curtsy and withdrew. A few minutes later, Gwen and Bess entered the headmistress's parlor, took in Mrs. Treadwell's ghastly pallor and the grim look on the countess's face, and exchanged a glance.

"You sent for us, Madame?" Gwen asked; "Madame" was the address the countess had instructed the girls to use.

"I assume," Christiane told them evenly, "I can rely completely on your discretion?" The girls nodded. "We've had some dreadful news from London. It seems Martha has . . . has . . ."

"We are ruined!" Mrs. Treadwell screeched.

"What in the world has happened?" Bess asked, bewildered.

"We aren't altogether certain. But we've had a letter from Martha's mother. It seems Martha made an attempt to—to end her own life."

"Martha?" Bess cried in shock. "Oh, no! That can't be!"

Gwen echoed her: "There must be some mistake!"

"As I say," the countess went on, as Mrs. Treadwell swooned on the settee, handkerchief pressed to her mouth, "the details are unclear. But Lady Westin makes reference to some scandalous rumor regarding Martha that reached Lord Fanning's ear, and had sufficient verisimilitude to cause him to question Martha as to—"

"Katherine," Gwen said suddenly, quite unexpectedly. "That *bitch*."

"Gwendolyn Carstairs!" Mrs. Treadwell exclaimed. "Such language!"

"What do you mean, Gwen?" Christiane demanded.

"I was afraid of something like this. Bess, you know you were, too! After that scene between them—"

"Oh, but Gwen! Think what you are saying!" Bess breathed. "Even Katherine surely wouldn't—"

"What scene?" asked the countess.

"It wasn't anything so grave as all that," Bess protested earnestly. "It was only Katherine being haughty and hateful, as she always is. She said something biting about Lord Fanning's family, and then Martha—and it was really most unlike Martha, you know, because she always *is* so sweet and kind—"

Christiane held her temper, with an effort. "What did Martha do?"

"She was only teasing!"

"It went beyond teasing, if you ask me," Gwen put in. "Didn't I say at the time, Bess, that I hoped Martha hadn't gone too far?"

"Yes, but—"

"What—did—Martha—do?" the countess asked from between gritted teeth.

"She . . . said some dreadful things about Katherine's stepmamma," Bess admitted. "Some really quite dreadful things."

On the settee, Evelyn gasped, "No!" And Christiane sagged a little at the knees.

"I don't understand, though," Bess went on thoughtfully, "why anyone would be ashamed of having Nanette O'Toole in her family. My father saw her play Cleopatra once. He said by the end, there wasn't a dry eye in the house."

The countess had recovered. "Thank you very kindly for the information, girls. You may return to your rooms. And would you be so good as to send Katherine down to me?"

"One doesn't 'send' Katherine anywhere," Gwen noted as they went out. "But we'll do our best."

"Just you let me do all the talking, Evelyn," the countess cautioned her old friend sternly after the young women were gone. "Not so much as a peep!"

"I am too shocked for words," Mrs. Treadwell declared, pouring a glass of sherry. "Would you care for some?"

"I rather think I had best be dead sober for this interview."

Katherine swept into the parlor in a fetching day-gown of embroidered Swiss muslin, her curls pulled to one side in a becoming chignon, her lovely face as radiant as spring. "You wished to see me?" she inquired of the two ladies, with a pert little curtsy.

Christiane restrained an urge to slap her. "Sit down, Katherine." The girl settled nonchalantly into a chair. "We've had some news from London."

"Have you?"

"Some news about Martha."

"You don't say. Oh, for gracious' sake, will you look at that? I have chipped a nail."

From the corner of her eye, Christiane saw Mrs. Treadwell gathering breath, and hurried to forestall her. "It seems some sort of innuendo regarding Martha reached the ears of her betrothed, Lord Fanning. Whatever the calumny was, he was sufficiently alarmed to question Martha regarding it."

"Sensible thing to do," Katherine murmured, still examining her manicure.

"Following their interview, Martha attempted suicide."

There was the merest twitch of the muscles in Katherine's throat before she said, "Dear me. How very melodramatic. I shouldn't have thought she had it in her. But then, with those quiet ones, you never know."

"Mrs. Treadwell and I wondered," the countess went on, with another warning glance at the headmistress, whose face was turning more red by the moment, "whether you had any inkling of indiscretion on Martha's part during the time she was here."

Katherine held her hand out to contemplate the effect of the broken nail. "I shall have to trim them all down; what a nuisance. Forgive me, what were you saying?"

"Oh, you unnatural, unfeeling creature!" Mrs. Treadwell exclaimed in horror. "The countess informs you one of your schoolmates has tried to kill herself, and you fret over a broken fingernail?"

Katherine shrugged prettily. "I really don't see what it has to do with me. If Lord Fanning is suspicious enough to believe what someone pens in an anonymous letter, and Martha isn't secure enough in his love for her to belie his qualms—" She glanced up. Mrs. Treadwell had gasped. "What?"

"No one made any mention," the countess said, "of an anonymous letter."

"Oh," said Katherine. "Really. I rather thought you had."

Mrs. Treadwell had risen from the settee to her full, if unappreciable, height. "Katherine Devereaux! What devilment have you been up to?"

Katherine stood, too, and her cool eyes flashed. "It is beneath my dignity to be examined and chastened like some common dowdy. I'll thank you to recall that I am the duke of Marne's daughter." She turned on her heel and glided toward the door. On the threshold she paused. "Had Martha recalled as much, she would not be in such straits now. Good afternoon." And she shut the door in her wake.

Mrs. Treadwell stared after her, openmouthed. "The—the brass of that girl!" she finally sputtered. "Why, she as much as boasted of it! She is a pernicious influence, Christiane! I won't have the other students exposed to her any longer. We must expel her instantly!"

"It is not so simple as that, Evelyn." The countess nibbled her lip. "You know that Richard and Nanette are in Russia on the Crown's business. They made me responsible for Katherine in their absence. She *is* a duke's daughter. I cannot turn her out on the street!"

"It would serve her right," the headmistress snapped, just before collapsing onto the settee again. "Whatever are we to *do*, Christiane? If Lady Westin should ever suspect that one of *our* girls is behind this mess . . . why, it would be the end of the academy!" And she dissolved into tears.

Christiane, too, was tempted to despair. But if life had taught her anything, it was that one could not afford to panic in a crisis. She squared her shoulders and raised her chin. "The first order of business, naturally, is to go and set things right with Martha and Lord Fanning. I shall leave for London immediately."

"Yes, of course," Mrs. Treadwell whimpered. "And . . . after that?"

"After that," the countess said darkly, "I intend that you and I, Evelyn, should put our heads together and come up with a plan to somehow, someway, tame our incorrigible shrew!"

A brisk shout from Stains roused the countess from her reverie. "There's the last signpost, mum! Five more miles is all!"

"Five miles . . ." Christiane put the problem of Katherine's chastisement from her mind, to plot and plan how she might make amends between Martha and her young man. After all, the best remedy for Katherine's mischief—though this time the girl had ventured far beyond mischief—would be to have the wedding go forward in triumph. And to achieve that, the countess would have to counter not just Katherine's poison, but the breach it had effected between two souls who, until this rupture, had loved and trusted one another for years.

"Think, Christiane," she murmured to herself, toes tapping on the floor of the carriage, fingers drumming on her knees in their demure gray traveling skirts. "Think. Think."

Two

Just four hours later, the countess d'Oliveri had the honor of conducting a very chastened, very hesitant Lord Fanning into Martha's mother's parlor, where Martha lay, appropriately ashen and fragile in white silk gauze shawls, across a pillowed divan. "Lord Fanning has something to say to you, Martha," she intoned, giving Lady Westin, who was hovering nervously at her daughter's head, the tiniest of nods.

His Lordship, a robust fellow with curling brown hair and broad shoulders, promptly threw himself on the floor at Martha's dainty feet. "Darling," he said huskily, "my darling, darling Martha! How could you ever have thought that I doubted you?"

Martha sniffled into a snowy kerchief. "Oh, Peter, I did not wish to think so! But when you confronted me with such a—such a vicious accusation—"

"Sweet, darling Martha! I never meant it as an accusation! I thought that you would laugh it off as I had! The gross absurdity . . . that you would give yourself to some feckless country youth, some nameless nobody—you, the flower of chastity, the very image of womanly virtue—"

Above the young people's heads, the countess and Lady Westin exchanged relieved glances.

"But the mere fact, Peter, that you would question me—"

"As God is my witness, Martha, I never for an instant believed it," Lord Fanning declared roundly, clutching her wan hand and pressing it to his lips. "But you, you little fool! Laudanum—what would drive you to do such a desperate thing?"

"The prospect of losing your love," Martha whispered, a tear sliding down her cheek. "Without which . . . I have no wish to live."

"Oh, Martha." Lord Fanning took her into his arms, kissing her pale forehead. "I do not deserve you."

"No, no, my love! I do not deserve you!"

They clutched at one another, murmuring endearments. Lady Westin, her furrowed brow considerably smoothed, patted her daughter's head and glided toward the doorway, motioning for the countess to follow. "And you and I," she murmured as they gained the hallway, "deserve a drink. What sorcery did you work with that thickheaded lug?"

"Merely told him one of the girls at the school had confessed to penning the letter . . . out of a jealous rage, because she was desperately in love with him."

Lady Westin snorted, opening the doors to the drawing room. "Of course. Always appeal to a man's vanity. Why did I not think of that?"

"And you, Violet—how did you ever convince Martha to forgive him for questioning her virtue?"

"I told her if she did not forgive him, her reputation was ruined forever, as he certainly would not keep silent about the poison letter's accusations if she spurned him."

"Hmm. There is something grossly inequitable about those two approaches."

"Yes," Lady Westin agreed glumly, heading for the sideboard. "I'd rather hoped more of your influence would rub off on Martha while she was at the academy."

"*My* influence! For heaven's sake, Violet, most mammas of the ton would be horrified to learn that I am schooling England's daughters."

"Most mammas of the ton are idiots. Bringing girls up to be no more than brainless things of beauty, and then wondering why they are unhappy in their marriages—I declare, if Evelyn hadn't let it slip that you were behind her academy, I'd never have entrusted Martha there. What can I get for you? Sherry? Madeira?"

"A very small whiskey, if you will."

Lady Westin affected a moue of horror. "Whiskey? For a woman?"

"Don't tease, Violet. It has been a trying day for us all."

Then she fixed her friend with a sharp glance. "How close did she come to succeeding?"

"Close enough. Another dram, Dr. Fennerly said, and she very well might have died."

"I shall have to add careful instructions for avoiding turning dramatic ploys into genuine tragedies to our curriculum."

Lady Westin, having just taken a large gulp of wine, sprayed it into the air. "Christiane, you are dreadful!" she said when she'd recovered. "Now, you tell me—and tell me honestly. Will they be happy together?"

"Oh, I don't see why not. They are certainly sincere in their mutual devotion. And as they practically grew up in one another's pockets, we can assume they know each other well enough. You like him, don't you?"

"What I think doesn't seem to matter. But yes, I like him. I don't happen to think he is particularly exciting, or vibrant, or intellectually stimulating. . . ."

"Which would make him," Christiane said with a smile, "a proper British lord. But he *is* the catch of the season."

"That is the one thing that gives me hope. Martha isn't enamored of his money or title. She genuinely loves the oaf. She always has. She told me when she was but six years old that she'd marry him someday. And then when the two of them began talking about dates for the wedding, I thought perhaps some time at your academy, with other girls of her own age, would broaden her horizons." She stared dolefully into her glass.

"I'm sure they will be wondrous happy together," the countess assured her gently. "I know that at the academy, she rarely spoke of anything but him."

"But that's precisely what I mean," moaned Lady Westin. "There's so much more to the world, isn't there, than finding a husband? And these silly girls today never seem to think of anything else. Do raise my hopes, Christiane. Tell me you have other students who intend to make their marks in life some other way than by bearing heirs and buying jewels."

The countess winked. "In faith, we do. But don't breathe

a word of it to the other mammas, or they'll withdraw their daughters instantly!"

"I so adore the notion of you and Evelyn installed down there in your antique Kentish monastery, fomenting revolution."

"And I so adore *you,* for being so forgiving of our charge's dastardly trick."

"Well, all's well that ends well, thank heaven." Lady Westin had drained her glass. "Care for another?"

"Alas, I must be on my way back. There is still the little matter of a proper punishment for our anonymous-letter writer."

"You aren't heading back directly!" Lady Westin cried in dismay. "I'd so hoped that we could spend a bit of time together. Perhaps do the town—"

"You forget, Violet. I am still persona non grata amongst the set."

"Oh, bosh. That silly old scandal—and it was all nothing but lies anyway. I don't see how you can stand educating the offspring of women who were so cruel to you."

"As I've often told Evelyn, I am nothing but grateful for 'that silly old scandal,' as you put it. True, if Lord Weatherston hadn't told the world he'd had his way with me, I never would have gone off in disgrace to France and Italy. But then I never would have had the opportunities I had."

Lady Westin giggled. "I'll wager you find it fearfully quiet down there in Kent, after owning your own gaming house in Paris and then being married to the richest man in Italy."

"On the contrary, Violet," the countess retorted, with a heartfelt sigh. "As the past day bears witness, there is rarely a moment's peace when one is caretaker for a score of girls!" She put aside her glass. "And now that this has been resolved so happily, I'll be on my way. Relish your triumph, Violet. Make her a lovely wedding."

"Surely you'll attend, Christiane!"

"I dare not, alas." The countess went and kissed her cheek. "You are a wonderfully forgiving woman, *chérie,* but I can guarantee you, should any other mother of the ton learn of my involvement in Mrs. Treadwell's academy, our grand experiment in teaching girls to think for themselves would abruptly end."

"Which is all the more reason that it must continue—and so I shall not press you. Forge on, Christiane!"

A scant half an hour later, the countess d'Oliveri was once more installed in her carriage as it clattered slowly through the dusky streets of London. She was achingly tired, and she wanted nothing more than to be home and in her bed. Still, her mind throbbed with the pressing question of how to deal with Katherine Devereaux. She turned the matter over and over until, still well shy of the city gates, she could not bear to think on it anymore. Traffic was quite dreadful; the regent must be out and about, she thought sleepily as Stains pulled close to the curb to let a long series of opposing coaches pass. Her head bolstered by a cushion, Christiane gazed idly from the window at the gaily lit establishment before which they'd paused. As she watched, the door opened to admit a trio of gentlemen dressed to the nines. Hard on their heels came a similarly tuliped-out quartet, also male. The countess roused herself a bit. That was a gambling hell if she had ever seen one. From within the place she even heard—or imagined she could—the familiar swish of cards against green felt, and the soothing *chink, chink* of falling chips. . . .

A solitary figure was approaching the entrance, tall and slim, but broad in the shoulder in his sweeping evening cloak. It was of deep blue-black, and matched the hair that was smoothed back into a tight queue beneath his hat. Christiane roused herself to press her face to the glass. There was something strangely familiar about the way the fellow carried himself—it would have been a swagger, had it not been so forcefully attractive.

"Movin', finally," old Stains called wearily from the coach box, gathering the reins as the last of the carriages rolled past.

The door of the gaming hall had opened to the man in the blue-black cloak. The team grunted as Stains clicked at them to move; they weren't accustomed to such crowds, or the lights. But they must have surrendered to the slight flick of the crop the countess heard; they pulled out, their harness jingling. Christiane turned her head, still staring at the doorway, at the tall man in the cloak, who was now mounting the step. And then, above the clatter of wheels, the jangling harness, the host of city sounds that made a constant clatter like crickets, she heard something that made her catch her breath.

The man in the doorway laughed, and it was, quite distinctly, what Christiane privately considered to be the most delightful laugh in all the world: that of Alain Montclair. "Stop, Stains!" she cried, so abruptly that the driver complied in a panic, calling out:

"Why, then? What's amiss?"

Christiane was already reaching for the door-latch. "Nothing," she assured him. "I simply need to stop here for a moment. You may pull into that alley there and wait."

"Here?" Stains said in dismay. "Oy, mum, don't you realize what that is there? That's a gaming house, or I'm a ruddy duck."

"Yes, I know," the countess said. "You must never, ever mention to Mrs. Treadwell that we made this detour. But I have just glimpsed an old, dear friend I have not seen in years."

"You can't go in there by yourself!" Stains burst out.

"Of course I can; why shouldn't I? Wait in the alley, Stains. I won't be long." She leaped down from the coach, glancing ruefully at her mussed skirts, reaching up to straighten her dusty chip-hat. Then—*Honestly, Christiane,* she thought wryly, *you are behaving like a stricken schoolgirl!*—she strode boldly up to the door and rapped the brass knocker. From the corner of her eye, she saw Stains craning to look back at her, an expression of the utmost horror on his face.

A liveried butler opened the door with a polite smile that faded instantly when he saw a woman on the step. "Wrong address," he said shortly, and pushed the door shut.

Christiane rapped again.

This time, he wasn't smiling. "Go on, get out; we don't want your sort hereabouts," he hissed at her. Christiane couldn't help it; she giggled—but not before taking the precaution of laying her gloved fingers along the jamb.

"You flatter me," she told the butler. "No one has taken me for a light-o'-love for a good fifteen years."

He hesitated, the door half-closed. "I meant no disrespect, mum. But you *must* have the wrong address. This is a *gentlemen's* establishment."

"And it is a gentleman I'm seeking."

He drew his liveried shoulders up, greatly affronted. "Not *that* sort of gentlemen's establishment!"

"That man," said Madame, nodding past him. "The one who just now came in. That is the one I am seeking. Monsieur Alain Montclair."

"But the card said his name was—"

"I do not care what his card said. And despite your lewd thoughts, I merely wish a word with him. We are old and dear friends."

"No ladies allowed on the premises," the butler intoned.

Christiane shook her head at him, smiling good-naturedly. "Come now, you cannot tell me there are no ladies inside." She looked beyond him at the stairs, gauging the dimensions of the building. "Two dozen in front, I'd say. And another dozen in the rear rooms—the *private* rooms."

He goggled at her. "How would you know a thing like that?"

She reached into her purse and plucked out a card of her own. "Will you at least give this to him, and ask him if he cares to see me?" Full-blown, in a sudden rush, the thought had occurred to her that Alain Montclair might prove the perfect instrument toward solving the dilemma of Katherine Devereaux. What had Lord Fanning told Martha? *The gross absurdity . . . that you would give yourself to some feckless country youth, some nameless nobody . . .* That was what Katherine had penned in her poisonous letter, because it was the greatest shame imaginable to her. Why the devil not pay her back in kind?

The butler took the ornately engraved card, glanced over his shoulder, then turned back to her. "One moment, if you will," he said uncertainly, and shut the door on her.

Christiane could only imagine how Stains must be rolling his eyes at her behavior. Ten years past, she would have found it demeaning as well, to be stranded on a doorstep, pleading to be shown in to a man. But one of the wonderments of growing older was the realization that the opinion of the world counted for very little; it was far more important to be at peace with oneself than with every butler and carriage driver in the world. So she waited, perfectly calmly, until the door flew open and the outstandingly handsome young man stepped through, caught her up bodily, and danced with her down the steps.

"Christiane!" he cried, in a voice just as thrillingly irresistible as that laugh. "Is it—can it be you?"

"If it is not," she noted dryly, "you have just embraced an utter stranger."

"But of course it is!" He held her at arm's length, staring into her eyes, and Christiane, despite a lifetime of experience with men, felt an unmistakable flutter. "My God. You look beautiful."

As do you, she almost told him, but held her tongue. The two men with whom she had had long-standing relationships while she lived abroad, General Jean-Baptiste Vouillard and the comte d'Oliveri, had been suave and brilliant and well-read and captivating. But they had not been *beautiful*—not like Alain Montclair. He had the most amazing sweep of blue-black hair curling back above a high brow; his cheekbones were gorgeously prominent beneath long-lashed eyes of a lapis so deep, it was positively unnatural. His mouth was wide and fuller-lipped than a courtesan's; he had a shadow of a beard gracing his strong chin now, though when she had first met him, he'd been a whiskerless boy. Even then, however, he had stood out in a crowd; even then, he'd been the sort of man women could not resist. His shoulders beneath the finely cut coat and blindingly white shirt were broad without being graceless; his waist was slim as a wasp's. And

the superfine breeches he wore fit so tightly that his . . .
Christiane hurriedly recollected herself. "Would you be so
kind as to vouch for me, Alain, to this exceedingly suspicious
fellow?" She gestured to the butler.

"Are you an ape, sir, that you do not admit the countess
d'Oliveri?" Alain promptly demanded, with such admirable
hauteur that Christiane stifled a laugh.

"She is not on the list," the doorman sputtered helplessly.

"The countess is *always* on all lists, *everywhere*," Alain
declared, leading Madame past him. "See you remember that
in future."

"I—I will," the man said apologetically, while the countess
nodded over her shoulder to Stains.

"Wait for me!" she called.

"Oh, no!" Alain protested, waving him off. "I intend to
keep her here forever!"

"Wait," Madame told the driver firmly.

"Spoilsport," Alain grumbled, escorting her into the gaming room. "How can you leave when I have only just got
you back? What will you have to drink? No—I won't even
ask. Dom Perignon," he told a passing waiter. "The bottle."

The man hesitated. "Mrs. Fourtenay has said your tab—"

"To bloody hell with my tab! Don't you know who this
is? The countess d'Oliveri!"

The waiter looked the countess up and down. Christiane
took care to assume as aristocratic a mien as she could—
which was considerable. Then he bowed. "Very good, sir,"
he declared, and bustled off.

"Well, Alain," Christiane observed. "If nothing else, my
visit here seems to have extended your credit."

"A temporary setback; nothing more," he assured her,
guiding her through the maze of tables.

"You know, the last place I should ever have thought to
look for you is in England. I know well enough your sentiments regarding my countrymen."

"I found France temporarily . . . overheated," the young
man told her.

"How can that be? The last time I saw you, you were the toast of Paris!"

"There was a certain unpleasantness surrounding a young lady." He held out a dainty gilt chair at a vacant table for her, then settled in beside her.

"Anyone with whom I was acquainted?"

He cocked his head at her. "Perhaps. Her name is Mimi Boulé."

She stared at him. "What? Jacques Boulé's sister?"

"The same."

"As I recall, she was a small, rather humpbacked creature."

"She still is. But with an exceedingly well-stocked jewel-case."

"And a brother determined to see her die unwed, so that her jewels come to him. Are you daft, Alain? Boulé moves in the emperor's highest circles."

"All the more reason for me to introduce la petite Mimi to the netherworld."

"No more suitable guide than you—except, perhaps, for Dante," the countess retorted. "So you have fallen from French grace."

"It does not take much to fall from grace under the current regime," Alain Montclair said darkly.

"No. I believe that." The waiter brought the champagne and glasses; she waited while he popped the bottle and poured it. "Still. You had such promise."

"I have promise yet." His tone bore a hint of resentment. "But—" He clamped his mouth shut for a moment, then began, in quite a different tone: "I believe when last we parted, I owed you thirty thousand francs."

"You know, Alain, that is why you are such a beguiling scoundrel. No other creditor of my acquaintance would have raised that topic so quickly."

He smiled his devastating smile. "It must be clear to you that I do not have it."

"And to you that I do not need it."

"Well, then! Cheers, by all means, as you English say!" He raised his glass to hers.

"Cheers," Madame replied, sipping the champagne and taking the opportunity to look about her. The house was hardly of the first order; the chandeliers were appallingly dusty, and the women on the laps and arms of the men were hunted and hungry-looking. "Who is Mrs. Fourtenay, anyway?" she asked softly.

"One of your regent's castoffs. You can see where her ploys and tangles got her with that revolting oaf."

"You should be careful, Alain," she warned him quietly. "Men have gone to prison for saying less."

"Not to you, surely. Anyway"—he paused, pushed back his black hair, grinning—"I do what I can for her. The silly creature seems to imagine that my presence here imparts some imprimatur of culture."

"She is silly indeed, then."

He laughed again and leaned toward her. "If you have not accosted me about the debt I owe you, what *does* bring you here, to such a second-rate establishment? Trolling for a new lover?"

She laughed despite herself. "You are such a rogue, Alain!"

"I wear the title proudly. And Mrs. Fourtenay is a widow, allow me to point out. I *have* progressed from seducing virgins."

"Pity."

His head came up. "What's that?"

"I said, that's a pity. I had just such a venture in mind for you."

He glanced at his glass, set it down abruptly, and sat back. "I've had a good deal to drink tonight, Christiane. Probably more than is wise. I thought I heard you say you want me to seduce a virgin."

"Perhaps 'seduce' is too strong," she mused. "To catch one's notice, rather."

"Who?"

"A young lady at my finishing school."

One of his black brows arched. "*You?* With a finishing school? It must be a most *unusual* place."

"I like to think it is."

"Where is it? In Florence?"

"Oh, no, no. I have returned, like the sea turtle, to the place of my birth."

Intrigued, Alain Montclair leaned forward on his elbows. "Tell me more," he said.

Christiane did. Briefly, she explained about her partnership with Mrs. Treadwell and the academy they had opened. Then she laid out Katherine's story—without naming her, naturally—with a sketch of her background and temperament. Alain listened with his eyes half-closed—a habit of his, she knew, not when he was bored, but when he was paying most attention to what was being said. When she had finished her summary, he rocked back in his chair and took a swallow of champagne, then refilled both their glasses.

"What is in it for me?" he demanded.

"The opportunity, of course, to be the instrument of future happiness for a young lady who might otherwise never find it."

After a moment, he laughed. "And?"

"She is the only heir to a dukedom. An exceedingly wealthy one."

He contemplated that briefly. Then, "No," he said.

"No?" the countess echoed, unbelieving.

"Sorry," he apologized. "It is just that I cannot abide the English."

"*I* am English," she pointed out, her mouth curving.

"And you are the exception that proves the rule. *Mon Dieu,* look at how this country behaved toward you! Making you a social outcast, abandoning you to the wayward French—"

"You've a dreadful inclination, haven't you, to pigeonhole entire nations?"

"Perhaps," he said negligently. "But the fact is, except for you, I have found the Englishwomen of my acquaintance to be hopelessly stuffy. Pale, prissy girls with no bosom."

"She *does* have a bosom—a rather considerable one. And she is generally regarded as extraordinarily lovely."

"By her compatriots," he pointed out, then closed his

sleepy eyes entirely. "Let me picture her. Yes . . . I have it now. Golden-haired, naturally. Blue-eyed. Aquiline nose. Porcelain skin. Rosebud mouth." The eyelids opened, barely.

"Yes!" she exclaimed, encouraged.

"Sorry. Not my type. And I foresee a considerable expenditure of effort—something to which, you know, I am constitutionally unsuited."

"Alain!" the countess chided. "An English innocent—why, you could crush her in two weeks without lifting a finger!"

"I should have to lift something else, though. Or at least pretend to." He grinned, hitching at his tight breeches.

Despite herself, Christiane laughed. "I must have been daft to think of you for this mission. A young lady of her quality would never give the likes of you a second glance."

That brought him up. "I could do it if I *chose* to. If I were not currently embarked on other business."

"I sincerely doubt your winnings in such sewers as this can measure up to the girl's father's coffers."

"Ah! But you don't want me to *seduce* her," he noted reasonably, "and thus you don't want me to marry her, either. And so I ask you again—what is in it for me?"

The countess fluttered a hand. "I don't suppose it is of any use to apply to your better nature?"

"None whatsoever," he said cheerily. The door opened beyond her shoulder; she saw his gaze dart toward the entrance to the gambling room, and she turned in her chair. A heavily veiled woman garbed in fur and brocade had appeared on the threshold. Alain sprang to his feet. "Must be going, Christiane. I have been fortunate enough to arrange a tête-à-tête with a certain young matron I desire to know more intimately." He bent to kiss her hand. "Lovely to see you again. Wish I could have been of help."

"Alain," she said with a sigh, "the way you carry on, you are certain to come to a bad end."

"Perhaps." He laughed that matchless laugh. "But what a journey I will have had!"

She laughed, too, and watched him go to greet the matron. He was stealing pinches and kisses even as he led her through the gaming room to a discreetly curtained back stair. The woman's voice floated back to her:

"Oh, no, Monsieur Montclair, not now! I cannot—we must not—"

"But we must . . . or I will die," Alain said with great solemnity, and pulled the curtain aside. The countess hid her smile in her champagne. When she had finished the glass, she rose from the table, pressed gold into the hand of the waiter, and made her way outside.

The carriage was still there; Stains hurried to open the door for her. "Let us go home," she said, suddenly weary. "It has been a most trying—" She broke off. A rider was coming down the road, his horse in a frightful froth. He reined in at the entrance to Mrs. Fourtenay's, leaped down, and stormed the door, already drawing both a gun *and* a sword. Stains's eyes went wide.

"Trouble in the air," he said curtly. "Best get you out of here."

"Wait," the countess told him calmly.

"Wait?" he echoed, voice rising.

"Wait," she said firmly, as the butler, confronted with a pistol barrel, evidently forgot about the list. The door flew open; there came a muddle of frightened female cries and outraged male voices. The door shut.

"I really think, mum . . ." Stains began nervously.

Pistol shots cracked the night air. Stains started toward his seat, but she caught him by the sleeve: "I said, wait."

"For what?" he asked in terror.

Two stories above them, a window was abruptly raised. More shots exploded. And then a body hurtled downward from the window, landing with a crash atop the cab. "*Now* you may go," Christiane told the startled driver, who froze in his tracks as she climbed into the carriage. She barked at him: "I said *drive*, damn you, Stains!"

He leaped up into his seat and spurred the horses off along the alley.

The countess took the opportunity to push back the window. A moment later, a face appeared in it, hanging upside down. "You may as well come in," she said with resignation, and Alain Montclair swung himself through the narrow opening with admirable athleticism. "Trouble?" she inquired unnecessarily, noting that he was coatless, and that his white shirt was unbuttoned.

"The idiot husband took issue with my pursuance of his little woman. How was I to know he cared for her? She certainly never intimated as much." He settled into the seat across from her, clutching the meat of his left arm, where red was seeping into the white.

"Sword or bullet wound?"

"Bullet. But only a graze." He let her bind it for him with her kerchief. Then he raised his sparkling gaze to her. "Like the old days, eh, Christiane?"

"Too *much* like the old days. You know, Alain, Kent might prove a most welcome haven for you, just for a fortnight or so. Until your paramour's lover stops pursuing you."

He shuddered, and not from the wound. "A girls' school . . ."

Hooves were thundering on the cobblestones behind them. Madame reached to knock to signal the driver to stop. "You wouldn't," her companion cried in dismay.

"Don't try me, Alain. I take my new role as doyenne very seriously."

"You *are* serious, aren't you?" He paused for a split second, considering. "Here, now. I don't have to marry the chit, do I?"

"Heavens, no! I'd never wish that on her! You only have to break her heart."

He moved to look discreetly back through the window, then abruptly dove to the floor, covering himself in the wide swath of her skirts. A rider drew abreast of the cab and leaned down to stare in. Madame gave the furious-looking gentleman on horseback a bland, polite nod. He scanned the coach's interior, cursed, and rode on. As his hoofbeats retreated into the darkness, Alain popped out again. "Oh, Christiane," he murmured, grinning devilishly. "I did not mind that at *all!*"

"You are incorrigible, Alain! Say you'll do it, or I'll call him back."

"Just break her heart?" He had his hand on his arm; it must have been throbbing.

"Think of it as a holiday," she urged.

"Holiday!" He snorted. "But—that noble fellow will no doubt be combing all of England for me, seeking to avenge his honor. Most unfair, really. She is quite the little tart." He hesitated. "A fortnight, then. No longer?"

"Not unless you require it."

"Hah! Not likely!" His spirits renewed, he reached into his rear pocket, drew forth a flask, and lifted it in a grinning toast. "Very well, Christiane! Bring your virgin on!"

Three

Katherine Devereaux was in a temper.

She'd just come from her *third* trip to the *hopeless* creature who passed for a mantua maker in the village of Hartin, in what appeared to be the unattainable cause of having the bodice of her new gown fitted to her liking. Really, was it so much to ask that the *peau de soie* shouldn't *gap* about the bosom? But apparently it was. Honestly, it seemed Mrs. Tattersall was purposely out to thwart her! Worst of all, *no one* at Mrs. Treadwell's academy seemed to take her troubles seriously. "I can't imagine what you are complaining about, Katherine," Bess had said, when Katherine pointed out the bodice's obvious inadequacies. And Mrs. Treadwell had suggested Katherine make the necessary adjustments herself— "As if," Katherine muttered furiously, "I were some wretched little clergyman's daughter!"

"What's that, Lady Devereaux?" inquired Stains, who'd accompanied her into the village.

"Nothing," she said curtly.

Unperturbed by her rudeness, he raised his long nose, sniffing the sweet summer air. "Lovely day for a ride, don't you think, Lady Devereaux?"

But Katherine was too preoccupied with her dark thoughts to take note of the buzzing bees, the lulling song of the river in the distance, the perfume of honeysuckle and wild roses. "For all the satisfaction this excursion earned me, I might as well have stayed home," she sniffed, and spurred her mount on, in no mood to make small talk with the help.

"Lady Devereaux!" she heard him call after her. "Wait, Lady Devereaux! Achilles is too winded to—" But the rest of his words were whipped away on the faint breeze. Her own horse, Maja, was a light-limbed pure white Arab from her father's stables, and *never* got winded. *Let him waddle home atop that pathetic old gelding,* Katherine thought most uncharitably, giving Maja her head.

Sometimes—not very often, but sometimes—when she was riding, with Maja gathering the miles beneath her strong hooves, Katherine was almost able to forget her miserable state. The fact, for instance, that while most young ladies of her exalted social sphere were at this very moment strolling the streets of Bath, turning parasols and catching the gazes of admiring gentlemen, she was mired in this Kentish backwater. The fact, for instance, that she had just that morning received another letter from her father, who had not so much as mentioned her increasingly desperate pleas to be removed from the hell on earth that was Mrs. Treadwell's academy. Or the fact—and here Katherine could not keep a self-pitying tear from rolling down her cheek—that on Tuesday next, she would turn nineteen.

Nineteen years old, and she had never had a beau. Nineteen, and she had not yet debuted! Oh, it was bitter as gall to be stuck here in the hinterlands while other girls her age— aye, and even younger!—were courting and having fun. Damn that Nanette O'Toole, who had ruined her life! Hadn't she always tried to be a dutiful daughter? To uphold the many, many responsibilities that her place in life entailed? And how did the duke reward her diligence? By marrying a commoner—an actress—an Irishwoman!—and in that single act depriving his daughter of all that was most dear to her. Of course her father had not been able to resume his place in society. Of course he'd had to head off to the most absurd destinations on the excuse of being a diplomat, and abandon her at dreadful Mrs. Treadwell's, where she was *each day* further humiliated by her parvenue suite-mates and the hopelessly egalitarian instructors, who simply *would not* call her "Lady Devereaux," according to her entitlement, and who expected her to perform the most shockingly humble tasks.

It was too much to bear at times. But when she felt overwhelmed by shame, when her unhappy state threatened to consume her, Katherine invariably straightened up and stuck out her lovely chin and forged on. Because really, to do anything else *would* be beneath her. To permit her school-mates even for a moment to glimpse the extent of her be-wilderment would be very bad form. And if there was one thing a Devereaux did not allow herself, it was bad form.

Except, of course, for her father. Katherine had grieved as honestly as he had when her mother, the duchess—the *real* duchess—had suddenly, unthinkably, died of an aneurysm. For a year, father and daughter had mourned together, brought closer than ever by their solitude. Then the regent, damn him, had demanded the duke's presence in London. And the next thing Katherine knew, she had a stepmother of the most unspeakable kind!

What could her father have been thinking of, to *marry* her? For the thousandth time, Katherine sought to understand this event that had turned her world upside down. Granted, Na-nette O'Toole was lovely. Granted, she was reputed to be extremely gifted. But she was a commoner! And worse, an Irishwoman *and* an actress, a brazen harlot who was said to have slept with half of England's nobility! For the duke, who had always stood so on custom, to have replaced his cher-ished first wife with a second who had no more to recom-mend her than a pretty face—and far more to *not* recommend her—was a tragedy of monumental proportions to Katherine. She had mourned every single day of the six years that had passed since the dreadful event—and she had not dared set foot in *proper* society.

Her father had changed so since this marriage! Where he had once demanded of her the strictest behavior, now he had consigned her to Mrs. Treadwell's, where she was quartered with the most common sort of girls. But they would not break her. No, they would *not* break her! Katherine would *not* de-scend to their level of despicable familiarity!

Heartened by this conclusion, Katherine straightened her backbone, thrust out her chin, and—

"My God," she gasped, catching sight of the figure stag-gering toward her from the wood along the road.

"Please!" the man called to her. "Please! I beg you, help

me!" He held out his hands to her, and Katherine shivered, seeing a great blotch of bright red—God, could that be blood?—on the front of his white shirt. She slowed Maja, who was shying at the stranger's approach. "I have had an accident," he told her, and now he clutched his arm. Blood. It was definitely blood. "I need—" He collapsed to his knees. Maja snorted, stepping daintily away. To Katherine's horror, the man grabbed for the reins, which she had let go slack. Hurriedly she drew them close, out of his reach.

"Don't you *dare* touch my horse!" she cried.

"God, have mercy, miss! I fear that I am dying!"

"Well, go off and do it quietly, then, and not while accosting your betters on a public thoroughfare," Katherine snapped at him.

"If you could spare a bit of water—"

"There's a whole entire river not a hundred yards away. Go get your water there." Whipping Maja emphatically, Katherine rode on with her head held high.

For an instant—only for an instant—she had an inclination to glance back. But she fought it, naturally. To do otherwise would be beneath her. Honestly, what was England coming to, she thought with chagrin, that dying men felt perfectly free to go about making such nuisances of themselves?

It was fortunate she didn't look back. If she had, she'd have seen Alain Montclair standing bolt upright where only a moment before he'd been expiring. She might even have heard him murmur, "*Mon Dieu,* Christiane! You have set me a hard case!"

"*Katherine! How went* your trip to Mrs. Tattersall's?" the countess d'Oliveri asked as she observed her student coming into the front hall.

"An utter waste of time," Katherine said shortly. "That woman has no more sense of style than a common hound."

"Dear me. I am sorry to hear it. Still, you had a pleasant afternoon's ride, I trust?"

"Hardly! Stains *would* insist on dragging behind me the entire way."

"Achilles grows old," Madame noted. "Still, it would be a pity to refuse him such simple pleasures as a journey to the village when he has put in so many years of devoted service."

"I don't see why. Such ancient, useless creatures ought to be shot."

Madame *tsk*ed. "You don't mean that, surely. It is possible that you yourself may become old and useless someday."

"If I do," Katherine said, pulling off her hat, "I shall shoot *myself,* rather than impose so on the convenience of others."

"You sound altogether wroth," Madame observed. "Nothing occurred on your trip to cause you to be in such a temper?"

"Of course not. What *could* ever happen around here?" Blithely, Katherine brushed past her and up the stair.

Madame bit her tongue to hide a smile. "Oh, Alain," she whispered. "I did warn you—"

"What's that?" Katherine demanded from the turn of the banister.

"I only said . . . perhaps life hereabouts will take a tilt toward excitement yet."

"I sincerely doubt that." Katherine paused, her elegant nose in the air. "Good God. Do I detect the scent of *cabbage*?"

"I believe Cook is preparing her renowned boiled supper," the countess acknowledged.

"Oh! Cabbage and crippled horses and mangled bodices— it is too much to *bear!*" Katherine declared with feeling, and swept haughtily up to her rooms.

This time, Alain knew, he had her.

He'd been entirely too nonchalant on his first try; indeed, he was embarrassed by the recollection of his artlessness. He had not made allowances for what Christiane had told him of the girl; he had relied on sheer shock and his charm. His charm, he knew, never, ever failed him. But he had taken the wrong tack for an English duke's daughter. This time, he'd laid his plans much more carefully.

He'd spent hours plotting out the precise spot in the woods along the road from which to release the rabbits. He'd procured them himself, good big Kentish hares trapped by a boy from the village to whom he'd paid a shilling the head. He'd hired a horse from the White Fox's stables, after trying out several to be sure he had the fastest. And he'd double- and triple-checked with Christiane to get the girl's schedule down pat.

Now he was waiting, in the pleasant summer sunshine— really, the weather here in England was not nearly so miserable as he had expected—for the sound of a carriage in the distance. He consulted his pocket-watch. A quarter to four. Any minute now, she should be coming along.

He'd dressed with a great deal more care for this second encounter. The peasant garb he'd affected the last time had been a dreadful error; one glance at the girl's blank expression and he'd recognized that. Granted, *most* Englishwomen he'd met would have found the pleading, bleeding figure he'd cut irresistible. Foolishly, he had not believed what Christiane had told him about this girl's character. Now he knew: It would take something far more heroic to catch her eye.

He settled his fist more firmly on the handle of the cage with the rabbits. Let it never be said that Alain Montclair made the same mistake twice!

There! There was the rattle of wheels, coming toward him from the village. He glanced quickly back at the horse tethered out of sight of the road. Not exactly greased lightning, but then, neither would the team be, Christiane had assured him. A nice, plodding pair of elderly geldings—and the curricle, he saw, as it came around the bend, nothing special in the way of speed. *"Eh bien, mes petits,"* he murmured to the rabbits, crouching low amidst the shrubbery. There were seven of them—his lucky number, seven. He blew them a kiss, and they stared at him with anxious eyes, noses wriggling in fright. He put his hand to the latch, waiting patiently until the curricle was almost upon him. At the precise moment, he jerked the cage open, shook the rabbits to the ground, and hissed at them: "Get on with you!" The silly things froze. He shooed them forward with the fir branch he had ready: "Go, damn you!" They didn't move. He swore at them, stamping his foot, making as if to chase them. Oh, bloody hell. It was almost too late. . . . Though he loathed the notion, he drew his boot back, ready to send them flying with a sudden kick. Fortunately, their leader seemed to grasp the seriousness of the situation and abruptly sprang out onto the road, his cohorts leaping after him. Alain crossed his fingers and murmured a prayer. Were they too late?

No. He'd actually overestimated the pace of the geldings; they had only just reached the turn. And they startled, perfectly, at the sudden spray of rabbits bounding across their path. "Whoa!" Alain heard the driver cry, and through the leaves he caught a glimpse of Katherine Devereaux's face beneath what really was an extraordinarily becoming chip-hat trimmed with rose-colored ribbons. Pity that her gown gaped so about the bosom. . . .

Recollecting himself, he seized the reins of his rented horse and leaped up into the saddle, ready to gallop to the rescue, his blood pumping furiously at the success of his plan. "Yah!" he cried, urging the horse out of the underbrush to dash after the out-of-control curricle—

Only to find, once he'd gained the road, that the driver's single caution had been enough to draw the team to a standstill. *His* horse, however, had caught the fever of his excitement; it pounded up beside the stalled vehicle with stirring élan.

Hmm, thought Alain, the feather in his cock-hat quivering as he yanked his mount to a stop. Well, might as well go for broke. "Are you in need of assistance, fair lady?" he thundered in a thrilling voice.

"Does it *look* as though I am?" Katherine Devereaux retorted curtly. "Ride on, Stains."

"Aye, mum," the driver muttered, looking askance at the elegantly clad figure who'd emerged from the wood.

"Please!" Alain protested, falling into step with the curricle team. "You must allow me to accompany you to your destination, fair lady."

"I *must*? Oh, I think not. *Do* drive on, Stains."

Alain thought fast. "But, milady! The danger that spooked your team might yet return!"

Her lovely mouth curled downward in disdain. "Danger? Surely you don't mean those bunnies."

"Those were genuine Kentish hares, milady! Known upon occasion to turn very nasty indeed!"

"Stains," Katherine Devereaux declared to the driver, "if you do not remove me from the presence of this madman now, instantly, I shall see to it that you lose your post."

"Very good, miss!" Stains slapped the reins and clucked his tongue. "Get on, Sammy! Gee-yah, Timothy!" The pair sprang out with surprising speed. Alain was caught unaware. Recollecting himself, he steered his own horse about, dug in his heels to pursue—and then felt his eyes widen as, just in front of him, a half-dozen-plus-one Kentish hares came careening back across the road.

"Whoa!" he shouted, but too late. The nag bucked and reared in terror. He grabbed for the pommel, but felt it slip from his hand. "Oh, damn!" He flew into the air, headed smack toward a thick growth of thistles. Worst of all, as he hit, he caught the merest glimpse of Katherine Devereaux craning from her seat to look back at him. Her high, bright laughter stung far worse than the thistles could.

Four

"You cannot say I did not warn you," Christiane observed, applying a pair of tweezers to Alain Montclair's exceedingly well-cut superfine trousers.

"Ouch," he grunted as she pulled out yet another sticker. "You warned me, *oui.* But you did not say the girl was inhumane."

"That's because I don't believe she is. Oh, insufferably proud, yes, and hopelessly vain. Mrs. Treadwell is ready to give up on her entirely. Her father is as well. But I . . . I cannot help but believe something more is there."

"I side with Mrs. Treadwell," Alain said curtly, gritting his teeth as she moved in with the tweezers.

"So. You give up, then? Admit defeat?"

He snorted. "Not likely. I merely have to rethink my tactics. And put no more reliance on English horses. Utterly untrustworthy creatures."

"That's been said of English women as well."

"Women are women," Alain announced with more confidence. "I have yet to find one who can resist me."

"So far, Katherine Devereaux has done so quite nicely."

"She has not seen me properly. In an appropriate venue."

"Well. A cheap French gambling hell is a bit much to expect me to import."

"I need to make a proper entrance," he grumbled. "She is clearly not the type to be impressed by roadside acquaintances."

"I could have told you that."

"If you had, you would have spared me a derrière full of prickles."

Smiling, she removed another. "If you require my help, Alain, just say the word."

"Do these young ladies of yours ever venture out into society?"

"Of course they do! Properly chaperoned, of course. Why, they are to make an appearance at the earl of Tatham's ball on Friday next."

"Aha!" Alain's troubled blue eyes cleared. "That is the sort of occasion on which I might make a proper impression! Could you arrange an invitation for me as well?"

"I suppose I could. But really, Alain. It has been eight days already, and you have made no progress whatsoever. I thought you told me two weeks was all you would need!"

"That is what you told *me*—and clearly, you were lying." She pinched the tweezers, and he winced, less from the pain than from the memory of Katherine Devereaux's mocking laughter. "But I *will* break that hard-hearted girl. I swear it on my *life.*"

"Gwen, that gown is absolute *perfection!"* Bess declared, her eyes aglow with admiration. "You look as pretty as a princess."

"Of what nation, I cannot imagine," Katherine Devereaux noted. "Slovenia, perhaps."

"Do shut up. And stop pigging the mirror!" Bess retorted curtly. "I don't see why you even bother. There are certain not to be any men you find worthy of *your* attention at the Tathams' ball."

"Truer words were never spoken." Katherine was twisting in front of the looking glass in an ineffectual attempt to get the wayward bodice of her new gown to sit right. "*Damn* that Mrs. Tattersall! I declare, this is worse than ever!"

Bess's green eyes narrowed as she contemplated her formmate's exquisite outfit, the diamonds that sparkled at her throat, her luxuriant golden ringlets. "Have you ever considered, Katherine, giving thanks for all you have, rather than bemoaning the merest trifles?"

Katherine whirled on her in a swirl of peacock-blue *peau de soie.* "I have no more than I *deserve,* by virtue of my birth. Indeed, I have a great deal less. If it were not for the unfortunate fact that my father chose this inopportune time to go and do the regent's business in Russia, I would be making a splash amongst the ton at the moment, not parading myself before a bunch of country bumpkins!"

"An earldom's not exactly small potatoes," Gwen observed quietly, pinning up her black waves.

Katherine's sneer was exquisite. "Not to the likes of *you,* of course. For you, an earldom's overreaching."

Bess, who was attempting to coax her thick red hair into some semblance of order, abruptly paused. "It's nothing more than accident, you know."

"What is?" Katherine asked blandly.

"One's birth. I mean, you always go on about it as if it's ordained by God."

"And so it is."

"I've done a bit of poking into your family tree. Do you know how your ancestor earned his dukedom?"

Katherine's mouth curved in a delicious smile. "Of course I do. Poppa has told me the story many times. Geoffrey de Vereaux, as the name was then styled, was granted the title in honor of his outstanding service to William of Normandy at the Battle of Hastings. He was serving under William's brother Odo, and he personally saved Odo's life by his valiant fighting."

"But do you know what he was *before* he became a duke?"

Katherine blinked. "Why—a soldier."

"He was Odo's valet."

"That's a filthy lie!"

Bess shrugged. "Read the history by Ordericus Vitalis yourself. It's quite conclusive. What's more, Geoffrey was illegitimate. The son, Vitalis says, of a Norman brewer and a barmaid named, by coincidence, Katherine."

"Oh!" Katherine was positively livid. "Ordericus Vitalis must be an idiot!"

"I believe the point Bess is making," Gwen observed in an attempt to soften the blow, "is that it was often nothing

more than being in the right place at the right time that
earned the nobility its honors."

" 'When Adam delved and Eve span,' " Bess quoted absently, " 'who was then the gentleman?' "

"That's an utterly subversive rhyme!" Katherine exclaimed.

"And utterly true," Bess countered. "Titles and such are
man-made honors. They've naught to do with God."

"I suppose *you* think they ought to be eliminated altogether—that we should all be 'citizens,' like the deluded
French!"

"Why not?" Bess said breezily. "A man's—*or* a
woman's—worth ought to be judged on what he or she has
done lately, not on what some lucky ancestor accomplished
five hundred years back."

Katherine raised a furious finger at her. "You—*you* are
what will surely pull this nation into the mire!"

"Katherine," Gwen put in quietly, solemnly, "there is
something that puzzles me. You know the truth about Madame—about the scandal that drove her away from the ton.
How that man claimed to have had his way with her—"

"Claimed? Oh, I'd wager all my jewels it's true!"

"But if you hate it so much here at the academy, why don't
you raise a fuss about it? Make Madame's presence known?
The mammas would withdraw their daughters instantly in the
face of such a scandal."

"You don't know how often I've been tempted," Katherine
declared hotly. "Only one thing holds me back. My own
chances of ever making a decent match would be utterly
destroyed were I to say one word about that—that harlot's
involvement here. And so I bite my tongue, and endure the
constant presence of such filth."

"Well." Bess did not seem particularly put out. "We all of
us began in the filth, didn't we? God fashioned Adam and
Eve out of common clay."

Gwen smiled. Katherine shot her a glare, then swept up
her handsome Paisley shawl. "Mock at the nobility if you
like," she said in a tight voice. "But you both know, deep in

your hearts, that given the extremely unlikely opportunity, you would marry up at the drop of a hat." She started for the door.

"Of course we would," Bess agreed. "The question is, would you ever marry *down*?"

"I'd sooner *die*," Katherine Devereaux declared. "Now, if you don't mind, I believe we are going to be late." She went out, closing the door behind her with a decisive bang.

Bess was laughing. Gwen, though, was nibbling her lip. "You ought not to taunt her so," she chided gently. "She is terribly unhappy."

"That's her own fault and no one else's," Bess declared. "And even if she is, does that give her the right to make *our* lives misery?"

Gwen glanced into the mirror. "Perhaps tonight will be the night. Perhaps some man will sweep her off her feet, and we'll be rescued. Ready?"

"As ready as I'll ever be," Bess replied, with a rueful glance at her own reflection. "It just galls me no end that she should be so lovely and so hateful. Why is life unfair?"

"Take heart," said Gwen, coming and squeezing her hand. "Somewhere out there is a man who desires nothing more in the world than a tart-tongued, red-haired rebel."

Bess burst out laughing again. "And another who is desperately seeking a sly, meek-as-milk black-haired miss!"

"Remember Martha," Gwen said in encouragement.

"Oh, I do. I do!" Bess's round face was wistful. "Do you imagine *we* will ever be so lucky?"

"No," Gwen admitted. "But I do have hopes that Katherine Devereaux will come to a very bad end!"

As the carriage rolled onto the earl of Tatham's long gravel drive, Mrs. Treadwell cast anxious glances at her trio of first-formers. "I trust all of you will recall your lessons in manners and deportment," she announced. "Granted, this is but a country ball. But it will give you one more glimpse at the sort of future that awaits you when you make your debuts."

Katherine Devereaux stifled a yawn. "I sincerely doubt that."

"The earl of Tatham," Mrs. Treadwell declared, with as close as she ever came to a chiding tone, "is quite an important figure in the government. He has friends in high places." Gwen and Bess began to look rather nervous, but Katherine only raised her chin.

"His title, I believe, is quite recent."

"It was bestowed on his grandfather for his military prowess," Mrs. Treadwell allowed. "Nonetheless, Katherine, there was a time when *your* ancestors' honors were new as well."

"Hardly an apt comparison. The Devereaux title dates back—"

"We are all quite aware of how far it dates back, Katherine," Bess noted, rolling her eyes. The coach came to a stop, and a liveried footman trotted to open the door. Bess rose to her feet, only to be bowled over by Katherine, who was already exiting.

"For your information," she cast back over her shoulder, "withdrawal from a vehicle *always* goes according to rank."

"After you, Mrs. Treadwell," Gwen said politely. "Where I come from, rank defers to the honors of experience."

Mrs. Treadwell laughed, even as Katherine stepped daintily down in advance of her. "A very gracious way, Gwendolyn, of referring to advanced age!"

The earl of Tatham's country home was quite new, like the family title, and in the Italian villa style. Gwen and Bess murmured admiringly as they crossed the marble threshold into an airy, much-windowed hall, but Katherine wrinkled her nose. "Predictable," she muttered. "The proportions are entirely askew."

"So is your bodice," Bess murmured mischievously, and had the satisfaction of seeing Katherine blanch and tug at it before giving her a withering glance.

"Mrs. Treadwell!" the lady of the house declared warmly, coming forward to greet them. "The earl and I are so delighted that you and the young ladies could join us for this evening's festivities!"

"Thank you, Mirabelle. Ladies, may I present you to the countess of Tatham. Miss Elizabeth Boggs." Bess dropped a curtsy. "Miss Gwendolyn Carstairs." Gwen did the same. "And Miss—"

"Katherine, Lady Devereaux," Katherine declared, remaining upright.

"You must be Richard's daughter!" cried the countess, a small, elegant figure in a ravishing emerald-green silk gown. "What a pleasure to make your acquaintance at last! I've heard so much about you."

"Really?" Katherine barely inclined her head. "I must say, the duke never made mention of you to me."

"Katherine," Mrs. Treadwell said warningly.

But the countess merely laughed. "And that's precisely what I've heard. Welcome, all of you. Won't you come this way?" Gwen and Bess couldn't help but titter; Katherine, however, saw no humor whatsoever.

"Why, of all the cheeky—"

"Katherine," Mrs. Treadwell cautioned again. The heir to the duke of Marne gave her golden curls a toss and stepped elegantly after their hostess, her peacock skirts sweeping the floor. Gwen and Bess heard Mrs. Treadwell let out a despairing sigh.

"Never you mind," Bess told the headmistress, reaching to

pat her hand. "Gwen and I will do our best to counter her effect."

"I'm quite sure you will," Mrs. Treadwell acknowledged. "But not sure you can!"

The ballroom of Tatham Hall was exceedingly elegant, and the company seemed so as well to Gwen and Bess. Katherine, however, had decided to sulk, rather publicly. Despite the headmistress's best efforts to engage her in the proceedings, she hung back, nose in the air, while a procession of eager young men approached to ask for introductions. As each swain was presented, Katherine's demeanor grew more haughty; she went so far as to yawn when she was presented to a mere viscount. Since Gwen and Bess could not, by propriety, be excluded from the meeting and greeting, Katherine's obnoxious behavior had the effect of earning them many, many offers to dance. They naturally obliged, Gwen shyly, Bess more robustly. Meantime, Katherine stood beside Mrs. Treadwell and observed their behavior with an occasional sniff.

"You know, Katherine," the headmistress felt compelled to note, "one catches more flies with honey than with vinegar."

"*Flies,*" Katherine retorted with a toss of her ringlets, "is precisely what this company consists of."

Mrs. Treadwell tried again. "Even if there are no young men present tonight who meet your exacting standards, some of them are certain to have friends among the higher echelon."

"Those amongst the higher echelon who have such friends are of no interest to me."

Mrs. Treadwell sighed. Christiane might have thought of something more to say under such circumstances, but she herself was at her wits' end. The polonaise the orchestra was playing finished, and she saw Gwen politely thanking the young man who'd squired her on the floor. Bess, too, was headed back toward her headmistress, her carrot hair already working free of its pins, the shoulders of her gown askew.

"Enjoying yourselves?" Mrs. Treadwell inquired, reaching to straighten Bess's sleeves.

Her green eyes were glowing. "Oh, very much so!"

"And you, Gwendolyn?"

Gwen blushed becomingly. "To tell the truth, I found Mr. Canthop a trifle . . . forward."

Bess perked up. "Really? I must dance with him!"

Mrs. Treadwell laughed. Katherine, however, was glowering. "I do wish, Bess, that you'd try to comport yourself with a trifle of dignity."

"Oh, do be hanged, you sour old grape," Bess said good-naturedly, turning to glance at the doorway as the footman announced a new arrival. Her jaw fell open as the newcomer stepped into the ballroom, and her voice went hoarse as she croaked, "My!"

"His Excellency, the comte de Clairmont," the footman intoned gravely, then stood aside. Mrs. Treadwell straightened and raised her monocle, and even Gwen let out a wispy sigh.

The young man on the threshold was without exception the most handsome creature in the room—perhaps in the universe, judging from Bess's expression. He was quite tall and impeccably slim, though his shoulders were more than broad enough to refute any impression of dandyishness. He had waving blue-black hair pulled back in a loose queue; his face was dark-tanned, or else his complexion was naturally quite olive. His cheekbones were broad and wide-planed; his forehead was high and distinguished, his mouth indecently full and sensual. Even at this distance, the hue of his eyes, a blue so clear and deep that it riveted attention, was plain. From all around the room came small murmurs of feminine appreciation. Then the countess of Tatham moved forward to greet her guest.

He made her a bow that quite took Bess's breath away, and that splendid mouth lingered over the countess's hand. They exchanged a few words, and then the comte de Clairmont broke into a laugh, deep and rich and wondrous, that made female knees go weak no matter their age. A few of the young men muttered at this sudden apparition in their midst, but the truth was, his beauty was the sort that drew admiring glances even from his own sex. The countess slipped her arm through his, cast a look about at the company, then led him toward her daughter Alicia and her intended, Lord Fisinger, who had suddenly put *his* arm around his fiancée in an unusually possessive manner. The music started up again, and one of the gentlemen approached Bess to ask her to dance.

"I'm dreadfully sorry," she said distractedly, "but I cannot."

When he'd gone, Gwen looked at her. "That, Bess, was Mr. Canthop."

"I know that well enough," Bess hissed. "But if I were to dance with him now, I might lose the opportunity to be presented to *him*."

"For glory's sake," Katherine snapped. "He is *French*, can't you tell that?"

"So what if he is?" Gwen asked curiously.

"French titles are notoriously unreliable anymore, since the Revolution. He might be anyone. Or no one."

"Oh, he is *somebody*," Bess declared dreamily. Then her eyes went wide with alarm. "Good God, she is bringing him this way! How do I look? My hair's a mess, isn't it?"

" 'Mess' would be charitable," Katherine agreed. Gwen shot her a look and did her best to push Bess's wayward red head into some semblance of order as the dowager baroness of Wentwhistle, who must have been eighty if she was a day, rose from her chair and blocked the countess's progress with her cane to demand an introduction.

"Young man," the ladies of Mrs. Treadwell's academy heard the octogenarian say, loudly and clearly, "where the devil have you been all my life?"

"In search of you, *ma chère* madame," the comte de Clairmont replied, with a smile that sent Bess swooning. His voice was as thrilling as his laugh, the touch of French to his English positively devastating.

"Oh, I am in love," Bess murmured, fanning herself with her hand.

Evidently, so was the dowager baroness. "I want to have supper with you, young man," she said roundly. "I want to look at you all night long. Indeed, I believe I'll have your portrait painted and hang it over my bed."

He leaned in close to her and whispered something that made the aged woman titter and blush like a new bride. Then he kissed her cheek, and she put her palm up to the spot, coloring again. The countess of Tatham intervened, saying jovially, "It is plain you two were meant for each other—so much so that I dare not leave you alone together. Forgive us, Gertrude, but I must present monsieur le comte to the rest of my guests."

"Alas, duty calls," the comte de Clairmont murmured. "But I shall hold you to that supper—Gertrude."

"Honestly!" Katherine Devereaux declared, with a toss of her head.

The countess, with her guest in tow, was coming straight for them. "Mrs. Treadwell, permit me to present to you the comte de Clairmont."

"Charmed, I'm sure," Mrs. Treadwell said with a breathy giggle. The comte made another of those exquisite bows over her hand.

"And these young ladies," the countess went on brightly, "are students at Mrs. Treadwell's academy for young ladies. Miss Carstairs." Gwen bobbed, eyes downcast. "Miss Boggs." Bess instantly thrust out her hand.

"However you just kissed the baroness of Wentwhistle's, I want *exactly* the same!"

"My pleasure," the comte said with a smile, obliging.

"And Miss—I beg your pardon—Lady Devereaux."

The comte reached for Katherine's hand. She drew it behind her back. His eyebrows arched in surprise. "I beg your pardon. Have I somehow offended? I am new to your country, and your ways are still somewhat unfamiliar to me."

"She—" Bess began in expiation. But Katherine, with

those amazing eyes trained straight at her, drew her shoulders up in their cocoon of blue silk.

"You have indeed offended, sir. If a lady does not proffer her hand, a *gentleman* does not presume to extend for it."

To his credit, the comte de Clairmont seemed not a bit disconcerted. "I must thank you, Lady Devereaux, for correcting my rudeness, then."

"Katherine, you are such a *stick*," Bess muttered in fury.

"I wonder," the comte went on, towering over them, smiling enchantingly, "if I might request the honor of a dance with you, Lady Devereaux? No doubt you would be able to correct any number of other errors in my comportment."

"I never dance with foreigners," Katherine said briskly.

"Katherine!" Mrs. Treadwell gasped. "Speaking of manners, where on earth are *yours*?"

For an instant, in the depths of the comte's azure gaze, Katherine saw a shimmer of something that made her . . . well, almost afraid. Something hard and dark and bitter . . . Then it passed, and the smile resumed. "It is of no account, Mrs. Treadwell," he said very softly. "Your young ladies do you honor, I am sure."

"Well, I am not at all sure!" the headmistress burst out, still furious with her arrogant charge.

The comte de Clairmont shrugged his magnificent shoulders in their form-fitting coat. "Lady Devereaux has a whimsy, that is all. They are very French, whimsies. I take my leave of you now, ladies." He bowed again and withdrew, the countess clutching his arm once more and murmuring to him beneath her breath.

"Well," Bess said flatly. "Thank you very much, Katherine, I'm sure, for spoiling *our* chances!"

"As if any decent young lady would *want* a chance with him," Katherine responded, wiping her hand on her skirts as though she had touched something unclean.

"Eh bien, Alain." Madame gazed at him as he lounged in an armchair in his rooms at the White Fox. "Mrs. Treadwell

delivered an account of your success—or lack thereof—with Katherine at the Tathams' ball. I apologize for her abominable rudeness. I imagine you are more than ready to pack it all in."

Alain had lit a cigar; he puffed at it now and watched the smoke float toward the ceiling. "*Au contraire,* Christiane. I find myself more engaged in the battle than before."

"I don't see why. I am inclined toward her own father's opinion—that she is an insufferable snob and deserves to be left to her misery."

"There has to be a way," Alain murmured, almost to himself. "There always is a way."

"If you are merely being stubborn because of how I egged you on—"

"I am being stubborn, yes. But of my own accord." His eyes slanted toward her from behind a curtain of smoke. "How much would this father of hers put up with?"

"I'm . . . not certain what you mean. You make me nervous, Alain, when you look like that."

"Like what?" he asked, grinning.

"Rather like a madman."

"Don't be absurd. I am simply intrigued. The woman is rare, you know, who can withstand my charms."

"I always assumed she was nonexistent," the countess said frankly.

He laughed, tilting his wineglass toward her. "You are immune enough."

"Only because I am old and wise. But were I nineteen, and without experience—"

"*There's* a wish to be wished."

"No," the countess contradicted. "I would not be nineteen again for anything in the world. Not even for you."

"Pity," he murmured, with a look of regret that nearly made her forget the difference in their ages.

She laughed at her own weakness. "There are times, though . . ."

"Only say the word," he declared devoutly.

"Stop it, Alain! We must put our heads together—"

"A position much to my liking."

"And resolve this quandary of Katherine!"

"Ah, yes. Katherine. The eternal English virgin." He made a grimace.

"That is precisely what her father is afraid of."

He moved his finger delicately around the rim of the glass, eliciting a faint hum. "You don't suppose, do you, that she is one of Sappho's daughters?"

Madame's eyes went wide. "*Mon Dieu.* It never occurred to me. I suppose it is *possible*."

"In which case," Alain noted shrewdly, "all her father's desperation is for naught."

"Not necessarily. Not in England. Most women so inclined are compelled by society to marry nonetheless. They make a brave show of it, produce an heir, and then are left alone by their husbands."

Alain shuddered. "What a country you have!"

"I was perfectly content to be absent from it for more than half my life." She glanced at him. "Do *you* think she is that way?"

"No," he said, so quickly that she could not help but take hope.

"Even though she has resisted you so entirely?"

"I saw a glimmer—the merest glimmer, mind you—of something like passion in that girl last night."

"You did?" Madame asked dubiously.

"I did. She is capable of hate, there is no question of that. It is only the opposite side of the coin, is it not, hate from love?"

"If you say so. But to answer your question, when the duke left the country for Russia, he told me that I had carte blanche in dealing with his daughter."

His blue eyes were gleaming. "Carte blanche."

"Those were his precise words."

"*Eh bien.*" He grinned, sinking back into the armchair. "We go one step further. That is all."

Six

"You must be pleased with your purchases, Katherine," Mrs. Treadwell observed from her seat in the carriage. The opposite bench was piled high with parcels tied in brown paper and string.

"Hardly," Katherine said blandly. "The selection in Hartin is not what I would call cosmopolitan."

"That length of plaid taffeta you procured—"

"Will no doubt unravel the instant Mrs. Tattersall takes shears to it. Which, considering Mrs. Tattersall's handiwork, is for the best." And she let out a yawn that she covered with a negligent hand.

Mrs. Treadwell leaned forward earnestly. "Katherine, there is something I have been meaning to broach to you."

"Is this to be yet another lecture on my high-handedness?" And she yawned again.

"Not exactly. It is more along the lines of . . . keeping busy."

"Busy?" Katherine echoed, perplexed.

"Aye. It occurs to me that much of your—well, your discontentedness might be laid at the feet of boredom. Were you to busy yourself in some way, find a means of occupying yourself, I honestly think you would find life more interesting and worthwhile."

Katherine examined a fingernail. "What sort of busyness had you in mind?"

"That doesn't matter so much as simply to be doing something. You know that Gwen has her scientific studies with Dr. Caplan—"

"I have been meaning to speak to *you,* Mrs. Treadwell, on that very subject. I overheard her recently telling Bess that she is anxious for Dr. Caplan to procure her a fetal piglet!"

"A what?"

"A dead unborn piglet!"

"Oh, my. No. That cannot be true. Why on earth would she want a dead unborn piglet?"

"So she can cut it up and examine it!"

Mrs. Treadwell's frisson of horror was extremely gratifying for Katherine to see. "I'm quite certain," the headmistress said, quite uncertainly, "that Dr. Caplan would never do such a thing!"

"You just wait until you stumble over its pieces in the science room. You'll see."

Mrs. Treadwell made an effort to regroup. "My point, my dear, is that surely there must be *some* facet of learning that engages you. Why, the world is so full of wonders!"

"Is it really," said Katherine.

The headmistress refused to be daunted. "Yes, it is! And the marvelous thing about learning is that the more you drink from the well of knowledge, the more thirsty you become!"

Katherine leveled her blue gaze at the headmistress. "Mrs. Treadwell. I am sure you mean well. But it is clear to me that due to your position in life, you can never understand. The entire *point* of being an aristocrat is to keep from doing anything. You have others do it for you."

"You are just like my daughter Vanessa," Mrs. Treadwell said sadly. "Mark my words, though. You and she both will wake up when you are fifty and wonder where your lives have gone."

"Vanessa has done remarkably well for herself, considering what she started with," Katherine observed, clearly without an inkling of how that sounded. "The earl of Yarlborough—and in her first season! I cannot comprehend why you think she has anything to complain of. Yarlborough Hall, and apparently infinite resources to spend on entertaining and wardrobe, not to mention the town house—what more could she want?"

Mrs. Treadwell started to say more, then decided against it. Instead she glanced from the window of the carriage at the fields that led down to the distant river. "Autumn will be here before we know it," she murmured.

"And then winter holiday," Katherine noted, with her first hint of animation. "This time, I *swear* it, Poppa won't send me back!"

"Perhaps that's for the best," Mrs. Treadwell acknowledged. "So long as nothing we have to offer at the academy engages your interest, you might do just as well to—" Something had caught her gaze beyond the window. "Oh, dear heavens!"

"What is it?" Katherine asked idly. "A stray cow?"

"I do believe," declared Mrs. Treadwell, going pale, "it is a highwayman!"

"Don't be ridiculous." But nonetheless, Katherine looked. "Where? I don't see any—"

"Whoa!" they heard Stains shout from the box. The horses pulled up with a suddenness that shuddered the staves. "Don't—don't—don't—" the driver was stuttering.

"Don't *you* be a fool, old man," said a male voice, cool and yet ominous. "Drop the reins. Nice and easy. Now kneel on the box, facing backward. Hands behind your head."

"Mrs. Treadwell!" poor old Stains shouted in warning. "There's a—"

"Shut up, fool!" the voice warned, still coolly but with less patience. The head of a tall white horse appeared beside the window; then a gloved hand reached down and yanked the window open abruptly. "Let's see what we have here." Mrs. Treadwell was cowering against the opposite side of the carriage. Katherine's face was unreadable.

A man with a black silk handkerchief covering his mouth and nose leaned down from the saddle and stared into the coach. He wore a black tricorn as well, pulled low to shield his eyes. "Two hens," he murmured, sounding pleased. "Two hens and one old cockerel of a driver. I'll have your jewels and your reticules, if you please."

Mrs. Treadwell scrabbled to unfasten her eardrops. "I haven't much," she said faintly, opening her bag and dropping them in. "Just these, and my cameo—oh, and this bracelet." She tried to unclasp that as well, but her hands were shaking so badly that she could not manage. "Katherine, would you kindly . . ."

Katherine had cocked her head and was gazing at their attacker. "What sort of highwayman attacks in broad daylight?" she demanded in annoyance.

"A daring one?" the horseman suggested from behind the handkerchief.

"More like an idiotic one, I'd say."

"Katherine, just give him what he wants!" Mrs. Treadwell pleaded, still struggling with her bracelet.

"I most certainly will not!"

"I would suggest, milady, that you follow your mother's advice."

"My *mother*?" Katherine burst out laughing. "Don't be absurd! This is not my—"

"*Hush,* Katherine!" Mrs. Treadwell hissed in a desperate whisper. "Do you want to be kidnapped and held for ransom? Give him what he seeks!"

Katherine crossed her arms firmly over the woven-wicker reticule in her lap. "Let him make me."

The horseman let out an impatient grunt. "Don't think I can't, pretty miss." And he thrust his hand right in through the window, making Mrs. Treadwell shriek in fear:

"For God's sake, Katherine! It is only money!"

"You are wrong there, Mrs. Treadwell," the girl said crisply. "There are principles at stake. If more folk would stand up to the likes of this coward—" The horseman growled.

Mrs. Treadwell hastily thrust her own reticule toward him. "Here! Take this, at least!"

Katherine snatched it back before he could reach it. "How *dare* you allow this creature to intimidate you!"

"Katherine, we are two women at his mercy!"

"Speak for yourself," Katherine said darkly. "I am at no man's mercy."

Mrs. Treadwell was on the verge of tears. "*Please,* Katherine! For my sake—for the sake of your parents who love you—"

"Father would never forgive me were I to part with these pearls," Katherine countered, fingering the strand at her throat. "They were a gift to his mother from the queen."

"Your father will never forgive *me* if you get shot by a brigand because of your fool pride!"

"I am out of patience," the horseman announced curtly. "Give me the bloody damned jewels and your reticules, or else."

"Or else what?" Katherine demanded, making Mrs. Treadwell come close to swooning.

"Or else you'll never see that father you're so fond of again."

Katherine stared at him, wishing she could see his eyes, hating him with every inch of her being. Mrs. Treadwell shrank into her corner, blubbering. The highwayman made a sudden impatient move, reaching for the purses Katherine still clutched. "Oh, very well, then!" she burst out in fury. "Here! Is this what you want?" She yanked the pearls from her neck, took off her earrings as well, and opened her reticule to shove them in. Mrs. Treadwell heaved a hugh sigh of relief—and then swallowed it in a gasp as she saw what Katherine drew from her bag, caught the glimmer of sunlight on a barrel of silver—

"Katherine! No!"

Too late. The girl held the pistol out and cocked it. The horseman withdrew his arm with startling swiftness. "Take *that!*" Katherine cried and fired, as Mrs. Treadwell clapped her hands to her ears. There was a sudden yelp of pain from the highwayman, before he spurred away. Katherine dug into the reticule again, eager to reload. "Aye, run, you miserable coward! Run like the wretched, worthless creature you are!" She crammed gunpowder into the chamber, stuffed in another bullet, and clambered out the door.

"Katherine!" Mrs. Treadwell screamed.

Another shot burst from the pistol, chasing the highwayman off down the road. "Dammit! Missed!" Katherine said in disgust, and reached for powder once more.

"Katherine, that is *enough!*" Mrs. Treadwell burst from the carriage as well, grabbing for her charge. "Stop! You've done enough!"

To her immense relief, Katherine lowered the pistol. "You're right. I'm not much good at a distance. Pity, though. I would have enjoyed blowing off his head."

"How long have you had that—that *thing* with you?" the headmistress demanded, eyeing the dainty silver gun in horror.

"Oh, I carry it always." Katherine told her. "Stains, do let's get going."

"Yes, miss," the shaken driver said.

Mrs. Treadwell, with some difficulty, climbed back into the carriage. "I declare, my heart is having palpitations! How *could* you, Katherine! You might have been killed! We both might have been!"

"We weren't, though, were we? And I'll wager that scum will think twice before he assumes women are *helpless* ever again," Katherine said with pride.

"You shot him," Mrs. Treadwell murmured, awed.

"Only a graze, I'm afraid. He was moving too fast." Katherine joined her inside the coach and pulled the door shut. "I wish I'd gotten *his* heart."

"Gee-yah!" shouted Stains, slapping the reins against the flanks of the horses. The carriage lurched forward. Mrs. Treadwell watched in amazement as Katherine tested the barrel of the gun to be sure it had cooled off, then slipped it back into her bag.

"Have you ever . . . shot anyone with that before?" Mrs. Treadwell asked with trepidation.

"Never. Rather satisfying to have all that practice with Poppa come to use at last, though." Katherine leaned back in her seat. "I'm feeling awfully hungry. It would be just like that wretch to cause us to miss tea."

*   *   *

"Oh, Christiane!" Mrs. Treadwell poured herself a very tall sherry. She and Madame were in the parlor, with the girls off to bed at long last. "It was perfectly dreadful! I was so frightened—not so much for me as for Katherine!"

"It sounds an utter horror," Christiane said, but with an odd air of distraction. "I am sorry for your scare."

"I've been thinking it over," Mrs. Treadwell declared, "and I really must notify the authorities at once. I understand completely what you said earlier about the academy's reputation. And it is true, the story might compel some parents to withdraw their girls. But I cannot bear the thought of that horrible madman still loose to wreak his havoc upon innocent travelers."

"I do wish, Evelyn, that you'd hold off."

"What—and give him the opportunity to attack again?"

"I find that notion dubious."

Something in her friend's voice caused Mrs. Treadwell to lower her sherry in mid-sip. "Christiane! You know something about this, don't you? Oh, don't try to hide it; I can tell. Who the devil *was* that man?"

"I am fairly sure he is the fellow I engaged in London to attempt to soften Katherine's temperament," Madame admitted.

"A *highwayman*?" Mrs. Treadwell fairly shrieked.

"He isn't a highwayman. He is more of an . . . adventurer."

"Hardly the sort of husband-fodder the duke has in mind, nonetheless!"

"He isn't husband-fodder at all. He was never meant to be. Anyway, you have met him on a prior occasion, Evelyn."

"I most certainly have not! I'd recall it if I had! Those rough manners, that insolence—"

"He attended the Tathams' last ball."

"Don't be absurd! The earl and countess would *never*—"

"What's more, I distinctly remember Bess informing me that upon introduction to him, you giggled like a schoolgirl."

Mrs. Treadwell opened her mouth to protest, then let it hang. "Oh, dear God. You cannot mean the comte de Clairmont!"

"Is that what he called himself?" Madame was amused.

"You must be mistaken," Mrs. Treadwell said dubiously. "The comte was perfectly charming! And so elegant! He would never, *ever* accost two women like a common hooligan!"

Madame reached for her shawl. "Well, I shall be calling on him tonight, so I will find out for certain."

"Calling on him *where*?"

"He is installed at the White Fox in Hartin. Has been for more than a month."

"Imagine that!" Mrs. Treadwell marveled. "But, Christiane, are you sure it is wise to visit him? He really did seem a dangerous sort."

"From what you tell me, our Katherine has shot him. I must at least apologize. But you do understand why I ask you to say nothing yet to the authorities? I'm quite certain the day's events will have quelled his willingness to continue with our experiment. He was not especially keen on it from the start."

"I hope she did not hurt him too badly," Mrs. Treadwell murmured, as Madame headed for the door. "Oh, but wait!" Her friend turned. "If you are right, and he calls it quits, then we will have our first complete and utter failure."

Madame smiled. "Make up your mind, Evelyn! One moment he is a monster, and the next our last hope! What you say is true. Still, you cannot expect any man who's had a pistol fired at him to remain ardent in his quest."

"I suppose not," Mrs. Treadwell said with a sigh. Then she brightened. "But perhaps you could encourage him? Persuade him to keep on?"

"I very much doubt that," Madame noted dryly.

"Pity," said Mrs. Treadwell, and gulped her sherry down.

Alain opened the door to his room at the countess's knock. He was clad only in his breeches and boots, and had a length of muslin wound around his upper right arm. Madame did her best not to stare at his bared torso. "I'm so very sorry for your trouble," she told him. "I came as soon as I could. Are you badly hurt?"

"Only a flesh wound . . . again," he told her, grinning.

"I'm surprised to see you able to smile. You must be dreadfully angry with me. I assure you, we had no idea whatsoever that she carried a weapon, or I surely would have warned you."

Alain shrugged, ushering her in. "Bordeaux?" he asked, and she nodded. He poured awkwardly from the bottle on the sideboard, then brought her the glass. She looked at him more closely. There was a strange glint to his eyes.

"I do hope, Alain," she said a bit nervously, "you aren't harboring some notion of revenge. All in all, I feel your ploy today was a mistake. You might have caused grave trouble. Mrs. Treadwell was frightened out of her wits."

"And how was Lady Devereaux?" he inquired, replenishing his own glass.

"Katherine? Why, she . . ." Madame paused as she sank into a chair. "She was remarkably composed, actually. You might have thought she'd enjoyed it."

"I had that same notion, even as she drew out her pistol."

Madame was unsettled. "Shall I have a look at that wound?"

"Oh, no. The landlady has seen to it admirably."

The countess clicked open her reticule. "I imagine you will want to settle up, after this unhappy incident."

"Settle up?"

"Why, yes. Let me repay you for the cost of your keep here in England, give you something to help you return to France."

"Who says I am returning to France?"

"I . . . I naturally assumed . . ."

"The task you set me to is not yet finished," Alain Montclair said gravely.

"Alain, she tried to kill you!"

"As coolly as could be."

"What hope do you have, then, for success with her? You have tried every trick in your book."

He sat on the settee across from her, leaning forward. "Not quite. I have been thinking. I could take her prisoner on a pirate ship."

"I sincerely doubt she's much of a one for men in rags and earrings."

"Only a thought. How about this, then? We could be caught together in the wilderness in a wild snowstorm. Forced to shelter in a cave—"

"Alain. It is July."

"Wild hailstorm?"

"Not likely, in Kent."

"On a very cloudy day?"

Madame burst out laughing. "Oh, Alain! Katherine Devereaux has no notion of what she is missing in you!"

He straightened on his seat. "But that is it, Christiane!"

"*What* is it?"

"I must make her miss me!"

"*Miss* you? She doesn't even know that you exist!"

"Ah, but she shall! She shall!" He sprang to his feet. "I'll need a slight advance. Shall we say five hundred pounds?"

Madame snorted. "Not likely. At least—not unless you tell me what you are plotting."

He arched innocent black brows. "Don't you trust me, Christiane?"

She looked at him, the sheer virile strength of his bared torso and arms, the gleam in his impossibly blue eyes. "I'm not altogether certain," she admitted. "In frankness, I came tonight expecting to find you ready to withdraw from the field. Why should you go on with the charade? You cannot tell me you *like* the chit."

"Let us merely say I find her intriguing. You said yourself, it is a rare woman who can withstand my charms."

"She continues to stand fast."

"Two hundred pounds?" he asked hopefully.

"One hundred," she replied firmly. "For now. Until I see some evidence of progress."

"You are a hard woman, Christiane."

Oh, if you only knew how soft I can be, the countess thought wistfully, and counted out the notes.

Seven

"Flowers?" Bess said excitedly at breakfast the next morning, seeing the bouquet of creamy roses and lapis-blue larkspur and something deep red and plumy atop the dining-room mantel. "Whoever are they for? You, Madame?"

The countess shook her head, pouring tea. "They only just arrived. There's a card, though." Bess needed no further invitation; she hurried to the hearth and poked among the blossoms eagerly.

"Whatever are those crimson flowers?" Gwen asked, contemplating the arrangement.

"Love-lies-bleeding, I believe," Mrs. Treadwell answered her.

"No one here has gotten flowers since Lord Fanning sent them to Martha," one of the lower-form girls said with a giggle.

"Would you pass the salt, please, Madame?" Katherine Devereaux asked from her place, then shook some over her eggs. "My yolks are broken again. I hardly think it too much to ask that Cook be able to prepare the *simplest* dishes with a *modicum* of—"

"They're for you, Katherine," Bess announced, having located the card.

There was a moment's pause. "For *me?*" Katherine echoed then.

"And there's a verse!" Bess went on in wonder. "It says—"

Katherine had risen from the table abruptly. "Give that to me!"

" 'White for the fairest face on earth, red for those lips divine'—"

"Bess!" Katherine screeched, in very un-Katherine-like fashion.

But Bess danced away from her, reading on:

> *"That I would give my soul to feel*
> *Only once touching mine . . ."*

"Bess," Mrs. Treadwell chided, with a curious glance at Madame. The lower-form girls were agog.

"Give that to me, damn you!" Katherine scrambled for Bess, nearly knocking the headmistress from her chair. Her quarry danced away, still reciting:

> *"Blue for your eyes, most radiant light*
> *Making the darkness shine.*
> *Roses, blue larkspur, love-lies-bleeding,*
> *Confessing what my heart is needing."*

Madame murmured something that sounded like, "I'll be damned."

"If you don't give that to me *now,* Elizabeth Boggs, I swear before God, I'll—"

"Stop teasing, Bess, and give it to her," Mrs. Treadwell ordered. "Let her see who they are from."

"Very well," Bess said archly, and relinquished the card. Katherine scanned it feverishly, lips moving as she reread the poem.

"Why—there's no signature at all!" she cried in dismay.

"Double-damned," Madame whispered.

"An anonymous admirer." Petra Forrester, a highly romantic sixteen-year-old, nearly swooned. "How marvelous!"

Katherine, still clutching the card, moved toward the mantel, staring at the flowers as though they might disappear. "He can't be worthy," she said doubtfully, "if he is too timid to sign his name."

"Worthy or no, he certainly has a turn for verse," Mrs. Treadwell noted, and clapped her hands. "Ladies, your breakfast is growing cold!"

Reluctantly the girls returned to their eggs and toast. Katherine drifted back to her place. "Very impressive, Katherine," Gwen Carstairs observed softly. "You have made quite a conquest."

"I wonder who he is," she responded dazedly. "I cannot think who it might be."

"Triple, perhaps," Madame murmured, smiling into her teacup. "Oh, Alain! Touché!"

All that day, the bouquet stood on the dining-room mantel. Though Katherine tried her best not to, she couldn't help sneaking glances at it throughout each meal. Whomever *could* the flowers be from? She'd folded the card very small and tucked it into her bodice; she could feel the edges press against her breast every time she breathed. *An admirer. She had an admirer at last, after all this time.*

Oh, it wasn't as though young men had never been attracted to her. They always clamored for introductions at the fetes and balls to which Mrs. Treadwell took the girls. But somehow, after she'd danced a set or two and engaged in conversation, or accompanied them in to supper, *something* went wrong, though she was never sure what. And while she'd heard Bess and Gwen giggle behind her back at her pride and lofty manners, that wasn't her fault, was it? She was only doing what was required—nay, demanded—of her as the daughter of a duke.

Occasionally, lying in her bed, Katherine wondered what life might be like without such burdens as she shouldered. To be as carefree and nonchalant as her form-mates, to be stripped of the awful duty to always, in every way, remain conscious of her birth . . . "Noblesse oblige," her father called it—the obligation of honor imposed by high heritage. Most folk tossed the term about as though it meant something else altogether, offering a license for profligacy and moral shame. They envied the highborn their riches, and their envy made them resentful. But Katherine had been schooled early on in how privilege demanded responsibility. And though her father, in wedding Nanette O'Toole, had clearly set aside the concept, Katherine was determined to stick to it. She owed her mother—her *real* mother—that.

Now, seated beside Madame as the supper plates were cleared away, she let her gaze wander once more toward the lovely bouquet. He likely *wasn't* worthy, her unknown admirer. Still, she searched her mind, wondering whom she might have met recently and charmed. There was that viscount at the Tathams' ball—what was his name? Lord Furst, something like that. He'd taken her in to supper. That was when she'd learned how new his title was—and that his grandfather had been a Lincolnshire wholesaler of wool. God. *Trade*. Not that there was anything wrong, of course, with making an honest living, if one was in a situation where one *had* to. But to expect her, the scion of men and women who had spent their days in service to king and country without recompense, as chancellors and parliamentarians and court advisers and ladies-in-waiting, to rub shoulders with such folk was a bit de trop.

The paper burned at her breast. *Roses, blue larkspur, love-lies-bleeding, confessing what my heart is needing.* The words made her tingle, set her head to pounding. Even Mrs. Treadwell had said her beau had a turn for verse. Who on earth was he? What did he look like? An image popped into her mind: the comte de Clairmont, that supposed French nobleman who'd been at the Tathams' ball. . . . Quickly she thrust the memory away, only to have it return, unbidden. He *had* been gloriously handsome. Of course, she'd spoken her mind to him, as she always did—the nobility did not hide behind pretense—and judging from the shocked reactions of Mrs. Treadwell and the other girls, that had been more than sufficient to squelch any attraction he might have felt.

It had been clever, though, the way he'd turned her rebuff to something like a compliment. *They are very French, whimsies.* Well. The first duke of Devereaux *had* been Norman. Though that had been hundreds and hundreds of years ago . . .

"Katherine?"

Katherine glanced up and saw that the dining room was empty except for her and Madame. "You seem lost in thought," the countess—another foreign title, that, and Italian, of all things!—observed gently. "You are thinking of your admirer, perhaps?"

For an instant, Katherine felt an overwhelming urge to confide in the petite woman, tell her how this unexpected, unprecedented gift had set her mind awhirl. Then she swiftly conquered the notion. It would be most unbecoming for her, the daughter of a duke, to pour out her hopes and dreams to a confessor who had, and for very good reason, been banished from the ton. "Not at all," she said crisply. "I was simply doing my best to recall the lesson on the rules of precedence in table seatings that Mrs. Caldburn gave us this afternoon." And she rose quickly from her place.

"I should think you would know such lessons well enough by now," Madame noted.

"I *believe* I do, of course. But the ramifications of a misstep are so serious, it cannot hurt to review the order regularly."

"Have you smelled those roses?" Madame asked.

"Roses? Oh, you mean the bouquet. I saw no need. I know what roses smell like." Besides, to have gone to the mantel and buried her nose in the profusion of blossoms would have been quite unladylike.

"These are particularly exquisite." Madame moved to the hearth, reaching up on tiptoe to take a long sniff. "Come. Come and see."

"I really don't think—"

"Katherine! A man has sent you flowers! Has any suitor ever done so before?"

"No," she admitted.

"Why do you think posies are such a part of the courtship ritual?"

"I've . . . never thought about it."

Madame touched a nodding rose. "Because they are beautiful and sweet, yes—but also because they are ephemeral. As fleeting as opportunity, Katherine. A gift of blossoms says—I cherish you now, today. Tomorrow, my fancy may move elsewhere. Grasp the moment while you can. Love while you may."

Katherine had taken a step toward the mantel; now she stopped. "You make it sound so . . . lascivious."

Madame shook her dark head. "No. Not at all. But this bouquet is a warning not to let life pass you by. Come." She gestured her forward again. Katherine moved reluctantly, almost fearfully. When she was close enough, Madame took her arm and pulled her to the vase. "Smell life, Katherine. This is what life smells of." She put her hand to the nape of Katherine's neck and forced her closer. The fuzzy fronds of love-lies-bleeding tickled Katherine's nose; their scent was faint and earthy. The larkspur smelled young, green. And the roses . . .

"Drink it in," Madame murmured.

Oh, they were heady, sweet-musky, like raspberries, ripe melons, but with an undercurrent that was dark and deep. . . . *I know what roses smell like,* she had said. But she never had smelled roses like these.

"They have a scent," Madame mused at her side, "like the body of a man after the act of love."

Katherine drew back quite suddenly, her cheeks flooded crimson. "My God! What a thing to say!"

"I beg your pardon. It was only what they put me in mind of. What do they put *you* in mind of?"

"Roses!" Katherine said in a fluster. "They just smell like roses!"

The countess shrugged. "*Eh bien.* As you will."

Eight

The following morning at breakfast, the maid, Clarisse, brought in the toast and tea and sliced pears and an omelet with mushrooms. Then she retreated to the kitchens, while Katherine contemplated the neat triangle of filled eggs on her plate. She poked with her fork, and the savor of the mushrooms wafted up to her nose. Intriguing odor, mushrooms had. Rich and yet subtle, a bit dunglike, clandestine . . . *Oh, you are growing fanciful,* she told herself sharply, and took a bite.

"This came for ye, miss." It was Clarisse again, laying something on the table at Katherine's elbow.

"Ooh-hoo!" Bess cried. "Another gift from your unknown admirer!"

Katherine stared. It couldn't be—could it? The parcel was rather long and flat, wrapped in brown paper and tied with blue ribbon. The attached card's envelope read: *Lady Katherine Devereaux, Mrs. Treadwell's Academy,* in a bold, slanting hand.

Trying to maintain her composure, Katherine pulled out the card and examined it. Bess craned to see, but Katherine quickly shielded it with her arm. "How can you be so *mean*?" Bess wailed. "None of us has ever had anything *half* so exciting happen to us!"

To her own surprise, Katherine relented, seeing the eager yearning on her form-mate's round face. "It is the same handwriting as the card with the flowers," she admitted. "But the message isn't poetry. In fact, it makes no sense." She passed the card to Bess.

" 'As I long to fit you,' " Bess read out, and her forehead furrowed. "You're right. It makes no sense at all."

"Perhaps," Gwen ventured from her seat across the table, "it would if you opened the gift."

By now, even the youngest girls were arching in their places, looking on avidly. Feeling self-conscious but flattered—it was rare for her fellow students to pay her much attention—Katherine reached for the ribbon. Then she stopped, glancing over at Madame. The countess gave her a small nod of encouragement, so she pulled loose the ribbon and uncrinkled the paper. Inside was a handsome gray-and-white-striped box. "Oh!" exclaimed Mrs. Treadwell, who was watching as excitedly as the girls. "I know that box! It comes from Farringdon's in London! A most exclusive establishment." Katherine lifted the lid to a cloud of pale ivory tissue and the unmistakable scent of leather, pungent and clean. It put her instantly in mind of horses and hunts and clear October skies.

"Go *on*," Petra Forrester breathed.

Katherine reached gingerly into the tissue paper, withdrawing a pair of dainty kid-leather gloves of the most remarkable workmanship, stitched just so, the hide as supple as silk. But the most amazing thing was their color. They were a rich azure blue, as blue as the skies she'd only just been imagining. Unthinkingly she laid them to her cheek, felt their soft drape. Then, abruptly, she let them fall to the table.

"Whatever is the matter, Katherine?" Gwen asked curiously.

"I—I cannot accept them. Gloves are too personal a gift. Do you not recall Mrs. Caldburn's lecture on the subject? 'Intimate objects of apparel may only be exchanged by couples who are betrothed.' "

"I'll take them!" Bess said promptly.

"I don't think they'd fit you," Gwen noted. "They look to be made for a very small hand."

"You're right." Bess glanced at her fingers. "They wouldn't, at that."

Katherine did have small hands, a fact she'd always been

proud of. Her gaze slanted to Madame. "Would it be wrong, do you suppose, just to try them on?"

"In my opinion, you may as well—and keep them. You can't very easily return them, since you've no notion who they are from."

"A point well taken," said Bess. "Did Mrs. Caldburn address that?"

"You were there," Katherine reminded her.

"So I was." Bess formed a moue that made the younger girls laugh. "But I never pay attention when she gets to rambling on about engagement etiquette. The idea that any man will ever want to wed me is just too far-fetched."

"Oh. She didn't, as it happens. Mrs. Treadwell, what rules apply in such an instance?"

"I—I'm not at all sure. But my instinct is that you should do as Madame says, and keep them. Or perhaps you might donate them to charity."

"*I* am in great need of charity," Bess declared.

Katherine smiled at her distractedly, then slipped her hand into one of the gloves. The smooth, lithe skin seemed at first as though it would be too snug, but as she tugged it on, it stretched and gave, allowing her to draw it down all the way to her wrist.

"Well!" Mrs. Treadwell declared. "Whoever he is, he gauged your fists perfectly!"

As I long to fit you . . . Looking down at the azure leather molded around her hand, Katherine blushed suddenly, deeply, with an intimation of why Mrs. Caldburn had said such a gift was improper unless a couple was engaged.

"They are so lovely," Petra Forrester sighed. "So *exquisitely* lovely."

"They truly are," Bess agreed. "It would be wrong, Katherine, for you to give anything away that fits you so well. I withdraw my bid."

"I—I shall have to think on the correct course of action. Apply to Mrs. Caldburn, perhaps."

"My goodness!" Mrs. Treadwell recollected herself with a start. "For how long, do you suppose, is our daily breakfast

to be consumed half-cold on account of Katherine's mysterious suitor?" Katherine blushed again, removing the glove
and laying it and its mate carefully back in the box.

"I'm sure this won't go on much longer," she assured the
headmistress with a hint of wry humor. "Generally, I've
found young men lose interest in me with astonishing rapidity."

Gwen had just lifted up her teacup; now it fell with a crash.

"Oh, dear. How clumsy of me," she apologized, hastily
blotting up the tea with her napkin as Clarisse rushed over
with a towel.

Later, after the meal was finished and she and Bess were
heading upstairs to dress for a riding lesson, Gwen said ruefully, "I certainly made a spectacle of myself letting go of
my teacup. But the truth is, I was *astounded* to hear Katherine say anything so self-effacing as she did."

"Had I anything in hand," Bess noted with a giggle, "I'd
have dropped it as well!"

Gwen's small, heart-shaped face was thoughtful. "Do you
know what else, Bess? Three times, you made the sorts of
observations that have always elicited rude comments from
Katherine. First when you said those gloves wouldn't fit you,
and then when you said the idea of any man wanting to marry
you was far-fetched, and then when you said you were in
need of charity. And not *once* did Katherine mock or insult
you! I call that downright miraculous!"

"Why do you imagine I went on saying such things?" Bess
grinned. "Whoever her beau may be, I wish him all success
in his courtship! I am almost beginning to like our Katherine,
now that she is in love."

The next morning at breakfast, it was flowers again, poppies,
paper-thin and blazing, and another verse:

> *You are my sun, my warmth and fire,*
> *My gentle swelling rain,*
> *The wind that whirls my wild hopes higher,*

My moon that will not wane.
Calm, when of life's cruel storm I tire;
My night, my silent pain.
All this and more I see in thee—
What, dearest heart, could you see in me?

Petra sighed audibly as Katherine, without much demurral this time, read the card out to the gathered girls.

"It's a curious verse form he has chosen," Bess observed. "Rather like that used by Molière in his early poems."

"Who on earth is Molière?" one of the younger students demanded.

"A French poet and playwright."

French. Katherine contemplated the poppies. No. It couldn't be. Not after she had been so disdainful to Clairmont. Still, it had to be *someone,* didn't it? And try as she would, she could not think of anyone except the handsome foreigner on whom she might have made *any* sort of impression of late.

Though there *had* been that curious incident with the highwayman.

Whom she had shot.

And that ridiculous fellow who had tried to save her from the rampaging rabbits.

Whom she'd laughed at.

Really, she thought, *considering my record with men, it is a positive miracle that any man could have written this poem for me.* Still, someone had . . . unless . . .

She glanced sharply at Bess, then at Gwen. Unless this was some sort of wretched practical joke by her form-mates, meant to make her look like a fool.

But Bess's face was nothing but wistful as she stared at the poppies with her chin on her hand. She wasn't *that* adept at playacting. And Gwen was as poor as a church mouse; she hadn't money to toss away on flowers and fancies for the sake of a jest.

Besides, Katherine felt in her heart that he was real, her

secret admirer. That somehow he could see into her soul, knew her hopes and fears.

Patience, she counseled herself dreamily. He would reveal himself in time. He'd have to, or what would be the sense in the gifts and poems? In the meantime, simply waking up of a morning had become the most marvelous adventure. She could hardly wait to come to breakfast on the morrow.

Alain Montclair sat at the desk in his hired rooms at the White Fox, scratching his chin, contemplating the note from the countess. The tone was quite unlike Christiane; she sounded positively giddy. *I strongly suggest you continue on your current course,* she'd written—and enclosed another hundred pounds. He was clearly making progress at last.

He would need another gift. Flowers? No, he'd done flowers twice already. He reflected on what he'd given women in the past, with more attention than was his wont. He had the sense he was treading a fine line. Should he presume too much, appear too intimate, this prickly Katherine creature would likely take offense. And yet he wanted something special for her, something intriguing enough to continue to pique her curiosity. He took a sip of wine and then crossed the room to his trunk, where he had, as usual, a store of the sorts of fripperies appreciated by the fairer sex.

There was a very handsome pair of gold and pearl eardrops that he'd pocketed from the boudoir of an admirer. But she had gold and pearls to burn, this daughter of a duke; he'd seen how fine was the necklace she'd worn in the carriage. He pushed that box aside, reached deeper, drew forth a pair of silk stockings. No, not those—at least, not yet. There was a volume of Dante's sonnets to Beatrice, but in French, and he had no idea whether she could read French. Christ, this was difficult, when he knew so little about the girl!

He closed his eyes, remembering the times he'd seen her. Christiane had told the truth; she *was* lovely. Ordinarily he found English blondes insipid, but this one had fire beneath her ice-cool. That she had shot at him—the notion still amused him. What courage that had taken! The way those blue eyes had flashed at him in fury as he demanded her reticule . . . there was passion locked inside her hard heart, but locked so tightly! He had stumbled across the first sequence in the tumbler, but where to go from here?

Once more he pawed through the trunk. Nothing but cheap trinkets, mostly, the sort that had always sufficed to gain him what he sought from women. Now, though, he needed something of value, something that would confirm his high opinion of her. A duke's daughter was not likely to be won by a string of glass beads, a cameo, a handkerchief. . . .

It occurred to him, briefly, that he was giving far more heed to the wooing of Katherine Devereaux than he had ever given to that of any other woman. But then, he wasn't accustomed to being rebuffed, much less scorned. Was that what intrigued him so much about this English schoolgirl?

Perhaps it was no more than that, he mused, reaching deeper into his cache of seductive baubles. On the other hand, that combination of fire and ice, disdain and steely nerve, was disquietingly familiar. In some strange way, the girl seemed like a mirror . . . of himself.

Ridiculous notion. He set it aside, along with an embroidered Oriental shawl. Why was he wasting his time here? By now, Jacques Boulé would surely have found more pressing matters to concern him than his sister's brief infatuation with a no-account womanizer. He should return to France. . . .

In the very bottom of the trunk, he glimpsed a crystal flagon. Perfume. Where had he gotten that? Swiped from some lover's dressing table? No—he remembered suddenly that he had actually *bought* it, when he had passed the doorway of a small Parisian shop and been struck by the scent emanating from within of distant lands, mysterious veiled women, caliphs and harems and palm-fronded fountains, the miracle of water after long, desperate thirst. . . .

But what would he say to this English miss if he sent it? He summoned up the image of her as she'd reached into her reticule for the pistol, the way her eyes had flashed, the way some part of his heart had constricted as he realized: *She wants me dead . . . and I want her in my bed.*

In all his experience with women, Alain had never encountered anyone like Katherine Devereaux. She was like the cherished daughter of some Eastern pasha, that distant, that remote.

He took the flagon in his hand, put it to his neck, felt the cool chill of the crystal. He unstoppered it, raised it to his nose, inhaled possibility, the soft silk of her skin, her sighs. He smiled to himself: *Ah, Katherine!*

He went back to his desk, took up his pen, and wrote.

On Tuesday, Katherine's present was a flagon of perfume—another forbidden gift, according to Mrs. Caldburn. On the card was a stark, aching sentiment: *For where I long to go.* That one, Katherine would not read out despite Bess and Petra's pleas. She took the crystal bottle to her rooms, and when no one else was there, she opened it. The scent was a subtle blend of Eastern woods and spices—patchouli, sandalwood, ambergris—married with softer notes of lavender and *muguets du bois.* Tentatively she touched the stopper to her left wrist, then raised her hand to her nose. She smelled of paradise, of mysterious, distant places she would never see. She inhaled more deeply, and then, with a cautious glance at the closed door, opened the throat of her gown.

For where I long to go.

Inside their chaste white-linen cocoon, her breasts felt warm and heavy. Very gently, she applied the stopper to each one in turn. The crystal was densely cool, the perfume even colder. Her nipples surged to hardness, making her draw in her breath. Slowly, softly, she swirled the glass around one rosy tip. *I must be mad,* she thought.

For where I long to go. She tried to imagine what it would be like to have a man put his hands on her bare flesh, touch her *there.* . . . The air in the chamber was thick with the exotic scent. She closed her eyes, pictured herself supine on a bed strewn with flowers, while her lover caressed her cheek, smoothed her breasts, kissed her longingly, lingeringly. . . .

A clatter of heels in the hallway made her start; her face flooded crimson. It was only the younger girls, rushing by on their way to some class. Still, the spell had been broken, and she went to the mirror, hastily straightening her bodice. If this was love, then love was stranger and more potent than she ever had dreamed. She was so wild to know her suitor's identity that she could barely contain herself; she wanted to run to the roof and shout to all of Kent: *Come out, come out, wherever you are!*

She hid the perfume away, deep down in the dresser drawer that held her unmentionables. But the drops she had touched to her wrist and breasts reminded her all that day of her admirer's ardor; she went about with a dreamy half-smile on her lips and a glow in her eyes.

Nine

"*It is just* plain *stupid*," Bess said shortly, poking her needle through the pillow slip she was embroidering. "He could be anyone. Or no one."

"True," Gwen admitted. "But I can't see what cause you have to complain. She's finally become bearable."

"If you call 'smitten' bearable."

Gwen laid her own needlework aside. "You didn't behave this way when Martha was being wooed by Lord Fanning."

"Martha deserved her success. She is a decent person. More than decent. A *splendid* person. Whereas Katherine is nothing but an intolerable snob. She already has everything anyone could ever desire. Why must she have such a delectable beau?"

"For all we know, he's not a bit delectable. He could be a hunchback. One-eyed. The worst sort of peasant."

"Don't be absurd. No peasant pens those poems."

"Aha! Now we get right down to it! It's the verses that have you green with envy!"

Bess laughed a little. "Well . . . perhaps. They are extremely good. And it seems to me that if anyone deserves a beau who knows his way around words, it ought to be me."

"I don't know. Two poets together is a frightening concept." Gwen's dark gaze slanted toward her friend. "It isn't you writing those verses to her, is it?"

"Not likely!"

"I only wondered. . . . I've been wracking my brain trying to think of where and when she might have conquered this mysterious stranger's heart. And I cannot—" Gwen stopped abruptly; Katherine had just come into the parlor.

"I beg your pardon," she said, hearing the conversation die. "I can go and do my work in our rooms."

"No, no! Sit down, please!" Gwen said warmly. "We were only discussing your anonymous suitor."

"As if anyone here ever talks about anything else," Bess noted rather glumly.

Katherine sank onto a settee, blushing a bit. "I am sorry for all the commotion he has caused. What beautiful stitches you make, Gwen! I love the way you've worked those violets."

Bess let out a small, strangled gurgle. Katherine hastily added, "Your piece is coming along quite nicely, too."

Bess cocked her red head. "I can't decide which is less tolerable, Katherine—the old you or the new."

Katherine looked up with a start. "I don't know what you mean!"

"I suppose I mean—which is real? The haughty aristocrat, or the tender lovestruck maiden?"

"Bess," Gwen said warningly.

"For all you know," Bess went on relentlessly, "he could be a humpbacked one-eyed dwarf!"

"It's possible," Katherine conceded.

"I'm quite sure he's *not*," Gwen said stoutly.

"Or the vilest sort of peasant."

"With money to burn on perfume and gloves and flowers and that exquisite music box he sent this morning," Gwen murmured.

"Well, there must be *something* wrong with him," Bess pressed on, "or why wouldn't he declare himself? Make an appearance in person?"

Katherine leaned her cheek on her hand. "I don't know, Bess. I wonder myself. Perhaps he *is* deformed in some way. Perhaps he is unworthy. All I can tell you is this. He *knows* me. He perceives things about me that no one ever has. It is as though he can see into my soul."

"What utter balderdash! As though *anyone* can see into another's soul!"

Katherine shrugged, taking up her needle. "I admit, it seems absurd. And the longer this goes on, the more I come to agree—there must be something dreadfully amiss about him. But at the same time, I begin to think it doesn't matter. What if he *is* a humpbacked dwarf, when he knows my thoughts, my longings, so perfectly?"

Bess frankly stared. "You cannot tell me you would marry such a man!"

"I think he is being very clever," Gwen put in.

"*Too* clever," Bess grumbled. "Mark my words, there is something definitely off about this."

"I know," Katherine said rather wistfully. "Still, I cannot help but enjoy it. At least for as long as it goes on."

"I'm sure he'll declare himself any day now," Gwen assured her.

"Oh, it is what I long for!" Katherine said, then nibbled her exquisite lip. "And, between us, what I am most afraid of."

"I cannot say I blame you," Bess said tartly, and nearly impaled her thumb as she stabbed another stitch.

The following morning brought orchids, the most truly glorious orchids, masses of them, with a poem even more intimate than its predecessors had been. Katherine read it silently as far as the line that began *Stone-cool, yet warm, thine alabaster breasts* before clapping the card facedown on the breakfast table, flushing so violently that even Bess dared not tease. The next day, her gift was a filigree hairnet, exquisitely worked in gold and silver wire and threaded with seed pearls. The card with that read simply: *When?*

Oh, God, anytime, anytime at all! thought Katherine, her heart blazing with longing. But she was at his mercy; she could only wait, since he had left her no clues as to how to contact him. Unless—

She stood up at her place. "Katherine?" Mrs. Treadwell said anxiously. "Is something amiss?"

"I—I must go and speak to Clarisse." And Katherine hurried toward the door to the kitchens, while her schoolmates stared.

"Clarisse must be in *big* trouble," one of the smallest girls said nervously.

Cook was sweating from the heat of the ovens as she bent

down to remove a batch of steaming bread. She straightened when she saw her visitor, and mopped a corner of her apron at her damp face. "Well?" she barked. "What is it now, *Lady* Devereaux? Eggs not cooked to yer liking? Too much salt in the butter again?"

"Oh, no!" Katherine assured her. "Everything is splendid! Simply delightful! I can't think when I've enjoyed a meal more." Cook stared for a moment, then turned the loaves out onto the table with a thump. "I only needed to speak to Clarisse for a moment."

"If she's spilled somewot across one of yer fancy gowns—"

"Of course she hasn't! Clarisse is marvelously adept at serving!" Clarisse, who'd just come up from the cellars with a fresh jar of lemon curd, stared as well.

"I am?" she said.

"Oh, you are! I don't know why on earth Cook imagined I was coming to complain."

"P'raps," Cook noted dourly, "on account of that's all wot's ever brought ye to my kitchens before."

"That's not true!" Katherine protested. "Why, I specifically recall complimenting you last Eastertide on your Banbury tarts."

Cook arched a brow. "Complimentin'? Is that what ye call it, then, tellin' me how yer *chef* at home puts more raisins in?"

"It was *only* a suggestion. To augment their perfection," Katherine said hastily. "Clarisse, may I speak to you for a moment? In private?"

"Why . . . er . . . yes, miss—m'lady," Clarisse said very nervously. "Will the pantry do?"

"The pantry would be lovely," Katherine told her warmly, taking the maid's elbow and steering her there. She closed the door behind them, then turned to see Clarisse making frantic pleats in the front of her apron with her fingertips.

"If this is about the ironin'," the maid began, "I'll have ye know, the girl is new and still bein' trained. And I told her ye would make her pay for it out of her wages, and she weren't happy, not a bit, but she's agreed to—"

"The ironing?" Katherine blinked. "What is wrong with the ironing?"

Clarisse's round, freckled face underwent an abrupt change. "Why—nothin' at all, miss. Not unless ye count that teeny-tiny scorch mark on the one pair of drawers."

"I didn't notice any scorch mark."

"Ye didn't?" Clarisse visibly relaxed. "Well, praise God for that!"

"I'll be sure and look for it after breakfast, though," Katherine declared, and laughed when the maid flinched. "I am only jesting! One would think I were some sort of ogre, the way you and Cook expect that I am bent on finding fault with you!"

Clarisse's bottom lip thrust out slightly. "Well, yer not one for tossin' bouquets."

Bouquets reminded Katherine of her mission. "That's just what I wished to speak to you about, Clarisse. The bouquets and gifts that have been coming for me."

"I don't know a thing, miss, about who sends 'em."

"But you must know something about *how* he sends them. Oh, I can't believe I didn't think of this before! How do they arrive, Clarisse? How do they get here? Who brings them?"

"They come with the milk," the maid responded.

Katherine blinked. "With the *milk*?"

"Aye, miss. On the milk-cart."

It wasn't what Katherine had expected. "And where does the milk-cart come from?"

Clarisse bestowed a pitying look on her. "The dairy."

"The dairy. And where, pray tell, is the dairy?"

"Farmer Brotton's dairy, of course. Halfway between here and the village."

"I see. And when does it come?"

"Four o'clock, most mornin's."

"There's a . . . driver?"

Clarisse rolled her eyes. "The dairy boy. Aye."

"And he brings the flowers and such."

"Said as much, didn't I? Ye'll excuse it, miss, but I've got work to do."

"I beg your pardon," Katherine said humbly. "I don't mean to keep you from it." She moved to open the pantry door, then shut it again. "This dairy boy . . . what is he like?"

"Wot's he *like*?" Clarisse looked as though her inquisitor were daft. "How the devil should *I* know wot he's like? He brings the milk! I leave him sixpence for it."

"I mean to say . . . is he young? Old?"

"I never much noticed. Most mornings, I'm still abed when he comes 'round. Somewheres in between. I'm sorry, miss, but Cook'll have my hide if I don't get out there now."

"Of course. Do pardon my foolish questions." Katherine made way for her, and the maid scurried quickly out to the kitchens again.

In the pantry, Katherine stood stock-still, surrounded by Cook's neatly labeled canisters and jars and bins, and thought: *The dairy boy?*

God. How ignominious.

Then she remembered what Gwen had said, about a peasant not being able to afford flowers and perfume and music boxes, and she took heart. The dairy boy was only a clue, a link in the chain. But she would have to speak to him.

When? the card with the orchids had asked. *Perhaps sooner than you think*, she thought, smiling.

Now the question was how she was going to awaken at the ungodly hour of four A.M.

The only way she could manage it was to stay awake the whole night through—and there had never been so lengthy and dreary a time in all her life. She sat cross-legged on her bed after Bess and Gwen were fast asleep, listening to their breathing, pinching herself when she grew drowsy. Only her fierce determination to learn her suitor's identity enabled her to make it through the endless hours. But at long last, she heard the village church bells pealing out four strokes, and then a rattle of wheels on the road through the dense predawn silence. She grabbed up her shawl, slipped into her boots, and tiptoed down the stairs to the kitchens and through the outer door.

She nearly knocked over the dairy boy; he was just bending down to set a can and several bottles by the doorstep. "Ye gods!" he cried, springing back in shock.

"I beg your pardon," said Katherine, conscious of her heart pounding. "Are you the dairy boy?"

"Nay, I'm the king o' Siam." He glowered at her from beneath his wide-brimmed hat, his hands full of butter and cream.

"That *was* a foolish question," she acknowledged. "I am Katherine, Lady Devereaux." There was a pause. "I was informed," she added, feeling unaccustomedly awkward, "that you are the bearer of my gifts."

"The wot?"

"The bearer of my . . ." She brought her hauteur down a notch. "Clarisse—you do know Clarisse?—she told me you bring the presents for me."

Beneath the hat brim, his face unclenched. "Argh, I *knew* that name was familiar. Aye, I brings 'em, all right. And a bloody bit of bother it be, too, atop all the *real* work I have to do."

"I'm so very sorry for the imposition. But I was hoping you could tell me about their provisor. The gentleman who gives them to you," she hastily amended, seeing him go blank again.

The face pinched once more, suspicious. "Such as wot?"

"Well . . . who he is, to begin with."

He burst out laughing. "Wot, then, ye don't know who he is?"

"As it happens, I don't," she said stiffly. "His gifts arrive anonymously. Without a name attached, that is."

"Don't know her own fellow." The dairy boy seemed infinitely amused at the notion.

Katherine straightened, gathering her nightdress with dignity. "As it happens, anonymous suitors have a long and illustrious history. It is precisely the way the romance between Romeo and Juliet began."

"I don't know no Romeo," said the boy, and aimed a stream of spit at the grass. "No more'n I know the name of yer fancy-love."

"Well . . . what he looks like, then?"

"Nope."

"Oh, but you must! How come you by the gifts?"

"They be set in the wagon when I come to the dairy. Before I ever stocks it, they be there."

"You mean—you've never seen him?"

"Not hide nor hair, miss. If ye'll excuse me now, I've got my rounds to make."

"Wait!" Katherine, made desperate by her need to know, grabbed for him and caught his shirt. "He must have made arrangements with you to deliver them. Paid you."

The face beneath the hat turned cunning. "He may leave me somewot for my trouble. But that be betwixt him 'n' me."

"Damn!" Katherine declared, and stomped her small foot, making him stare. "Your master, then. Whoever owns the dairy. Farmer—what the devil is his name?"

"Brotton," the lad said reluctantly. "Never mentioned it to him, did I? He'd only skim half the shilling I'm given, wouldn't he? And why should it go to him, I'd like to know?"

"I see." And Katherine did; it was clear the boy was not a whit inclined to share the news of his daily windfall with his employer. With a growing sense of despair, she contemplated the situation. Then a notion came to her. "See here. You could leave a message for him, couldn't you? In the wagon?"

"For who? Farmer Brotton?"

"No, no. For whoever is sending me the gifts. I could give you a message, and you could leave it there for him when you have made your rounds. He'd find it in the morning, when he brings another present."

The dairy boy scratched his chin. "I don't know. I'd run

the risk, wouldn't I, of Brotton findin' it? I don't think he'd be happy to learn I've been deliverin' flowers 'n' such with the butter."

"I could make it worth your while," Katherine said shrewdly. "Another shilling, say?"

"Oh, well, if that was the case, I might find a way."

"Wait here," Katherine ordered, and she flew back up the stairs to her rooms, extracting the coin from her purse, then taking a sheet of stationery from her writing-drawer and pausing over it with her pen. What on earth would she say? If only she were a poet! Perhaps if she woke Bess, the girl could come up with a verse . . . but no. That would never do. She couldn't bear for anyone to learn the lengths that she was going to.

What had his last note read? *When?* Suddenly inspired, she scrawled across the page: *Tonight. In the courtyard at midnight.* Then she folded the paper over several times and scrambled down the stairs.

The boy was waiting, whistling impatiently. "Here." Katherine thrust the note and shilling at him. "There'll be another shilling in it for you if you don't read it—not that you can likely read—and if you hold your tongue."

He cocked his head at her. "Hold my tongue about wot, miss?" Then he laughed again at her flustered expression, tucking the note into his shirt. "Argh, never fear; I'm not one to rock the boat, am I? I'll leave it in the wagon, as ye say." He turned back to his cart. "Gor, I near forgot. Here. Today's delivery." He tossed her a package, tipped the hat, and climbed into the seat, clucking to the team: "Gee-yah!" They clattered off across the yard and through the gate, leaving Katherine staring down at the parcel in her hands.

She'd done it. She could scarcely believe she had done it.

The door swung open behind her, and Clarisse, yawning, stumbled out onto the step. The maid's eyes went wide as she saw Katherine. "Why, Lady Devereaux! Wotever are ye doin' up at this hour?"

Katherine clutched the package to her breast. "Just making

the dairy boy's acquaintance," she murmured, brushing past Clarisse and rushing back to her rooms.

Inside the brown wrapper was a box containing a single beeswax taper, long and slim, its wick already blackened. The attached note made Katherine infinitely grateful she had not opened it in front of her classmates. *As I burn for you . . .* She hurried to hide the gift and note away with the others— then went and fetched the slip of paper out again, to trace the magical words with her fingertip.

He would find her note. He had to. Tonight, he would come to her in the courtyard, and at long last she'd meet him, this lover who knew her so intimately but whom she did not know at all. What would she say to him? What would she wear to their assignation? Suddenly panic-stricken, she went to the wardrobe and began to paw through her gowns.

"Katherine?" Gwen's sleepy voice called from her bed. "You are up and about early."

Katherine, blushing madly, was struck by a desperate urge to confide what she had done. Then a great, wide wave of shame stopped her dead. *He could be anyone,* she reminded herself, willing her wild heart to calmness. It only made sense to learn his identity before revealing anything, even to sympathetic Gwen. She backed out of the wardrobe. "I had . . . some trouble sleeping," she confided.

"God, you look it," noted Bess, who had awakened as well. "Tormented by dreams your mystery beau might be a peasant after all?"

"Bess, don't tease," Gwen chided, as she took in Katherine's tousled nightgown and wan face and mussed hair. "You *have* had a night of it, haven't you, Katherine?"

"It doesn't matter," Katherine murmured. And it wouldn't—not after midnight. Then a thought struck her. The note she'd left with the dairy boy wouldn't be found by her suitor until the *following* morning, when he came to leave another gift. She would have to bide her time until midnight the *following* day. "Oh, damn!" she burst out, and chewed on her lip. How would she ever endure it?

"Katherine, I am *shocked,*" Bess declared, in such a perfect imitation of Mrs. Caldburn's round tones that even Katherine had to laugh.

"You really are so good at mimicry," she said, and noted absently that at the compliment, Bess's face lit up with pleasure, so that she looked almost . . . attractive. Then she recollected herself—she must not tread too far down the path of friendship with these girls; it simply wouldn't suit. "Pity it's not a talent likely to help you land a husband."

"*There's* the Katherine I despise and have missed so lately," Bess declared, tossing her carrot curls.

"Missed? I haven't changed a bit!" Katherine insisted, as she crossed the room to take command of the mirror, patting her long blond ringlets with shaky hands. She felt the need to reestablish supremacy. "Gwen, how fare your efforts to have that despicable Dr. Caplan find you a calf to slice up?"

"Fetal piglet," Gwen informed her with dignity. "Their physiology is remarkably close to that of humans, I'll have you know. And experience with them is absolutely vital to any sort of proper medical knowledge."

Katherine shuddered extravagantly. "I would sooner die than touch a dead thing! And what do you mean, proper medical knowledge? What possible use could *that* be in the marriage mart?"

"There's more to life than marrying," Gwen observed.

"Well," Katherine noted airily, "in your case, it's just as well you feel that way." The proper equilibrium restored to her relationships with her inferiors, she took a deep breath, preparing herself for the long wait until midnight the next day.

Ten

At the stroke of midnight, Katherine pushed open the door to the courtyard, just a crack, and peered out into the darkness. The moon was a slim virgin crescent in a star-ripe sea of black. A cool breeze ruffled the tufts of Mrs. Treadwell's daisies around the fountain, and the academy windows were fathomless blanks. All was silence. *He didn't come,* she thought, and was swept with a strange mixture of sadness and relief. His absence confirmed her worst fears. He did not dare confess his heart in person. He was a coward—or somehow lacking, deformed. Indignation billowed up in her throat, tasting bitter, like iron. How dare he lead her on so, when he knew all the time he was unworthy of her love?

A star burst and flared in the sky. No, not the sky—on the far side of the courtyard, hard by the cart-gate. How could a star be there? She stood and watched the faint, distant glow. Then the night wind wafted the unmistakable scent of a Havana cigar toward her, and her knees buckled, so that she had to clutch the door latch. He *had* come, after all. He was waiting for her there.

Anxiously she tried to pierce the night's veil, make out his figure and form. The darkness was too absolute, though. She sought to summon up the memory of the sweet rhymes and words he had sent her, but she seemed gripped by a strange malaise that kept her from stepping out of her hiding place. *What is the matter with me?* she thought desperately. *He knows my hopes, my fears, my innermost feelings.*

And he could be anyone.

Oh, she wished she'd never arranged this meeting, never asked for him to come in the flesh! How much more comfortable it would be simply to let his pursuit go on as it had, and bask in her schoolmates' breathless admiration of his cards and gifts! *I can go back,* she realized. *I have only to close the door and slip away.* She could send the dairy boy with another note for the wagon, explain that she'd been ill, or that Mrs. Treadwell had kept close watch on her. . . .

Across the courtyard, the cigar tip burned more brightly as he drew on it. How long would he stay there if she did not make herself known?

A thousand doubts crowded in on her, making her tremble. Why had she chosen this solitary midnight assignation? Why had she not asked him to meet her in sunlight, where she might take proper gauge of him? If she stepped forth, she would be at his mercy. What if he meant to harm her in some way, to assault her? In the time it took for her to wake someone with her screams—if she even managed to scream; if he did not prevent that—anything might happen. Wracked with misgivings, she drew back into the hallway, silently pulling the door closed—

And then abruptly pushed it open again, just far enough to ascertain that the tobacco beacon was still there.

It was. He had not moved from where he stood. What, she wondered, was *he* thinking? Was he as wary as she? Had he forced himself to work up the nerve for this meeting, afraid of her rejection—or, worse, that she might not, in person, live up to his lovestruck imaginings of what she was like? Something very profound sliced through Katherine's heart as she recalled how men at parties and balls inevitably drifted away from her upon furthering their acquaintance. What if he found *her* lacking? The notion was enough to cause her to yank the door shut.

Better, *wiser,* surely, to leave matters as they stood. That way, she would be safe, insulated from disappointment or rejection. And her dream-lover would remain just that—a lovely, distant dream, a cipher she could form and re-form according to her fancies, imagining him blond, were that her whimsy, or tall and slim, or dark and dangerous, a prince or duke, a tulip of the ton, as rich as Croesus, with the voice of an angel, and the pure, singleminded devotion of a monk, and a poet's rapturous, burning heart. . . .

That *burning* reminded her of the cigar. Though she knew by now it must be finished, that he must have concluded she did not intend to keep their appointment, she could not resist inching the door open. Just to be certain, she told herself. To be sure he was gone. . . .

The star still shone. Even as she watched, though, she saw it tumble to earth; its golden glow blazed for a moment from the grass before he must have ground his boot heel down, extinguishing it with the last of his hopes. Then there was only darkness, and the desolate groan of the cart-gate latch being raised. . . .

"Oh, wait!" she cried, astonishing herself. "Oh, do wait! I'm sorry. I am here. I was just . . . just . . ." She had moved into the courtyard, propelled by some force infinitely stronger than her wavering fear.

"Katherine," he said, and her name on his tongue was as sweet as the chime of a church bell. "My Katherine . . ."

"Yes," she breathed, taking a step toward him. And then, against all odds, she was running, flying to him beneath the wide night sky, and he had spread his arms in welcome; she collided with him, and he grasped her tightly, his mouth seeking hers. His kiss was as boundless as that sky, and it made her lips burn and her cheeks flush and her eyes fill with inexplicable tears.

He brought his hand to her face, his touch warmly possessive. "Ah, Katherine. If you knew how I have longed for this—"

"And I also," she whispered, all her qualms vanquished by the sensation of his strong arms around her, by the scent of him, tobacco and leather and laundry soap mingled most alluringly. He was tall; she could tell by how he towered over her. And he did not seem misshapen. . . . Tentatively she ran her palms from his back up to his shoulders. No. Not misshapen at *all*. When he shuddered and claimed her mouth once more, she felt the most remarkable sensation of puissance, of the power she held over him. Gingerly she stroked his hair, her eyes straining to make out its color. Dark, she was nearly sure. And his face . . . she traced the line of his cheekbones with her fingertips. He turned and kissed them, frantically eager. "Who *are* you?" she wondered aloud.

"Do you not know?" She shook her head shyly. "One who has watched you from afar . . . for too long a time."

"You must have a name," she said. "What am I to call you?"

"Whatever you will. 'My love' will do. Or 'my dear heart.' Or—"

"Don't tease," Katherine chided, giggling as he kissed her ear. She could feel his breath against her skin, and it tingled mercilessly. "If you do not tell me your name now, this minute, I will go back inside."

"I do not think you will." The calm certainty with which he spoke the words sparked her temper; she was about to give him a piece of her mind when he bent down and whispered, "But it is a chance I would rather not take. You may call me Alain."

"Alain what?" she asked suspiciously.

"Alain my dear heart, of course."

She laughed again, despite herself. "You are very cock-sure, Mr. Alain My Dear Heart."

"Why shouldn't I be, when you send a note asking that I meet you at midnight in this desolate place?"

"It is not so desolate as *that*," Katherine quickly protested. "Mrs. Treadwell's rooms are just over *there*, and Madame's are right *there*. Not to mention all of the girls, who are very *light* sleepers." His arms were tightening around her; she was suddenly afraid he meant to carry her away. "*And* Stains, the driver, who sleeps above the stables. He is very strong and bad-tempered. He—" She broke off. He was kissing her again, with a force that left her breathless. His tongue insinuated itself between her lips, ran along her front teeth. "I don't," she started to say, intending to mention Mrs. Caldburn's caution against such disgraceful goings-on. But he had pushed his tongue right inside her mouth, was tasting her, savoring her as though she were a fine wine.

"Mm," he murmured, withdrawing. "Peppermint tea. And cakes—almond cakes, no? Delicious."

Katherine was thanking God she'd been too tense to eat Cook's supper of boiled beef and cabbage. "I don't think you are supposed to remark on how a person you kiss *tastes*."

"Why not? If I am thinking it, why not say it? Here." He laid his finger to his lips. "Come. Tell me what I taste of."

"I can tell you now. Your cigar."

"Taste me inside," he challenged.

"I don't think Mrs. Caldburn would approve."

" 'I don't think Mrs. Caldburn would approve,' " he mimicked, catching her prim tone so precisely that she let out a faint laugh. "Let me tell you," he went on, "about Mrs. Caldburn. She has gray hair that she strangles in a bun, and she wears pince-nez, and her bosoms are large and unwieldy—"

"Oh!" Katherine let more of the laugh escape. "You are perfectly *dreadful*. How do you know her?"

"I don't," said Alain. "I simply know the type to whom the English entrust the education of their daughters."

She pulled back from him a bit. "You . . . are not English?"

"Certainly not! What Englishman would court you as I have?"

"I knew it!" she declared. "I know who you are! You are the comte de Clairmont, that I was so rude to at the Tathams' ball!"

He drew himself up. He really was very tall. "I most certainly am not the comte de Clairmont."

"Oh, but you must be!"

"I swear I am not, on my love for you."

"Well, if you are not, then I can't think where or when we might have met!"

The moon had slid lower in the sky, so that his eyes caught its shimmer and glowed like a cat's. "We have met numerous times, Katherine."

"Now I *know* that you are lying."

He turned his head a little, and his eyes lost the glow. "I never lie. You will learn that about me. It is something you must tuck away here"—his fingers tapped the bodice of her gown, just above her breasts—"and hold to, whatever might happen."

"Goodness!" Katherine breathed, her heart pounding at his solemnity, the intimate gesture.

"Now, will you tell me what I taste of, or no?" He clasped her to him, pressing his mouth to hers, his lips parted a little, as though to dare her. Very tentatively, Katherine let her tongue flick between them, then hurriedly withdrew.

"Cigar," she affirmed.

"And?"

She paused, licked her own lips. "Cognac. *Petite champagne.*"

He laughed, delighted. "Very good indeed! Can you tell the year?"

"Of course I can't! Could you have?"

"But of course."

"Liar."

"I already told you—I never lie."

He was holding her close, very close, so that she could feel his heart beating against her, and could feel something more, a pressure at the front of his breeches, mysterious and hard, where they pressed her thighs. He brought his mouth down to hers, one arm encircling her shoulders, the other fast at her waist. Katherine closed her eyes, let herself lean against him, into him, drinking in the heady tastes and scents. . . . " 'Ninety-eight!" she suddenly declared, yanking away from him.

His eyes were full in the moon again, and glittering. "Oh, Katherine," he said, in a tone of astonished admiration.

"I only know," she explained, almost apologetically, "because it is my father's favorite."

"You, *chérie,*" he murmured, wagging his head at her, "are a creature of infinite possibilities."

"If that is so, you are the only one who has ever thought it," she said ruefully.

"Perhaps . . . I am the only one whom you have ever let see it."

His words brought back to her in a rush the startling intimacy of his poems, the cards he'd penned to her that had laid her heart bare. "How can you know me so well," she whispered, "when I do not know you at all?"

"I believe there are souls that are twinned at birth," he whispered, his voice very low. "Whose destinies are entwined by some power beyond human imagining. Do you believe this as well?"

"I—I've never given it thought," Katherine said hesitantly.

"You must contemplate it now," he told her, drawing her to him in the darkness. "Because I know, I sense, that you are my destiny." Again he put his fingertips to her heart, but this time he let them trail lower, to the swell of her breast. She could feel their heat straight through her dimity gown, just as she felt again that intriguing mass pressing into her thighs. His fingers caught in the bodice of her gown, started to inch it downward.

"I—" Katherine began, her mind a muddle of Mrs. Caldburn's lectures and Mrs. Treadwell's cautions about reputation. But what had such cold counsel to do with the fire in his hands, the searing blaze of his kisses? He put his mouth to her mouth, then to her throat, and then, as his hand drew the dimity away, to the tip of her breast, which was tight and round and hard as a rosebud.

"You are wearing the scent I gave you." He sounded pleased and proud as a boy. Then he took that taut bud between his lips again, and was instantly all man.

"Ohhh," she murmured, half enthralled, half aghast at the liberty she allowed him.

"Oh," he agreed, catching her up in his arms and then laying her down in the soft, thick grass. He knelt beside her, slipped one arm behind her head to cushion it, let the other trail upward from her knee to her thigh, all the while plying her with kisses, until at last his mouth closed on her breast again. He sucked at it, first softly, then with growing ferocity, his tongue teasing the sweet bud, his lips hungry and wild. He leaned over her, his free hand pulling at the shoulders of her gown, baring the white expanse of her bosom to the night sky.

Katherine was very much aware that what he was doing

was *wrong,* that she ought not to permit it, that she really
must speak up and put an end to this at once. But, oh, his
touch was so heavenly! How did he know to kiss her there,
and *there,* and draw just *so* at her nipples while his hand
made slow, tantalizing circles against her belly? He stretched
out beside her, pulled her half atop him while he scrambled
to find the hem of her skirts and reach beneath it. The sensation of his fingers against her bare calf was electric; she
expected lightning to erupt in the air.

"Ah," he murmured, his mouth at her breast. He reached
higher, to her knee, beyond, until he met the downy softness
of her drawers. He slipped his hand inside them, covering
her buttock. Katherine tensed in his embrace, and he instantly
withdrew—only to bring his fingers around to her belly, letting them play across her skin. "I want to pleasure you," he
whispered.

"No," she told him—and then confessed, blushing, "You
do pleasure me."

She felt him smile against her breast. "I could do so much
more . . ."

"What?"

"This." Again his hand plucked at the edges of her drawers, slipped upward until it settled on her mound of Venus,
caressing the curls there. "Ringlets." He sounded pleased.
"So those are natural!"

"I don't think . . ." Katherine began hesitantly.

"Don't," he told her, the motions of his fingers so gently
seductive that she lost all will to resist. As if in a dream, she
felt him part her knees with his, felt his hand slide between
her thighs, felt one long finger touch her—

There. Oh. God. Her legs closed around his hand of their
own accord as a bolt of fire surged through her. Oh, no. Oh,
God! *There . . .* He was probing her most secret places, eagerly exploring. She was reminded in a rush of how hesitantly she had put the stopper of the perfume bottle to her
breast. But that had been only a pale premonition of this, of
the terrible excitement that seized her as he caressed her and
murmured her name. Her nipples were tight and swollen; the

bud he touched was pulsing with his eager ministrations. The sky was swirling, clouds charging across the moon, stars flashing and flaring, and all the heat and light in the universe seemed concentrated between her thighs. And still his hand sought her, searched her, stroked her, until she could no longer bear the flood of sensation, until she wanted to cry, to scream, to shriek like an animal. One moan, harsh and low, escaped her.

"Yes," he whispered into her ear. "Yes, my love. Don't be afraid . . ." She moaned again, half-turning so that her body pressed to his, so that she felt the mass in his breeches that had surged to rock-hardness against her. She buried her face against his chest and let the ecstasy she felt engulf her, gave rein to her need to express it with wild sighs that mounted in a crescendo. She felt him answer her, his mouth tight to her hair. He groaned and shuddered, his whole body going rigid in her arms just as the stars above them collided, exploded. She screamed then, the sound muffled by his jacket, her back arching, her insides washed with fire. The fire pulsed in bright waves, spreading out like the circles from a stone thrown into the sea, sweeping through her head to toe and then slowly receding, fading bit by bit until only scraps of tantalizing memory remained.

He had his fingers inside her still. He withdrew them now, delicately, and flopped back onto the grass, tugging her to his chest. Katherine, bewildered by the storm of sensation she had just experienced—what had happened to her? *How* had it happened to her?—closed her eyes, fighting to catch her breath. Her heart was beating so mad a tattoo that she feared she was swooning, or dying. Would she ever be the same after this, after what they had done?

There was a dampness between her legs, and another at the front of his breeches; she felt it, cold, against her bare knee as she lay atop him. What had *he* felt, while those wondrous waves roiled through her? She was about to ask when he shifted, moving his arm behind his head as a cushion. "Are you positive you are English?" he asked.

Her uncertainty made her giggle. "Of course I am. The

first earl of Devereaux came here with William the Conqueror."

"Aha! Came here from *where*? From France!" He sounded oddly smug.

Her patriotism impelled her to protest. "Surely eight centuries is long enough to erase any Gallic traces from my blood."

"From your blood, perhaps. From your soul . . . I think not." He flopped over again, onto his side, and stared down at her, head propped on his hand. "Did you like that?"

"Did I—" She felt herself blushing.

"Tell me true, Katherine! I said I would never lie to you!"

"I liked it very much, then."

"Mm. Do you like cherries, Katherine?"

Perplexed, she blinked. "I like cherries very much."

"Did you like this more than you like cherries?"

She scrambled to sit up in the grass, grasping his point. "Oh, very well! Yes! I liked this more than I like cherries. What would you have me say?"

"You might say that you love me."

She dropped her gaze. "I . . . don't know you."

"If I asked you to come away with me, what would you say?"

She felt as though he'd struck her a blow. "Come *away* with you? Away with you *where*?"

"Anywhere." He plucked a piece of grass from the turf, sucked at it thoughtfully. "Anywhere I might be going."

Another blow, redoubled. "Are you going away?"

"If I had to, would you come with me?"

"I . . . I couldn't," she felt compelled to say.

"Why not?"

"I don't even know your true name!"

"You know how I feel about you."

"Yes, but—" Her head was whirling. "That's not the way it's done. You are supposed to court me—"

"I have courted you."

"Not in any *normal* way, you haven't. What about meeting my father?"

"Why should I meet your father? What has he to do with you and me?"

"Why, he . . ." She stopped, unable to think of an answer. Then it came to her: "I *am* the daughter of a duke, you know. In any marriage, there are all sorts of arrangements to be made. Legal this-and-that. Property considerations. I—"

"Who said anything about marriage?"

The deepest blow of all. She sucked in her breath. "I can't imagine what *else* you might be proposing!"

He lolled toward her, his hand stretching for her thigh, caressing it intimately. "I am proposing more of what we just enjoyed. Endless nights of it, in fact. And with addendums I believe you would find most . . . fulfilling." His head came down to her breast once more; his tongue flicked against her nipple.

Katherine fought against the tide of still-lingering passion his touch threatened to unleash, jerking away as though he was the devil himself. "What sort of girl do you think me?" she demanded in fury.

To her horror, he laughed. "The sort who has made me come in my breeches, like a fourteen-year-old boy. Oh, Katherine, don't take offense! Not when every word I ever wrote or spake you is true!"

"If—*if*—you love me," she began.

"Can you have any doubt of it?"

"Then you must behave properly about it! Go through the correct channels!"

"But what if the correct channels are closed to me?"

"Why? Why should they be?"

He shrugged, pushing back his dark hair. "You said yourself . . . you are the daughter of a duke."

"And what are you? *Who* are you?"

"Alain My Dear Heart." He saw her start to protest with a slap, caught her hand in his, looked into her eyes in the darkness. "The twin to your soul, Katherine." And the way he spoke it, the tremor in his voice, was almost enough to cause her to break.

Almost. Not quite. Because it had been dawning on her

slowly that her behavior with him had been irredeemably shameless and wanton; that she had very nearly given herself to this man who had no name, no honor, certainly no title, and who had won her with no more than a few pretty trifles and some lines of no-doubt-stolen poetry. She knelt up in the grass, throwing off his hands. "I don't know who you are," she said heatedly, "or why you've tried to—to *humiliate* me this way—"

"Humiliate? That is what you call it?"

"You have caused me to behave in a most unladylike fashion this evening!"

"I made love to you, Katherine."

"You *tried*," she said with a return of her hauteur. "You did not succeed."

He moved, so suddenly that she flinched, fearing he meant to strike her. But he only knelt up beside her. "You think that I could not have? While you moaned and writhed beneath me, you do not think I might have gone on to do what another man—nay, any other man—would have?"

"I *never* would have allowed that!"

"Oh, Katherine. Do not deceive yourself. Had I wished, I could have made you beg me for it."

"You think so highly of yourself!" she cried, yanking up her bodice, tugging down her skirts. "Or so little of me!"

A strange calm came over him. "Never that, *chérie*. Never so little of you. Indeed, I do not think it likely you will ever meet a man who esteems you the way that I do."

She was no longer afraid of him, now that his anger had passed. "And you show it this way?" she demanded. "With such—such *dishonorable* intentions?"

He reached his hand out, smoothed her tangled curls in a gesture that constricted her heart. "There can be no dishonor in true love, Katherine. But that is another lesson you have yet to learn." Very swiftly he pressed his mouth to hers in a hard, fast kiss. "I must go now."

The prospect of his leaving made her forget all her indignation. "Go where?" she asked plaintively. "When will I see you again?"

"Who knows?" He rose from the grass.

Katherine stood as well, fully intending to reclaim some vestige of dignity. "Well," she declared. "I can always leave another message for you with the dairy boy."

"You can try," he allowed.

She faltered. "If I do . . . will you get it?"

"Perhaps."

His nonchalance was infuriating . . . and frightening. "I don't see how you can—can breeze in and tell me that you love me, that our souls are twins, and then just go along your merry way!"

For one last moment, his eyes met hers. "I do not think, Katherine, that it will be so merry. Not without you beside me." He bowed to her, and she could not decide if his manner was mocking. *"Au revoir, ma chérie."* He headed for the cart-gate, moving very quickly. Katherine stood rooted, her shoulders squared.

Just before he opened the gate and slipped out, she very nearly gave in, very nearly ran after him. But in the end, she did not. Whatever had passed between them, her amazing, enthralling mystery lover had made it plain with his *despicable* offer, not of marriage, but of concubinage, that he was *not* worthy of her.

Eleven

"What, no gift this morning, Katherine?" Petra Forrester inquired in surprise, as Clarisse cleared away the last of the breakfast dishes.

Katherine, who had spent what little of the night remained after her return to her rooms tossing miserable and sleepless, snapped out at the girl: "Why don't you mind your own business?"

"I—I beg your pardon, Lady Devereaux!" Petra quickly murmured, put in her place. But her eyes were wide. Bess's, at her seat across the table from Katherine, were narrowed.

"It's rather odd, isn't it," she mused, ignoring a cautioning kick from Gwen, "that he should miss a day?"

"He isn't the postman," Katherine threw at her, flinging down her napkin.

"He's been a good deal more regular than the mail delivery, though, these past days, hasn't he?" Bess said irrepressibly. "You don't suppose he's ill?"

"How the devil should I know?" Katherine shoved back her chair, casting a sweeping glare at the roomful of goggling girls. "And I should think the lot of you would have better ways of spending your time than prying into my affairs!" She swept out of the room, slamming the door.

"She was only too grateful to have us pry into them yesterday," Bess pointed out, with perfect truth. "She seemed positively *delighted* to rub our noses in her mystery suitor."

"Bess, do hush," Gwen told her, nibbling her lip. Mrs. Treadwell was looking at Madame with both eyebrows raised, and the very slight shrug the countess gave in response did not escape Gwen's dark gaze.

At Mrs. Caldburn's morning lecture, on the scintillating topic of engraved stationery, Katherine was uncharacteristically silent and withdrawn. When the instructor posed a question to her regarding the proper styling of the calling card, she responded with, "Oh, who cares?"

"This is serious," Bess murmured to Gwen.

"I'm afraid it is. When Mrs. Caldburn's done, do a favor for me, would you? Engage her in some conversation out in the hallway. Give me a chance to have a word or two with Katherine alone."

Bess stared at her. "I don't see why you'd bother. If he's thrown her over, it is only because he's recognized what an utter and complete pain in the—"

"Did you have a question, Miss Boggs?" their instructor demanded, glaring through her pince-nez.

"No. Not really," Bess said airily.

"Then I'll thank you not to whisper to your neighbor."

"Yes, Mrs. Caldburn." Bess assumed a somewhat unconvincing expression of contrition, then read the message Gwen had penned on her page of scanty notes: *Just do it!* "Oh, very well," she mumbled gracelessly.

When Mrs. Caldburn had imparted everything the girls might have wanted to know about writing paper and envelopes and cards—and a great deal more besides—she finally released them. Katherine started for the door but was blocked by Bess, who, true to her word, was charging toward the teacher. "Forgive me, Mrs. Caldburn," she said cheerily, "but I want to pursue what you said today about colored papers. Oyster or ivory, you suggested. Would ecru be suitable as well?" She started for the hall, so that their instructor naturally followed her, noting testily:

"It comes as a surprise, Miss Boggs, to see you professing any interest whatsoever in my lectures."

"Mrs. Caldburn, how can you say that? I find your lectures most edifying. I've no doubt they will spare me no end of embarrassment when I make my debut. But what about that ecru?" Their voices faded away down the corridor.

Gwen gathered up her notebook and went to Katherine, tentatively laying a hand on the girl's shoulder. "Katherine? Are you all right?"

Katherine raised her gaze. Her face was drawn and haggard, though she did her best to assume her customary superciliousness. "Of course I am. I merely . . . didn't sleep well."

"I'm sure it was simply some confusion in the delivery that kept you from hearing from your young man this morning."

"No doubt." Katherine yawned, then covered her mouth. "I beg your pardon."

Gwen had her notebook clutched to her chest. "If . . . if you should ever need a friend, Katherine, someone to talk to . . . I know that I am not of your milieu. But I've been told I am a good listener."

For an instant, Katherine's blue eyes swam, Gwen could have sworn, with tears. But she quickly blinked them back. "I . . . no. No, thank you. I simply couldn't."

"If you change your mind," Gwen said softly, "I am here." Then she, too, started toward the door.

"Gwen," Katherine said suddenly, making her turn. "If you had a . . . a quandary. A moral dilemma. To whom would you go—Mrs. Treadwell, or Madame?"

Gwen thought for a moment. "That would depend on the quandary, I suppose. They are very different sorts of women."

"Which one, do you think, would be more likely to . . . to keep her counsel about something one said?"

"Oh," Gwen said instantly, "they are both utterly trustworthy!"

"But whom would *you* choose?"

Gwen took a shot in the dark. "If it were a matter of the heart, I should go to Madame. I believe she is infinitely more experienced with men than dear Mrs. Treadwell."

" 'Experienced with men.' " Katherine's pretty mouth was drawn. "According to the ton, she is nothing but a common tart."

"The ton," Gwen said steadfastly, "has on occasion been wrong about things."

She expected her form-mate to wax huffy. But there was

a note almost of plaintiveness in Katherine's voice as she said haltingly, "It's just that there are certain customs. Mores. Ways of doing things in a civilized society. If people such as me don't uphold them, then whoever will?"

Gwen looked at her with surprise, and something like pity. "I'm glad *I* don't face such conundrums."

"That is the luck of the lesser classes," Katherine said with her blithe unself-consciousness.

But for once, Gwen didn't bristle. "I suppose it is."

"Well?" Bess demanded eagerly when Gwen appeared in their rooms. "What did you find out?"

"Gossip," Gwen noted, "is sinful."

"Oh, for God's sake! You are starting to sound like *her!* Didn't I do exactly what you asked me?"

Gwen relented. "Lady Devereaux is faced with a moral quandary."

"No!" Bess fell back onto her bed, convulsed with laughter.

"Stop it!" Gwen said sharply. "It isn't a bit funny! The poor creature is in agony!"

"Good! It couldn't happen to a more deserving soul!"

"If you don't stop scoffing, I won't tell you any more."

Instantly, Bess sobered. "I am the picture of sympathy. Tell on."

"She wanted to know, were I faced with such a quandary, whether I would go to Mrs. Treadwell or Madame for advice."

"You ought to have suggested *me*. I could tell her a few things," Bess noted darkly. "But whom did you suggest?"

"Well—it *must* have to do with her suitor, mustn't it? And so I said Madame."

"Hah! Let me guess her response! 'Madame is a harlot.' "

"Close enough," Gwen acknowledged. "The phrase she actually employed was 'a common tart.' "

"Ooh!" Bess pounded on her pillow. "If you ask me, she

deserves every moral quandary the universe has to pose for her!"

"There was something else she said, though," Gwen mused, "that made me feel quite sorry for her. Something along the lines of, 'If folk like me don't uphold the mores of civilized society, who will?' "

Bess fluffed the pillow she had flattened so decisively. "To hell with civilized society. Titles are completely antiquated and arbitrary, Gwen! You know that! You long to be a scientist, don't you? I should think you'd be the last one to claim some sort of mystical basis for that rigmarole."

"I'm not saying it's rational. Just that it must be a tremendous burden. I mean, once you have bought into the thing, been born and raised in it, it's only natural you would take it to heart."

Bess had too often been the victim of Katherine's mockery to sympathize. "That girl hasn't *got* a heart."

"Oh, yes. She has. And unless I miss my mark, she has had it broken."

"Well, I say bully, then, for the mystery suitor," Bess said darkly. "It can only do her good."

Mrs. Treadwell was alone in her parlor after supper that evening when there was a rap at the door. "Do come in!" she sang out cheerily, reaching for her sherry glass. She quickly set it down again when she saw that her visitor was Katherine Devereaux. "Why, Katherine," she said more carefully. "What a pleasure! You have not often called on me for tête-à-têtes."

The heiress to the duke of Marne seemed uncharacteristically ill at ease. "I hope I am not disturbing you, Mrs. Treadwell."

"No, no, not at all! Any number of the girls drop by in the evenings for a chat. I'd always hoped you would, too."

Katherine glanced at the door with something like alarm. "Are any likely to drop by now, do you suppose?"

"Probably not. It is very late, isn't it?" Mrs. Treadwell

glanced longingly at her sherry, then had a sudden notion.
"Would you care for a drink? You are certainly old enough
to have a bit of sherry."

"I'd appreciate it ever so much," Katherine said gratefully.
When Mrs. Treadwell had poured her a glass, she snatched
it up and drank half in a gulp. By force of habit, the headmistress nearly reminded her charge that a lady always *sips*.
But something odd, some wildness in the heiress's eyes,
made her hold her tongue. "Won't you sit down?" was all
she said instead.

Katherine sank onto the plush settee in the corner, her
knuckles white on her sherry glass. "Mrs. Treadwell," she
asked abruptly, "do you believe in love at first sight?"

The headmistress blinked. "Well . . . all things are possible."

"I thought not," Katherine noted. "And neither do I."

Mrs. Treadwell was aware of a need to rise to the occasion.
"I certainly believe in *attraction* at first sight," she added.
"My daughter Vanessa and her husband are perfect proof of
that. From the moment they met, they—"

"But he is an *earl*," Katherine interrupted rudely, perplex-
ing her listener.

"Yes . . . yes, so he is." Uncertain where to go from there,
she waited.

"Do you believe in noblesse oblige?" Katherine demanded
then.

"I suppose that depends on what one means by the term."

"I *mean*," Katherine said impatiently, "that the ruling classes have a God-given responsibility to maintain moral order
in the universe."

"Goodness!" Mrs. Treadwell exclaimed. "What a burden
that would be!"

Katherine's lovely face was drawn and earnest. "I am not
explaining myself well. I mean . . . to propound by example.
To lead those less fortunate along the paths of righteous-
ness."

"I've always looked to our Lord Jesus Christ to do that."

"But that's precisely my point!" Katherine cried. "Honors

and titles are presented by the sovereign. The sovereign is God's own anointed. Therefore, haven't those whom God so favors a responsibility in return?"

"Oh, Katherine." Mrs. Treadwell took a hearty sip of sherry, in the vain hope it might clear her head. "Perhaps if you were to offer more concrete examples . . ."

Katherine's smooth brow furrowed. "Do you think it is wrong for a person to marry outside of his or her class?"

Mrs. Treadwell closed her eyes, then opened them. "Actually, I do. As a general rule. But not because of honors and titles being granted by God. Simply because marriage requires a . . . a sympathy between husband and wife that is most easily attained when they are of the same station in life."

"Exactly!" Katherine exclaimed.

"However," Mrs. Treadwell continued, then paused.

"Yes?"

"Oftentimes, love has a way of overcoming such considerations."

Katherine leaned forward on the settee. "Well, tell me this, then—how does one know when one is in love?"

Mrs. Treadwell sighed. "That's a question the poets and playwrights have wrangled with for ages. I hardly think I can answer it for you, except to say . . . when you are, you know."

"But *how*?" Katherine pressed. "What if, just for argument's sake, you had never been in love before, and suddenly a man paid you attention, and you . . . felt some *tendresse* for him, felt *something* for him, but weren't certain it was love?"

Here, Mrs. Treadwell was on more solid footing. "I believe I have tried my best to impress upon you girls how dangerous such infatuations can be. They can only lead to downfall and disgrace. If a young man's love for you is hallowed and pure, he will *never* entice you to dishonor. True love rises above venality."

Katherine let out a sigh of her own, half of relief, half of wistfulness. "You are correct, of course, Mrs. Treadwell. And I am grateful to you for your wisdom."

"You are most welcome, Katherine. I am glad I was able to help."

"It *was*, of course, strictly a hypothetical question."

"Of course. More sherry?"

"Oh, no, I mustn't." Katherine was looking very tired indeed, but less glum than when she'd come in. She stood and curtsied. "Thank you again. It is such a *relief* to find that we are in agreement. Good night, Mrs. Treadwell."

"Good night, Katherine," said the headmistress, with an uneasy intimation that as correct as her advice had been, she had just performed a grave wrong.

In his chambers at the White Fox, Alain Montclair was packing his belongings when the countess d'Oliveri burst through the door. "Damn you, Alain!" she cried furiously. "What did you do to her?"

Alain calmly laid a shirt inside his trunk. "What you bade me do, Christiane. Nothing less. Nothing more."

"I specifically told you seduction was beyond the pale!"

He looked at her, his blue eyes very dark. "I did not seduce her."

"At her age, in her innocence, even consensual intercourse—"

"No intercourse took place."

She looked at him dubiously. "You swear that?"

"I do." He folded a pair of breeches. "Have you reason to think otherwise?"

"I—forgive me, Alain. No. I do not. Other than the way she looked today."

He picked up a boot, found a spot for it. "And how, pray tell, did she look?"

"Wounded," said Madame. "Wounded and confused . . . and wise. Wise in the ways of men and women." She suddenly took notice of what he was doing. "What are you up to?"

"I am leaving England."

"Leaving . . ." She registered shock. "You cannot leave her now!"

"Our agreement, I distinctly recall, was that I break her heart." He brushed a tendril of leaf from another pair of breeches. "I believe I have achieved that. Or close enough."

"You've certainly done *something*. Oh, but Alain, consider! If you walk away from her now, after such attentiveness—did you write that poetry yourself?"

He shot a smile in her direction. "Do you think me incapable of it?"

"No, not at all! But it was very lovely!"

"English is an easy language in which to seem sincere. Everything rhymes with everything else. French would have been far more difficult."

"Have you anything to drink?" Madame inquired rather breathlessly.

He had a bottle of cognac. He poured her some and watched as she sipped. Then he set the last of his clothes in the trunk. "You seem disappointed in the outcome of our enterprise. Would you not agree I have fulfilled my duty to the girl?"

"I suppose you have. But it seems rather harsh . . . to woo her so warmly, then break off so abruptly. . . ."

"I have business that awaits me in France. I cannot be expected to forgo it to attend to the whims of some silly English schoolgirl."

She looked at him, her dark eyes shrewd. "You could have her if you tried."

"That was never part of the plan."

"No," she acknowledged reluctantly. "It wasn't. Still, somehow I hoped—"

"What? That I would find her devastatingly lovely? That I would lose my heart to her? Christ, Christiane! I should think you'd know me better than that." He slammed the trunk shut. "Women are playthings, meant to be enjoyed and then discarded."

"What a noble sentiment."

"And anyway," he went on heatedly, "she does not—"

He'd broken off. The countess stared at him. "Does not what?" He made no answer, but there was a spot of color high on each of his cheekbones. Christiane suddenly wished she'd interviewed Katherine before coming here. "You met with her, didn't you?" she said slowly. "It wasn't just the gifts. You met with her. That would explain—"

"It is very difficult," Alain noted, "to break a heart from afar. Yes. I met with her last night in the courtyard of the school. She had sent me a note asking for the meeting. I would not have presumed, of my own accord."

"What happened?" she demanded breathlessly.

"We kissed," he said with some reluctance.

"And what else?"

He turned away, busying himself with the trunk straps. "Some fondling. Nothing that went beyond your strictures."

"And then?"

"I . . . discouraged her."

"How?"

"See here, Christiane. I cannot see what difference it makes. I have accomplished what you asked of me."

"And so you are going back to France."

"I have pressing business. I have dallied too long here as is."

Pressing business . . . he meant Mimi Boulé, or another one like her. "Still, Alain! After you have been so tender with her, so attentive . . . do you not think it would be more honorable to let her off politely?"

"If you wanted honor, Christiane, you ought to have called on some other man."

Madame was picturing Katherine's normally horrid temper magnified by this abrupt reversal of fortune. "One last gift?" she ventured. "With a farewell poem? Something to explain your absence . . . give her some hope?"

"Hope?" He laughed, and the sound was not at all charming. "Hope for what? Let me give you some advice, Christiane. Tell her father to take her to London and toss her hat into the ring. Beauty like hers won't last."

Christiane stared at him. He was angry. She could not

recall ever having seen Alain Montclair so angry with anyone or anything. What the devil had gone on between Katherine and him? She sensed there was no use in further appeal, yet she could not keep from prying a little further. "I thought blue-eyed blondes were not your type, Alain."

"Here." He went to the mantel, found his purse, pulled out notes. "What remains of your two hundred pounds."

She felt the bulk of the roll. "There can't be this much left over," she protested. "Those gifts were very costly!" She thumbed through the notes. "Why, nearly all—nay, all of it is here!"

"Do you forget? I owe you thirty thousand francs. Think of it as a donation. To the altar of the eternal English virgin. And now, if you have finished your wine, I must ask that you excuse me. I leave quite early on the morrow."

"Alain," she began, thinking to implore him again to discard Katherine more gently. But his blue eyes were so distant that she reconsidered; he did not even seem to hear her, appeared already to be back in France—or at least not here, in this room. She hesitated, shrugged. "At any rate, I must thank you."

He jerked back to the present. "Thank me?"

"Aye. For having accomplished our goal."

"I was glad to be of service." With some semblance of his accustomed nonchalance, he kissed her hand. "*Au revoir,* Christiane. The pleasure was all mine."

I doubt that, from the way Katherine is behaving, she thought, but wisely held her tongue. Something was at work here far beyond the simple schoolgirl crush she had imagined. But she was not going to learn anything more from Alain Montclair. "*Au revoir,* Alain. I presume I may call on you again should another such exigency pop up amongst my students?"

"Christ, no," he said, so flatly that she could think of nothing else to do but take her leave.

* * *

Breakfasts at the academy for the remainder of that week had an aura of breath-held anticipation. As morning after morning ticked by, though, without any resumption of the mystery suitor's gifts, something very odd occurred. Katherine, prickly, proud Katherine, was treated by the other girls as if she were suffering from some awful disease; they tiptoed around her, spoke in whispers in her presence, were quick to offer her the bacon or jam. Christiane, observing this, expected the duke's daughter's temper to flare at any moment; how galling it must be to have commoners condescend to her! But the fire had gone out of Katherine Devereaux. She was pale and silent and withdrawn, picking at her food, never once displaying her legendary hauteur. All the kindness and solicitousness seemed to wash straight over her, leaving her completely untouched.

Mrs. Treadwell was deathly worried. "Do you suppose she is ill?" she asked Christiane anxiously. "Should we have Dr. Caplan attend to her?"

"I scarcely know what to do," her old friend confessed. "This is not at all what I had in mind when I engaged Alain."

"Perhaps he will come back?" the headmistress proposed anxiously.

Christiane shook her head. "No. He is gone for good."

"I shall take her to Vanessa's," Mrs. Treadwell decided. "For a long weekend in the country. I shall take all the upper-form girls. Some attention from other beaux is all she requires to set her right again." When the headmistress returned from this venture, however, she appeared more discouraged than ever.

"She was . . . not herself?" Madame inquired.

"On the contrary. Most folk would say that she was much improved. She actually danced with a viscount whose father manufactures rugs. But it was as though . . . as though she were in a daze," Mrs. Treadwell confessed, nibbling at her lip. "Even Vanessa remarked on the change in her, said how frail and wan she looked. Christiane, I am extremely concerned. I believe she is in a decline. We *must* bring in Dr. Caplan. Or at least inform the duke."

"Dr. Caplan first." Madame's expression was grave. True, Alain had said he'd not had sexual relations with the girl. But what if he'd lied? What if he'd passed something on to her—syphilis, or the pox?

To her enormous relief, the black-bearded physician gave Katherine a clean bill of health. "She's a bit gaunt and pale," he told the countess and Mrs. Treadwell after his examination. "But I can find no medical explanation for her condition. Whatever ails her, I suspect it is all in her head. Has she suffered some disappointment of late?"

"She had a suitor who spurned her," the countess said.

Dr. Caplan's brow cleared. "Ah! That would certainly explain it. Classic symptoms, really. She'll come about. I prescribe activity—plenty of activity, to keep her mind off her loss." He snapped shut his bag and prepared to depart.

"Doctor," Mrs. Treadwell said suddenly. "Something has been brought to my attention. . . ."

He adjusted his eyeglasses and peered at her. "Yes?"

"One of the girls mentioned that you might be procuring a . . . good heavens, I scarcely know how to put this. I believe the term is *fetal piglet*."

"Ah, yes!" Behind the glasses, the doctor's gray eyes brightened. "For Miss Carstairs. So I am."

"Really, Leon?" the countess asked with interest. "Has she come so far along in her studies as that?"

"She is a most remarkable young woman," the doctor said gravely. "Her curiosity . . . her intellectual hunger . . ."

"Yes, but—a dead pig!" Mrs. Treadwell interjected. "Here—in the academy! Just imagine if word ever got out!"

" 'What each girl needs,' " the countess murmured, " 'in order to achieve her potential in life—' "

"I know that is what we agreed, Christiane! But I was not thinking of dead pigs at the time. And I'm quite certain dear Admiral Carstairs did not expect us to include dissections in the curriculum!"

"If you insist, Mrs. Treadwell, I will curtail that part of Miss Carstairs's education. Though I must point out," said the doctor, "that there is no substitute in medicine for hands-on examination. And Miss Carstairs shows extreme promise in the physical sciences."

"But where is that to get her," Mrs. Treadwell wailed, "in the matter of a husband?"

The countess stood up. "I'll see you out, shall I, Dr. Caplan?"

He took her arm, then paused, smiling at the headmistress. "Mrs. Treadwell. You know how greatly I admire your academy. Never—*never*—in the history of England has a school for girls taken education so seriously. What you are performing here, you and the countess, is nothing short of miraculous. Your willingness to smash down barriers on behalf of your students—"

" 'Smash down,' " Mrs. Treadwell murmured. "You make it sound so . . . so violent!"

"You are revolutionaries, both of you," the doctor declared.

"I'm not at all sure I *want* to be a revolutionary," Mrs. Treadwell fretted.

The countess shot a pointed glance at Dr. Caplan, who put on his hat. "Well. Be that as it may—my suggestion for Lady Devereaux stands. Keep her busy. Attempt to engage her."

Mrs. Treadwell appeared perfectly willing to change the subject from Gwen's medical studies. "That we will," she promised. "Good night, Dr. Caplan."

He took his leave. On the threshold, Madame smiled up at him. "You must have known a dead pig would throw Evelyn for a loop, Leon."

"You think it best that I not procure one?"

"Oh, no. I would just make certain you are extremely discreet about it when you do!"

In accordance with the doctor's advice, Madame and Mrs. Treadwell stepped up Katherine's schedule of riding, took pains to arrange excursions, asked Mrs. Caldburn and the other instructors to tailor their lectures to the girl's special interests. Katherine acquiesced to the flurry readily enough, but her strange demeanor did not change.

After a month, Mrs. Treadwell was at her wits' end. "I really think, Christiane," she told the countess over sherry, in her parlor, "that you must confess."

"No!" Madame said violently. "How can I do that? To inform her that I paid a man to court her ... why, it would destroy her!"

"Better she should pine after him without knowing that he is a highwayman?"

"He's *not* a—"

"Very well—an adventurer, then! Whatever you care to call him, it is plain you made a terrible mistake in judgment!"

"As I recall, *you* had no ideas whatsoever on how to cure her of her haughtiness. And you were ready enough to agree to mine!"

Mrs. Treadwell's plump face crumpled. "Oh, I *don't* want to argue with you, pet! And I will admit—you did achieve our goal. Only somehow, it has all gone too far." She raised her handkerchief to her eyes. "She is the only *true* upper-echelon girl to be entrusted to us, and look how we have failed her!"

"I'm not yet willing to admit failure," Christiane announced, with a gleam in her eye that made Mrs. Treadwell wince.

"Oh, dear, I do hope you haven't got *another* brilliant notion!"

"Tell me again, Evelyn, what she said when she came to speak to you in private the day after ... the day the presents stopped."

Mrs. Treadwell mopped away tears. "I can hardly recall now. It was all such a muddle. She asked how one could know love was true. And—and whether I thought marriage between social classes was wrong."

Madame perked up. "And what did *you* say?"

"Well—I told her the truth, of course! That it is! *Not*," she added hastily, "because I am a snob. I trust you know that well enough by now. I took care to explain that successful marriages are based on shared experience, and that without such a basis—"

"Oh, Evelyn. You didn't!"

"You cannot blame this on me!" the headmistress cried in agitation. "Not after it is all *your* fault!"

"It *is* my fault," Madame said thoughtfully. "Perhaps you are right after all. It might be best if I told her the truth about Alain Montclair."

Mrs. Treadwell was swift to backtrack. "She is so young yet. Young and resilient. Don't say anything to cause further harm. I'm certain that in time . . ."

"Are you?" The countess shook her head. "You've met Montclair, and still you say that?"

"*She* never met him, though! Except in passing, at the Tathams'. She only had his cards and presents! So I really cannot understand . . ." The headmistress's voice trailed off as the countess, against all odds, blushed deep red. "Oh, dear heavens. There is something here you haven't shared with me, isn't there, Christiane?"

"I'll have a talk with Katherine."

The headmistress glowered at her. "I think that you had better. As for the rest of what went on between them—well! If I've any hope of ever looking the duke of Marne in the eye again, better I shouldn't know!"

Twelve

The countess d'Oliveri took a deep breath, then turned to the girl seated in her parlor. So much depended on what she said in these few moments—Katherine's happiness, yes, but the future of Mrs. Treadwell's academy as well. The duke's daughter *would* get over her lost suitor in time, just as Dr. Caplan had promised. But what if she should prove so offended by Madame's well-meaning efforts that she decided to raise a scandal, bruit the story of her presence here to the world? The countess knew enough of Katherine's temper not to take such a possibility lightly. How was she to convince the girl that she had only her best interests in mind?

"Thank you for coming to see me, Katherine," she began—because she really *had* to say something. "No doubt you are curious as to why I sent for you."

"Not especially," said Katherine.

Madame moved a little closer, perched on a chair beside the girl's. "We are all concerned for you, Katherine. Your headmistress and I most of all. There is no sense in pretending that you haven't suffered a grave disappointment." She waited, but Katherine made no response. "I mean, of course, with your young man." Still nothing. "Believe me," the countess said with feeling, "I know just how wrenching it can be to think that someone knows you intimately, cares so deeply about you, and then find out it isn't true."

Finally, Katherine spoke. "Who says it isn't?"

Somewhat nonplussed, Madame blinked. "Isn't what?"

"Isn't true."

The countess spread her hands. "Well, *chérie,* one has only to look to his behavior. To encourage you that way and then break it off so abruptly, without a word of explanation . . ." The briefest flicker of animation brushed over Katherine's face, like a shadow, an autumn breeze. *Oh, dear,* thought Madame. *I ought to have pressed Alain further.* What had gone on between them in the courtyard? She felt she was groping her way down a long corridor in the dark.

"He does love me," Katherine said then, making Madame's heart constrict.

"Oh, child. He may have *said* so—"

"He didn't need to. I could tell it," Katherine said simply.

"From his poems and gifts and cards, you mean."

"Yes."

The countess sighed, deeply. "But if he *did* love you—"

"There isn't any question." Now the girl's voice was sharp.

"Then why would he disappear as he did?"

"He is punishing me."

Deeper and deeper into the darkness . . . "Punishing you for *what*?" the countess demanded.

"For not trusting him. Not believing in him."

Madame felt like tearing her hair. "Well, now you see how correct you were *not* to! No worthy gentleman would punish a respectable young lady in so reprehensible a way!"

It was at this point that Katherine said the most amazing thing of all. "I have broken his heart," she told the countess, who could not help but gasp.

"Oh, *chérie!* Of course you haven't!"

"How would *you* know?" Katherine asked, so dismissively that the countess made a sudden decision.

"Because I know *him,* as it happens. Know him quite well." Really, she could not allow the girl to harbor such a misapprehension!

"Know him how?" Katherine asked without much surprise, and then answered her own query: "Oh. Of course. He is French. You must have known him in France."

Now that the worst was over, Madame wanted only for this uncomfortable interview to end. "He was a frequent visitor to the gambling house I owned in Paris," she explained. "He had quite a dreadful reputation with the ladies there. *And* with the authorities, I might add. He is a—a blackguard, Katherine. A scoundrel. A rogue of the first realm."

"*Was*," Katherine said implacably.

Madame didn't know whether to laugh or to cry. "You think one midnight assignation with you has changed his nature forever?"

That made Katherine sit up. "How do you know about that?"

"He told me himself. I *said* I knew him well."

"What is his name, then?" Katherine asked breathlessly.

"His name is Alain Montclair. But he goes by any number of other monikers when it suits his—"

"The comte de Clairmont!" Katherine cried. "So it *was* he whom I met at the Tathams' ball!" Then her face, newly animated, all its startling beauty regained, turned puzzled. "But he said we had met numerous times. Whatever did he mean by that? I'm sure had I encountered him elsewhere, I would have remembered it!"

"Think back, Katherine," the countess ordered. "Think back more than two months, to a hapless, bleeding soul who asked your mercy while you were riding home from Hartin." Katherine looked at her blankly. "You had left Stains and poor Achilles behind," Madame went on impatiently. "He came out of the woods, begged you for water. You pointed him to the river and rode on." Still Katherine stared. "Oh, for heaven's sake! Do such things happen to you every day? How can you not recall it? What about the time when you were in the coach with Stains and a flurry of rabbits crossed your path, followed by a dashing stranger who came to your rescue?"

"That was Alain Montclair?" Katherine's blue gaze had widened. "Oh, I think you are mistaken! Why, he fell off his horse into a prickle patch!"

"Who do you think pulled out the prickles for him? And the highwayman—you do recall that incident in the coach with Mrs. Treadwell, I trust?"

"I—I *shot* him? *Him*?" Unaccountably, Katherine began to laugh. "And still he pursued me as he did? Oh, his love is immeasurably strong, is it not?"

The countess felt like shaking her. *No, you little ninny!*

she nearly said, then bit her tongue. She had dearly hoped to avoid revealing *why* Montclair had pursued her as he did. But she saw now, all too clearly, that she must tell everything. Somehow Katherine, in her self-centeredness, her pride, had managed to construe what Christiane had admitted so far in completely the wrong way. She swallowed and prepared for the storm. "What you must understand, Katherine, is that Montclair wooed you at my instigation. It was a sort of a . . . wager. Well—not a wager, precisely. But we were so worried about you—Mrs. Treadwell and your father and I. Concerned that you might never find true love because of your . . . your haughtiness, if I may be frank."

Katherine was taking all this in with remarkable calm. "I see! And so you brought me Montclair!" She smiled enchantingly. "I must say, I am very grateful to you for explaining it all."

"You aren't angry?" Madame asked tentatively.

"On the contrary! I find it most touching that you and Mrs. Treadwell and my father should go to such lengths on my behalf."

"You . . . you do?"

"Absolutely," said Katherine, and reached out to pat Madame's hand reassuringly. The gesture unnerved the countess completely. She could only stare as Katherine rose gracefully to her feet, looking a different creature altogether from the morose, brooding girl who had entered the parlor not half an hour before. The sparkle was back in her eyes, her cheeks were rosy with color, and even her glorious ringlets seemed to have more bounce. "Thank you, Madame. Thank you ever so much."

"Why—you're most welcome, Katherine. I must say, you are taking this very well indeed."

Katherine laughed again, and shrugged. "Why not? What's done is done, isn't it? One can only go on from here."

"That is a very *mature* attitude for you to take. I expected you to be furious with me—or to burst into tears."

"That would be rather a waste of time, wouldn't it?" Katherine said gaily. "Now, if you'll excuse me, I'll be on my way."

"Certainly. Good night, Katherine."

"Good night, Madame." And then, impulsively, the girl bent down and swiftly kissed the countess on the cheek—an action so against precedent that the recipient burst out coughing. "Best have a bit of sherry," Katherine advised thoughtfully.

"Thank you, I believe I will," said the countess—and she did, the moment the door had closed.

After a brief pause, a knock sounded. "Christiane?" Mrs. Treadwell hissed. "Is the deed done?"

"Do come in, Evelyn, and raise a toast with me."

Mrs. Treadwell entered, looking most downcast. "To the end of our academy, I suppose. Oh, well. It was splendid while it lasted, wasn't it?"

The countess, now that it was over, was quite giddy. "You have nothing to fear, Evelyn. Nothing at all. She took the news splendidly."

"You told her you put Montclair up to this? To all of it? And she didn't smite you?"

"On the contrary. She thanked me."

"She didn't!"

Madame laughed and pressed a glass of sherry on her old friend. "*And* she kissed me. Right here. On my cheek."

Mrs. Treadwell was so astonished that she very nearly missed the edge of the chair she was about to sit on. "No!"

"God's truth," Madame said smugly, and crossed her heart. "If you ask me, she was genuinely relieved to discover the truth behind Montclair's siege to her affections. She left here in quite opposite spirits from the way she came in."

"I can scarcely believe it!" Mrs. Treadwell marveled. Then she reconsidered. "But perhaps I can. After so much uncertainty, so many doubts and questions, it must have been rather reassuring to discover that the entire episode was no more than a sham."

"And," Madame noted happily, "from her behavior this evening, it is clear as day to me that having her heart broken has made her a new person. Oh, we have been lucky, Evelyn! So very lucky indeed!"

At breakfast the following morning, Madame noted that Katherine's accustomed seat was empty. She smiled at the sight as she buttered toast. Finally enjoying a decent night's sleep, the poor thing, after all that tossing and turning on account of Alain Montclair. . . . She was actually disposed to feel quite kindly toward the rake himself, considering that he had accomplished everything she had intended. On Katherine Devereaux's next visit to Mrs. Treadwell's daughter's estate, she suspected, the young men would be in for quite a pleasant surprise. And dear Richard and Nanette would be ever so pleased. . . .

Lost in her happy daydreams, she was not at first aware that Bess was addressing her. But as the girl continued to speak, her words came into focus, slowly, as through a warm summer haze: ". . . Katherine finally got what she deserved, and I for one am happy for her."

"Well." Madame smiled at the redhead affectionately. "Perhaps not what she deserved, precisely, but what's best for her. She came around to see that at last. And if I'm not mistaken, we will all see a very different Katherine Devereaux from now on."

"But not see her *often*, I trust," said Bess, drawing a frown from Gwen. "Oh, really, now, Gwen! She's been perfectly beastly to us both from the day we all arrived here."

"I'm inclined to agree with Madame," Gwen murmured. "Katherine *has* changed. And it might have been quite nice to get to know her now that she has stepped down from her high horse at last."

"You girls must go on being very kind and gentle with her," Mrs. Treadwell interjected from the end of the table.

"I'm sure that will be much easier," Bess noted, reaching for the jam, "since our paths are not very likely to cross after this."

Madame, about to bite into her toast, felt an odd little

shudder in her soul. "After this *what*?" she demanded of Bess.

"Well, now that she's gone. I mean, I suppose we will still encounter her in London now and again, but I don't imagine she will have the time of day for—"

"Gone?!" Mrs. Treadwell screeched, so loudly that the lower-form girls all dropped their forks as one. "Gone *where*?"

Bess shrugged, slathering jam on her bread. "Home, isn't that so?"

Mrs. Treadwell stood up, glaring at the countess. "You said nothing to me about her going home!"

"She said nothing to *me* about it!" Madame said dazedly. "What makes you think, Bess, that she has gone home?"

"Why, when I woke this morning, her clothes weren't clogging up the wardrobe. And for once, she wasn't pigging the mirror."

"What *was* she doing?" Mrs. Treadwell asked in rising consternation.

Bess shrugged again. "She wasn't there at all."

As one, Madame and Mrs. Treadwell rushed out of the dining room and up the stairs.

Sure enough, Katherine's bed did not look to have been slept in. "Her clothes *are* here," Mrs. Treadwell said hopefully, peering into the wardrobe.

"Not all of them," Madame said at her elbow. "Not the dimity. Not the peacock *peau de soie*. Not the rose-pattern muslin. Nor her favorite periwinkle jacket, or the lavender-ribboned hat. And her riding boots are gone." She ran to the bureau, searching for Katherine's jewel-box. "So are her bijoux."

"I don't understand." Mrs. Treadwell stood in the doorway to the wardrobe, her forehead wrinkled. "If she has gone home, why wouldn't she take *all* her things?"

"She hasn't gone home." Madame's voice had a note of wild despair to it that Mrs. Treadwell had never before heard.

"Why—where has she gone, then?"

"To France," the countess told her with dreadful certainty. "To France, to find Alain Montclair."

Thirteen

The docks at Dover were bustling on that Tuesday dawn, with sailors clambering high into the rigging of ships, and stevedores loading artillery and cannon and materiel, and soldiers embracing their wives and mothers and more casual female acquaintances from the many taverns and brothels in the town. Katherine stood for a moment on a little rise above the commotion, taking in the scene. She had made it this far. But what in God's name was she to do now? She had to get aboard one of those ships, and it had to be one that was willing to take her to Calais.

All her life, Katherine had been accustomed to having others do her bidding. But as she gazed at the bustle on the docks below, she recognized, belatedly, how *extremely* unlikely it was that a ship's captain would agree to take a solitary, baggageless girl to a foreign nation, no matter how forcefully that girl insisted she deserved to be taken simply because she was the daughter of the duke of Marne.

Damn. She chewed her lower lip, bemoaning her impetuousness. If only she'd taken time to think this through, lay plans! Rushing off like this, heading hell-for-leather toward the unknown, wasn't at all the sort of thing she did; it was behavior more becoming to Gwen or Bess. Or to her stepmother, for that matter, who'd married her father just weeks after having been introduced to him.

Nanette would know what to do, Katherine mused; she'd simply pull some appropriate scene out of a play by Shakespeare or Goldsmith or Aristophanes and perform it. Hadn't she recommended often enough that Katherine try to do the same in social situations, in her pathetic attempts to become her new stepdaughter's friend? "Just put aside for the evening the fact that you're a duke's daughter," she'd counseled—as if Katherine ever could! "Make believe that you are someone else. I do it all the time, you know—not just when I used to be on the stage. It's a handy trick for dealing with an awkward social situation. You can pretend. I know you can, if you only try."

Katherine recalled very clearly what she'd responded to the overture: "A true lady never encounters an awkward social situation."

Nanette ought to have found that cutting; instead, she'd laughed. That was the most infuriating aspect of Nanette O'Toole, Katherine had long ago decided; she did not take offense. No matter how cold and haughty Katherine was, her stepmother kept trying, went on seeking for points of connection between them despite the obvious fact that there were none and never would be.

Still, Nanette's advice might prove suitable for this, which by any reckoning surely counted as an awkward social situation. Katherine surveyed the decks of the various vessels, searching the faces of their officers, contemplating what role she might play. Her initial instinct was to choose a young, attractive commander, flatter and flirt with him. But then she noticed that one of the older captains, a stout, bearded fellow in the king's colors, reminded her quite strongly of her Uncle Paul.

She had always been able to wrap Uncle Paul around her finger. She tightened her grip on her valise and hat-boxes, drew a deep breath, and strode boldly down to the dock, taking care to note the name of Uncle Paul's trim warship: the *Mary Anne*. Just before stepping onto the gangplank, she caught the sleeve of a seaman who was looking rather grim. "Excuse me, sir," she said, turning her smile on full-blaze. "Do you sail on the *Mary Anne* this day?"

He tipped his hat to her, his expression brightening. "Aye, that I do, pretty lady. First mate on the *Mary Anne,* I am."

"Under Captain . . ." She paused, clearly searching her mind. "Captain . . ."

"Bressler, miss." He dropped her a wink. "And ye'd best call him *Admiral* Bressler, or he'll chew off your ear."

"Of course." More of the smile. "Thank you ever so kindly. You have saved me from a most embarrassing mistake." God, this was humiliating, to be thanking a common sailor!

"No problem at all, miss. Glad to be of service."

A young woman he'd just left at the end of the dock was glaring at the two of them. "Johnny! Johnny Farraday!" she cried out, waving her kerchief. "If you've time for *that,* I should think you'd time for one more kiss!"

Johnny Farraday grinned ruefully at Katherine and tipped his hat again. "My wife," he said in explanation. "As of yesterday. Can't say the fellows didn't warn me against it, but she sweet-talked me so . . ."

What would the girl she was pretending to be say to that? Katherine wondered. And then it came to her: "Go on and kiss her," she urged him.

He glanced up at the admiral, then decided to do so, running back along the quay to embrace his bride. Katherine, meanwhile, proceeded up the gangplank, balancing herself gingerly.

It didn't take long for Admiral Bressler to take note of her. As she stepped on deck, she saw him frown in the midst of firing off an order and stride toward her with the rolling gait of a man who'd spent his life at sea. "What's this, then?" he demanded as he approached. "I've a war to win; I can't be burdened with—"

"Admiral Bressler!" Katherine cried warmly, cutting off his objection in midbreath. "How lovely to see you again! Is my father aboard yet?"

"Your father?" He squinted down at her through thick crow's-foot wrinkles, seeming to reconsider his belligerence as he took in Katherine's elegant plissé gown and cunningly cut periwinkle jacket, the height-of-fashion beribboned wickery perched atop her curls, and the bandboxes she carried, clearly marked with the best London names. "I—I beg your pardon, miss, but I've no recollection of ever seeing you before in my life."

"And to think," Katherine said with a pretty pout, "that I

believed I'd made such a favorable impression!"

"No doubt the mistake is all mine, Miss . . ."

"Devereaux—*Lady* Devereaux," Katherine said with quiet emphasis. "My poppa is the duke of Marne."

"The duke of Marne!" Admiral Bressler's brow cleared. "Well, I know Marne, naturally. Fine man. Upstanding man. Still, I cannot say that I recall—"

"Oh, it was many years past," Katherine assured him. "I was practically in short skirts. It was at court that I was presented to you. I insisted upon it. 'Poppa,' I said, 'whoever is that handsome gentleman with the blue eyes, who walks as though he has just gotten off a horse?' He hushed me, of course, afraid you might overhear and would be offended. But you were ever so kind, whether you'd overheard or not! Poppa brought me up to you, and I made a curtsy—" She made another now, imbuing it with childish awkwardness. "And you leaned down—I thought you were quite the *tallest* man I ever had seen!—and you kissed my hand, just as though I were a princess, and said very gravely, 'How do you do, Lady Devereaux?' And when Poppa had drawn me away, I told him straight out that when I grew up, I intended to marry you!"

My God, she thought in astonishment. *Where did that come from?*

Admiral Bressler had listened to her rather breathless recitation with the undivided attention of a man put on the spot and seeking desperately to place the moment in time. But then his brow cleared, and he nodded slowly.

"Aye, now that you tell me the story, I believe I *do* remember. You were much younger then, as you say. Not nearly so . . . well. Grown-up."

Katherine's smile was of pure enchantment. "Oh, I *am* glad that you remember me! For when Poppa told me we'd be crossing to Calais with the admiral, I was quite overwhelmed with joy! Though I don't suppose you'll have waited all this time for me without taking yourself a wife." With the pout again . . .

"I've been married thirty-four years. Have six children, all grown themselves," the admiral confessed. "But—see here, Lady Devereaux. I've had no orders whatsoever about taking His Grace to Calais."

Katherine looked flustered for a moment. Then abruptly she put her fingers to her lips. "I suppose that is because this is a diplomatic mission for Poppa—very on the quiet and all that."

"Even so," the admiral noted, "someone would have said *something* to me."

"But surely you've received our baggage? I had seventeen trunks," Katherine burbled, "and my maid, Mary An—" *Anne,* she'd almost said, the name of the ship in her mind. "—gela," she finished quickly. "And my spaniels? I do hope my babies are comfortable here aboard the ship."

"None of that's arrived," Admiral Bressler declared, on firmer footing now. "I can assure you. No trunks, no maid, and certainly no spaniels."

Katherine stared at him in openmouthed wonder. "Why, however can that *be*?" she asked plaintively. "The letter I had from Poppa distinctly assured me my belongings would be here, aboard the admiral's ship, on the twenty-first of August."

"Aha!" the admiral said, looking much relieved. "There's your problem right there, Miss Devereaux. This is the *twenty-sixth* of August."

"No! It can't be! It simply *cannot* be! I *never* would have made so foolish a mistake!"

"Well, I'm afraid you have," the admiral said very gently. "Tuesday, the twenty-sixth of August. No doubt about it at all. Here, Jonas!" he cried to one of the crowd of sailors who'd gathered around them, avidly eyeing their captain's attractive visitor. "What's the date?"

"Tuesday, the twenty-sixth of August," Jonas answered quickly. "Though I wish to *hell* it was the twenty-first."

Sweet like Martha; as emotional as Bess . . . Katherine formed an expression of alarm. "But what's become of my babies?" she cried in dismay. "Flopsy and Mopsy, and—" She was making herself somewhat nauseous, but bravely pressed on. "You don't suppose they've gone to sea without me?"

"If your poppa was on a diplomatic mission, as you say, it's entirely possible," Admiral Bressler told her. "It must have been another admiral he meant. Perhaps he sent a message to you at home after you failed to appear, with further instructions?"

"If he did, I would not have received it. I left home a fortnight ahead of schedule, and stopped on my journey to visit with the earl and countess of Tatham. Such a *lovely* fete they gave in my honor—though a tad countrified, if you catch my meaning. Still, they did quite well with so little advance notice," Katherine said judiciously. "Harlem cherries, which are altogether rare now, on account of the embargoes, and the most *scrumptious* oyster pie, and—" She broke off in midsentence, her eyes suddenly welling with tears. "Oh, *dear,*" she sniffed, bringing out her kerchief. "Poppa is going to be *ever* so cross with me!"

"Ach, 'tis an honest mistake, lass," one of the sailors assured her in a round Scottish brogue.

"I think the best thing for you to do now, Lady Devereaux," advised the admiral, "is to return home at once, and discover what plans your father made for you once he found you'd missed your rendezvous."

Katherine dabbed at her eyes. "But I *cannot!*" she cried in dismay. "We are due to be in Calais on the twenty-eighth! Poppa mentioned it *expressly!* I am to help him entertain the French ambassador there, since Mamma is indisposed."

"Nothing serious, I trust," the admiral automatically observed.

"Actually—" Katherine made the tears spill over. "It is. Very serious indeed. She has a—" *Dammit, what should she have?* She tried desperately to recall the sorts of diseases Gwen was always talking about after her lessons with Dr. Caplan. "A . . . a cancer," she said, dropping her voice to a whisper. "Of the womanly sort." Several of the sailors crossed themselves in horror.

"In that case, Lady Devereaux, your place is at her side," the captain noted gravely.

"But it was Mamma's special insistence that I go with Poppa! Oh, I argued against it. I know that I shall never be able to live up to her standards for courtesy and etiquette! But she told Poppa: 'The fate of thousands of good English soldiers and sailors is hanging in the balance, Richard. We dare not chance offending the ambassador by offering any slight at this desperate juncture. If we have the opportunity at long last to put an end to this dreadful conflict through diplomatic means—' " Her voice broke off; she sobbed into the kerchief. "Oh, God! To think that more lives may be lost because I am too *stupid* to take proper note of the date!"

"Here, now, Admiral, sir," murmured one of the crowd on deck, which by now was quite large indeed. "Could we not take the poor girl to Calais? We have time and enough before we're due at Lisbon."

"It would be quite outside regulations," the admiral said briskly.

" 'Twould bae a mission o' mercy," the Scottish sailor growled.

"She has no chaperone," the admiral pointed out, "and more than likely no passport or papers. *Have* you a passport, Lady Devereaux?"

"No," she blubbered miserably. "Poppa had all of that. He said he did not care to entrust it to me, because I am too— too flighty. And all of this only proves how correct he was! Oh, I shall never be able to look him in the face again! And what am I to tell poor Mamma?"

Several of the sailors seemed close to tears themselves at Katherine's plight. Johnny Farraday stepped boldly forward from the throng. "Admiral. Sir. As for the lack of chaperone—" He looked at Katherine, his eyes burning with fervor. "Any man here who would take advantage of this poor soul isn't worthy to serve God or England! I myself will take pledge for her safety, and kill any man who dares even to imagine breaching her honor whilst she is in our care!" This heady speech rendered him nearly breathless; he compounded the effect by dramatically throwing himself at Katherine's feet.

Time to back away, Katherine thought, for best effect. Noble and brave, like Cordelia in *King Lear* . . . Smiling through her tears, she reached down and drew noble Johnny up again. "I thank you, kind sir, for your words and your devotion. But it would be wrong of me, terribly wrong, to urge upon your captain a course contrary to his orders." She heaved a heartfelt sigh. "I shall return home to Momma and confess my mistake. I only pray she will forgive me. I am quite sure Poppa will not." And she gave a little flinch of her shoulders, as though she could feel the beating she was sure to receive from him.

For a moment, she feared she'd gone beyond the pale. The notion that a duke of the realm might actually beat his daughter . . . surely these men would realize the absurdity.

What she hadn't counted on was that they themselves were all too acquainted with the flail, and flinched with her collectively. "Oh, Admiral, sir," one cried, only to be echoed by a host of voices: "Let us take her to Calais!" "We must take her to Calais!" And the Scotsman growled again: "I would nae have the woundin' of the wee lass on *my* conscience, Got wot!"

Admiral Bressler was twisting uncomfortably between the winds of sympathy and duty. Katherine bowed her head, but flashed one last brave smile at the assembled men. "Nay, you must not blame the admiral," she said clearly and stoutly, "when the fault is all mine. I will wish you *bon voyage,* gentlemen." She picked up the valise and hatboxes and started for the gangplank, treading as though she went to meet her executioner. And that much of her performance, at least, was not feigned. . . .

She did not dare glance back, but she sensed the sailors were all holding their breath, eyes trained on the admiral. Should have gone for the young captain after all, she thought regretfully, putting one foot on the gangplank. And then suddenly, miraculously, the admiral called after her: "Lady Devereaux! Wait!" She turned, with a tremulous, sad smile. "You really told your father that you wanted to wed me? Back when you were a child, I mean?"

"God's truth," she told him. "And you cannot imagine the lecture it earned me on a duke's daughter's duty in marriage!"

"Hmph!" said the admiral, taking off his plumed hat and scratching his head. "Oh, what the bloody hell. We'll take you to Calais." The sailors let out an earsplitting cheer. "She can have the first mate's cabin—if, that is, Mr. Farraday, you don't mind bunking with the crew."

"It would be an honor," Mr. Farraday declared devoutly, his hand on the hilt of his sword. "And woe betide the man aboard that so much as looks at her askance!"

Katherine dropped to her knees, kissing the highly embarrassed admiral's hands. "You have saved my life, sir," she said simply.

"Hmph!" Admiral Bressler said again, and covered his fluster with a flurry of orders: "See to that mainsail, then, men! Set the stays! Let's be off, for we've dallied too long as it is!"

By the afternoon of the following day, Katherine was stepping ashore in France with her valise and hatboxes, wondering how far it might be from Calais to Paris, where Madame had said Alain Montclair was from. But she was *here*. By some sequence of miracles, she had achieved her first goal. The admiral, once the anchor was down, scanned the waterfront quays. "See your poppa?" he asked brusquely.

"Of course not," Katherine replied, with a calm she was far from feeling. "He does not expect me to be here."

"Hmph. How will you find him, then?"

"Take a hired carriage to the embassy. They have them in France, do they not?"

"I'll have Farraday hail one for you."

"That would be ever so kind," Katherine murmured, and took her leave of the sailors, all of whom looked as though they had faced down lions for her. And perhaps they had.

She smiled again at their commander. "Let me assure you, Admiral Bressler, your decency and thoughtfulness will be well recompensed by my father, once I tell him all you have done for me. Your children are fortunate indeed in having such a poppa as you."

"Hmph," said the admiral again, clearly anxious to have her gone from his care. "You have all your belongings?"

"Well, not my darling spaniels, of course! But I've no doubt they will be overjoyed to see me again. Poppa doesn't see much use in spaniels."

"Sensible man," the admiral declared, and waved her over the gangplank. "Farraday! See Lady Devereaux to a cab immediately!"

"Very good, sir!" the first mate responded, with a snappy salute. "The English embassy," he told the driver he hailed. "On the double! And see you do whatever she wishes!"

The driver grumbled something inaudible in French, then spurred his horse. Katherine leaned back against the worn leather seat and let out the breath she'd been holding for the past two days. If this was what Nanette had felt at the end of a stage-play, Katherine was beginning to form a new respect for her stepmother.

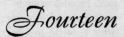

Fourteen

As soon as they were out of sight of the quays, Katherine called to the carriage driver: "Stop at once, please! Do you speak English?"

"Not a word of it," he said in a most surly manner.

"Why, you certainly do!"

"When in a foreign nation," the driver informed her, "it is the visitor's duty to make herself understood."

"I am willing to try," Katherine said pleasantly enough, "but my French is quite dreadful, or so Monsieur Jacquet informs me, and it will only slow us down considerably to have me hobble along in it. I need for you to take me to Paris instead of to the English embassy."

"To—" The driver whipped around to stare at her and let out a rapid stream of words, *none* of which, Katherine was quite sure, had ever been in Monsieur Jacquet's vocabulary lessons at the academy.

"Does something about my request disconcert you, my good fellow?"

"Have you any notion," he said in his perfectly intelligible English, "how far it is from Calais to Paris?"

"None," Katherine admitted.

"Nearly two hundred miles. Five days' ride, hard ride, requiring overnight accommodations, changes of horses, not to mention meals and wine—" His eyes narrowed; he was watching Katherine unclasp the diamonds she wore at her ears.

"I imagine that the fare you'd charge would be considerable," she said calmly, and held the drops out to him. "Would this cover it?"

He reached out gingerly for the gems. "Paste?" he demanded, half dubious, half hopeful.

"You may stop at a jeweler's, if you wish, to have them assessed. But they are insured by my father for three thousand English pounds."

The French economy, Katherine had heard Madame sigh often enough, had been completely devastated by the chaos of the Revolution and the subsequent years of war. It was a fact she had been counting on. She could almost see the driver performing currency conversions in his head. "Enough to retire on," she heard him murmur. "Buy a bit of land as well, a few head of cattle—" He caught himself abruptly and resumed his glare. "I suppose it's enough," he said brusquely. "You may count yourself lucky, though, it was *my* carriage you happened into. Any other driver in Calais would have laughed at such an insane proposal!" He clicked his tongue at his team, flicking the reins, and they were on their way.

By the afternoon of their fifth day of travel, Katherine was wishing she'd had the foresight to hire a closed carriage for the journey. She was so choked with dust that she could barely draw breath, and her clothes were nothing less than a disgrace. She didn't dare change them, though; her surreptitious leavetaking had required that she pack only the barest minimum. She could always stock up on gowns and stockings and shoes, she had figured, in Paris, which was, after all, the fashion capital of the world.

"Is it much farther now?" she asked the driver, craning in her seat in hopes she might glimpse the city's spires and roofs in the distance.

"Far enough," was all he answered, which was all he ever did.

For long stretches of the lovely, verdant late-summer countryside, it was easy to forget that France was a nation at war with most of Europe—well, with what of Europe Napoleon hadn't conquered. Every now and again, though, as they entered a town, they'd be met by white-and-blue-uniformed soldiers. The first time it had happened, Katherine had gone pale. Apparently, though, the driver had been whiling away his hours at the reins with dreaming of that little farm, and his greed made them companions in deception. "Look ill," he'd hissed to her at the soldiers' approach, "and keep your mouth shut"—orders that, in her dusty disarray and terror, were easy to fulfill. He greeted the men with a salute, offered up his papers, then gestured to Katherine, who was sinking, white-faced, in her seat. Whatever he told the men was enough to make them cluck in sympathy and step back a few paces as they waved him on.

"What did you say to them?" Katherine demanded when they were out of earshot.

"That you are dying of consumption, and I am rushing you home to your poor grieving mother so that you can expire in her arms."

"How awfully clever of you!"

"You needn't sound so surprised," he'd said dourly. "Folk with jewels aren't the only ones with brains." It was rather a novel notion to Katherine—but then she reminded herself that *he* was the current possessor of a fistful of jewels. No doubt that had inspired him.

She roused herself now from the reminiscence and repeated the question she knew irritated her unlikely cavalier but could not keep from asking: "Is it much farther?"

"Five minutes less than when last you asked," he grunted, and then relented: "Another three or four hours at most."

"So little as that," Katherine marveled, suddenly chilled at the prospect of the journey's end.

Thus far, she had been unaccountably fortunate—in her choice of Admiral Bressler, in this aspiring driver, in the fact that no one at the academy had sounded an alarm in time to stop her at the Dover quays. But now that she was so close to her objective, her feet were slowly turning to clay. However would she find Alain Montclair in that great foreign city? And if she *did* find him, what would she say? *I am sorry. I was wrong. I love you.* All of that had seemed so easy when she'd first conceived her scheme. As the miles rolled past, though, and the bright, imagined future moved inexorably toward a far more muddled present, second thoughts were crowding her mind.

Still, she could hardly demand that the driver turn about—he would surely have her consigned to an asylum. She'd traveled this far along the course of hope and faith—two road signs that, before Montclair began his siege of her heart, had never held much meaning for her. But only look at the strength he had instilled in her! *I believe there are souls that are twinned at birth,* he had whispered to her. *Whose destinies are entwined by some power beyond human imagining. Do you believe this as well?* She hadn't, there in the courtyard. She did now, though, with all her heart. For what else could have compelled her to set out so recklessly, flouting every convention, every speck of decency and modesty?

For the first time in her life, she had burst free of the burden of her ordained role. And while just now she felt she was sailing straight over a waterfall to disaster, she clung to the memory of that moment in the courtyard ferociously. Once she found him, all would be well. Once she was in his arms again, they would laugh together at her qualms. He would kiss her, and all her doubts would vanish at the touch of his lips on hers. *Happily ever after . . .*

Honestly, she thought, *I am as silly as that romantic fool Bess!*

Then she pictured again the entrance he had made at the Tathams', how all eyes had turned to him, his impossibly broad shoulders, the silky black hair, the impeccable way he'd worn his evening clothes, with all the elegance of a prince. Regardless of how Madame had tried to convince her he was nothing but a rogue and a scoundrel, her heart knew better.

She smiled, her confidence restored, and asked the driver: "How much longer is it, then?"

They reached the outskirts of the city just as dusk was falling. Her driver performed another miracle of subterfuge to get her past the guards at the north gate, which was far more heavily secured than the country villages had been. Once inside the walls, he twisted on his seat, and she noted how drawn and exhausted he appeared. Poor man . . .

"Get out," he told her.

"Get *out*?" She glanced about nervously at the shadowy tangle of streets. "I cannot just get out! I've no idea where I am!"

"Our agreement was that I take you to Paris. I've fulfilled it. Now, if you don't mind, I've a farm to buy."

"But—" What had happened to her comrade-in-arms? "I cannot even speak French! What will become of me?"

"You seem resourceful enough. Go on, now! Get your stuff and get out!"

"See here!" Katherine huffed, folding her arms across her chest. "I am not going anywhere! You have a responsibility to see me safely installed at one of the finer hotels!"

"My responsibility to you ended the moment we entered those gates."

Eyes narrowing, Katherine reached into her reticule for her pistol—then remembered she had packed it inside her valise. Damn! Well, she would not make that mistake again. "I won't get out," she vowed. "You will have to make me." Two minutes later, he'd done so, depositing her and her baggage beside the curb, then bounding into his seat again and whipping his team. "I hope your cattle die! I hope your farm is a wasteland! A wasteland, do you hear me?" Katherine raged at him as he rode off. "A pox on you and your crops!" Then, noticing that the people in the street around her were staring, she shouldered up her valise and bandboxes and grimly started to walk.

It was the most terrifying journey she had ever made. The twilight deepened to darkness as she plodded along through stunted, twisting passageways between squat houses with unwelcoming facades. Now and again, some denizen approached her, murmuring suggestively in French, offering God knew what aid or haven. Katherine withered all such proposals with disdain, at which, fortunately, she was very practiced. At long last, as her feet were aching and her spirits were at their nadir, the streets widened; gaslights appeared; and the passersby were far more elegantly dressed. There were hired carriages as well, though Katherine, from recent experience, was loathe to hail one. She stood for a moment, taking in the scene, glancing up at the street name posted on the corner of the nearest building. RUE DES PETITES CHAMPS—it was a name she thought she vaguely remembered from Monsieur Jacquet's discourses on Paris. That was a good omen. A row of coaches was pulling up in front of a tall, stately edifice, disgorging chattering passengers, the ladies like swans in their gossamer gowns, the gentlemen impeccable in cloaks and tall hats. Slowly she approached, sticking to the shadows—like, she thought ruefully, some sort of common tramp. She was close enough now to read the sign above the entrance—the Palais Royal. It wasn't a hotel at all, blast it, but an opera house; the din of an orchestra tuning up confirmed what she'd gleaned from the ornate letters. And then, at that moment, someone seized her by the shoulder, so roughly that she gasped. A hand whirled her about, and she stared into the glittering eyes of a dark-skinned, mustachioed man.

He barked something at her in French.

"P-parlez-vous anglaise?" Katherine stuttered.

Evidently not; he barked again and thrust her back in the direction from which she'd come. Katherine was about to slink off into the shadows when something in her just snapped. Whether it was her carriage driver's perfidy, or the hours spent wandering these unknown streets in terror, or just the unspeakably crude way in which the man had laid hands on her, she decided she had had enough. She drew herself up, squared her shoulders, tossed her mussed, dusty hair, and glared right back at the man.

"Now see here," she announced as grandly as though she were addressing King George, "I don't know who you are, or by what right you accost me. But I will have you know that I am Lady Katherine Devereaux, daughter to the duke of Marne, and I am *not* accustomed to being manhandled by the likes of *you!*" Her sapphire eyes flashed. "Through a series of circumstances that are no doubt beyond your comprehension, I find myself alone and friendless in this city, and I must say, so far the reputation of the French people for rudeness is proving entirely accurate. If you've any decency whatsoever, I would appreciate your directing me to the nearest of the fine hotels!"

Somewhat breathless, she finished. The man—she noticed now, belatedly, that he was dressed in the same epauletted livery as the opera house footmen—had let his jaw drop open. He closed it abruptly, held up a finger in a gesture that clearly meant *Wait here,* and rushed off to the opera house steps. She watched him engage in a brief, passionate discussion with another of the footmen, pointing at her across the cobblestones. The other man glanced her way, spat with noisy derision, and laughed. Katherine glared furiously at him. The mustachioed man looked back at her, shrugged, and darted inside the opera house. Katherine, sighing, had just picked up her hatboxes when she saw him emerge, this time accompanied by a short, dapper fellow in evening dress. As they descended the steps toward her, Katherine set down her belongings and assumed her most regal stance.

"Ma'm'selle." Doubt was plain in the little fellow's voice as well; clearly he thought this a fool's errand. But he spoke English! "Bertrand informs me that I have a lost duchess on the doorstep of my opera house."

"Not a duchess. The daughter of one," Katherine said airily. "To whom have I the pleasure of speaking?"

Somewhat taken aback, the fellow made a belated bow. "I am Monsieur de Braquefort, manager of the Opera House of Paris. And you are . . . ?"

"Katherine, Lady Devereaux." She did not curtsy, any more than she would have to the doorman, and she saw him register the fact behind his carefully neutral features. "Daughter of Their Graces the duke and duchess of Marne."

Unexpectedly, his eyes lit up. "The duke of Marne's daughter—*oui, oui,* I see the resemblance now, as plain as can be!" He bowed again, much more obsequiously. "I beg your pardon, Lady Devereaux! Many, many times I had the pleasure of greeting your father when he came here to my house! His especial favorite, I recall, is Mozart. He is well, I trust?"

"Quite well," Katherine said crisply, not at all certain if she was glad or not to be recognized. Still, anything was better than this aimless wandering. She forced a smile. "I can remember Poppa remarking on his enjoyment of the performances here."

"Naturellement," Monsieur de Braquefort said, puffing out his chest. Then he peered at her anxiously. "But how does it come to be, Lady Devereaux, that Bertrand finds you here in such a state?"

Katherine had been thinking of just what to say to this inevitable question. "As I attempted to explain, through a most unfortunate sequence of events, I became separated at the gates of the city from the school group with which I was traveling. My French being somewhat uncertain, I was unable to make myself understood in my predicament. And so I was reduced to making my way on foot, hoping against hope that I would come to some landmark and thus find our hotel."

Monsieur de Braquefort was shocked. *"Quel dommage!"* he clucked. "My poor child, I apologize for my city's inhospitable reception! I only thank God you were delivered to me! At which hotel are you staying?"

Katherine felt a stab of panic. She ought, she really *ought*, to be able to think of the name of a hotel in Paris. But her mind had gone blank; she was suddenly exceedingly weary and hungry and actually felt on the edge of tears. She reached deep down within herself for a reserve of strength, and found it. "I am ashamed to say, Monsieur de Braquefort, that I cannot recall the name. I do remember, though, my headmistress telling us that it was the most elegant hotel in Paris. And," she added hastily, "that its staff spoke English exceedingly well."

"Ah! That, of course, would be the Hotel Luxembourg. We must see to it that you are taken there at once, must we not, Bertrand?" He issued a volley of instructions in French that resulted in Bertrand disappearing again. "May I invite you into my offices, Lady Devereaux, for some refreshment? A glass of wine, perhaps? His Grace the duke always stops by for champagne."

Katherine's mind boggled at the notion of her father sipping champagne with the manager of an opera house. She shook her head. "That's very kind of you, monsieur. But my headmistress must be frantic at my absence."

"Ah, yes. So she must! I would not care to have on my head the misplacing of such a jewel as you!" A carriage, a very ornate one, its gilded wheels and green paint gleaming in the gaslight, clattered into the street, with Bertrand on the driver's box. He reined in beside them, and Monsieur de Braquefort caught the leads and held them while Bertrand hopped down to install Katherine and her belongings. "Bertrand will see you safely returned to your party at the Luxembourg," the opera manager continued.

"I am most grateful for your assistance."

"*Ce n'est rien,* my dear child! *Pas du tout!* But I shall see you again, no doubt. No tour of Paris is complete without a visit to my opera house," he said—rather smugly, Katherine thought. Then she imagined coming here with Alain Montclair, joining that glittering line of fashionable Parisians, and her heart softened; she actually extended her hand to de Braquefort to be kissed.

"Now, off you go," he said avuncularly, "before your poor headmistress calls out the city guard! Bertrand—" One last stream of vehement instructions, to which Bertrand nodded again and again. Then she was up into the coach, and sinking into cushions of the softest velvet, fighting the urge to fall asleep then and there in order to conquer in a greater fight— that of hoodwinking the management of the Hotel Luxembourg.

But after all that had happened thus far, that proved blessedly simple. She dismissed Bertrand at the entrance as the hotel's doormen swooped down on her. Inside the lobby, she felt herself on solid footing again. The staff of any fine hotel was accustomed to idiosyncratic arrivals, and her relative lack of luggage didn't register so much as a blink from the clerk as she engaged a room. She paid for a week's stay in pounds, from her somewhat meager store—only just before she'd left England, she'd written to the duke asking that he increase her allowance. She requested that roast chicken and bread and wine be sent up to her as soon as possible. And she followed a deferential servant to her room, which was nearly as expansive and elegant as her chambers at Marne House, with wonderfully thick carpets and a sitting area and a wide, curtained bed.

She could do no more than pick at the excellent chicken and sip one glass of wine before that bed beckoned irresistibly. She sank into it gratefully, and left for the morrow the troubling question of just what, exactly, her next step should be.

The instant she awoke, though, stiff and sore despite the admirable mattress and pillows, she knew what would come next—a bath. A bath, and then she simply *must* procure more clothes. She accomplished the first in a lingering fashion, taking time to soak away the dust and mire of her journey and wash out her hair. She'd had the foresight to send her spare day-dress for pressing when she'd ordered the bath, and it arrived, in the hands of a smiling young maid who gave her name as Marie, along with her boots, freshly blacked. Katherine did recall, very well, the name of her stepmother's favorite Paris couturiere, Madame Villeneuve, and that was sufficient to get her by cab to the establishment in question, where she was fussed over greatly and encouraged to order extravagantly—encouragement to which she was happy to acquiesce once Madame Villeneuve had agreed to bill the duke for his daughter's purchases. Katherine felt a brief qualm at leaving such plain traces of her whereabouts. But then she considered the pace of mail between two countries, plus her father's less than careful scrutiny of Nanette's dressmaker tabs, and decided the duke might very well think these bills simply latecomers from his last diplomatic journey to France.

Madame Villeneuve was, in fact, so accommodating that Katherine steeled herself to pose the question she must ask of *someone* in order to find Alain. "What would you say, Madame, is the premier gambling establishment in this city?" she inquired casually, in the midst of a discussion, half in French, half in English, of Paris's attractions.

The dressmaker, her mouth full of pins as she fitted an absolutely stunning gown of swansdown crepe over Katherine's slim hips, considered. "In the old days, it would have been La Maison de Touton—run by one of your compatriots. A most charming woman—the comtesse d'Oliveri, she is now, though she was simply Christiane Haversham in those happy times. Now—" She paused, applied for support to the young woman who was adjusting the gown's bodice in a way, Katherine noted happily, that Mrs. Tattersall in Hartin could *never* have achieved. "What would you say, Anne?"

"La Maison Grecque, je suppose," her assistant replied absently, making a tuck that showed Katherine's bosom to devastating advantage.

"And where is that?" Katherine asked, fighting down the pounding of her heart. Hadn't Madame said that Alain Montclair was a great rogue, a rakehell? Surely *somebody* at this Maison Grecque would know where he could be found.

"Sur la rue de Rivoli," Madame Villeneuve informed her, then winked and smiled. "You are your stepmother's daughter indeed, are you not? Just arrived in Paris, and the first amusement you wish to assay is the roulette wheel!"

I am not *my stepmother's daughter!* Katherine nearly blurted out, but stopped herself in time; instead, she managed to giggle girlishly in response. Odd, how playacting grew easier and easier the more you did of it. "Oh, I doubt that I shall manage to slip away from my chaperones in order to visit such a place. Still, one likes to be informed, does one not?"

"Certainement," the seamstress agreed, a glint in her eye as she tacked up the hem of the gown.

Two days later, Madame Villeneuve's breathtaking confections had been duly delivered to the Hotel Luxembourg;

Katherine had also acquired, with the couturiere's aid, a number of fetching new shoes and hats and items of lingerie. Never had noblesse oblige seemed so gratifying; simply scrawling her name across the bills ensured they would be directed to her father, and every tradesman and tradeswoman she visited fawned on her delightedly. It was almost enough to make her forget that she was on a mission. But the sooner she took the plunge, the sooner she and Alain would be reunited. That evening, she requested that the pretty maid, Marie, dress her in Madame Villeneuve's white swansdown evening gown and put up her hair. She donned her sapphire neckpiece and the matching eardrops, added and then subtracted a pair of gold-and-diamond bracelets—really, she *was* in a foreign country, and if some swarthy hoodlum accosted her, she could hardly afford to lose so much of her jewelcase—checked that her pistol was inside her reticule, let Marie settle the most becoming new cap of curled ostrich plumes atop her ringlets, and set out for La Maison Grecque in a hired cab, the driver of which did not so much as blink at her destination. Some facets of French culture, Katherine mused, were *most* peculiar. She could only imagine what Mrs. Caldburn would have to say about an unaccompanied young woman visiting such a place.

The cab stopped before a nondescript sequence of darkened doorsteps, and the driver helped Katherine to alight. She tipped him well before asking, "Which one is it, exactly?" More than her words, her uncertain expression made him nod toward the middle door of the row.

"*Là-bas,*" he said.

She thanked him and strode resolutely up to the door, which had a brass knocker that clanged when she let it fall. A small shuttered window slid back, and she found herself staring into an impassive set of eyes. "*S'il vous plaît,*" she began haltingly, "*je—*" What the devil was the verb for "search"? But before she could say any more, the door opened, and the eyes became part of a face, a young man's face that was smiling in admiration.

"Bonsoir, ma'm'selle," he announced, reaching for her wrap. *"Bienvenue à la Maison Grecque."*

Katherine grabbed the new ermine back from him. "Oh, I am not staying! I am only looking for a man." She flushed as he laughed uproariously and said in English:

"You have come to the right place, then, *ma petite!*"

"No, no! What I mean is—" Hopelessly flustered, she tried to summon up hauteur. She was so disconcerted, though, that it only came across as nervousness. "A *particular* man. One named Alain Montclair."

The expression on the young man's face altered abruptly. "Oh, *non, non*," he clucked in disapproval. "Not you also, *ma petite*. Not one so lovely as you."

"I don't care what you say about him," Katherine said more confidently. "I intend to find him, wherever he may be." What had he meant, she wondered, when he said, "Not you also"? But she scarcely had time to form the thought before he went on:

"I tell you, then, what I know of Alain Montclair. He is in the Bastille, imprisoned on charges of murdering the sister of Citizen Boulé."

"Murdering—" Katherine faltered, there in the foyer. "No!" she cried, shaking her head vehemently. "It isn't possible! There has to be some mistake!"

He looked at her with pity. "There may indeed be some mistake. These days there often is. But there he is, nonetheless. And I would give you any odds you name that he will die by the guillotine."

Fifteen

Katherine made her way back to the Hotel Luxembourg in a dim haze of horror. Alain . . . in prison . . . the Bastille, for God's sake! And for murder! She felt as though a curtain of lead had fallen onto her chest; she could scarcely breathe. Her informant was wrong; he had to be wrong. So pale and distraught did she appear as she alighted from her cab that the doorman took her arm. *"Ma'm'selle?"* he asked anxiously. *"Sont-vous en besoin de l'aide?"*

"I need—" Katherine gasped out, clinging to him tightly. "I need—"

"Du vin, peut-être?" he suggested.

"Yes," she said gratefully. "Some sherry, if you please."

He blinked, leading her to the stair. "But I have already sent sherry to your room."

"That was wine, with my luncheon," Katherine contradicted him, in no mood for idiotic servants. She shook off his arm as well. "Bring my key at once. And sherry."

"Bien sûr, ma'm'selle." He bowed, retrieved the key, and then hurried off as she climbed the gleaming inlaid steps.

At the landing, she paused. Her eyes had filled with tears; she could barely see. She groped her way blindly down the corridor to her room, somehow managed to fit the key into the lock and turn it. Soft light fell in a flood as the door swung open. How odd, she thought, that Marie should have lit the lamps. . . .

"Bonsoir," said a dry, droll voice. Katherine rubbed at her eyes with the back of her hands. There in the chaise longue was the countess d'Oliveri, sipping a glass of sherry, the bottle close at hand.

To her complete astonishment, Katherine found herself unspeakably grateful to be discovered. "Oh, Madame!" she cried, bursting into tears. "The most dreadful news! Alain is—"

"I know." Madame patted the chair at her side, but Katherine collapsed at her knees instead. "I spoke to Guillaume, an old friend at La Maison Grecque, as soon as I arrived. He informed me of Montclair's . . . predicament."

"It is a mistake, don't you think?" Katherine asked anxiously. "Surely some mistake has been made!"

But Madame merely shook her head in sadness. "I always warned him he would come to a bad end, playing hard and fast as he did."

Katherine looked up from the floor, her eyes desperate. "They say he killed a woman!"

"Mimi Boulé. I know. I got the entire story from Guillaume. She most assuredly is dead. Strangled in an upstairs chamber at a gaming hell—a chamber she had entered with Alain Montclair, in full view of a dozen citizens."

"He is not capable of murder!" Katherine insisted.

"I did not think so, once. Now that I see what he has done to you, though, I am not certain at all."

Katherine's cheeks went red. "I do not know what you mean!"

"Don't you?" Katherine had never heard the countess sound so severe. "You run away from your home, you make your way to a foreign nation, chaperoneless, companionless, moneyless—"

"I *did* have my jewels—"

"*And* shameless, I might add!"

The scarlet stain on Katherine's cheeks was from fury now. "You are a fine one to talk of shamelessness! The former proprietress of a gaming hell—"

"That is neither here nor there, Katherine! The salient facts are that you have terrified poor Mrs. Treadwell, thrown a dreadful scare into the girls at the academy, and behaved in a way that would *kill* your father if he only knew!"

"So!" Katherine cried triumphantly. "You haven't told him! I might have guessed. You are so intent on preserving the reputation of your precious academy—"

"Did it ever occur to you, Katherine, that the reputation I am so intent on preserving is *yours*?"

Katherine stared for a moment. "I did not think you cared anything about my reputation—or about me, for that matter."

"And why should I? You are headstrong, you are rude to your subordinates and positively *evil* to your classmates, you are conceited and impossibly proud and—Jesus in heaven, in light of all that, how did you ever manage to get to France?"

Stumblingly, Katherine explained about riding to the Dover docks, and choosing Admiral Bressler's ship, and Johnny Farraday and the other sailors, and the carriage driver and his traitorous conduct, and her hazardous walk through the streets of Paris, and the way Bertrand had accosted her outside the Palais Royal, and de Braquefort's miraculous intervention, and—

It was at this point in the story that she realized the countess was laughing—laughing quietly, true, but quite mirthfully. Affronted, Katherine broke off and said bitterly, "I am glad my travails provide you with such amusement."

"Oh, Katherine. Forgive me. It is just that—who would have thought you, of all people, capable of such resourcefulness?"

Katherine paused. "I *was* resourceful, wasn't I?"

"Astonishingly so." Madame set aside her sherry glass. "You were wrong just now when you said I did not care about you. I have always cared about you, against all likelihood. I think . . . because you remind me so strongly of myself when I was your age."

"*I?*"

Madame laughed again at Katherine's nonplus. "Yes. You."

"But you created a *scandal*."

"What did you imagine *you* would create when you ran off to find your lover?"

"He isn't my—" But she stopped, her eyes growing wide. "Oh, God. Oh, dear God, forgive me, what have I done?" And then the awful import, the repercussions, overwhelmed her; she crumpled in a heap on the floor. "What *could* I have been thinking of?"

"I imagine," Madame said calmly, "you were thinking of his arms about you, and his lips on yours. That is the way it usually is."

Katherine stared at the carpet. "You make it sound so tawdry. Common."

"Only in the motivation," the countess assured her. "Not at *all* in the lengths to which you went. Those were quite uncommon indeed." There was a knock at the door. *"Entrez,"* Madame called in her perfect French, and a servant entered, bearing sherry. *"Oh, merci, mais nous avons de plus."* He bowed his way out again, and the countess reached to raise Katherine into a chair. "Let me pour you some wine." She did so, and held out the glass. Katherine took it absently.

"There is no hope for me, I suppose."

"Oh, I shouldn't say that. You tell me you explained to Monsieur de Braquefort that you were in Paris with a school group. I *am* associated with your school. As for that folderol you handed Admiral Bressler about your father—well, I daresay in the press of war he isn't likely to think much about it, nor will his sailors. After all, they've gone straight off to Lisbon—how are they to know whether or not your poppa is in Calais?"

Katherine took a tiny sip of sherry. "What would you advise me to do?" she asked very humbly.

"So long as we have come all this way, I think that we should see the sights of Paris, then return to England. But not," the countess added, "before we visit Alain Montclair."

"Oh, no! I mean—that isn't possible, is it? He is in prison—"

"I very much regret to inform you, Katherine, that I have numerous contacts at the Bastille."

Katherine was shaking her head. "I mustn't. I couldn't. It would not be at all proper."

"It is why you came to France," Madame reminded her gently.

"But only because I was besotted—bewitched!"

"What better way to break the enchantment than to confront your sorcerer face-to-face?"

"I don't dare."

"I think that you must." Madame looked at her. "What are you afraid of, child?"

"That he might do it again," she whispered. "That he might . . . sorcer me."

"I hardly think that likely. Not now that you have come to your senses."

Her senses. In the courtyard . . . her senses. Alive and warm and engaged as they had never been before . . . The scent of him, cognac and tobacco. The taste of his skin on her tongue. His hand probing, gently stroking. The flow of love between them . . .

Katherine drew herself upright, much more assured now that she was not alone. "You think it so necessary as that?"

"I think it vital," Madame told her, and took a sip of sherry. "I tried to tell you what he is. You can see for yourself, now that he is where his destiny ordained him to be."

"Very well, then. But after I see him—please, may I go home?"

"Of course," Madame said soothingly, patting Katherine's hair.

"I'm so very tired," Katherine confessed, letting out a yawn.

"You must sleep now," the countess said, and led her to her bed as though she were a child, undressing her and then tucking her in with a hug and a kiss.

For the next week, Madame took Katherine on a grand tour of the French capital—to Notre Dame, to the Louvre, to the place des Vosges, to the Tuileries, to Versailles, even, one long afternoon, to the Empress Josephine's famed rose garden at La Malmaison. It was all very splendid and exotic and grand, and the countess was a matchless guide. She always seemed to know some guard who could show them the crown jewels without waiting on queue, or a boatman who would take them for a picnic on an island in the Seine, or a café that served extraordinary pastries and ices.

She was also, in some odd way, impressive. At first Katherine was embarrassed to be seen about town with a woman who seemed to be recognized by every Parisian they passed. But Madame's delight in being back here in the city she so clearly loved was infectious, and the regard in which her adopted countrymen held her was profound. One afternoon, as she and Madame strolled through the Jardin des Plantes, Katherine blurted out the question that had been weighing on her mind for days: "Why did you open a gambling hell?" The countess's dark gaze slanted toward her. "I mean," Katherine said quickly, "you could not have known much about business matters. You were only a woman, after all."

"*Only* a woman?" Madame sounded bemused. "Do you think women are lesser creatures than men, *ma petite*?"

"Not—not lesser creatures, exactly. But certainly less able ones. You don't see female ministers of government, or barristers, or statesmen."

"No. You don't," the countess agreed. "But contemplate, Katherine, what a woman who runs a major estate, such as your stepmother, does. She has a budget. She hires and fires employees. She keeps track of what is needed for the household—wine, food, creature comforts. She is responsible for maintaining the morale of her troops—not to mention that of her husband. Now, consider what men of the upper echelon do with their time. They gather and meet, and talk, and talk some more, and drink, and play cards, and wench. And then they talk again. Which background do you think better prepares a human being for the role of, say, prime minister?"

Katherine was staring. "Women are not qualified for high offices."

"According to whom? To men, *ma petite!* And why do they say so? Because we are emotional. We cry too easily; we laugh too readily. We take too great an interest in the lives of those around us. We are listeners, not talkers. When women gather, they search for common interests. They seek out similarities—how many children do you have? Did they suffer from the colic as babies? Isn't it difficult to find a good cook? Don't you hate the new sleeves? Whereas when men gather, they butt heads. They throw out challenges to one another. They are like goats in a pasture, bucking for position, recognition, superiority."

"I have observed that tendency," Katherine said slowly, "among my father and his friends. Even a simple hunt becomes a competition—who will get off the first shot? Who can ride the fastest? Whose dogs are best?"

"Precisely," said the countess. "Women and men have widely divergent philosophies of life. Ask a man what matters most to him, and he will reply: rank, or money, or the respect of his peers. Ask a woman, and she will tell you: my family and my friends. Which set of priorities makes a soul more suited to governing a nation?"

"You," Katherine declared, "have some very peculiar ideas."

The countess laughed. "Yes. I have been told so. But it seems a shame to me that what women have to bring to the table at, say, negotiations over peace between nations should be discounted out of hand. It is one of the reasons I convinced Mrs. Treadwell to found the academy. Our sex has much more to offer, Katherine, than the world is as yet ready to receive."

"Women will never be accepted as heads of state," Katherine said quite firmly.

"Our Queen Elizabeth did rather well at the job for more than forty years."

"Yes, but look at what she sacrificed to do so—her womanhood! She never had a husband, never had any children—" Katherine broke off abruptly; the countess's eyes were suspiciously bright.

Madame recovered her composure, though, to say: "She played by the rules of men, because she had no choice—not in that day, that age. The time is coming, though, when we will change the rules, Katherine. You and I may not live to see it, but the time *will* come."

In all her life, Katherine had never been party to a conversation such as this. "You are quite a . . . a revolutionary, aren't you?" she asked hesitantly.

"I suppose I am. But I have not answered your question, have I? I opened a gambling hell because I knew I would prosper. Because I understood enough of the ways of men to use them to my advantage. They are simple creatures, really. They want to be thought well of, to be flattered. To believe we women find them irresistible, even when they are bald and fat and drunk and stupidly eager to throw their money away."   .

"Don't you *like* men?"

"I like some men very much. But most of them I find to be great ninnies."

Katherine couldn't help but giggle. "You are precisely right!"

"Every now and again," the countess went on thoughtfully, "a man does come along who really is irresistible. And it has been my experience that such men think like women, not like men. They understand the value of listening, not just talking. They pay attention in a conversation. And they have a way of touching a woman . . . the way we touch one another. Softly. Gently. Frequently. Not only when they are frantic to make love."

Katherine blushed wholeheartedly, thinking of Alain Montclair's fingers brushing against her cheek. She rushed to change the subject: "Do you ever regret that you never had children?"

Madame shot her an amused glance. "I used to. Until I got to know you girls, and realized how impossible raising a child could be!"

Katherine's enjoyment of the time she spent with the countess could not help but be marred by the thought of the interview at the Bastille that still loomed ahead. She did not speak of it, hoping against hope that Madame might forget about it in her joy at being back in the land of her exile. But over a breakfast in the hotel restaurant of delightful almond croissants and perfectly ripe melon and big cups of coffee stirred with sugar and cream—really much preferable, Katherine thought, to the disgusting English habit of beginning the day with sirloin and ham and eggs drenched in butter and thick slices of bread dripping with marmalade—the countess said quietly, "I have arranged for us to visit Montclair tomorrow."

"Tomorrow?" Katherine nearly choked on her croissant. "I really don't think it necessary, Madame. I am quite over my infatuation with him—and unspeakably grateful that you went to so much effort to spare me from my idiocy."

Madame calmly broke off a bit of her croissant. "It would be remiss of me not to insist that you see him. Otherwise, how am I to be sure you will not pine and long for him after our return to England, and repeat your giddy behavior in three months, or six months, or a year from now?"

Katherine started to bristle, then recognized that from the countess's viewpoint, the fear was justified. "All I can tell you is that I have learned a great deal from my mistake."

"So you seem to have." Madame considered her curiously. "I fear you may have learned *too* much. Your ability to find your way here, alone and unaided, leaves me quite in awe."

"Oh—" Katherine waved a hand dismissively. "It was not so difficult as it might seem."

"That's precisely what I mean. Who knows what you are capable of if you put your mind to it?"

"Madame, all I intend to put my mind to, once we return home, is studying my lessons and being kinder to my classmates and—I hope—finding a nice, *respectable* young man to wed."

"You don't think a respectable young man might prove a bit dull in the wake of Montclair?"

"Absolutely not! I am positively *craving* a lifetime of dullness and respectability." As she spoke the words, Katherine meant them absolutely. Yet in a hidden corner of her soul, something fluttered in protest, as though it had wings it was trying to unfold. Mentally, she tamped the thing down firmly, laid atop it the considerable weight of public opinion and social acceptance and her miraculous avoidance of scandal.

"When I consider," Madame murmured, "what *might* have become of you, amongst those rough sailors, or with that unscrupulous driver who hauled you clear across the country, or in the midst of the rabble of Paris as you wandered in the dark—I confess, I am nearly overcome. As many times as I have rued your hauteur, I cannot help but think that was what kept you safe. It would take a very courageous man indeed to attempt to breach the walls of your contempt."

Katherine colored, remembering with what ease Montclair had successfully scaled them.

Madame contemplated her once more, and Katherine hid her discomposure behind the oversize coffee cup. "I shall leave it to you," the countess finally declared, "whether you wish to see him again or not."

That *thing,* dark-winged and dangerous, nearly managed to escape from beneath its crushing load. Nearly, but not quite . . . "I should prefer to bow to your wisdom," Katherine confessed. "I only wish I had done so a fortnight ago."

"In that case, we will go," Madame decided. "He may be a scoundrel, but I have known him since he was very young indeed. It is only right that I bid him adieu. And you may as well accompany me."

"If that is what you think best." Katherine gave a final, forceful downward thrust to that unruly thing. "I suppose I owe him some sort of debt, for proving to me that even the loftiest among us are capable of base errors in judgment."

"*There's* the old Katherine," Madame noted, smiling with mingled exasperation and relief.

Sixteen

The Bastille was a building at once beautiful and formidable, gray and august and looming, with a sort of sepulchral magnificence. Far less attractive to Katherine's mind were the miserable French citizens they passed as their carriage approached the fortress, who were busily attempting to bribe or wheedle or bluster their way inside with gifts of bread and sausages and wine for their loved ones. The guards, Katherine could not help noting as Madame engaged in animated conversation with one through the cab window, appeared to view the supplicants' desperation with whimsical amusement. Sometimes they took the gifts intended for the prisoners but turned the grieving families away; sometimes, especially when the supplicants' hands were empty, they drove them off with their pikestaffs; very occasionally, some lucky soul was let through. And that soul's good fortune was enough to revive the spirits of the entire crowd, so that they pressed forward ever more eagerly despite the odds against them. It was, Katherine thought, like some peculiar game of roulette, with a heavily weighted wheel.

Madame had no trouble at all progressing through the ranks to the doors of the prison. "How does it happen that we are so readily let in," Katherine asked the countess, "when so many are turned away?"

"A number of the guards served under my former lover in the war. We entertained them."

"You entertained prison guards?" Katherine was astounded.

Madame looked at her with some surprise. "You must be aware that in France, the social order is turned all topsy-turvy. That first fellow I spoke to is a former viscount. And the commandant of the prison was once seigneur of half the Rhône Valley."

"Imagine that," Katherine marveled. "How do they come to find themselves here?"

"Under the Revolution, rank was eliminated. Estates were ripped from the aristocracy and given to newcomers. The men of France are now expected to rise and fall according to their abilities. It helps, of course, to have the wherewithal to purchase a desirable post. That of commandant here, for example, is quite lucrative, what with stripping the prisoners of their belongings, accepting bribes from grieving relatives, and offering preferential treatment—windows, baths, decent meals—to those who can afford to pay."

"I cannot *believe*," Katherine said quite firmly, "that any aristocrat would ever behave in such a way."

A shadow passed across Madame's face. "You'd be amazed what an aristocrat will do with a pistol to his head."

"But that just goes to prove, does it not, that the very idea of the Revolution was an abomination?"

The countess considered for a moment before speaking. "Great notions," she said then, slowly, "are like upheavals of nature—earthquakes, or volcanoes. There is a certain unavoidable amount of profound misery attached to them as they shake themselves out, erupt, and then subside. The throwing off of privilege and rank seems to have been quite successful in America."

"And no wonder," Katherine sniffed. "That land is peopled by the scum of the earth. Religious deviants, indentured felons, opportunistic riffraff of every sort—why, there was never any nobility there to speak of!"

"That," Madame said with a smile, "may be precisely why egalitarianism has succeeded there and is still causing mayhem in France. But we have arrived." One of the guards had opened the coach door. The countess alighted, in her elegant patterned muslin and tight-fitted sarcenet jacket and dainty half-bonnet cocked above her glistening black hair. Katherine followed tentatively. She'd spent most of the night wide awake, wondering what to wear. She wanted very much to

look her best—*not,* she had told herself, for Alain's sake, but for her own, so that she would stand tall and proud as she told him what she thought of him. Now, as she stepped toward the barred entrance in her new day-gown and open-work linen wrap and ostrich-crowned bonnet, she felt oddly conspicuous before the doleful peasants crowding the gates. Not daring to glance backward, she lowered her head, sneaking toward the open door for all the world like some sort of—

"Souillon!" someone shouted from amidst the muttering throng, and Katherine yelped as she felt a blow at her back.

"What in heaven's name—" She turned, then ducked as a missile came shooting toward her out of the crowd. Nay, not a missile—a ripe plum, that spattered against her skirt in a horrid purple-green blare. Madame grabbed her hand and yanked her into the prison, while the angry shouts pursued them:

"Coureuse!"

"Coquinne!"

"What are they saying?" Katherine demanded, trying without any success to wipe away the plum-stain with her glove.

"They are calling us whores," Madame explained.

"But why?"

"Two women in fancy dress, admitted to the Bastille . . . it is a reasonable assumption," Madame noted dryly. "Your gown is ruined, I'm afraid."

"Of all the utter nerve!" Katherine's nascent sympathy for the throngs at the gates had evaporated completely. "How *dare* they assault me! I shall press charges! I shall see them imprisoned! I shall—"

"Do hush," the countess admonished, "and come along. It is best not to make waves in this place."

Katherine would have argued it, but a shaft of chill, clammy air had suddenly enveloped her, making her stagger on her feet. "God, what's that smell?"

"Despair," the countess said briefly. The guard beckoned, like an augur of doom, and Katherine pulled her lavender-scented kerchief from her reticule and pressed it to her nose as she followed in Madame's wake.

They went along seemingly endless corridors of mossy, moist stone, then down a curving, slippery staircase so steep that Katherine felt a sweep of vertigo. "Not at all a good sign," the countess murmured regretfully, "his being so low. He had friends once. I wonder what has become of them."

As they made their way into the bowels of the prison, the dreadful stench intensified, until Katherine's head was swimming. She grabbed unsteadily for Madame's arm: "I don't think . . . I can go any further." From somewhere below, there arose a howl of almost animal nature that echoed wildly against the stone walls. Katherine's knees buckled. Madame calmly drew her up again.

"It is best you see him this way, so that any romantic notions you still might harbor—"

"God! How could I?"

Inexorably, the countess pulled her on.

The jailer paused before a low, inconspicuous door, wood barred with iron, indistinguishable to Katherine from the dozens of others they'd passed. *"Ici,"* the man intoned, taking the heavy iron ring of keys from his belt. Then he waited. Katherine was wondering what for, then saw Madame dig into her reticule and take out a large wad of notes—English pound notes. Once she had turned them over to the man, he put the key to the lock.

"I'll go in first, if you like," Madame offered, "to explain matters, while you remain here in the hall."

Katherine cast a nervous glance at the lowering jailer. "I'd prefer to come with you," she said, and crowded after the countess through the portal. She had never in all her life heard anything so desolate as the creak of that door closing behind them, and the clank of the key turning the lock once more.

It was pitch-black inside the cell except for a single narrow rectangle of flickering torchlight that fell across the floor from a slot in the door. Katherine clung to the shadows, but the countess strode boldly into the darkness and called out, "Alain? Are you here?"

Katherine could just glimpse some formless shape rising from the floor, like a monster disturbed in its lair. *"Qui est là?"* came a croaking voice she did not recognize at all, and for a wild instant, she was sure the creature they'd conjured into consciousness was not Montclair—that there had indeed been some mistake, and that the handsome young man who'd invited her to run away with him in the academy courtyard wasn't here after all, was safe and hale at a baize table in some Paris gaming hall.

But then Madame said, *"C'est moi,* Alain. Christiane."

And the yearning disbelief with which the creature echoed the name—*"Christiane?"*—left her with no doubt of his identity. He stumbled forward, then stopped abruptly, like a fish yanked on a line, as the stone walls echoed with the rattle of a chain.

The countess obligingly went toward him—*very* obligingly, Katherine thought, considering the way he stank. There ensued a low-voiced conversation in extremely rapid French, which she was unable to follow. She was quite sure, though, that she did not hear her own name mentioned—an impression confirmed when Madame interrupted Montclair's impassioned discourse by saying, in English, "Even in such straits, we must not forget our manners, Alain. You have another visitor, one who does not share our tongue."

"Another—" She could sense him peering past the countess. "Who? Is it the ambassador?"

"The ambassador?" Madame broke into a laugh. "The *English* ambassador, do you mean? Why should he take an interest in you?"

"I . . . forgive me. No reason in the world. The solitude—it has made me imagine strange things. Who, then, is your companion?"

"Lady Devereaux."

"Lady—" Did Katherine only dream it, or did he recoil from her, slink back toward his corner at the mention of her name? He let out another burst of vehement French, against which Madame murmured in the same language. When he ran out of words, there was silence in the cell.

Then Madame said in English, very clearly and slowly, "Because I had no choice, Alain. I gather you made some sort of proposal to Lady Devereaux that the two of you run off and find eternal happiness in one another's arms. So potent were your charms that the silly thing took you up on it. Against all odds, in the midst of wartime, she managed to make her way to Calais aboard a troopship, then cajole a hired driver into taking her to Paris—alone, mind you, without a single chaperone or companion—and then, after adventures better left untold, install herself at the Hotel Luxembourg and scour the underbelly of the city seeking you out. It was at the hotel that, God be praised, I caught up to her at last and impressed upon her the complete *lunacy* of what she had done." Montclair had sucked in his breath. "She was willing to risk everything—her repute, her status in society, even her tender innocence, considering the rough company she fell in with—in order to find you. Since she has gone to such lengths, I thought it only right that she see you in your present circumstances, so you could tell her yourself exactly what sort of man she allowed herself to become infatuated with. Now—go on and tell her." The countess's voice again bore the dreadful sternness Katherine had remarked in their interview in her hotel room.

Montclair seemed at a loss. It was several minutes before he found his tongue and said haltingly, "She knows what I am charged with?"

"She does. The murder of Mimi Boulé."

"I . . ." In the blackness, Katherine thought she saw him hang his head. "You should not have brought her here."

"But I had to," the countess said implacably. "I could not let her go on pining away for some mad, romantic vision of you that is so far from the truth."

Another silence. Then, "Could I speak with her . . . alone?" Montclair asked softly.

"That is up to her, I suppose. Katherine?"

All reason argued against it. And yet Katherine heard herself murmur faintly: "Yes."

The countess bustled toward the door. "I shall be in the corridor. Do not hesitate to cry out, my dear, if he frightens you." She rapped against the wooden barrier, and the key clanked again. The door swung open. Katherine fought against an overpowering urge to bolt—but she did take care to stay well out of reach of him on his chain.

When the door had closed, she realized she'd been holding her breath, and let it out slowly. Through the gloom, she almost imagined she could see his impossibly blue eyes, and she wondered what he might say—in excuse, explanation, expiation. What he did say, when he spoke, was the last thing she could have expected. "Katherine. Have you your reticule?"

"Have I my—" Katherine was enveloped by bewildered rage. "For the love of God! I follow you halfway across the world—"

"It was not nearly so far as that," he said infuriatingly, deprecatingly.

"—risk life and limb—"

"I hate to think of that—especially the limbs. You have such lovely limbs."

"—find you imprisoned on the *vilest* of charges—murdering an innocent woman—and you have the *audacity* to ask, have I my reticule?"

"Well, have you?"

He was beyond decency. "Of course I have!" she snapped.

He lowered his voice to a whisper. "And is that pretty little pistol still inside?"

Katherine's head jerked up like a puppet's. She gripped the bag tight to her chest. "Perhaps I ought to use it on *you*," she hissed at him.

"I have a better notion. Where are you staying? No, no— Christiane already let that slip. You need only tell me the number of your room. And," he added, "leave me the pistol, of course."

"What do you imagine might happen if I did?"

"I would come to you there. Not tonight. Tomorrow. The next night, at the latest."

She was beyond protest. She was dumbfounded.

"Does Christiane sleep in the same chambers?"

"She—she—" Her rage overflowed. "What difference does that make? If you think I have any inclination toward aiding you to escape, you are sadly mistaken! For all I care, you may rot in here until the authorities have the good sense to chop off your head!"

Her eyes had grown accustomed to the dimness now; she could see him smiling, or thought she could, and shaking his head. "Katherine, *ma chérie*. So long as you *have* come halfway across the world—or what the world is to you, at any rate—it hardly seems sensible to waste the journey. Not to mention the impetus behind it."

"Which was?" she asked, steely-voiced.

"You want me," he said simply.

"Want *you*? A filthy, lice-ridden, flea-infested—"

"Come, come. Let's not be melodramatic. A bath and a bit of tar soap, and I will once again be the man you love. The man you desire." His voice was a silken caress, and she nearly forgot the stench and the squalid surroundings. Nearly—but not quite.

"You're mad," she told him.

"*I* am not the one who risked so much to come to France. I really do long to hear more about how you convinced those sailors to let you tag along with them. Did you employ tears? Or did you hike up your skirts and show them those delectable ankles?"

"I am going for the guard," Katherine announced, turning for the door.

"I believe," he went on inexorably, "there are souls that are twinned at—"

"How *dare* you try that rigmarole with me twice!" she cried, scandalized.

She thought she saw him shrug. "It worked well enough once."

To her horror, Katherine heard a giggle push itself up from

her belly. She squelched it as soon as she realized it—but was not quite quick enough. It burbled forth into the fetid cell, fresh as violets, heady as vervain. When he heard her laugh, he laughed, too—and they were laughing together, helplessly, without inhibition. Shocked at her own dissoluteness, Katherine bit down on her hand to stifle the sound. She looked at him and saw him spread his arms in the darkness. She walked into them and was locked in his embrace.

His mouth brushed her hair. "God. The way you smell— of life, of hope. Of a future."

"The way *you* smell," she said, and giggled again.

"I dreamed of this, you know. Dreamed every night—and every waking moment."

"You must think me the most foolish girl in all of Europe."

"I think you are the bravest, rather." His mouth had found hers, was pressing it tentatively.

The taste of him—rankly alluring, like mushrooms grown in dung—made her draw back. She stared into his eyes, wished she could see him more clearly. "You are taking advantage of me. Again."

"You seem to have enjoyed it the last time," he murmured.

Someone knocked at the door. "Katherine?" The countess's voice. "Are you ready to go now?"

"In a moment!" she called back, then pushed him away from her, to arm's length. "Did you kill that woman?"

"What would you have me say? If I did, there were reasons for it."

She shivered once more. "You might lie to me. Tell me you did not."

"I said once—and I meant it—I would never lie to you."

"What sort of 'reasons' could you have for murdering a woman?"

"Leave me that pistol," he whispered, "and I'll tell you. Tomorrow night. Or the next." His hand caressed her breast, then moved downward, toward the reticule she clung to. She heard him unfasten the clasp, reach inside. "Is it loaded?"

"There are bullets in the bag beneath."

"Katherine?" The countess sounded increasingly concerned.

"I am coming!" she reiterated, as Montclair found the ammunition and withdrew his fist. "Will—will you have to kill someone?" she whispered breathlessly.

"Perhaps many someones. But only because if I do not, they will kill me."

"Is that why you killed Mimi Boulé?"

"I never said I did. I only said if I did, there were reasons. I never will lie to you, Katherine."

"You say that and *say* that, but—"

"Katherine, I am coming back in," the countess announced.

"If you did not believe me, would you be here?" Alain Montclair whispered, and kissed her again, frantically, as the door swung slowly open. The instant the spreading flow of light threatened to reveal him, he faded back into the shadows. Katherine wished devoutly that she might have had just one clear glimpse of him.

"I trust, Alain," the countess said crisply, "that seeing you here, in these circumstances, has fully disabused Lady Devereaux of whatever misconceptions she may have been harboring as to your character. The guard informs me you are to be executed at the end of the week. I had always hoped for better from you."

"I know you did your best to look after me, Christiane." Montclair's voice was so hollow that Katherine was taken aback. She'd given him the gun and the bullets. What could possibly go amiss now? "I am sorry . . . that I disappointed you."

"Have your parents been to see you?"

"I . . . have not informed them of my circumstances."

"Oh, Alain." The countess sighed. "Your pride is nearly as insufferable as Lady Devereaux's." But she crossed the cell to embrace him anyway. "Make a good death," she told him, causing Katherine to shiver once more.

"Why not? I have had a most splendid life," he declared, so gaily that Katherine wanted to cry. "*Au revoir,* Christiane.

Adieu, Lady Devereaux. It was very kind of you to call on me."

It was then that Katherine reflected on the many, many soldiers guarding the Bastille, and their impressive weaponry, and the chances a lone pistol held against such force. Did he intend to kill himself with her gun before he could be brought to the guillotine? It seemed extremely likely—and she was simultaneously elated that she had provided him with the means to avoid the blade's disgrace and horrified at her un-witting acquiescence to his plan. What did one say in such circumstances? She could only echo the countess's words: "Make a good death, monsieur."

"Thank you. I intend to," he said—and, she could have sworn, winked at her.

The guard growled from the corridor: *"Eh bien, c'est fini!"*

Christiane hugged Alain tightly. Katherine, her eyes well-ing with tears, could not bear to. The door clanked shut in their wake like the last trumpet call.

"So much promise," Madame murmured as they climbed back up the endless stairs. "Such a pity. A waste."

"Yes," Katherine agreed, the tears pouring down her cheeks. "Yes. Indeed it is."

Seventeen

He did not, of course, appear at her rooms the following evening, or the next one, either. Katherine fully expected the countess to bring her word that he'd been killed in an attempt to escape. But perhaps the Bastille guards did not care to let news of even failed unscheduled departures pass through those thick stone walls. Friday, the date on which he was to die, dawned cold and gray, to match Katherine's mood. She and Madame were due to leave Paris on Saturday morning, after a final Friday evening reception at the embassy.

She tried her best to maintain her composure as she dressed for the affair, in her latest acquisition—a new gown from Madame Villeneuve, of glorious teal-blue velvet, with small off-the-shoulder sleeves. She wore her sapphires as well, and white lace gloves, and very high-heeled teal shoes; her golden hair was caught in a tiara. The fog and chill had made her curls tighter; they defied Marie's best efforts to tame them into a chignon, and so the maid finally left them to tumble into a mad cascade down her mistress's bared back.

Madame told her she looked stunning, but she felt unbalanced, bereft. Though she longed desperately to ask for news of Alain, she recognized that the countess considered their duty to him discharged by their prison visit; it would not be fitting to inquire any further. So she tagged along to the reception, where any number of eager young Frenchmen and English attachés vied to make her acquaintance. She forced wan smiles and made small talk and agreed to proposals of dancing—earning herself a very sizable rush. All of which caused her to reflect that if what it took to be supremely popular in elevated circles was such spiritlessness, she might almost rather be a dairymaid.

At midnight, the countess made their excuses, explaining

that they were leaving Paris in the morning. A dozen crest-fallen swains swept forward to plead for a last dance with Katherine. Rather than offend any, she turned them all down.

"Well!" Madame declared as they settled into their carriage for the trip to the hotel. "I must say, you seem to have turned over a new leaf, Katherine. I did not hear you once insult anyone tonight, not even the French."

Katherine rubbed the nap of her gown absently. "It did not seem worthwhile. After all, I shall never see any of them again."

"I wouldn't be so sure of that. Diplomats travel in the highest echelons of society. Some of those gentlemen will certainly turn up in London when you make your debut. And it will very much redound to your favor that you made such a splash tonight. Lord Dalrymple seemed very smitten with you."

"Who?" Katherine, her face turned to the window, was watching the mist swirl above the Seine.

"Lord Dalrymple, *chérie*. The tall young man with the blond hair."

"I don't recall him."

"He will not forget *you*. Not only has he made a most respectable name for himself as an aide to Ambassador Nevins—he is also the heir to a dukedom."

Katherine at that moment was wondering if anyone would wash Alain Montclair's body before he was buried. Would his head be stuck up on a pole along the Bastille walls, to be nibbled at by crows? The carriage went over a bump, and she feared she would retch. She pressed her kerchief to her mouth, her head spinning. Madame leaned toward her, concerned. "Do you feel ill, *chérie*?" Katherine nodded miserably. "I shall stop the carriage." The countess moved to knock, but Katherine waved her off.

"I . . . perhaps I ate something at supper. . . ." Then she could bear it no longer. "Oh, Madame! He is gone, isn't he?"

"Yes," the countess said gently. "I had word the order was given this afternoon. I did not want to spoil your last evening in Paris, though."

"Do you think he . . . made a good death?"

"I am sure he did. So his soul is at peace." She reached for Katherine's hand. "And so must yours be. It is finished now. He has no hold on you."

His mouth at her breast. His fingertips wandering . . . His blue eyes staring into hers in the darkened cell . . . Why had he not used the gun? "Was he a Catholic, do you know?" she asked intently.

"I believe he was."

That explained it, then. Had he killed himself, he never would have earned his salvation.

Yet he had told her that if he had killed Mimi Boulé, it had been to save his own life. Did God make such fine distinctions? It seemed doubtful. She was beginning not to look very fondly on God.

"When we return to England," Madame was saying, "I shall send word to the duke and duchess that you are ready to make your debut. You proved tonight that you have learned your lesson. Pride, Katherine, always goes before a fall."

They went into the hotel. Madame kissed her good night at the door to her rooms. Katherine let Marie undress her, dismissed the maid, and then collapsed on the bed.

Weary though she was, sleep evaded her. She lay perfectly still in the darkness, mulling the countess's words. Pride hadn't brought her to France; what had drawn her here was quite the opposite. She had humbled herself totally, unimaginably, for the sake of Alain Montclair. So what lesson *was* she to take away from this debacle?

That one's heart was not to be trusted, just as she'd always suspected up until this brief stint of madness. That duty and honor would not be flouted. That the French were quite mad.

Still, for the length of her sojourn here, straight up until she'd heard Montclair was imprisoned, she'd believed her quest was high and romantic, worthy of Iseulte or Juliet or some other great heroine. It only goes to show, she thought wryly, that I am more foolish than I ever thought I could be. Then an image of the guillotine blade slicing into Montclair's neck, severing that handsome queue of glossy blue-black hair, overwhelmed her; she wrapped her arms around herself and began to cry.

The skies, which had been lowering all that day, at last matched her misery, and let forth matching torrents of rain. She heard it pound against the windows, clatter onto the streets below in a fitful flood. The wind had risen; it was buffeting the casements. Katherine buried her face in the pillows, enveloped in grief. God, what a storm! It seemed to shake the rafters. . . .

One of the windows shattered. Katherine did not even flinch. Let nature rage! she thought bitterly. Let it give him his due. He'd been a force of nature, too. . . .

The wind seemed to be calling her name, so plainly that she trembled, fearful of ghosts. Would he haunt her forever? Was she doomed to hear his voice, see his flashing eyes, in every storm?

"Katherine!"

Another edge of the broken window burst inward in a shower of glass. This time, though, she saw the stone that had caused the damage, plainly saw it sail past the scattered shards to land, solid and thudding, against the carpet. What—

"Katherine!"

She flew to the broken casement and stared down into the street, at the rain-drenched, wind-whipped figure there. "Alain?" she whispered, not trusting her own eyes.

He had his hands on his hips. His head appeared to be quite firmly attached to his body. "I am going!" he shouted up at her. "Are you coming, or no?"

"Coming *where*?" she asked in disbelief.

He threw his arms wide. "Anywhere! I don't know! Will you come with me? Will you, this time?"

If he was a ghost, he was a remarkably good-looking one. Dashed with rain as he might be, she had never in her life known so handsome a man. For a moment, she contemplated all she would be leaving behind. But only for a moment. Then she called back: "Just let me pack!"

"There isn't time for that! Come as you are. Or don't come at all."

"But I am in my nightdress!"

He shrugged his broad shoulders, starting away.

"No!" she screamed down at him. "Don't—don't leave me! I am coming!"

He glanced behind him into the street, made vacant by the storm's fury. But that very rage worked against him; the heavens could not long sustain such intensity. "Bring nothing with you," he called to her. "Nothing of the past—"

There was a knock at the door connecting her room to Madame's. "Katherine? I thought I heard a crash. Is everything all right?"

"Everything is fine," she replied, grabbing a shawl from the closet. He could not begrudge her that much. Oh, wait! And her jewels—they would need the jewels.

"Last chance, Katherine!"

She was fumbling with the lock to her jewel-case but could not get it open. God! She grasped the casket, meaning to carry it away with her. It was dreadfully heavy. His voice echoed through the storm:

"Good-bye, Katherine!"

She left the box, left everything, yanking open the door and flying into the hallway. A knot of gray-haired ladies returning from some proper society outing stared at her as she flew by. She flapped down the stairs barefoot, her nightdress sailing behind her. A startled doorman rushed to do his duty, though his expression showed he clearly thought her insane.

"Alain!" She could just glimpse his back; he was hurrying away from the hotel. "Alain! Wait for me!" He turned, paused, taking in her garb, her empty hands.

Then he smiled at her, and it was as though she'd been reborn, as though that smile would suffice to keep her happy for the rest of her life. He came toward her across the cobblestones and seized her arm.

"Don't look back," he warned, kissing her as they ran together through another burst of showers.

"I never will," she promised, ignoring the ominous thunder in the skies.

Eighteen

They spent what remained of that night crouched beneath one of the city's bridges, in the company of the most disreputable characters imaginable—drunkards and harlots and madmen and rogues so evil-featured, she expected to be robbed at any moment. Then it struck her: She had nothing for them to rob her *of.* Alain seemed perfectly at home; he leaned against the ancient stones of the pont, his arms around her, his head nodding against her hair, until the first light of dawn. "Come," he whispered then, pulling her to her feet. "We must be on our way. Unless . . ." He searched her face in the cold fog rising up from the Seine. "Unless you have changed your mind."

"No. I am coming with you."

His smile slashed through the haze. "*Bien.* I am glad." He kissed her forehead, and the touch of his mouth made her burn.

He led her through the mazelike streets of the city. The stones dug at her bare feet, and she wished she'd had the sense to put on boots, at least. Twice he sighted soldiers and drew her into doorways, holding her there until the danger passed. He said little, and she was so preoccupied with imagining what a sight she must make stumbling along in her nightdress that she kept her head down and followed him, mute as a lamb. Gradually, though, she began to recognize that no one was staring, or even taking much notice of her at all. She raised her chin a bit, looking about cautiously. They were in the Halles marketplace, and the folk come to sell their chickens and carrots and lettuces and butter and eggs were not dressed much differently from her or Alain. The men wore no fancy coats or cloaks; they were in shirt-sleeves and breeches. And many of the women, in their shapeless shifts, had nothing to cover their toes.

Still, she felt conspicuous, and feared that at any moment Madame would appear with a passel of constables. She was glad when Alain stopped in front of a stall displaying crates of cabbage and addressed its proprietor in a whisper: "*Bonjour,* Thomas!"

The cabbage seller, busy arranging his produce, glanced up, then frankly stared. "Montclair?" And then he went on in rapid French to say something that made Alain laugh. God, he had a wondrous laugh. The man beckoned them behind the stall, and he and Alain had a hurried conversation that she could not follow. It concluded, however, with Alain the possessor of a broken-down drab of a workhorse and a two-wheeled cart.

He helped her onto the seat, then climbed up beside her. Katherine eyed the horse dubiously. "He does not seem built for speed, does he? Should we not hurry away from the city? Won't they be searching for you?"

He'd wangled two straw hats, too, and plunked one onto her tangled curls. "No doubt. But they will not suspect a simple farmer and his wife heading home from the market." He contemplated her, then adjusted her brim. "You look very fetching."

"I look like hell," she said ruefully.

"No. You do not. At all." His blue eyes glowed. Katherine blushed and examined the mud that caked the hem of her nightdress. What would Mrs. Caldburn have said?

The cabbage seller was beaming at them like a proud father. He spanked the horse's rear to set the creature off at a leisurely amble, then called something after them. "What did he say?" Katherine wanted to know.

"He was congratulating me."

"Oh. On your escape."

"On my bride."

"You told him we were *married*?"

He shook the reins, grinning. "The French, you know, are very odd. Thomas would not scruple at aiding an escaped murderer. But to lend his horse and cart to us without my assurance that my relationship with you is honorable—now, *that* is quite a different matter."

"So. We are to be Monsieur and Madame—what?"

"You choose a name."

She thought about it. "Clairmont?"

"No. Too close to the bone, in this situation."

They were passing over the Pont de Bercy. Katherine was amazed by how coolly he tipped his hat to the guards there. "There must be a French equivalent of Smith. Or Jones," she noted nervously.

"There is. 'Le Bon.' "

" 'The Good'?" She giggled despite her nervousness. "It hardly seems appropriate."

He put his arm around her, pulling her closer on the seat. "But it fits you. *And* me, as you shall discover. Alain and Katherine Le Bon. I rather like it." And that was the name he gave to the soldiers at the Porte d'Ivry. Katherine was fearful they would ask to see papers, but apparently folk leaving the city were of far less concern than those entering; they were waved on without a second glance. And somewhere, in a dark corner of her mind, Katherine thought, *He would have had a far harder time of it had I not been with him.* Then she thrust the notion away and leaned into the warm curve of his arm.

By the time they'd reached open countryside, the sun was high and blazing. Katherine longed to open the laces at the throat of her nightdress but did not dare. She was suddenly aware of how little she really knew of the man seated beside her—and of how completely she had put her trust in him. He *had* been convicted of murder. What if he'd only used her to make his escape? What if he planned to abandon her now—or even worse? She must have drawn away from him unwittingly, for he glanced down at her, his expression grave.

"Do I frighten you?" he asked.

"A—a little."

"You are thinking of Mimi Boulé."

"Perhaps I am. And—of how you got away from the Bastille. How *did* you get away from the Bastille?"

He sighed, stretching his long legs. "Better you shouldn't know."

"Did you—kill anyone?" *Many someones?*

Alain glanced over at her. "I cannot decide whether you would like for me to have or not. But I have told you—I never will lie to you. So . . . no. I did not."

"But then how—"

"Katherine." He reined in the horse, turned on the seat to look straight into her eyes. "If we are to be together, there will be some questions that I cannot answer. If you cannot accept that, it would be best if we stopped now."

"I only thought," she said, her voice small, "that you might trust me. As I've trusted you."

"Oh, *chérie*." He reached to stroke her cheek, push a wayward curl from her throat. "Don't ever think I am not aware of your sacrifice. That it does not fill me with awe."

His solemnity embarrassed her. "It is not so much, what I have given up."

"Nonsense. You have relinquished everything for me. You know, don't you, that now there is no going back? To Mrs. Treadwell's? To your parents? To the life you would have had?"

"I—" She swallowed, tears welling. He was right, of course. When she'd turned that pistol over to him in the Bastille, she'd gone beyond silly schoolgirl crushes. She had become an accomplice to a criminal act. The realization was chilling. "I know."

"I will make it up to you," he vowed, his eyes the deep blue of the cloudless sky. "I swear that to you, Katherine. You will never regret it." He paused, reconsidered. "No. You *will* regret it at times. That is inevitable. Let us say—you will regret it less often than not."

"Sometimes," she whispered, "I wish you were not quite so honest."

"Your mistake, then, in choosing the only honest murderer in France to fall for." He grinned and chucked the horse on.

*   *   *

They drove all that day, and stopped for the night at a country tavern of which "humble" would have been too generous a description. Alain introduced himself as Monsieur Le Bon, and Katherine as Madame. The regulars sipping *vin ordinaire* at the tables glanced at the new arrivals, then went back to their gossip and drink. The proprietress showed them to a room beneath the upstairs rafters that was airless and drab.

"You must be hungry," Alain said solicitiously when she had left them, then added, "Have you any money?"

Katherine stared. "You told me to bring nothing with me."

"Ah. So I did. Well, Thomas lent me a few sous, but I shall have to sing for our supper. Would you prefer to rest, or watch?"

"Watch," she said, fascinated. Did he really mean "sing"?

They returned to the common room, where he ordered wine. She saw him observing the company covertly while he sipped from his glass. In a corner, two men, rough-hewn, monosyllabic, were playing at cards. Alain wandered over and engaged them in conversation, in French she could not follow. She did note, though, that his accent was considerably more raw than it had been in Paris. After a time, the men invited him to play. He dug his few coins out of his pocket and sat down with them.

The game was some form of hearts, she thought, but the precise rules were unfamiliar to her. They must have been to Alain as well; he lost again and again, quite congenially. Then, suddenly, he won a hand. The men were more surprised than she was. They laughed and clapped his shoulders, and he smiled broadly, raking in a small mound of coins.

The cards were shuffled and redealt. He lost the next six hands. Katherine, her stomach growling from hunger, observed the dwindling pile of coins in front of him with mounting resentment. Really! He might have paid for their room and meal both from that single win! It was just like a man to go on playing when the cards were so clearly against him. She had resigned herself to making do without supper when the game turned intense. Whatever hand Alain held, he was betting everything on it. And the farmer across from him was doing the same on *his*.

Intrigued, she got up from the table and started to move toward Alain's chair. He waved her off, though, with an impatient glance that made her cheeks burn. Well! If he was going to be that way, she would go upstairs to bed! Just as she reached the door, she heard Alain's opponent let out what was unmistakably, in any language, an oath. She whirled around. The man was leaning over the gaming table, staring at the cards Alain had laid out before him. Alain had his shoulders raised in a sort of dazzled shrug. Muttering, his opponent shoved back his seat, grabbed his hat, and stomped out of the roadhouse, trailed by his companion. Alain watched them go, then gazed about the room as if to say, *Who could guess?* to the curious onlookers. Then he gathered up the coins from the table and sauntered back to the table Katherine had just left, beckoning for her to join him again.

Reluctantly, she went back and plunked herself down. "What will you have to eat?" he asked expansively. "We can now afford the best in the house—though I daresay that will be quite humble. The roast chicken smells good, though, don't you think?"

"I'm not hungry," Katherine said curtly.

"Come now, you must be, after such a long day of riding!" He called an order to the landlady, who bustled off to the kitchen. Then he looked at Katherine. "Have I done something wrong?"

"I am not accustomed to being dismissed the way that you dismissed me just now!"

"The way I *what*?"

She was seething. "When I started over to your table! You just—" She mimicked his impatient wave. "As though I were some serving girl!"

"Ah." He nodded. "I beg your pardon. It is just that I was counting."

"Counting *what*?"

"The cards."

"How hard could *that* be?" she sniffed. "You had only seven in your hand."

He burst into that marvelous laugh. "No, no, *chérie*. All the cards in the deck that had been played so far."

"Why on earth would you want to do that?"

"To have a better idea of what might be in my opponents' hands, of course. Not to mention what I am most likely to draw. It paid off, as you see."

"How could you possibly keep track of so many cards?"

"It is only a matter of training oneself," he said modestly. "I can count up to three decks at once—so long as I do not have the most beautiful woman in all of France distracting me. And *that* is why I waved you away." He reached across the table to cover her hand with his. "You must stay far from me when I am gambling, *chérie*. Promise that you will."

Katherine blushed, ashamed that she'd been cross with him. *The most beautiful woman in all of France* . . . The landlady arrived with their suppers, heavy trenchers piled with thyme-scented roast chicken and mashed potatoes and the most remarkable green beans, slim as a baby's finger. Alain made a great fuss of complimenting the landlady, who giggled like a girl. Meanwhile, Katherine dug in. The food tasted as splendid as it looked.

"I thought you said you weren't hungry," Alain observed as she forked up a hearty mouthful of potatoes. "I see that I must teach you not to lie to me." If she hadn't been so busy eating, she would have stuck out her tongue.

He had admirable manners at table, she noted, watching him covertly—not flashy or showy, but compact and refined. The beard he'd grown in prison was rather attractive, or would have been, trimmed down a bit. His hair wanted cutting as well. He—

"Thinking I am in need of grooming?" he broke into her thoughts, and laughed when she turned scarlet. "You are right, I suppose." He stroked the beard thoughtfully. "But it will have to wait."

"I like the beard," Katherine said shyly.

"Do you? I shall leave it on, then, by all means. More wine?" He raised the bottle.

"Just a bit," she said, suddenly nervous at the prospect of the meal's end. Having come so far for this, for him, she supposed she ought to be wild with anticipation for their return to that drab room upstairs. Instead she suppressed a shiver. *I wish I knew him better,* she thought. *I wish this had not happened so fast.*

The landlady came to clear the trenchers away, and Alain engaged her in a brief discussion. "There is cherry tart," he told Katherine then. "I recall that you are very fond of cherries. Would you like some?"

"I couldn't possibly. I am stuffed. But you go ahead," she said quickly. When the tart came, he fed her bites from his fork. It was extraordinarily good. He poured the last of the wine, sharing it between them, then leaned back in his chair.

"What did you think of the supper?" he asked, reaching for a cigar, then grimacing as he realized he hadn't any.

"You would never get a meal so fine as this in an English commonhouse."

"Naturally not. You English butcher food. You boil your vegetables until they are mush, roast your meat until it turns to leather—why, you do not even make wine!"

"That is because of the climate," Katherine pointed out patriotically. "There is too much rain."

"It's a poor bit of earth you call home," he agreed with a grin.

Katherine did not want to speak of *home*; it made her think she might never see hers again. Seeming to sense her mood, he hastily called for the landlady to settle their tab. Katherine felt weary and disheartened. She had to stifle a yawn. "You go on up," Alain urged. "I am going to try to locate a cigar. Though I have not much hope."

As she climbed the stairs, Katherine was grateful for his thoughtfulness. At least she could wash and change into her nightdress in privacy. Then she realized that she was *wearing* her nightdress, and the extent of what she'd done overwhelmed her; she sank down onto the landing, drowning in remorse. Her clothes, all her lovely new clothes from Madame Villeneuve's . . . her shoes and her bonnets . . . What had she been thinking of? How could she live like this? She stumbled to her feet, made her way to the room, and collapsed on the bed in a flood of regretful tears. She was still crying when the door opened behind her and Alain came in.

"Chérie?" He sat on the bed beside her, gently rubbing her taut shoulder blades. "Are you unhappy?"

"No. Yes. It is just . . ." But how could she explain? *I miss my dresses.* It was more than the dresses, though. It was all that was accustomed, familiar. The life she'd left behind.

The bedstraw crackled as he stretched out beside her on his back. He reached to pinch out the candle, and she edged away from him in the darkness, as far as she could. He did not touch her, though. He locked his hands behind his head, staring up at the ceiling in the moonlight that peeked through the single window. Katherine waited, heart pounding, muscles coiled. Still nothing happened. What was holding him back? Why did he not kiss her, reassure her, say he loved her, that their souls were twins?

With shock, she realized that he was snoring. And in that instant, all her wistful nostalgia vanished, replaced by a rush of wrath. Oh, she'd been right! He had only used her to effect his escape; he had no more regard for her than for the drab that pulled their cart. Furious, she flounced over onto her side, yanking at the bedspread—filthy thing, no doubt rife with fleas and lice! The notion made her skin crawl. She was hot and homesick and miserable, and at that moment she wanted nothing more than for him to hold her and kiss her and set her mind at ease. So what did he do? He fell asleep, the insensate oaf! Why, he owed his life to her! If not for her gun, he'd have lost that handsome queue *and* the neck it fell upon by now!

He can go to hell for all I care, she thought malevolently. *I'll turn him in to the authorities myself. If I do, they might even forgive me for having aided him in his escape. I could go downstairs now, tell the landlady who he is, and have her send for—for whatever they have in this godforsaken country that passes for the law.* The prospect of seeing him hauled away in chains was tremendously satisfying. She reveled in it for a few moments—before her mind turned in another direction.

Why did he not want her? What could possibly account for his coldness now that they were finally together, when he'd been all on fire for her that night in the academy courtyard? What had changed? Hadn't she done what he'd asked of her then—hadn't she come away with him, on *his* terms, dishonorable though they were? She remembered her little fit of pique in the common room, after he'd waved her away from the card table. Was he holding that against her? Oh, *why* had she been so haughty to him? He was not the sort of man, she recognized belatedly, who would stand to be scolded or carped at. She had rebuked him as she would a servant. She had offended his pride.

And what about my pride? The question surged up, refused to be quelled. Here I lie in a filthy bed in a disgusting roadhouse, with no more to my name than the clothes on my back—for what? For *him!* And how does he reward me? By falling asleep on this, our first true night together! Regardless of any mistakes she'd made downstairs, she did not deserve such scorn! Tired though she was, her angry thoughts made sleep seem a distant dream. She rolled onto her back and dared to dart a glance at him. The moonlight played over his face, over his bared chest as it rose and fell with his heavy breaths. God, but he *was* a handsome man! Covertly she studied the high, splendid curve of his cheekbone, his long black lashes, his full-lipped mouth, and the sight reminded her of why she'd come to France for him.

His kisses, velvet and wine. The touch of his fingers inside her . . . She caught her breath as the memory of that ecstasy swept through her, so true and strong that she could feel wildfire kindling in her belly. Tentatively, as though reaching toward a burning coal, she let her hand stretch to his shoulder, drew it back. He *was* asleep. He would never know. . . .

Her fingertips brushed his skin in the lightest caress.

He flipped over in the bed and fell on her, crushing her in a kiss.

"Oh! You!" she cried, pushing him away in fury. "You were only pretending!"

"And you were feeling sorry for yourself." He licked a languid line from her mouth to her cheek.

"Well, what if I was?"

"I was not about to take you while you were in such a state," he whispered. "I was waiting to see if you would come to your senses. Waiting to see if you . . . wanted me. As I want you." His tongue tasted the curve of her ear.

Katherine was blushing madly. That he'd caught her doing just that was dreadfully embarrassing. A woman wasn't supposed to have such urges, was she? Mrs. Caldburn had always said . . .

He was unfastening the laces at her bodice. She could feel the strange bulge in the front of his breeches pressing at her thigh. He lowered his head, put his mouth to her breast, sucking at its tip. Katherine froze, torn between the notion of punishing him by refusing to respond—he'd played a terrible trick on her!—and a mad desire to strip off her clothes.

He nuzzled against her, letting out a groan of pleasure. His tongue flicked across one nipple and then the other, while his hands kneaded her firm, sweet flesh. Of their own accord, Katherine's arms wrapped around him, drawing him closer. He looked at her then, the moonlight turning his eyes to pale fire. "Now," he promised, his voice hoarse with passion. "Now I will finish what we began in the courtyard. Now I will make you mine."

He drew the nightdress down from her shoulders, kissing her with abandon. She returned his kisses, shamelessly eager, hopelessly aroused. He thrust his tongue between her lips; she welcomed it, letting her own tangle with it, trading tastes, exchanging caresses. He shifted so that he lay half atop her. The pressure of his manhood was impossibly beguiling. She trailed her fingertips down his chest to his breeches buttons, heard him draw in his breath.

"Oh, *chérie* . . ."

Emboldened by his reaction, she put her hand to him there, felt his hard rod pulse against her palm. He grabbed for her nightdress's hem. "Don't tear it!" she cried. "It is all I have!"

"Best get you out of it, then, or I will not be responsible." She sat up, and he eased it off her slowly, his grin widening as more and more of her was revealed. "*Chérie,* you have a body"—he threw the dress aside—"that was made for loving. And since you have no spare drawers, either—" He tugged at their string, slid them down over her thighs, her knees, her ankles, his mouth trailing the snowy cotton's retreat. When he'd reached her toes, he began to lick between them. She tried to draw him up again:

"Alain! The dust!"

"I am not so fastidious as to be able to resist." And he finished, then started back up her calves. At her thighs, he paused, parting her knees, and for an instant his tongue swirled against the bud of her desire. Katherine gasped as flame shot through her.

"Oh, no! You must not—"

"Ah, but I must," he said gravely, raising his head to meet her gaze. "I want every part of you, Katherine. I want nothing hidden, nothing reserved."

"If you feel that way," she managed to murmur, "you might at least take off your breeches."

"Splendid suggestion. Better yet, you take them off for me." His eyes, blue ice in the moonlight, challenged her. But it was no challenge; she ached to see him naked, as he saw her. She unbuttoned the eight shiny buttons, her gaze never leaving his. Then she knelt on the bed and pulled the breeches down.

His manhood sprang up as she released it from the rough serge. Katherine stared in fascination at the long rod. She ran her finger along the broad vein at its front, and his whole body shuddered. "Katherine—"

"Nothing hidden, you said." She put her tongue to its broad tip, where a single bead of moisture had formed. She licked it away. Alain groaned, from his soul. She considered the taste—salt-sweet, warm, like nothing else she ever had tried. She liked it. She took the tip between her lips, sucked at it. He convulsed beneath her.

"God, *chérie!* No more! You forget—I am just come from prison. I have been without a woman for a very long time!"

She pulled away. "Have you had a lot of women?"

She could have sworn *he* blushed. "What would you have me say?"

"Whether you have had a lot of women."

"Too many," he muttered. "Does that satisfy you?"

"I don't know. Hundreds? Thousands?"

"Not thousands," he demurred.

"Hundreds, then."

"No, no. Not hundreds, either."

"Dozens?" He was mute. "You *said* that you would never lie."

He caught her by the shoulders, held her there. "Forty-three."

"Forty-three?"

"Very well. Forty-four."

"You are teasing, aren't you?" she asked dubiously. "No man could possibly have relations with forty-four women."

"Why not?"

"Well . . . some of them would be *bound* to know one another, wouldn't they? Once you got into numbers like that? And women talk about such things. It seems to me it would be terribly awkward to have so many women telling their friends about you and finding out that you'd made love to them, too."

"There have been a few awkward moments, as you put it." He released her, falling back onto the pillows. "Must we discuss this now?" His manhood, she noted, had gone limp.

"I was only curious. Do *all* men sleep with so many women?"

"How the devil should I know?"

"Don't men talk about it?"

"It is *all* they talk about," he said ruefully. "But they are dreadful liars."

"Except for you."

"Except for me."

"Am I number forty-three, then, or forty-four?"

"Katherine Devereaux," he exploded, "I find this discussion in very poor taste!" She began to giggle. "What? What is it?"

"That," she declared, "was to pay you back for feigning sleep."

He sat bolt upright. "You don't care, then? Whether you are forty-three or forty-four?"

"You are still the first for me," she told him with a shrug. "And Poppa always said, if you are going to buy a hunter, you do want one that's proven."

"You," he declared, "are the most peculiar, most provoking woman I have ever had in bed. Regardless of number."

His manhood had gone taut again. She curled against him, and he pushed her over onto her back—then kissed her, hard and long. "Proven, eh?" he murmured at her throat.

"It has always worked with Poppa for hunters."

He arched above her. "I love you, Katherine," he said. He kissed her cheek. And then he pushed inside her, slowly, carefully.

Katherine willed herself not to go tense at the unfamiliar sensation. He brought his hand down to stroke her, ease the way. As marvelous as his ministrations were, she could not relax; his rod seemed so big, and her sheath small and inadequate. He took his time, though, lowering himself and then withdrawing, all the while using his fingers to tantalize her. With each caress, she felt her body widening, releasing a flow of moisture from some hidden spring. He felt that as well; he sighed with anticipation, playing with her, teasing her, pushing deeper inside. He moaned, his hilt sunk half into her: "Oh, *mon Dieu!*"

"Oh," Katherine answered shyly as he thrust further, as his eager fingers played against her flesh. Then he pushed all the way into her, lost himself in her warmth.

He stayed there for a long moment, looking down at her. He smiled, and she smiled back, tentatively. "A fine fit," he pronounced, and drew a long, curling strand of hair from across her face.

"You think so?"

"I do." He started to withdraw.

She blinked. "Is that—all?"

"Was it not enough?" he demanded.

"Oh, I did not mean that!" she said hastily. "It was wonderful. Splendid!"

"You felt the earth move?"

"I believe I did."

He sank into her once more. "Liar. I really do have to teach you not to lie. Even to be polite. But first—" He pulled back, drove down again. "First I will teach you about the earth moving." His hands slipped to her buttocks, cupping them, drawing her to him. His skin in the moon-glow was slick with sweat. His queue had worked loose, and his black hair tumbled over his shoulders, a mass of midnight brightness. He kissed the tip of her breast, then the side of her throat, his loins pressing tight to hers, withdrawing, pressing tight, withdrawing. There was a rhythm to his motions like the swell and ebb of the sea. She was reminded of the sensation of being rocked to sleep aboard the *Mary Anne*. But this rhythm was far from lulling; it awakened all her senses, seemed to intensify them, so that the scent of him, sweat and red wine and dust and cherries, swirled in her head in an intoxicating muddle, so that the sheen of his hair and the gloss of his skin looked blindingly bright. Her bare flesh registered every ripple of his muscle, each brush of his mouth and hands, and the walls of her sheath were so exquisitely animate that his slow thrusts were a tantalizing blaze of pleasure. She heard his breath coming faster, catching in short moans—then realized in surprise that she was moaning as well, the sounds drawn from deep within her, an involuntary echo. He glanced down at her, smiling in approval, but the skin was drawn tight across his cheekbones; his eyes were narrow with need.

"C'est bien?" he whispered.

Miraculously, she managed to recall enough of Monsieur

Jacquet's lessons in the heat of the moment to answer him: *"Oui. C'est bien."*

Reassured, he quickened his pace, began to push more frantically, that hard rod pressing so deep that their bodies seemed conjoined, the borders between their flesh and blood falling away until they were a single being—one heart pounding, one skin glistening, one voice rising in escalating ecstasy. He let out a maddened groan, just as she whispered: "Oh!" She clenched her eyes shut against the almost unbearable assault on her senses. Something was happening inside her at that point where they were united, something wild and profound, so that it was almost as though—

As though the earth was moving. She could have sworn she felt it shift crazily beneath them just as a tide of fire so high, so strong, swept through her that she bit down on her lip so as not to scream. His hips rose, fell, rose, fell, his whole body straining, thrusting into her with irresistible force. She tilted to meet him, holding to him desperately while the tide broke over her, crashed through her, drenching her, body and blood and bone. She did scream then, but the sound was swallowed in his own wild cry of release. They rode the crest of that wave for a long, fierce stretch of rapture, clinging to one another, before it finally began to subside.

In its wake, it left filaments of light and wonder. Alain collapsed atop her, chest heaving, fighting to catch his breath. Katherine lay beneath his welcome weight, feeling the tide's slow, glittering withdrawal. Inside her, his manhood convulsed in a final surge of lingering brightness, like the afterglow of fireworks against a black sky.

"You," he whispered then, his mouth hard against hers. "You—"

"What?" she whispered back.

He fell onto his side. "Just that. You."

"*I* didn't do anything," she demurred. "You did it all."

"Nonsense," he murmured, pulling her to him, cradling her in the circle of his arms.

"I—I think I did feel the earth move then," she said tentatively.

He laughed. "Move? God, it tilted so far, I'm astonished we didn't fall off!"

"Is it always like that?" Katherine asked, thinking of Mrs. Caldburn's dry cautions.

"It never has been before," he said, and kissed her.

"No doubt you said the same thing to the last forty-three."

He raised his head then, to look into her eyes. "You are wrong about that."

She plucked at the nubby bedspread with her fingers. "Really?"

"Really. I—"

"I know. You never lie."

"Not to you. But that wasn't what I was going to say."

"I beg your pardon. What were you going to say?"

"Only . . . if it had been like that with the first, there never would have been more."

"What was it like with Mimi Boulé?"

He flinched as though she'd struck him. "There's not much mercy in you, is there, Katherine?"

She was so sorry she'd said it. But though he kept telling her he didn't lie, there was this between them—his time in the Bastille, the evil deed for which he'd been sentenced to die. "It doesn't matter," she murmured abjectly.

"It matters to you, evidently, since you raise the subject in the afterglow of our first lovemaking."

"You . . . lay with her?" A long, long pause. "You said that you would never lie."

He sighed. "I did not say I might not avoid certain subjects. Katherine. *Chérie.* I can tell you only this. It would be dangerous for you to know."

"I see." She contemplated that. "More dangerous than having helped you to escape from the Bastille?"

"Much, *much* more dangerous."

She shifted so that she looked into his eyes. They were hooded, veiled—but there was in their depths a wrenched sort of pain. "Who are you, Alain?"

"Alain My Dear Heart."

But she was not wooed by his humor. "No, I mean it. Who are you?"

"The man who loves you. Adores you." He seized her fingertips, kissed them. "Forever. For all time."

She sensed there was no use in pursuing it, so she changed the subject. "Where are we going from here?"

"To the Côte d'Or. Wine country."

"Why?"

"It is the harvest season. There will be work for me."

"And what for me?"

"Me."

It seemed little enough—and yet it seemed sufficient. Why? she wondered. What was there about this man that made her trust him against all odds, made her willing to relinquish so much for him?

He had begun to stroke her thigh, very gently. He kissed the tip of her breast. She felt a flash of longing for him, for more of what they'd just shared. He sensed it and smiled. "Twinned souls," he told her.

"I begin to think you must be right. There certainly is no logical reason!"

" 'The heart has its reasons, of which reason knows nothing,' " he told her gravely. "Pascal said that. A Frenchman." Then he made love to her again.

Nineteen

It took them five days to reach the Côte d'Or, and in Katherine's memory, the journey would always have a golden haze to it, a sun-drenched glow. They rode at the drab's leisurely pace through lush valleys and across green hills, past fields of glorious blue flax and ocher mustard and sweet-scented rosemary, with Alain explaining to her the uses of each crop: linen-making, condiments, perfumery. "Not a very practical employment of the land," Katherine observed, as he showed her a vast expanse of acreage dedicated to lavender that would one day grace the wrists and throats of well-to-do ladies.

"Beauty has a purpose in this life," he retorted, sniffing the herb-sharp air. "What would you have us do—turn it all to sheep pasture?"

"Oh, no. That would never suit the frivolous French."

He glanced at her sidelong. "Oil of lavender fetches twenty-three times the price per pound of mutton on the market."

"How would you know such a thing?"

"I am a receptacle of vast stores of useless knowledge."

And he was. He knew the most astonishing arcanery—how many crocus stamens it took to yield a gram of saffron, how many beatings made the best linen paper, what feed produced the finest foie gras. "One might almost think you were a farmer," she teased him, "instead of an aristocrat."

"Who says I am an aristocrat?"

"Oh, Alain. Don't be coy. You are no peasant."

He looked down at her and seemed on the verge of replying. Then he just shook his head, tossing back his silky black hair. "Look. There." He pointed into the distance.

She strained to see. "At what?"

"The master of that manor is hawking."

Now she could see the little knot of mounted figures in the distance, and the peregrine soaring high above them. "My father keeps falcons," she said.

"Mine prefers chickens," he told her, with an odd smile.

They passed ancient stone churches and tiny villages of whitewashed houses roofed with thatch and orchards heavy with harvest; they bought bread and fruit and cheese to eat as they rode, and washed them down with local wines. To pass the time, Alain sang or told her tales of the countryside through which they passed or tried to help improve her French, but more often than not those lessons ended with him bursting into laughter, hugging her close to him on the narrow cart seat.

"If the language only made some *sense*," Katherine would say, "and had less neighing and braying in it, I might do better."

"Ah, yes. English is so noted for the beauty of its sounds."

"English is the most beautiful language in the world!" she would tell him stoutly. But she had to admit, the French he spoke to the folk they passed on the road and the proprietors of the roadhouses where they slept was seductively mellifluous, though it went over her head in a rush of elongated vowels and strange, slurred consonants.

The roadhouses were a revelation. Though the accommodations were invariably humble, there was always some unexpected touch of grace: a bowl of roses set beside the bed, or candles scented with citron, or hand-loomed linens like suede to the touch. And the food was simply marvelous. They ate rich stews scented with basil and garlic, and rabbit pie with crust layered like the finest pastry, and lamb shanks braised with wine and mushrooms and tiny green peas, all paid for with the takings from Alain's gambling bouts. Each night, he made love to her again and again, until, sated with food and wine and passion, they fell asleep clinging to one another, their limbs entwined.

On the afternoon of the fourth day, he reined the horse in beside a glistening stretch of river and jumped down from the cart. "Why have we stopped?" Katherine asked, gazing about at the desolate surroundings.

He grinned, producing a cake of soap from his coat. "I thought you might care to bathe."

She eyed the river dubiously. "In that?"

"Have you never washed in a river before?"

"Certainly not!"

"It is a good deal more enjoyable than a tub. Come." He reached for her hand, but she held back.

"Anyone could come along and see us!"

"It is a possibility," he admitted.

She touched her hair, which was matted with dust. Still, to step into that raging torrent . . . "You go ahead," she demurred. "I'll watch."

"As you wish." He stripped bare with efficiency, standing naked in the sunlight. Katherine glanced away, blushing, then heard a splash. He had jumped right in.

"The water's lovely!" he called to her, up to his chest in the swirling current. "A trifle cold, perhaps, but most refreshing!"

"I'll take your word on it." She was scanning the road ahead and behind them. No one was in sight. Still, he was absolutely shameless to be without his clothing in so public a place!

She looked back at him. He was floating, his long feet sticking straight up as he lathered the soap, whistling. She rubbed her forehead, which was damp with sweat. It had been longer than she cared to think since she'd bathed. She watched him lave his long arms, then rub suds through his hair. She felt itchy. The cake of soap drifted away from him; he leaped after it in a bright spray.

"Sure you don't care to join me?"

"Quite sure."

He shrugged and dove deep, leaving a foam of bubbles on the rippling water. Katherine waited anxiously for him to resurface. He did not. She counted to thirty, then to sixty. There was still no sign of him. Seized by panic, she stumbled down from the cart and stood at the river's edge, trying to see beneath the sun-spangled surface. Had he hit his head? Snagged himself on a root? What would she do if he died? Terrified, she plunged in fully clothed, slipping on the rocky bottom, sliding toward the spot where she'd seen him go down. Just as the freezing water reached her waist, she heard a nonchalant whistling from a hundred yards down the river. Whirling about, she saw him swimming toward her, his black hair slicked to his head.

"You—you *bastard!* You did that on purpose!" she sputtered furiously.

"I am extremely touched by the rapidity with which you came to my rescue." He reached her side, smiled down at her. "Does not the water feel fine?"

"I am never speaking to you again so long as I live!" Katherine declared, starting back for the bank. He caught her by the waist, though, and pulled her tight against him.

"You may as well let me wash you, since you are already in." He slipped his hand inside the drenched nightgown's bodice, rubbing soap against her breast. Katherine caught her breath as his fingers found her nipple, stroked it enticingly.

Still, she clung to reason. "Alain, please!"

"Mmm." He was kissing the nape of her neck, his hand wandering lower. His manhood pressed at her buttocks, slipped between them, making her gasp. "Let's be rid of this, shall we?" He pulled the nightdress over her head in a whoosh and flung it toward the shore, leaving her naked except for her drawers. "And these." He yanked at their tie, dove low to slide them down over her legs. She stood in shock beneath the wide blue sky.

He popped up again. "Now," he said in great satisfaction, "I shall wash you properly."

He did, too—every inch of her body, very thoroughly, and then her hair, cupping water in his hands to wet and rinse it, since she refused to duck down. The air filled with the scent of the soap—sweet bay and citron. Dragonflies buzzed past them, their wings like rainbows in the sun.

"You already washed there," Katherine reminded him, as his hand meandered between her legs.

"I believe I may have missed a spot."

She could not help laughing. He stroked her, gently at first, then with more urgency. She sighed, hopelessly enamored of him, and let him make love to her in the water, her legs wrapped around his waist. His rod was slick and hard within her; his hands cupped her buttocks, pulling her close, and the river swirled and eddied around them in a silver rush. He came in a burst of fire even the water could not quench; she felt his seed flow into her and cried out his name. His arms tightened around her; he kissed her wet cheek and hair, licked silver droplets from her lashes. "You are shameless," she whispered.

"I am, when it comes to you." He withdrew from her, beaming with contented pleasure. "That was marvelous." Cleansed and sated, he led her to the bank and retrieved her clothes. "These will dry in no time at all," he assured her.

"And what am I to do until they *are* dry?"

"This," he said, laying her down beneath him in the soft grass on the verge of the river, taking her once more. And despite her fears, no one disturbed them; they lay naked beneath the cloud-studded sky, the sun soaking their bodies, the dragonflies flitting, the river rushing onward toward the sea.

On the afternoon of the fifth day, they cleared the crest of a wooded hill that gave onto a wide valley. Opposite them were endless low hills, lined by impeccably neat rows of a plant Katherine did not recognize that was supported by miles and miles of wooden trellises. "What is growing there?" Katherine asked, shielding her eyes from the sun.

"Grapevines. That is the Côte d'Or. The Golden Slope." He had raised his head and seemed to be drinking the air, breathing it in as though intoxicated. "Still a day or two until harvest, I'll wager. We are in time." He clucked to the nag and started down into the valley, leaning forward eagerly.

Katherine had not failed to note the elegant spired château

in the distance. "Are you from hereabouts?" she asked, carefully casual.

"I grew up here. Yes."

She bit away her smile.

He drove the cart straight to the château gates. Then he looked at her, his straw hat tilted over his eyes. "Do you mind waiting for a bit? I need to speak to someone."

His father. Oh, she'd known it, she had always known it! She nodded happily, the château, unspeakably grand and lovely, looming over their heads. "Of course. Take as long as you like." He kissed her swiftly, then leaped down and opened the heavy iron gate, striding purposefully toward the house along the gravel drive.

Katherine curled her toes in anticipation. It was better even than she'd dreamed! To be the mistress of so glorious a home as this . . . She stared up at the dizzying towers, bent forward to see the handsome gardens, tried to imagine the splendors that must lie inside. *His house. Our house.* They would make such a marvelous life.

A pair of towheaded children had appeared out of nowhere, sidling up to the cart to stare at her. Katherine smiled at them, and they giggled and skittered away. She looked after them fondly, beneficently. His peasants, soon to be hers. They seemed healthy and happy, which made her glad.

She hoped Alain was not having too hard a time of it with his father. Of course there would be explanations, apologies. He would have to humble himself, poor dear. But in the end, she was sure, the prodigal son would be welcomed home. She would try her best to get along with his family. Oh, she hoped they would like her! Surely they would be glad to see Alain settled down. She started counting windows, trying to picture how the interior of the château might be laid out—how many rooms, how many servants. She'd just reached thirty-four casements when she glimpsed Alain coming back down the drive, whistling cheerfully. So fast as that—the interview must have gone well!

She was surprised, then, when he shut the gates after coming through them. "That is that," he declared, and climbed back onto the seat. He flicked the reins. "Get on, now!" And he steered the horse about, away from the château.

"Where are we going?" Katherine asked.

"To our new home."

She sat up, scanning the landscape, but no other buildings of consequence were visible. "And where is that?"

"Not far." He was still whistling. He seemed very pleased with himself. Suddenly he glanced over to her. "You did not imagine we'd be staying in the château, did you?"

"Of course not," she lied.

She was dumbfounded when she saw the tiny thatched cottage to which he drove, deep down in the valley. "Here we are!" he said gaily, jumping from the cart and holding out his arms to her.

"This is where we are to stay?" she asked dubiously.

"For the length of the harvest. After that," he shrugged charmingly, "who knows?"

Katherine had a blinding flash of revelation. The prodigal son had returned, right enough, but his father had determined to make him prove himself, as in some ancient fairy tale. Still, Alain did not have to seem so happy at the prospect! She let him lift her down and carry her inside the hovel, his face buried in her hair.

She stared about her. One room. A dirt floor. An open hearth. Two small windows, shuttered, unglazed. There wasn't even a bed! "Where are we to sleep?"

"I'll go and get some straw for a pallet, borrow a blanket from the neighbors. I was told there was a cooking pot." He opened a rugged cabinet. "And so there is!"

"And who is going to cook in it, pray tell?"

"You are, *chérie*."

"I don't know how to cook!"

He cocked a black brow at her. "You don't? What did they teach you at that fancy school?"

"Household management!" Katherine said defensively.

"I suppose, then, you will have to manage." He turned to glance through the open door. "Getting late. I'd best see about the straw and blankets." He went out again, leaving her alone in the ghastly place.

Something small and sleek and brown scuttled out from the cabinet. Katherine stifled a shriek and hugged herself tightly as it disappeared into a chink in the wall. Oh, this was impossible! He could not be serious, could he? She took a step toward the hearth. Another mouse scampered across the dirt. Katherine stood, willing her heart to stop fluttering, trying to gain her breath.

She'd been right—it was a fairy tale, though not the one she'd thought. It wasn't Alain on trial; that was plain enough. It was *she!* She was going to have to playact Cinderella, lowly and dowdy. He meant to make her prove her fitness to be his bride—or else his father did. He meant for her to *cook!* God! He likely meant her to launder! To darn his breeches, scrub his plates—where the devil was the water closet in this place? With a rising sense of despair, she saw the enameled chamber pot behind the door.

Then, from the corner of her eye, she glimpsed the tall, imposing château through the window. She squared her shoulders, staring at those glorious spires silhouetted against the sky. It was a ludicrous test, of course—but one she meant to rise to, just as the heroines always did in those old tales. East of the sun and west of the moon, clean the stables, comb the giant's hair, steal the golden egg . . . all for their own true loves. It was only playacting, after all. And it would not last long. She could be Cinderella—for a few days, at least.

He bustled back inside, arms piled high with straw. "Let me help you with that," she said evenly.

"Thanks, *chérie*." Together, they pushed the bundle into a corner. He shook out the blanket he'd brought, laying it over the top. "Comfortable enough, don't you think?"

"Marvelously comfortable," Katherine lied. No—not Cinderella. The Princess and the Pea. "There are mice in here, Alain. I have seen two of them already."

"Really? You will have to set traps." She could not keep from shuddering. "I'll empty them, of course," he offered chivalrously. Then he paused, looking down at her. "Is it all right? Really?"

"Of course it is," she said through gritted teeth.

"It will only be through the length of the harvest."

At least her quest had an ending. "And how long does that last?" she asked, flinching as a spider spun dizzily from the ceiling not two feet from her face.

He grabbed the pest and pinched it dead between his fingers. "Three weeks or so."

Three weeks. She took heart. Three weeks, and she'd be bedding down in comfort. She thought of Nanette's advice: *You can pretend, Katherine! I know you can, if you only try!* "I'm sure we'll be very contented here," she told him, even though she knew she was lying to him again.

He left her at dawn. Katherine lay wide awake atop the rough blanket he'd borrowed from their nearest neighbors—Joseph, he'd said, and Veronique. Her tongue twisted trying to wrap around the unfamiliar pronunciations. That night, for the first time, Alain had not made love to her, had simply kissed her and then fallen asleep, and she wondered if she had already failed his test.

Breakfast had been what was left of the bread and cheese and wine they'd brought with them in the cart—as had supper the night before. She was hungry and cranky, though he seemed contented enough as he dressed for the fields. "Here's a knife. You'll need it. I'll be back home for dinner," he murmured, and she'd nodded sleepily. Only after he'd pulled on his boots and gone did she recognize that he meant she should have a meal ready for him.

Now she could think of nothing but the impossibility of that task. She had, perhaps, five hours. She had no food and no money. Did he think she was a conjurer, to summon up a supper from the air? And what about firewood? Water? Utterly disheartened, she flopped down onto the straw and buried her head.

But despair wasn't going to help her prove her fitness as

a château mistress. Resolutely she got up from the makeshift bed, straightened the blanket, combed her fingers through her tangled hair. There had to be a way. He meant to challenge her to find it, that was all. And she'd come too far now to give up. He'd told her himself: She could never go back. She would have to make do.

There was a tentative knock at the door. "Come in," Katherine said curtly. Nothing happened. "I said, come in!" she snapped again. Still the door stayed shut. Muttering beneath her breath, she crossed to it and flung it open, to find a perplexed-looking older woman with two thick black plaits standing there with her hand raised to knock again.

"Bonjour!" the woman said brightly. She had, Katherine noted, a chicken—a live one—by the neck in her other hand.

"Uh, *bonjour.*"

"Je m'appelle Veronique," the woman announced, entering and glancing about curiously. She clucked her tongue at the sight of the lumpen bed and launched into a burst of fast French. Dazed, Katherine tried to break in. The woman talked straight through her. Not until she'd wound down, quite some moments later, was Katherine able to say self-consciously:

"Pardonnez-moi, mais je ne parle pas français."

The woman blinked. *"Vous ne parlez pas français?"*

"Well . . . *je parle un* peu *de français,"* Katherine qualified it.

Her guest brightened and started up again, so quickly that Katherine could not follow a word. She held up a hand. "You must go more slowly! *Plus—plus—*" Oh, what the devil was the word for "slowly"? She put her palms together, stretched them out. *"Plus . . ."*

"Ah! Lentement!"

"Yes. Thank you. *Merci,* I mean. *Plus lentement."*

Veronique thrust the chicken at her. *"Pour votre déjeuner,"* she said very slowly and loudly.

"I'm not deaf, for heaven's sake," Katherine said, recoiling from the flapping, beady-eyed bird. "I just don't—here, I don't want that! Take it away!" More confused than ever,

Veronique shrugged and turned to go. *Pour votre déjeuner.*
Katherine was still translating. *For your*—"Dinner!" she exclaimed, so excitedly that her visitor turned back. "For our
dinner! Oh, I beg your pardon! Thank you! Thank you so
very much! *Merci beaucoup! Pour le déjeuner!*"

"*Oui, oui! Pour le déjeuner!*" Veronique agreed, nodding
happily, holding the chicken out again.

"But—what am I to do with it?" Katherine said, staring at
the bird's angry, glittering eyes. Veronique contemplated her
for a moment. Then, very gently, she reached with her free
hand for Katherine's palm, gazed down at it. "Are you a
fortune-teller?" Katherine asked, intrigued.

Her guest pressed her own callused fingertips against
Katherine's soft white ones, raised her blue eyes, took in
Katherine's tousled ringlets and sunburnt nose. She clucked
her tongue. "*Oh, mon Dieu, Alain,*" she said slowly, regretfully. Then she released the hand and, as Katherine watched
in horror, snapped the neck of the chicken with a single quick
motion. The squawking and flapping stopped, at least.

Veronique let the corpse fall to the floor and caught up
the heavy iron cooking pot. "*Allons,*" she said with an air
of resignation, and tugged Katherine out of the cottage, rolling her eyes.

An hour later, after the water they'd fetched from the river
in the valley had been brought to a boil over the fire Veronique had built in the hearth, Katherine learned how to pluck
a chicken. She watched the older woman's movements
closely. So long as her teacher spoke very slowly and clearly,
Katherine found, she could catch the gist of her French. The
chicken, headless and footless and degutted and hacked into
pieces with Alain's knife—an incredibly messy business—
then went back into the simmering pot. Katherine insisted
that they fetch clean water for the cooking, even though the
path up from the river was really quite steep. "*Allons,*" Veronique said again, and led her from the cottage to a sizable
kitchen garden down in the valley, where a number of peas-

ant women were busy weeding and crushing beetles and
picking vegetables. They pushed back their straw hats to
stare at Katherine curiously. Veronique told them something
in extremely rapid French that made them stare even harder.
Blushing, Katherine toed the rich brown earth with her bare
foot. Veronique pulled some carrots and onions, and picked
snippets of what Katherine thought might have been chives
and thyme. Those went into the pot back at the cottage. Then
Veronique disappeared, to return a few moments later with
a paper-wrapped cache of salt. Katherine started to pour the
contents into the pot.

"Non, non!" Veronique cried, staying her hands. She
showed Katherine how to add just a pinch and fold the rest
away. A bell clanged out then, from the direction of the
château. *"Pain et vin,"* Veronique said obliquely. "Bread and
wine"—Katherine knew that much. She followed Veronique
outside once more, joining a line of women and children
heading up from the valley to the château gates, where shiny
brown loaves of bread and jugs of wine were being distrib-
uted from a cart by aproned serving girls. Katherine waited
patiently in the queue, and clasped her long baguette and jug
tightly once she had them in her hands.

She was in considerably better spirits than she had been
upon waking. It seemed she would have dinner on the table—well, on the floor—for Alain after all. Back at the cottage, she followed Veronique's instructions to pour a goodly
dollop of wine into the bubbling pot, which was beginning
to give off the most wondrous smell.

She would have liked butter for the bread, but none
seemed to be on offer. Veronique vanished again, back to
her own hut, and returned with two bowls and two spoons,
which she set by the hearth. She then lifted the pot lid,
sniffed the savory steam, nodded in satisfaction, and went
out again, with a little wave. "Thank you!" Katherine called
fervently. *"Merci beaucoup*—so very much!" From the doorway, she could see the menfolk parading down the hillside
from the vineyard, shirts drenched in sweat as they shouted
jovially to one another. In every cottage doorway, she no-

ticed, women were waiting, while the children swarmed up
to meet their poppas. It was really a very charming, bucolic
scene—the sunlit hill, the straw-hatted men, the barefoot
children being swung up on shoulders or hips. And there was
Alain, his hair glistening, his skin with a new sheen of brown
to it, smiling at her as he drew near.

"So," he said, and kissed her—right there on the doorstep,
in full view of everyone around. "I smell dinner."

"Chicken," she said shyly. "With wine and carrots and
herbs."

He raised his black brows. "You don't say! You got along
all right?"

She hesitated, then confessed: "I would not have without
Veronique. She showed me what to do."

He seemed pleased by the admission. "Part of learning
what to do is knowing how to accept help. From whatever
quarter."

She scooped him out a hearty helping of the chicken and
broth. He spooned up a taste while she watched fearfully.
Her first test . . .

"Delicious," he declared, savoring the chicken on his
tongue. "Careme himself would be proud."

Antonin Careme was chef to the regent. It was a heady
compliment. "It cannot be so good as that," Katherine demurred.

"Try it," he proposed.

She filled her own bowl, sipped a bit of the broth. Her
head came up. "It really *is* good, isn't it?" she asked in
amazement. "Imagine that." Suddenly ravenous, she dug in.
Alain broke the loaf of bread in two, handing her half.

"Oh, no. You have worked so much harder than I have,"
she told him, trying to give it back.

"I'm not at all sure of that." He smiled at her. "You did
well, Katherine."

They ate what was left of the by-then-very-tender chicken that
night, for supper. Veronique had been back, with an apronful

of flour, to demonstrate how to make dumplings. Katherine was very proud of the result. "But I cannot imagine what I'm to do tomorrow," she said ruefully as Alain wiped broth from his bowl with a bit of dough. "Surely Veronique will not come every day with a chicken."

"There are eggs to be had from the château. You can make omelets. Cheese, too. And mutton is shared out every now and again." Omelets! She eyed the cooking pot dubiously. "The women go out to gather mushrooms." He sucked up a carrot. "And you've seen the garden plot."

"It's very odd, I know," Katherine said tentatively, "but in all my life, I never once wondered how the fieldhands ate."

"No reason why you should have. It was not your concern."

"The seigneur seems to have it all most well managed. The distribution of victuals, I mean." Giving him the opportunity, of course, to admit the château owner was his father . . .

He glanced at her. "So he does. You can get butter and cream and milk from the dairy, if you wake early enough. Veronique can take you tomorrow, if you wish."

"I'll be sure to wake." She gathered up their spoons and plates, then looked about ruefully. "I don't know where I wash these."

"You take them to the river. Along with the chamber pot." Her shoulders slumped—all the way down there again? He laughed, seeing her expression. "I'll do it for you tonight."

She straightened, unwilling to fail the test now that she'd come so far. "No. You had the harder day. I'll take them."

His blue eyes were soft in the dying sunlight. "We'll go together," he proposed.

That night, on their pallet of straw, he made love to her with a fervor that left her breathless. "Life in the hinterlands suits you," she whispered when she could speak. She felt him smile at her breast, and she curled tight against him.

"It suits you as well, Katherine."

For now, she thought, but held her tongue.

Twenty

By the end of that first week, Katherine had mastered the making of mushroom omelets, had grown accustomed to rising at the crack of dawn to head for the dairy, and had sprouted calluses on her hands from hauling the cooking pot to the river and back. It was astonishing, she thought, that time passed so quickly. If you had asked her, a month before, who had more leisure, noblewomen or peasant women, she'd have answered the latter, without hesitation. All fieldworkers' wives did, she'd have said, was sit about and wait for their husbands to come home. Whereas her days had always been *stuffed*—with fittings for gowns, correspondence, lessons, social calls, fetes. But a fieldhand's wife worked from sunup to sundown. How could it be otherwise, when simply preparing a meal took half the day? Not to mention the laundering—though she'd been spared the first laundry day at the river, since she'd had naught to wear while she washed the nightdress. Instead she'd hauled the cooking pot to the river late one evening, dragged it back to the cottage, then stripped and scrubbed her clothes and Alain's shirt and drawers and hose with a bit of soap she'd begged from Veronique. She'd hung the garments up to dry overnight on the shutter pegs, while Alain watched her through narrowed eyes. When she'd finished, he'd beckoned her to him and made love to her, sweetly and gently, while crickets sang at the closed door.

He was pleased with her, and that egged her on, compelling her to ask Veronique for culinary tips, submit willingly to stints at weeding the garden in the hot sun, even wring the neck of the next chicken herself. If, for some reason, Alain and his father had decided she must assay such humble tasks, by God, she'd show she could excel! But as the days wore on, she discovered a curious sense of self-satisfaction.

Granted, creating a passable stew wasn't on the level of or-
dering up a ball for two hundred guests. Still, the results were
much more immediate—and far more delectable.

On Sunday, she went with Alain to church, at his insistence. The service was Roman Catholic, in Latin, and she
felt like a fish out of water, unsure of when to kneel or stand,
embarrassed that the priest, Père Bertrand, a small, thin fellow, must know she was living in sin. But he greeted her
warmly when they exited the church, kissing both her cheeks,
and slapped Alain on the back with familiar heartiness. Odd.
She'd never thought much about the matter of his religion.
For her, as for most of her set, churchgoing was little more
than another social obligation, a chance to show off hats and
gowns and ogle young men. She asked Alain as they strolled
back to the cottage: "Do you believe in God?"

He glanced down at her. "Don't you?"

"Of course I do. I am only surprised that you would. And
that you are a Papist."

That amused him. "I don't see why."

"Well. My understanding is that Catholics must make con-
fessions. Admit their sins."

"I did so last night, on my way home to you."

She colored, recalling how eagerly he'd come for her on
their pallet as soon as the washing-up was finished. "What
did you tell Père Bertrand, then?"

"That I had committed the sin of fornication. Ninety-three
times in the past ten days."

"I think you exaggerated," she said dubiously.

"As did he, I'd wager—until he met you."

"Well—what did he say you should do?"

"Sin no more."

"And what did *you* say?"

"That wasn't possible."

She giggled. "You must have scandalized him!"

"I don't think so." They had reached the door. "He's heard
worse, no doubt. He told me in that case, I should say ten
Hail Marys. It is a very practical religion, you see."

She stepped inside, went to check on the pea soup she'd

left simmering. "Did you say the Hail Marys?"

He came up behind her, catching her around the waist. "Nine. So far." He rubbed his groin against her. She set the spoon down and turned to him. "Holy Mary, Mother of God," he murmured, slipping the nightdress from her shoulders. "Pray for us sinners."

"Amen," she said breathlessly, as he kissed her breasts.

When they were alone together—when it was only the two of them—she was unspeakably happy. He was amusing and clever and attentive, and as passionate as any woman could wish. It was only when they were among the hands and their families that she felt strange and conspicuous, nervous even, afraid she would embarrass him by what she said or did. And how odd *that* sensation was—thinking that she, of all people, might commit a faux pas! But this wasn't the ton, and these folk had matters on their minds other than the cut of a sleeve or the seating arrangements at a state dinner. She kept silent, mostly, to avoid mistakes, and she could feel Alain watching her, sensed that he wanted her to be more outgoing. She simply could not; she was too self-conscious, though Joseph and Veronique and the others were all very kind, and a great deal smarter than she had expected—Joseph, especially.

This most senior of the fieldhands was tall and sinewy, gray-haired, gray-eyed, and he wore his open-throated shirt and cambric breeches with a raffish air. His hands were brown and strong, and his voice boomed as he laid out opinions on politics and philosophy and the progress of the war that she could barely follow, with her lamentable French. There were even books in his cottage, she noted with amazement—big books, heavy books, leather-bound. He was polite to her, but he maintained his distance. His reticence reminded her that she was only in the midst of this jovial company temporarily, until Alain and his father concluded she was ready to take on the château. And so she marked time, waiting for the future to unfold.

One night, as she finished the washing-up and then took her place beside Alain on the straw pallet, he said there was a market the next day. "We'll try to purchase something more for you to wear, so you can go to the laundering," he murmured. "You don't want to miss the laundering. It is where, I am told, all the best gossip takes place. And shoes for you. And ribbons for your hair." He ran his hands through the mass of her ringlets. "And our own spoons and bowls, so we can return the ones Veronique has lent us. And another pot, too, for washing. And goosedown pillows. And—"

"How will we afford all that, peasants that we are?" she asked coyly.

"I make a wage, you know, picking the grapes. I don't labor for free."

"You cannot make much."

"There will no doubt be an opportunity to augment my earnings with a spot of gambling."

"I see." If he wanted to pretend he could not buy the entire market and more with his father's money, what was that to her? She hid a smile, burying her face against his chest.

"Mind you stay out of my sight while I do. You are a terrible distraction."

"Am I?" she whispered, feeling his manhood surge to hardness.

"The worst I ever have known," he told her. His hands came up to knead her breasts, and he groaned with pleasure. "The worst by far."

For an instant—only for an instant—her mind formed an image of those loving hands stabbing Mimi Boulé, plunging a knife into her heart. Then his caresses overwhelmed her; she slipped into the oblivion of ecstasy. But later, after he had brought her to a soaring climax, when her thighs were damp with his seed and he snored quietly beside her, the image returned, and she stared at him as he slept.

They rode to market in the cart, with Joseph and Veronique and half a dozen other vineyard workers and a passel of their offspring, who all sang and jested and generally behaved, Katherine thought, like schoolchildren on holiday. And why not? For this space of time, they would be spared the backbreaking picking, the drudgery of chores, the harsh shouts of the overseer, and the ennui of the lines for bread.

The market was in Flavigny, which passed for a town in those parts, though Katherine, as they approached, was unimpressed. There was a wreck of a convent, a slightly less decrepit church, and a small cluster of stone houses. There was also, however, a crossroads, just outside the town, at which numerous stalls and tents had been struck. The way was clogged with goats and pigs and sheep and their drovers, not to mention assorted jugglers, gypsies, craftsmen, and a procession from the church of painted wooden statues of the Virgin Mother and the Christ Child carried by bisque-robed monks.

Alain found a spot to leave the wagon, and a boy to watch it. His passengers clambered down, excited and eager. He lifted Katherine from the seat, pressed a kiss to her forehead, then thrust a thick wad of Continentals into her hand. "Buy anything you like," he urged her. "I mean it. Anything."

Katherine nearly laughed. What would she find here to buy? "Where will you be?" she asked.

He gestured vaguely toward a spot at the far end of the stretch of stalls, where knots of men were hunched over makeshift tables of crates. "Playing cards. I'll come and find you for dinner." He kissed her again, then set off across the grass.

Katherine stood still while the bustle of the market swirled around her. Then she glanced down at the bills in her hand. It was a lot of money, even given France's state of inflation. Buy whatever she liked, eh? Well, why not? She wended her way through the stands.

What she needed most was a gown—several gowns. She paused in front of a table manned by a grim gray-haired woman on which was displayed an array of drab peasant smocks. The woman's small eyes ran over Katherine's well-worn nightdress. Then she reached under her table, for a bundle of cobalt-blue linen. She spread it over the smocks. "Straight from Paris," she said in gutteral French. "The latest fashion."

Tentatively, Katherine ran her hand over the gown. "Paris fashion" was a gross exaggeration. Still, the color was lovely, and the size seemed right. *"Combien?"* she demanded—"How much?"

The woman shrugged. "You tell me."

Katherine pondered it, then pulled five bills from her cache. The woman stared at her, expressionless. Katherine offered two more. Still no reply. Another five. The woman gazed up into the sky, her mouth pursed a little. Well, really! Katherine thought. The gown was not so fine as that! She turned to go. "Wait!" the woman said abruptly, then grabbed for the bills. "It is enough. It will do." She wrapped the dress in brown paper and handed it to Katherine, who felt quite pleased with her bargaining.

The package tucked under her arm, she wandered through the stalls. She found another simple gown, this one the deep red of claret, and bought it. She bought a lemonade, and then a sausage roll. She purchased a handful of ribbons, since Alain had mentioned them, and another nightdress, of downy white cotton, with smocking at the bodice. She bought a broom, and bowls and spoons, and forks as well—no sense not trying to maintain some modicum of civilization. A hat-maker's stall beckoned seductively. She bought a very fetching straw hat, wide-brimmed, suitable for church if she added a ribbon. She still had a lot of money in her hand.

A tablecloth of slubbed linen striped yellow and white—that would brighten up the house, especially if Alain ever got about to building the table and chairs he kept promising. Spices . . . seduced by the marvelous aromas at that stall, she loaded up on peppercorns, salt to pay back Veronique, and, for her own store, cinnamon, piney sage, tarragon, a tiny paper of precious saffron, sugar, and coffee. She bought two real glasses, sick to death of drinking out of tin, and a coffeepot. She bought a ladle, and a sharp knife of her own, so that she would not have to go on borrowing Alain's, and a wooden chopping block. She lingered over a display of jewelry, but it was all cheap baubles, glass beads and tin and nickel. She bought Jordan almonds and—she could not resist—a thick bar of shiny dark chocolate. She suddenly realized she had bought too much to hold.

Bowed beneath her packages, she looked about for Alain. It took her some time to locate him. He was outside the marketplace proper, sitting on the ground across from a man in a bright red shirt with dirty-blond mustaches and hair. They were playing cards. Katherine sighed, remembering his caution to keep her distance. She headed back to the cart, and gave the boy who was minding it a Continental to watch her packages as well. What else had Alain told her to buy? Oh, yes. Another pot. She sought out a tinker, paid what seemed an exorbitant price for a stout iron vessel, and hefted it up. She would have to go back to the cart again.

She hadn't taken two steps, though, before Alain appeared beside her. He looked very cheerful as he took the pot from her and asked, "Amusing yourself?"

"I always enjoy spending money. How went your game?"

"Well enough. Country bumpkins are such trusting folk." He winked at her, flicking his queue back over his shoulder. In the sunlight, his eyes were the same glorious shade as the sky. "Did you find shoes?"

"Not yet." They'd reached the cart. He set the pot down, contemplating the array of packages.

"*Mon Dieu,* you do like shopping, don't you?"

"You *said*—"

"I know. Quite right. But we must get you some shoes." Taking her arm, he led her through the crowd to a cobbler's stall. Katherine dutifully perched on a sawn-off log while the man measured her foot and then presented several samples. They were hideous, stiff and clunky, and Alain apologized: "Not exactly Farringdon's, is it?"

"No. But they will do—for now." He grinned at her—a conspiratorial grin—and paid the cobbler for a pair. She wore them away. It felt very peculiar to be shod again, even in such clumsy things.

"Hungry?" he asked.

"I had a sausage roll and lemonade," she confessed. "But

I could eat again. It's quite lovely eating someone else's work for a change."

"You've been a good sport, Katherine," he told her, his eyes darkening. "A *hell* of a good sport." He hesitated, and she thought for a moment that he meant to end the charade. All he said, though, was, "I appreciate it. More than I can say."

"It has been an interesting experience," she allowed with a smile. "Though I cannot honestly tell you I would be contented to live this way forever."

"You won't have to," he promised, a catch in his voice.

"Yes. I know." She squeezed his hand, secure in their shared secret. Far in the distance, the spires of the château rose against the sky.

"Well!" he said more heartily. "What are you in the mood to eat? Chicken? Lamb? I saw a man with skewered fish."

"Anything at all. So long as I am with you."

He stopped then and there and kissed her, his mouth warm and enticing. "Perhaps we should just go back home," he murmured.

"But what about Joseph and Veronique and the others?"

"Let 'em walk." He pulled her back toward the cart, his arm tight at her waist.

From the far side of the marketgrounds, there arose a wild scream.

"Goodness!" Katherine declared, craning to see what might have caused the commotion. Folk were running toward the sound in a swell. More screams erupted, and then there was a brief silence. "What do you think it can be?"

"Drunkards fighting over a woman, no doubt." He tried to tug her away, but Katherine resisted.

"Can't we go and see? Everyone else is."

It was true; even the proprietors of the stalls were abandoning their wares. "Whatever it is," Alain said flatly, "it's no place for you."

"Oh, don't be such a stick." Katherine pulled free of his arm and started toward the hubbub.

"Katherine!" he called sternly. "Come back here! Don't—"

But she'd been swept into the rush of the crowd. "Katherine! Come back!" she heard him cry again. She couldn't have obeyed if she'd tried. Whatever was happening, the entire market was rushing to be there.

She glanced over her shoulder, shrugging a little, wishing she'd heeded him. The press was very thick, and smelled strongly of garlic. Riding the wave of humanity, she trotted in her new shoes. At the far side of the market, the swell abruptly stopped, pushing her up against a sea of backs. *"Que ce que c'est?"* she demanded of a tall young man standing next to her, who could see above the throng: "What is going on?"

"Je ne sais pas," he said, and shrugged.

Then a pair of blue-and-white uniformed men on horseback—the emperor's soldiers—plunged through the crowd just ahead of her. In their wake, she had a clear view of a woman who was kneeling—it had to be she who'd screamed—above a figure in a red shirt. Just before the masses closed in, Katherine saw one of the soldiers leap down from his mount and push the prone man over with the tip of his boot. His head lolled back in the most peculiar way.

"Christ! His throat's been cut," the young man beside her murmured.

It took a brief moment for Katherine to translate his French. Once she did, she stared at the corpse. He had a dirty-yellow mustache, and a thatch of dirty-yellow hair.

Alain had caught up to her. "Come," he said intently, not even glancing toward the body.

She looked at him. "You were playing cards with that man, weren't you? You ought to come forward. Perhaps something you noticed would help the authorities. You—"

"Shut up. Come with me."

She glared, about to say just what she thought of such high-handedness. But then she saw the expression in his eyes, and it made her shiver. He was afraid. She'd never seen him afraid. "Alain?" she said tentatively.

"Come," he ordered again, pulling her by the arm, tugging

her through the throng in a rush. They reached the cart; he paid the boy, handed Katherine up, and leaped onto the box beside her, snapping the reins. When they were a few hundred yards down the road, he turned, looking back.

Katherine sat quietly, miserably, all the day's pleasures puddling. She watched his arms, his lean, strong arms on the reins, and his lovely hands. Impossible to imagine that those hands had wielded the knife that sliced the life of the red-shirted man. And yet—

It was on the tip of her tongue to ask him. But how would she frame the question? "Did you kill that man you played cards with?" She knew by now what he'd say: *If I did, I had my reasons for it.* Just as with Mimi Boulé . . .

She shuddered suddenly, realizing that she was afraid, too—of him. How could she be afraid of him? She loved him madly, spent each night in his bed. . . .

She knew so little about him. How could she trust him?

After all she had given up for him, what choice did she have?

He glanced down at her. The fear had left him. "Katherine," he began.

"Don't tell me!" she said fiercely. "Don't lie to me! Don't—don't *not* lie to me. I just . . . don't want to know."

"I did not do that to him."

I never will lie to you.

"You don't believe me, do you?"

"I don't know what I believe anymore," she said.

He brought the cart to a halt. He seemed to be warring with himself, on the verge of something like confession. And that, strangely, was worse than anything to her—that he might admit to his sins. How, she wondered, did priests ever bear it? She would never hold on to her sanity beneath such weight.

"Look at me, Katherine."

She kept her head down.

"Look at me, Katherine!" He forced her chin up, forced her eyes to meet his. "I am not a murderer," he said. His gaze was forthright, clear with conviction.

He might be mad. Insane. Perhaps he could not help himself.

He swore furiously in French, seeing her avert her gaze again. "I played cards with the man! I won a handful of sous from him. That was all. When I left him, he was as hale as— God, there's no talking to you, is there? You think I did it."

"Perhaps," she said tentatively, "perhaps you do things and you don't recall them."

"You, too? It was bad enough when Christiane bought the lies about me. But if you have no faith in me, Katherine, after all we have been through—better I'd been guillotined. Better I'd lost my head." He grasped her hands. "I love you, Katherine. From the first time I saw you, I loved you. We are—"

"Twinned souls," she whispered.

"Twinned souls," he affirmed, kissing her fingertips. For an instant, her heart warmed. Then he said, "He was only a drifter. A nobody. What does it matter what became of him?" He had picked up the reins. "He was bound to meet a bad end, that one. Let's not speak of it anymore."

They didn't. But Katherine could not keep from thinking of it, from seeing that dandelion-haired head lolling back, and the great, gaping cut, and the blood. . . .

When they reached the cottage, he unloaded her packages, admired the gowns profusely, complimented the tablecloth, swore he'd set to work on a table to go beneath it as soon as he could. Katherine made an omelet, with the tarragon and black pepper she'd bought, and he said it was the best he'd ever tasted. She made chocolate instead of tea for their after-dinner drink. He went with her to the river for washing-up water. He was in fine spirits, singing. Katherine oiled the new pot and left it out to dry.

"Coming to bed?" he asked as the sunlight faded.

"Soon enough now. After I sweep the floor." She reached for the new broom.

"Leave that till the morrow." He had his arms around her waist; his mouth was pressing at her hair.

"I am tired, Alain," she said softly, pushing his hands away.

For an instant, she feared she'd angered him. And angering him had taken on a new potency, far beyond losing the château, even beyond losing his love. He let his arms drop, though, and when he spoke, his voice was wrenchingly sad. "You do know that I love you?"

"You tell me often enough." She grasped the broom like a weapon, ready to wield it if he came at her.

"I want to show you. I want . . . to prove it to you. Katherine, don't turn away!"

"I am tired," she said again, wretchedly.

"Come to bed. I'll just hold you."

"Oh, Alain—"

"If you stop believing in me, what will I have?" he asked, with a crooked smile.

"It would be easier to believe in you," she whispered, "if so many bad things did not happen to you. Around you."

"I am a bad penny," he admitted. "Come to bed with me."

She did—half out of fear and half out of desire. Her own ambivalence was frightening. He worked furiously to bring her to climax, but the fire had fled. "Katherine—"

"I said I was tired. You go on. Take your pleasure."

"It is not pleasure unless you share it."

"I don't mind."

"I do." He turned his back on her and went to sleep.

She lay awake, though, still haunted by the memory of the red-shirted man's lolling head. The future that had seemed so bright and assured only that morning had turned bleak, clouded. A hard sweep of wind rushed through the windows; she heard on the roof a slow patter of rain. She began to cry, grateful for the storm that covered the sound.

If you stop believing in me, what will I have? More frightening to her was the question of what *she'd* have. Somehow, at some point, she had pinned everything—her happiness, her future, her life itself—to Alain Montclair. What if she'd made a fool's decision? How had she thought she could trust, could love, a man who gave so little of himself away?

When had he been honest with her, ever? He'd come to her in so many different guises—as a wounded peasant, a highwayman, a nobleman, a wronged innocent, a simple vineyard laborer—that she had no notion at all what he was at heart. What had gone on today made her wonder if even *he* did. If he'd had nothing to do with that man's death, wasn't the obvious recourse to go to the authorities and offer what help he could? Then she pictured the armed soldiers on horseback, remembered the guards at the Bastille dressed in that same blue and white, and realized that a murderer, even a falsely accused one, who'd managed to escape from prison would have reason enough to bolt under such circumstances.

He moved closer to her in the darkness, reaching for her, pulling her toward him. She fit herself against the curve of his thighs while lightning flared through the shutter cracks, hating her doubts and fears. Either you believed in someone or you didn't; there wasn't any halfway. She could not *almost* trust him, or trust him most of the time, or trust him about some things and not others. He'd told her he hadn't killed Mimi Boulé. He'd told her he hadn't killed the red-shirted man. He'd told her that he loved her. Unless she swallowed it all, trusted him wholly without ever looking back, she would have no peace.

She thought of that day when he'd gone bathing in the river and disappeared, and how in her terror of losing him she'd plunged in blindly, without qualm. It was in that same spirit that she'd followed him to France in the first place, forsaking everything and everyone she knew, abandoning all for his sake. And she recognized, with flashing clarity, that life with this man was going to consist of another and another and another of those mad, blind plunges, that time and again she would have to silence her nagging doubts by simply plunging in.

The prospect was frightening and at the same time liberating. To have a plan, a scheme for the future, at least gave her some illusion of control, made her feel less as though her life was spinning into chaos. She made her decision—recognized that she had really made it long ago, when she fell in love with him that night in the academy courtyard. She remembered how he'd touched her then, and her body's amazed awakening, and she needed desperately to feel that way again.

She turned to him, ran her hand along his arm to his shoulder. "Alain," she whispered. She kissed him, tasted the savor of his sleeping mouth. "Alain—"

He murmured something, still more asleep than awake. She let her fingers play across his chest, stray to his taut belly, slide to his groin. She wrapped her hand around his slack manhood, felt it swell and tighten, and rubbed the smooth tip with her thumb. A crash of thunder pealed out, and he sat up abruptly. She smiled, knowing he could not see it, still stroking him gently. "I thought—that I was dreaming," he told her.

"I love you, Alain. Make—make love to me. Please."

"But you said—"

"I need you to make love to me."

He did, without another word, and it was the best that they had ever shared, slow and sweet and then fast and wild. She came again and again, clinging to him, moaning her pleasure, each impossible surge of ecstasy swallowed by the next, and still he came at her, plunged inside her, soothed her, caressed her, kissed her, until she thought she could bear no more bliss. "Now, Alain," she begged him. "I swear, I cannot stand it!" He laughed and hitched her hips toward him. Her legs encircled him, holding him close. The storm that raged in the skies swirled around them and then entered them, consumed them, so that every slash of lightning was a blast of internal fire. They came together in one final convulsion, to a mighty thunderclap that could not drown out their cries.

As the storm subsided, as the fire faded, he held to her tightly, his hand smoothing the mad tangle of her hair. "I will never forget this, Katherine," he whispered haltingly. "If ever I am alone and afraid, I will remember this—what you did for me now—and it will be enough that I will go on."

"You will never be alone. I will always be with you."

"God, I pray that you will." He kissed her fervently, one

hand on either side of her face. "I don't know what I might have done to deserve your love."

"You asked for it," she told him frankly. "No one else ever has."

"Marry me, Katherine."

She drew back a little. "Do you mean that?"

"With all my heart. My soul. Say yes."

"Yes." He hugged her close, kissed her eyelids and then her mouth, a solemn, holy sealing of the covenant. Which made Katherine think . . . "I suppose—I shall have to become a Catholic."

He laughed at that. "No. Marriage is a civil matter in France now. The Corsican has seen to that."

She was much relieved. "I *would* have done it, you know. Converted. If I had to."

"Given up your God for me? Katherine, I am awed."

"I'm not so sure I haven't already," she said ruefully.

He laughed. "And made a pact with the devil? I am a *lucky* devil, but I'm not Satan himself."

Katherine yawned. She was enormously weary, and enormously contented. She fell asleep in his arms, while the rain flung itself fitfully from the wide, black sky.

Twenty-one

When she awoke, the rain was still falling. Alain was pulling on his boots, frowning, and Katherine was aware of a bustle outside the cottage, an unfamiliar morning hubbub of voices and footsteps. "What is going on?" she asked sleepily.

"The rain. It is bad for the grapes. Very bad, this late in the season. The seigneur has ordered everyone to the fields—women, children, all."

She pushed the blanket away. "Then I must come, too!"

He looked pleased. But then he shook his head. "It is hard work. You will be wet and cold and miserable—"

"I will be with you."

That made him smile. "*Bien,* if you like, come along. Bring a knife." She paused only to fetch the new one, put on her clogs, and tie back her hair. Then she followed him outside, into the gray, drizzling dawn.

The men looked grumpy and red-eyed in the aftermath of their market holiday, and the children were shivering in their shifts. Katherine climbed into the cart beside Alain, her skirts already slick with mud. They rode halfway up the Golden Slope. "The best grapes," Alain explained as he guided the horse, "are not at the top or the bottom, but at the middle. So it is these we must first see safe in." The workers took baskets from the cart and fanned out along the terraces carved into the hillside. The earth smelled chalky and damp; the vines gave off a heady, heavy scent. Alain showed her how to test the grapes between her fingers to see if they were ripe, then slice away the surprisingly tough stalks. He picked with one eye on her progress. She was nervous at first, and his basket was full long before hers. He emptied what she'd gathered so far into it, then took it to the cart.

Jolted early from their beds, the pickers worked in silence

in the beginning, still half asleep. But as the sky slowly lightened and a fine mist began to swirl up from the valley, someone started a song, and a dozen voices chimed in. Katherine could not make out the words, but the tune was lilting and lovely. Alain sang, too, in his rich, smooth baritone. She loved the sound. "What is the song about?" she asked in a lull between stanzas.

"Love. What else?" He stole a kiss from her beneath the dripping grape leaves. Veronique saw, and smiled. She called something in very rapid French to Alain that made him laugh.

"What did she say?" Katherine demanded.

"That you are a good influence on me."

Katherine glanced at the black-plaited woman, who was picking nearly as fast as Alain. "Have you known her long?"

"All my life. Wait until she hears that we're to be married."

"Do you think she will mind?"

He looked at her curiously, his knife slicing through stems with practiced ease. "Why should she?"

"Because I am not French."

"Oh, no. She's far more likely to hold it against you that you are a duke's daughter. I think perhaps I will not tell her that. She is a fervent supporter of the Revolution."

Katherine pondered that, contemplating the long rows of peasants picking in the steady drizzle. "I cannot imagine it has made much difference in their lives."

His eyes, gray in the rain, met hers with a glint. "Not in how they live them, perhaps. But in how they think about them, yes. If they wanted to now, they could leave this land. Go away to Paris, or Marseilles—anyplace they like."

"But they haven't," Katherine said after a moment.

"The difference lies in knowing that they could."

Katherine had a glimmer of understanding. It was not so unlike throwing off her own bonds of nobility. How very odd. Was that what freedom consisted of, then—the ability to dream beyond the confines of what had always been, whether one chose to act on it or not?

Alain's basket was full again. He took her meager portion

and his own to the cart. Far away across the hillside, Katherine could see the château's towers swaddled in mist. "What did the Revolution mean to you?" she asked him when he returned.

"To me? Nothing much. I would have gone to Paris or Marseilles or wherever I pleased regardless."

Of course he would have, as the seigneur's son. She risked probing a little deeper. "What about to your father?"

He was suddenly very busy with picking, and she thought for a moment that he did not mean to answer. But then he said slowly, "He was not so much in favor of it. He is very much . . . the traditionalist. He was glad when Napoleon made himself emperor. It was more what he was used to dealing with."

"And Veronique? What does she think of Napoleon?"

"Like most French, she would like to see him conquer the world. She is not fooled by him, though."

"Fooled by him how?"

"Napoleon is for Napoleon. Far more than he is for the French." He hesitated. "And she has lost two sons in his wars."

"She might have been happier," Katherine suggested softly, "had they not had the opportunity. If they were still here beside her, picking grapes."

"No," he said with quiet force. "Opportunity is all. Without it, there can be no dreams. With no dreams, the soul is dead."

"My father," Katherine began haltingly, "takes very good care of the folk who live on his lands."

"I am certain he does."

"When there is a peasant who shows particular promise, Poppa makes certain he is sent to school, for training in the clergy or estate management or animal husbandry or the like."

"That is most decent of him."

Katherine hacked at a particularly difficult stem. "There's been no such revolution in England. I daresay that's proof enough the people who serve Poppa and those like him are happy."

"Perhaps so."

"Well, what else could it be?" she demanded, pulling the bunch free at last.

"That the English are sorely lacking in dreams."

She straightened her stooped back. "That is a cruel thing to say."

"It is a cruel thing to do, to hold great masses of people enthralled—"

"The English are *not* enthralled!"

"To a system based on the vagaries of birth," he went on quietly. "After one of your father's peasants who excels at animal husbandry is duly educated, can he then buy land? Start up his own farm? Extend his holdings?"

"He can if he has money."

"Ah. And where would he earn this money, pray tell?"

"By working for . . . by working for my father!"

"Who would then sell him parts of *his* land?"

"There are many English families who have had to sell off portions of their estates. You have no notion how dreadful the death taxes are. Why, entire *legions* of parvenus who have made fortunes in trade have bought up manors and halls and are made barons or viscounts by the regent."

"And these clever newcomers are, I trust, embraced by society?"

Katherine blushed. "Well—they are *not,* actually. The true aristocracy—"

"Aha! The *true* aristocracy! Have you any notion what that means, Katherine? It is nothing more than the parvenus who got there first!"

She cocked her head at him. "You are a solemn believer, aren't you? In the Revolution?"

"I am."

"I cannot see why you would fall in love with me, then," she said tartly, "if I am everything you despise."

"Silly girl. The Revolution was not about discounting human worth. It was about valuing it wherever it might pop up, whether in peasant or noble. Not about dragging everyone down to one level, but about lifting up those who would otherwise have no—"

"Opportunity."

"Precisely."

She sighed. Her hands stung from the juices of the grapes; her spine felt permanently bowed. "If I were Veronique," she declared, "I'd have long since taken off for Paris or Marseilles. This is a miserable way to make one's living."

"You think so? I rather like it," he declared, and sliced another bursting cluster from the vine.

By late afternoon, Katherine was stumbling with exhaustion. Alain urged her to rest in the cart, but she kept on doggedly, not about to admit that French peasants had more fortitude than she. She sliced and picked and piled, sliced and picked and piled, until her hands were raw red and she had blisters all along the edges of her forefingers and thumbs. Her clothes were streaked with mud; the rain sluiced down her hair and face and chilled her ceaselessly. She worked in a mindless, unthinking daze, far beyond the efforts of conversation, beyond anything but the grinding routine.

From one terrace to the next they moved, in a long, winding line. No one was singing now. No one had been singing for hours. All one heard was an occasional grunt or curse, the sloshing suck of the thick mud, and the constant patter of the rain on the leaves. Then, just as darkness was falling, a shout went up from the head of the line on the Golden Slope, which would more accurately have been called the Muck-Brown Slope just then. The knife slipped from Katherine's hand. She glanced up disinterestedly, wondering what had caused the ruckus, and saw Alain vaulting toward her over the rows of vines. "It's enough," he told her, reaching her side. "We are finished for tonight. We have saved the heart of the crop. Come along." He held out his hand for hers and caught it just as she collapsed to her knees.

"Finished?" she croaked. "Are you certain?"

"My God, Katherine." He lifted her and carried her down the hill toward the cart. "I never should have let you come."

"I'm all right," she insisted. "I am fine." And then she fell asleep, right there in his arms.

She did not awaken until he laid her down on their bed and began to ease her out of her wet clothes. Then she tried to push herself up: "Your supper. I must make your supper. I've made nothing for your—"

"Hush, *chérie*. We have bread, and some olives and cheese. Shall I bring you some?"

"Yes, please," she murmured, snuggling down into the blanket. She was asleep again before he returned with the food.

Sometime before dawn, she woke, needing urgently to use the chamber pot. She stumbled up from the straw, her muscles aching and stiff, and found her way in the dark. When she was finished, she was terribly thirsty. She groped for the water bucket they kept on the floor by the hearth, but couldn't find it. "Dammit all," she muttered under her breath. There were matches in a box on the mantel. She struck one, blinking at the small conflagration, then glimpsed the bucket over by the door. She crossed to it, drank two full dippers— then froze where she stood. Something was different. Something was wrong. She heard the rain, and a whistle of wind, but she did not hear Alain's soft snores.

In a panic, she went back for the matches and lit another. Her hand was trembling. In the thin scrim of light, she saw that the bed was empty. She held the match until the flame singed her fingers, staring at the emptiness.

Where could he have gone at this hour? She could only guess at the time, but the night felt far advanced, as though it might be three or four o'clock. She was wide awake now, and frightened. Perhaps he'd simply gone to the river for water—but here was the bucket. Or he'd had to help someone in need . . . She went to the window and looked out. None of the surrounding cottages showed any light. Perhaps there was more picking to be done after all? But that was absurd; no one could pick in the dark. With a dreadful fear clawing at her heart, she looked to see if he had taken his clothes. But of course he had. He only owned what he had on.

She lit a candle, thinking that perhaps he had left a note. Not that there was anything to write it on, or with . . . He might be in trouble, though. He might have gone down to the river—who knows what for? Perhaps to bathe?—and slipped and hit his head. *I must go out to look for him,* she thought, and started out the door. But the candle she clasped sputtered out instantly in the rain, and the wall of night was so thick and dark that she turned back.

If he had left her . . . But why would he leave her? He was happy. *They* were happy. Weren't they? He'd been proud of her today, proud and concerned; she'd seen it in his eyes. She lit the candle again, set it in its stick, and sat on the floor by the doorway, clutching her hunched-up knees.

Unwillingly, her mind turned to the image of the man with the red shirt. If Alain had killed him, might he not run? But Alain *hadn't* killed him; he'd told her so. And he'd said he never would lie. She trusted him—didn't she? She'd decided that she *had* to trust him.

And as soon as she had, he had disappeared.

He will return, she told herself. *Wherever he is, he will come back to me.*

And what if he didn't?

That prospect was so unutterably bleak that she could hardly bear to consider it. That he would abandon her after enticing her away and seducing her . . . oh, he would not! Could not! Could he? What would be the sense of it?

That he'd needed a cover, a willing "wife" to get him past the guards in Paris. That he'd needed someplace to hide until the clamor over his escape died down. Why, even now he might be headed back to Paris, disguised by the beard, using some other name—he was familiar enough with using other names—to game and wench and wallow in dissoluteness. Hadn't Madame warned her? Hadn't she said he was a notorious rake?

And only the night before, he had asked her to marry him.

Stone-faced, she stared at the closed door in the flickering candlelight. Despite the refrain in her heart—*Trust him, trust him*—she could not stop the scattered thoughts that flitted through her head. Mimi Boulé. The man with the red shirt. The ugly bulk of the Bastille, and those dank, close corridors smelling of misery and despair . . .

The door burst open, so suddenly that she screamed. Alain paused on the threshold, rain dripping from his hat. "Goose," he said, perfectly calmly. "What are you doing there?"

"I—I woke, and you were gone. I didn't know where you'd gone. Where *did* you go, Alain?"

He tossed the hat across the room. "To play cards. With some fellows I know."

"To play *cards*? After the day we spent on the slope?"

He shrugged and grinned abashedly, with something of the air of a schoolboy caught at truancy. "You forget—I'm accustomed to the labor. Come off the floor, for heaven's sake, and get back to bed."

Katherine could not decide if she was furious or relieved. She let him raise her up, and as she did, caught the scent on him of brandy and tobacco. "Do you often leave when I am fast asleep?" she demanded.

"No. Of course not. Only this once. You were so tired, I thought for certain you would not miss me. I'd not have gone if I'd known you would worry." He shook his head, sending a shower of bright droplets flying. "Though I cannot think why you *were* worried."

"Because—because—" *I feared that you had left me. I feared you had killed Mimi Boulé and the man with the red shirt, and you had no further need of me, and you'd abandoned me.* But that would never do. "I was just . . . afraid. To wake without you here."

He wrapped his arms around her. "You *are* a goose." Then he yawned luxuriantly. "I am weary *now*. And I will pay dearly on the morrow for the few sous I won!"

He kissed her forehead, used the chamber pot, and then undressed, while she crawled back beneath the blanket. He pinched out the candle and lay down beside her, with a heart-felt sigh of peace. He drew her close to him, kissed her once more, and fell asleep.

Katherine lay awake and listened. The accustomed night noises were all there now: the rain, the wind, his snores. Still, she could not help thinking that something had subtly shifted, realigned in a way that she could not yet fathom. She felt tired and disspirited.

He grunted and stretched, his hand seeking her thigh and, finding it, settling there like a heavy weight. Katherine watched the darkness lighten to another rain-gray dawn beyond the shutters, her heart more raw than the blisters on her hands.

Twenty-two

"*Let us see* where we stand," growled the duke of Marne, seated at the table in the countess d'Oliveri's suite at the Hotel Luxembourg. A tall, thin man with a great sweep of silver hair and the same fine bones and striking blue eyes that made his daughter so alluring, the duke was plainly not happy. His cravat was askew, and deep lines furrowed his high forehead; he looked as though he had not slept in some time.

The countess d'Oliveri, her lovely face unaccustomedly wan, contemplated her clenched hands. "All of this is my fault," she said miserably.

Only Nanette O'Toole, a fetching brunette some ten years younger than her husband, seemed perfectly calm as she assured the countess: "Christiane, you must know that Richard and I do not blame you."

"You should," Madame said bluntly.

"Nonsense!" Nanette had a glorious voice, rich and reverberating even in quiet conversation, with a hint of Irish still lingering in it. "How were you—how was any of us—to know she had it in her to do this?"

"I should have told you when she first ran off to find him," Madame moaned. "It was wrong of me to keep that from you."

"So it was," the duke barked.

His wife turned her clear gray gaze on him. "Why?" she asked quietly. "Christiane tracked her down quickly enough. No harm had come to her."

The rebuke, gentle though it was, hit home. "The fault's not all yours, Christiane," the duke rumbled. "I ought to have known something was amiss when I got that letter sent to me by Admiral Bressler. Couldn't make hide nor hair of what he was prattling on about!"

"But by that time," Nanette put in, "you'd already sent us word, Christiane, that you had Katherine safe and sound in Paris."

"You will at least admit I ought not to have taken her to see Montclair in prison!"

The duke turned to his wife. "You'll not argue with that, Nan!"

The duchess shrugged. "Christiane's logic in doing so seems perfectly clear. It would have been my instinct as well, to have her see firsthand the depths to which he had sunk. Who would ever have suspected Katherine might aid him in his escape?"

Madame looked dazedly at her old friend. "One might almost think you were proud of her, Nanette."

"Well—I'm not, of course. But perhaps in a sense I am. When you have spent years despairing over a girl who has never done *anything* the least bit shocking or out of the ordinary, it comes rather as a relief to discover that she has a mind of her own after all."

"She is certainly bedding with him," Madame noted bluntly.

That shocked the duke; he covered his discomposure by clearing his throat. But as he did, Nanette waved a hand. "Come now, Richard. She would not be the first English girl to lose her maidenhead to a comely wooer. Nor will she be the last."

"My wife, as you see," the duke put in, glowering, "is quite liberal in these matters."

"That is a masterpiece of understatement!" Christiane said, dazed.

"Don't be a hypocrite, Richard," Nanette chided. "Young men have always sown their wild oats—and, if you want my opinion, are all the better for it, since it prepares them to settle down. Monogamy is hardly a natural state for the human race. Better, I say, for Katherine to purge such wildness *before* marriage than after."

"All *I* can say," the countess declared, somewhat dumb-founded, "is thank heaven it was Katherine who came to such straits! Any other parent would have the law down upon Mrs. Treadwell's and my heads!"

"If Richard were not being so stubborn and belligerent," the duchess noted, "he would have to admit that you have more than fulfilled what we requested of you in regard to Katherine. Had it been up to me, we would not even have come to Paris—we would have let the infatuation run its course."

"So you said in Russia, Nan. But this news that he is a murderer," the duke noted grimly, "puts a somewhat different slant on the matter."

The French lieutenant who was seated with them at the table had been following the conversation with a highly affronted air. "I should say so!" he declared now, roundly. "This Montclair is a dangerous scoundrel! You have only to look at how adeptly he won his freedom from the Bastille!"

" 'Adeptly,' " the duchess said drolly, "is the operative word there. Not a single man killed or even wounded, despite Montclair's possession of the pistol he seems to have gotten from Katherine. Hardly a rampage of bloodthirstiness."

The lieutenant colored slightly. "Do I detect some insult to the courage of the Bastille guards?"

"Not at all, monsieur! Faced with a loaded pistol, I myself would willingly open any door asked of me." The lieutenant did not seem placated, and Nanette rushed on: "But what matters now is that we assess the current situation. Christiane—the countess—seems to feel it is possible Katherine is being held by Montclair against her will."

"Though how anyone could make that girl do *anything* that was against her will," the duke rumbled, "is beyond my ken."

"Well—if not against her will, then against her better judgment," Madame sought to explain.

The duke raised a brow. "There's not much question of *that.* The chit's judgment seems to have gone straight out the door from the moment she first encountered Monsieur Montclair."

The duchess smiled at him fondly. "Rather like yours when I met you, eh, Richard?"

"Very like," he agreed.

She smiled at him. "And that was not the end of the world."

The lieutenant—his name was Giacauld—had stiffened. "I do not think, Your Graces, that you grasp the danger your daughter is in. Montclair *is* a killer. There is no doubt of that."

"With all due respect, Lieutenant Giacauld," Nanette declared smoothly, "there *is* some doubt. We have read the transcripts of what passed for Montclair's trial. It appeared to me the only souls in the courtroom more confused than the witnesses were the government's representatives. Richard, don't you agree?"

The duke seemed torn between emotion and honesty. "Montclair made a defense that in England would certainly be considered to leave reasonable doubt as to the murderer's identity," he finally said.

"He was alone with Mademoiselle Boulé in the room!" Giacauld burst out in fury.

"He said not," Nanette countered. "He said there was another man—her brother. And that the brother killed her to protect the family name."

Giacauld laughed. It was not a pleasant sound. "What else would you expect him to say?"

"If," Madame quickly interjected, "we might get back to Katherine, I honestly believe we ought to find her as soon as we can, and at least ascertain whether she is accompanying Montclair willingly."

"You are right, of course," Nanette admitted. "If for no other reason than to set your mind at ease."

"What about *your* mind?" Madame demanded. "You cannot tell me a mésalliance with a convicted murderer is what you wish for your stepdaughter!"

"Of course not," the duchess said with quiet force. "But

that is the way it is with children, isn't it? You do your best to teach them what you know, bring them up to be the sort of people you admire. There is a point, though, at which you must let go. Besides, you told us, did you not, that this Montclair is of noble lineage? The son of a rich seigneur in the wine country—"

"I don't know that for certain," Madame corrected her. "It is only what he told me when I first met him. When he was no more than a boy." For a moment, her mind flitted back to the proud, self-possessed youngster who'd been dragged to her by Guillaume, the doorman who had worked for her at La Maison de Touton. *This one*, Guillaume had said, clenching the boy by the ear, *will not go away*. . . . And Alain Montclair had made a bow worthy of a musketeer, his black hair sweeping across his amazing blue eyes. . . .

"It is what our friends here say as well," the duchess assured her. And the countess had to bite her tongue to keep from shouting: *Well, who do you think* they *heard it from? From me!*

Lieutenant Giacauld cleared his throat: "If we might return to the matter at hand—"

"Do let's," the duke growled. "His present whereabouts."

"Yes. As I noted, we have arrested one Thomas Venday—"

"The cabbage seller," the duchess of Marne murmured.

"Who confessed to having provided Montclair with the means of his withdrawal from Paris. *And* who told us—"

"Under torture, no doubt," the duchess said blithely. "I must say, this Revolution that began with such high hopes has guttered down miserably."

Giacauld stood up from the table. He was a tall, reed-thin man with black hair shot through with gray and a long, elegant hooked nose. "I resent that remark, milady!"

" 'Citizen,' " Nanette corrected him absently. "We are all citizens now that we are in France."

"Nanette, *don't* provoke," the duke said sharply.

"You were saying, Lieutenant?" the countess offered as a palm branch.

It took Giacauld a moment to recollect. "Ah, yes! Who

told us that a young woman matching your daughter's description most definitely was with him. We have traced them both to a roadhouse near Mallaume, where Montclair made himself memorable by fleecing several peasants of their last sous at cards, and where he and your daughter shared a single bedchamber—and the maid found blood on the sheets."

"Oh, don't hesitate," the duchess murmured, "to hold back any lascivious detail."

"Their trail then leads to the east, where they stayed at several other roadhouses. Our last confirmed sighting of them was by a shepherd lad, who witnessed them bathing nude together in a river near Montbard ten days ago."

"Katherine?" said the duke, eyes widening.

"At least—a young woman matching her description."

"Imagine that! Katherine, nude in a river! Do you know," the duchess mused, "I begin to admire this Alain Montclair!"

Giacauld seemed about to explode. And Madame shared his sentiments. "Nanette. I cannot help but feel you are being all too sanguine about this," she said sternly. "Your stepdaughter has been abducted—"

"Has absconded," the duchess corrected her mildly. "The doormen here seemed clear enough about that. How did that one fellow phrase it, my love?" she appealed to her husband.

" 'She looked as though she were going to paradise,' " the duke said grimly.

"Ah, yes. Quite poetic, that."

"She is only nineteen years old!" Madame said desperately.

"Hardly a child," Nanette noted. "You, Christiane, certainly knew your own mind by nineteen."

But I did not have a man like Alain Montclair to mold my thoughts for me. To win my heart from me. To seduce me, to use me . . . Madame tried to consider whether Alain the murderer might have murdered Katherine. She could not dismiss the possibility. He had already moved so far beyond the boy she'd known that she wondered whether she *ever* had known him. All she could reiterate, as forcefully as she could, was, "We must find Katherine. She must be found."

Nanette sighed. "Yet Lieutenant Giacauld assures us all that can be done in such a situation *is* being done. Is that not so, Lieutenant?"

"Certainly, Your Gr . . . citizen."

The duchess shrugged. "In that case, we ought to make the most of our wait. The opera house has *The Magic Flute* tonight. And we owe a debt of thanks to Monsieur de Braquefort, for aiding Katherine as he did. I'll go and dress, shall I?" She stood.

Lieutenant Giacauld cleared his throat again. "Pardon me. But there is one more tactic we might try."

"And what is that?" asked the duke.

"A reward."

The duke of Marne's blue eyes narrowed. "There, Nan. Did I not tell you? Did I not say finding Katherine would come down to money in the end?"

Giacauld's hand went to his sword. "If you mean to imply that French justice is to be bought—"

"Well, what in hell did you just tell me?" the duke said irritably.

This confounded the lieutenant slightly. He recovered his composure, though. "As matters stand now, *citizen,* we have only the military searching for your daughter. Offer a reward, though, and every soul in the land will have his eyes out for her."

"If Katherine is in trouble," the duchess noted calmly, "she will have the good sense to get out of it. If he is abusive . . . if she does not trust him . . . she will leave him. Christiane, wouldn't you agree?"

The countess darted a glance at the duke's furrowed forehead. "I—I'm not certain, Nanette. His personality is so overwhelming—"

"Oh, bosh."

"You have not met him," the countess said again, hollowly.

The duke of Marne looked at her, hard and long. Then he turned his gaze to Giacauld. "Very well. Let us say ten thousand."

"Ten thousand—*English pounds,* milord?"

"No—Greek drachma," the duke said irritably. "Of course English pounds, you nincompoop, what do you think?"

Strangely enough, this time Giacauld took no offense. Instead he straightened where he stood, the epaulets on his blue-and-white uniform springing to attention. "I think it fair to say, Your Grace, you will have your daughter back within a matter of days."

Twenty-three

After three days, the rain had finally subsided, leaving the Golden Slope damp and shining from its thorough wash. The top and bottom terraces had been harvested at a more leisurely pace than the crucial center, and no one went to the vines now except the old women, to search for late-ripening bunches and fruit that might have been missed. The business of winemaking had begun in earnest, and it put the seigneur's workers back into a holiday mood.

First, the gathered grapes were stripped from their stalks— a tedious chore, but also a sociable one, with everyone assembled together in the huge, barnlike press house at long tables stained by centuries of juice. Katherine enjoyed helping in this task, and even gained compliments from Joseph for her deft, quick hands. The stalks and any blemished or moldy fruits were flung onto the floor, then swept up by boys for use as pig fodder. As each table's worth was finished, the stronger men—Alain among them—tipped the surface up from one side, so that the mounds of grapes rolled down into great oak vats, eight and ten feet across. In these vats waded women with their skirts kirtled up and men with breeches rolled past their knees. They moved in circles, singing, the grapes squishing between their toes. The first time Katherine saw this, she was horrified. "It does not seem very clean," she whispered to Alain. "All those feet—and half those folks have been going without shoes for the entire time I've been here!"

"It is how the finest wines in the world are made," he told her indignantly. "There are those who say the reason French wines are so highly regarded is that French peasant feet impart a certain *je ne sais quoi* to the juice."

"I could jolly well say *quoi*," Katherine muttered, picturing the mud and refuse those toes tracked through every day.

"Besides, the alcohol in the wine vanquishes any impurities," he reassured her. "Would you like to try it?"

"What—me? Tread in there?" She laughed, shaking her head. "I don't think so. I don't care to have my feet stained purple. And anyway, surely English toes would give the vintage an off taste."

"Not your toes. I happen to know your toes are quite delectable." He caught her hand. "Come. Let's. When will you ever have a chance like this again?" Still she hesitated. He leaned his head close. "And imagine the fun you might have announcing at the regent's supper table that your feet were once standing in the Nuits-Saint-Georges he so proudly pours!"

"I'm not going back to England." Katherine's eyes abruptly widened. "Is *that* what we are making? Nuits-Saint-Georges?" He nodded, enjoying her astonishment. "Why, that *is* a fine wine! One of the very finest! My father serves it often on state occasions!"

"You must remember to mention to him that the 1813 vintage has a special savor."

"He never would believe me," Katherine said absently. "No one I know would." She wished the subject of her father had not come up. Surely by now the countess had informed the duke of her disappearance. He must be beside himself with worry. And he would blame Madame, which was so very unfair. . . .

Alain seemed to recognize that they had broached a sore subject. "Do come," he urged her, his blue eyes beguiling. Katherine glanced over to the vat. Veronique was among the treaders; she smiled and waved, beckoning:

"*Allez, allez!*" she cried to Alain and Katherine. "*Nous avons besoin de vos pieds gigantiques!*"

"I do *not* have big feet!" Katherine answered her in French.

"No—but I do," Alain told her, bending to pull off his boots.

"You *do* mean to wash before you—oh! Oh, Alain, don't!

Stop!" He'd lifted her in his arms and was removing her countrified clogs, even as she kicked in protest. The workers paused in their labors, grinning and shouting encouragement at him. "Don't you _dare_—"

"Best hike your skirts up," he warned, clambering over the edge of the vat.

"_How_ can I hike them when you are—Alain Montclair, I warn you, I will never speak to you a—oh!" She grabbed frantically for the edges of her gown—thank God it was only the worn old nightdress!—as he set her down. The juice sluiced over her ankles to her calves; she could feel the whole grapes suspended in the liquid mass, felt them squishing beneath her soles. It was like walking in a river full of tadpoles. The expression on her face made Veronique double over in laughter.

"_Oh, chérie!_" she cried, clutching her belly.

Alain, meanwhile, was placidly stomping, raising his feet and setting them down again in a steady rhythm. "Nuits-Saint-Georges," he reminded her. "Your contribution to civilization—"

She glared at him, tentatively lifting one foot. There was no means of staying clear of the juice without holding her hems disgracefully high.

He pulled her into the circle, starting to sing. The laughing men and women joined in. It was a song she hadn't heard before, raucous and lively, and as she caught snatches of the verses and refrain, she blushed mightily. It concerned a man who glimpsed the knees of a fair maiden treading grapes— she _hoped_ it was the knees; she was not quite certain of the word—and fell hopelessly into her thrall. Alain's arm was around her waist; his hand held hers tightly. She looked back over her shoulder at him, and he smiled. His pleasure made her forget completely that she was calf-deep in smashed grapes; she sloshed through the mess in a daze of joy, untouched by fear of what had gone before or what might be to come. Her heart seemed about to burst with happiness. The press house rang to the rafters with the riot of voices; the late-day sun poured through the wide doors, casting a gilded glow over the tables and vats, sending the shadows of the treaders dancing against the far wall. Alain bent to kiss the nape of her neck through her tangled hair, and her contentment was so complete that she was suddenly apprehensive. Bliss such as this could not last. . . .

"Je t'aime toujours," Alain whispered. *I love you forever.*

As Katherine twisted her head to return his kiss, in the corner of her eye she saw a man in the open doorway, a tall man, very lean, his dark hair shot with gray. He was hovering covertly, as though he did not want to be seen. The seigneur, she realized. Alain's father. It had to be; they shared the same height, the same build, though the father's nose had a hook where Alain's did not. His clothes were not those of a peasant; he wore a frock coat and smooth, well-fitted serge breeches above handsome tall boots that gleamed.

She started to smile in his direction, but stopped herself. It was his business if he chose to linger at the edges of his workers' idylls; she would not give him away. It was a pity, though, that he could not partake of the joy the way his son did. Perhaps that was his curse of noblesse oblige.

The turning circle hid him from her sight. By the time she'd come around to the same spot, he had vanished. Katherine was unspeakably glad he had seen her in the vat, had witnessed her willingness to perform whatever task Alain set her to. It would not be long now, she was sure, before she was invited to the château to make his acquaintance. And then all the deprivations of these past weeks would be no more than a dream. Did he know that Alain had proposed marriage to her? Could Alain have gone to tell him on that night he'd vanished from the cottage? Playing cards, he'd said—she realized now how ridiculous his excuse had been. He'd been to visit his father. Of course. It made perfect sense. She remembered the lingering smells on him of brandy and tobacco. Where else would he have gotten cigars?

"The vats," Alain chided, nudging her along, "are no place for daydreams. If you cannot keep up with the pace, back to the stripping table you go."

She was overwhelmed with love for him, with her dreams

of their future. *"Je t'aime aussi,"* she told him. *"Toujours."* Forever . . .

Touched and surprised by the tremor in her voice, he stopped her, held her at arm's length. "Katherine? What is it?"

"Only that—I have never been so happy before," she whispered.

He stared down at her, his blue eyes shining. "Nor have I."

That evening, Katherine took the cooking pot to the river to wash it. She'd made a potage of green peas and carrots and onions—humble fare, but Alain had complimented it extravagantly, and it *had* tasted fine after the long day in the press house. He'd made love to her after supper, so she was later than most of their neighbors. She waved and exchanged greetings with two women, Anne and Marceline, who were finished with their scrubbing and heading home. "You did well today!" Anne called to her, laughing.

"Thank you," Katherine said humbly. "I don't imagine I helped much. But it was a new experience."

And Marceline, gray-haired and wizened, told her cheerfully: "That is as it should be. Life should be filled with new experiences!"

Katherine laughed, wading barefoot into the river with her scrubbing rag and pot. Monsieur Jacquet would have been quite taken aback, she mused, at her current grasp of idiomatic French. And when it came to that, she very much doubted he was French at all, the charlatan. The accent he'd so tediously exacted from his students at the academy had really been completely—

"Oh!" The word escaped her in a gasp as the moonlight ignited a tall figure standing by the shore. "Alain?" she said tentatively. He was tall enough, but he seemed rather slim.

"Bonsoir, ma'm'selle." Not Alain. His voice was altogether different, deeper-pitched, grating. Who, then, could it be?

He took a step toward her down the riverbank and skidded on the slick grass. In keeping himself from falling, he turned sideways, and she glimpsed his long, beaked nose. The seigneur . . . Feeling more calm—it had been rather unnerving to have him creep up on her that way—she relaxed. "I saw you today. At the press house," she told him in French.

"Did you, now?"

She was embarrassed that she had her skirts raised up, just as she had then. She stepped onto a rock and let them fall. "Yes. You were watching your son and me."

"Watching my—yes. So I was."

"I do hope," Katherine rushed on, "you won't think me unworthy. I would not ordinarily behave that way. But Alain seems to think I must prove myself. I can only assume the impetus comes from you."

"I suppose it does."

"He is a wonderful man," Katherine said shyly. "You must be very proud of him." He said nothing. "And no doubt you would have preferred it had he chosen a Frenchwoman. I can only tell you—I will try my very best to live up to what is expected of me."

"No doubt," he said in that low, grave voice. Just then, she heard Alain calling from the cottage:

"Katherine! Katherine, where are you!"

"I must go," she said, grabbing up her pot.

"Katherine!" Alain shouted again.

"I am coming!" she called back, gingerly stepping over the moonlit stones.

The seigneur caught her arm as she passed him. "It would be best," he said, "if you did not mention to him that you have spoken with me." His fingertips dug into her skin.

"Of course not," Katherine said nervously. "If you think that best."

"Katherine?" Alain was coming toward them, down the bank. For a moment longer, the seigneur held her fast. Then he let her go and slipped away as quietly as he'd come, disappearing into a stand of pine trees. Katherine dropped the pot and stared after him, rubbing her sore forearm. But here was Alain, sounding cross and tired. "Where the devil have you been?"

"The—the peas were stuck to the bottom of the pot," she told him, and instantly regretted the lie. Hadn't he sworn he would never lie to her? Where was her allegiance, anyway? Why would his father demand that she not tell him they'd met?

He laughed, putting his arm around her. "My poor Katherine. A day spent treading grapes and scrubbing burnt peas—you must be altogether ready to be rid of me."

"You know better than that." The pine branches rustled. Alain went for his knife, his mood changed instantly.

"Who's there?" he barked.

"It is only the wind," Katherine told him—another lie on top of the other. He had his nose stuck in the air, sniffing like a fox. Frantic lest her falsehoods be discovered, she tugged him toward the cottage. "Come. Let's go to bed."

That prospect was enough to make him forget his qualms. He took the pot from her and clasped her tight to his side. "You insatiable thing!"

Katherine blushed in the darkness, hoping his father had not heard that.

Later, though, after he had made love to her with heart-stirring yearning, she regretted the lies she had spoken. "Alain?" she whispered, from within his strong, sure arms.

"Mm?" He was half asleep.

"I . . . what I told you about the peas and the pot, there at the river? It wasn't true."

"Mm."

He sounded so weary that she nearly stopped. Only honor made her press on: "I *was* speaking to someone. It was your father."

There was a long pause in which she felt his muscles tense, from head to toe, in the oddest way. All he said, though, was, "My father?"

"Yes. The seigneur. I'd seen him peeking in at the press house. He came up to me at the river, and we . . . we spoke."

"I see. And what did you say?"

"Just—how wonderful you are. And that I hope he doesn't think me unworthy of you because I am not French."

"And what did he say, pray tell?"

"That it would be best . . . if I did not mention to you that we had spoken."

"How did you know him to be my father?"

"He was as tall as you—even, I think, a shade taller. And dressed ever so elegantly. At least, he was at the press house. I couldn't see much of him at the river, because of the dark." She laughed nervously. "I must say, I am glad you did not inherit that hooked beak of his!" He had rolled over onto his back and was staring up at the ceiling. "I hope you are not cross with me."

He gathered her against him, smoothing her hair. "No. Of course I am not."

"I know you mean for me to prove my—my fitness to be your wife with living here, and helping with the harvest, and pretending to be a peasant. I think I've done quite well, don't you?"

"Very well indeed."

"Does—does your father know that you have asked me to marry you?"

"Yes. I told him several nights past."

"That explains, doesn't it, why he would have come to see me?"

"It might."

Why did she have the impression she had somehow done wrong? "I am sorry I did not tell you the truth at first," she said abjectly. "It was only that he said I shouldn't. And he has such a grand manner about him—it was rather like when you are speaking to a minister or priest, if you know what I mean. You never think to contradict them, whatever they say."

"All that matters is that you told me the truth now," Alain assured her, and kissed her.

"I'm so glad. I simply couldn't bear it if you were angry."

"I'm not angry. Get some sleep, *chérie*."

Relieved that her conscience was clear, she snuggled down

into the straw, her arm across his taut stomach, her head nestled on his chest. She sank into a deep, dreamless slumber. When she woke, the sun was high, and Alain was gone.

This time, she knew better than to panic. She thought only of how kind he was to let her sleep in late. She rose, put on her claret-colored gown—she'd stick to stripping today; no need to assay that stomping more than once—ate some bread and cheese and a handful of warm, sweet cherries, then hurried to the press house, ready to tackle her share.

It took her several moments to ascertain that he wasn't among the workers busy at the tables and vats. She joined Veronique at a stripping table and asked, "Have you seen Alain?"

The older woman shook her head. "No. Not all this morning."

"How very strange," Katherine said, and then shrugged. More than likely, he'd gone to his father at the château. Alain, too, must be tiring of sleeping on straw and going barefoot. Soon, very soon, this living-as-a-peasant business would come to an end. Cheerfully she pulled the plump grapes from their stalks, flinging the refuse over her shoulder with a practiced air. The sun was shining, the stompers in the vats were singing, and everything was very much as it had been the day before. And would be the day after, and the day after that . . . *Only not for me,* Katherine thought, with a secret smile that made Veronique smile at her.

"You are in high spirits this morning," the black-haired woman observed, her eyes kind and indulgent. "You have the look of a woman who has been well-loved the night before!"

Katherine blushed and giggled. "Goodness, Veronique! What a thing to say!"

Veronique calmly went on with her work. "When does he intend to make an honest woman of you?"

The blush deepened. "He has already asked me to marry him," Katherine confided.

"Oh, we know that. But you must make him set a date. Youth and high spirits are fine for a time. In the end, though, you must settle down. Have babies."

"I should like to have his babies," Katherine said shyly, even as she wondered why Alain would have told Veronique and Joseph—Veronique *had* said "we"—of his proposal to her. Or perhaps the woman meant that everyone at the vineyard knew?

Veronique laughed and gave her a quick hug with her juice-stained arm. "The two of you will have beautiful children. I am certain of that." Then she went back to the stripping, joining in the grape-stompers' song.

Katherine concentrated on her work. It was growing warm in the press house, and she rubbed her forehead with her sleeve. Without Alain, the aura of wonder she'd felt the day before had dissipated. She began to feel a trifle cross with him. Really, if he insisted on subjecting her to this charade, he might at least endure its tribulations with her. Why, she—

Beside her, Veronique stopped singing in midsyllable. Katherine turned to her anxiously. "Have you cut yourself?" she asked. Sometimes the stalks could be surprisingly sharp. But the men and women in the vats, she noted, had gone silent as well. They were frozen in place, their eyes trained on the wide doors. Veronique was turned in that direction, too.

Katherine glanced at the doorway and saw the small, thin figure of Père Bertrand. Behind him were men on horseback—men who wore the blue-and-white uniform of Napoleon's soldiery. That was very odd. Perhaps they had come to arrest someone for the killing of the man with the red shirt. The priest's eyes swept the assembly of workers—then settled on her. He came toward her through the maze of tables and discarded stems and boys with brooms. The men behind him had dismounted. She saw the priest's brown robe and high white collar, and his wide brown hat, and his face beneath it, pinched and pale.

"Katherine Devereaux?" he said, when he was only a few feet from her. She stared. "You are Katherine Devereaux?

The daughter of the duke of Marne?" he said again, more urgently. There was a commotion beyond the doorway; more men on horseback had come up, hard against the mounts of the blue-and-white soldiers. At the head of this second group of riders was a tall, thin man with a sharp-hooked nose. The seigneur . . . only he could not be the seigneur, because he, too, was in uniform.

Father Bertrand stepped to her, caught her by the hands. "Are you Katherine Devereaux?" he demanded.

"Halt!" shouted the man with the hooked nose, leaping down from his saddle. "How dare you interfere—"

"Oh, my child," the priest said sadly. "Do say yes. Believe me. You must."

The hook-nosed man was striding toward her, his face a study in fury. Katherine was suddenly afraid of him, afraid to her soul. "Yes," she whispered. "Yes."

"Say it!" the priest commanded. "Speak your name, so that all here can witness it."

"I am Katherine Devereaux, daughter of the duke of Marne!" Katherine cried, just as the hook-nosed man reached her. Veronique very bravely stepped in front of her.

"You are too late," she told the tall, thin soldier.

"We'll see about that," he snarled, reaching for Katherine's arm. She remembered well that viselike grip.

The little priest had spun around on his heel and was confronting the much larger officer. "She is right. You are too late," he said calmly. "I have a hundred witnesses who will testify I found her. Give it up, Giacauld." He tucked Katherine's arm into his. "Come along, my child."

"Where—where are we going?" Katherine asked, mystified.

"To your parents, of course. You are going home."

Katherine wrenched away from him. "But I don't *want* to go home! I am *not* going home!" She turned to Veronique. "Where is Alain? I need Alain!"

"He is halfway to Marseilles by now, I imagine," the dark-haired woman told her, her head held high as she stared at the man the priest had called Giacauld. "Or to Nice. Or to Paris, perhaps."

"We *will* find him," the man spat at her. "We found the girl. And we will find him, too."

"*You* did not find her," the priest corrected him. "*I* did. And the ten thousand English pounds—they will go to me." The hook-nosed officer raised his arm as if to strike the little man. "One hundred witnesses," Père Bertrand reminded him.

"*What* ten thousand pounds?" Katherine demanded, her head spinning.

"It is the reward your parents set, child," Père Bertrand explained. "For your safe return."

Wild-eyed, Katherine turned again to Veronique. "You must find Alain—you must tell him! He will not allow this to happen!" But there was a strange distance in those eyes that had been so warm.

Père Bertrand put his arm around her, leading her past the fuming Giacauld to the door. His touch was very kind. "No more of that, child. Who do you imagine it was that told me who you were but Alain Montclair?"

Twenty-four

Katherine was seated in a velvet-cushioned armchair in a suite at the Hotel Luxembourg, wearing the white swansdown gown Madame Villeneuve had made her, and her kidskin boots. She was freshly bathed; her hair had been washed and dressed by the maid, Marie. Across the room from her, her father and stepmother shared a settee. Madame was there as well, as were a French officer—a short, swarthy man with hair cropped close to his head—and an aide to the English ambassador. The latter happened to be Lord Dalrymple, with whom she'd danced on what was to have been her last night in Paris, a million years before.

The French officer cleared his throat. "You understand, Lady Devereaux," he said in heavily accented English, "why you are here." Katherine stared at the patterns in the carpet. Its border was the color of Nuits-Saint-Georges wine.

"You're so very brown," her stepmother murmured. "Dark as a walnut. Didn't you once think to wear a *hat*?"

"Leave her to me, Nanette," the duke told his wife in an ominous rumble. "Let's have this over and done with."

Lord Dalrymple leaned forward in his chair, looking earnestly at Katherine. "If there is anything you can tell us, anything at all that will help us apprehend the man who did this to you—"

"I don't know where he is." Katherine's voice was small.

"Did he never discuss where he meant to take you once the wine harvest was over?" the French officer demanded.

To the château. As his wife. But she did not say that. She was quite certain now that he was no relation to the seigneur, whoever that might be. And as for his never having lied to her—he'd done nothing *but* lie, from the first time she'd met him.

"Did he never discuss—" the French officer began again, more sharply.

"General Fremont. Please." That was Lord Dalrymple, the words polite, but his tone frankly warning. "She has been through enough. Must you badger her?"

"She is the best chance we have for capturing this dangerous criminal! Two times a killer at least—"

"What two times?" Katherine asked idly.

"The woman named Boulé," Dalrymple explained, "and a drifter—a cardsharp—at a country fair."

Alain had sworn he'd killed neither of them. More lies. "He never spoke of what would come after the harvest," Katherine said.

Fremont muttered furiously beneath his breath.

"General . . ." Lord Dalrymple cautioned.

"Does she know we can charge her as an accessory to that drifter's murder?"

"Here, now!" The duke shot up from the settee. "What the devil are you talking about?"

"She was there with him, was she not?"

"I think you are going a bit too far, General Fremont." That was Madame, who looked very thin and frail. "Since when has French law permitted that a victim of a kidnapping be accused of complicity in her tormentor's acts?"

Fremont's swart face twisted with scorn. "Kidnapping? Don't be absurd. She went with him willingly."

"He had impaired her reason," Dalrymple said stoutly.

"Precisely how did he do that?"

"Did he give you wine to drink, Katherine?" her stepmother asked. Katherine nodded. "Well, there! You see! He got her intoxicated."

"The French drink wine with breakfast," Fremont noted disdainfully. "You will have to do better than that."

"Lady Devereaux is nothing but an innocent victim," Dalrymple declared, with surprising passion. "How can you suggest otherwise? That a young English girl, so carefully brought up, so tenderly cared for, could possibly have gone with Montclair of her own free will—"

"If she was so carefully brought up and cared for," Fremont said, "perhaps you can explain how she made her way to France in the first place."

Madame spoke up again. "That was my fault. Entirely my fault."

"Oh, no, Christiane!" the duchess demurred.

"But it was. If I had only fulfilled my duties as her guardian in your absence, she would never—"

"I don't see," Dalrymple broke in, "what any such assigning of blame can contribute. *Just* as I cannot see, General Fremont, why you would even *think* of pressing charges against Lady Devereaux."

The general rose from his chair. "Because she knows where he is."

Katherine started to speak, but Dalrymple silenced her with a swift, pointed glance. "She has already said she does not."

"Then she has some idea, at least." The Frenchman was like a mastiff with a glove; he would not let it go.

The duke had settled back into his seat; he was rubbing the bridge of his nose. "What I cannot comprehend, General Fremont—with all due respect—is why the army should even be concerned with Montclair's whereabouts. He's nothing but a common criminal."

"He escaped from the Bastille!" the general snapped.

Lord Dalrymple, diplomat that he was, attempted to elaborate: "That is considered an affront to the national pride, Your Grace, and—"

"The devil take the national pride!" the duke said impatiently. "It's got nothing to do with our little girl! We have her back safe and sound, and we want only to return her to England. Now! Yesterday!"

"That is not possible." General Fremont was implacable. "She will have to be examined by the police."

"Isn't that what *you* are doing—examining her?" the duchess cried, clearly shaken. "What do you mean—'examined'?"

"Now, see here, Fremont," Dalrymple began. "There is

such a thing as diplomatic immunity. His Grace the duke holds credentials—"

The general brought his fist down on the table beside him with a thump that made them all jump—all but Katherine. "We want Montclair," he reiterated, "and we mean to have him."

"Katherine." Her stepmother looked at her, imploring. "If you know anything . . . anything at all . . ."

"She is covering up for him," Fremont said coldly. "She is in love with him."

"There'll be none of *that* talk!" Dalrymple announced, going livid.

Fremont looked at their horrified faces. His sneer had returned. "What? You think because she is a duke's daughter, she is above such a thing? You think she does not feel the pull of his masculine allure? That she did not—"

Dalrymple actually put a hand to his sword. "One more such insinuation, Fremont, and I'll be forced to challenge you!"

Katherine stared at her unlikely champion. Clearly he was in earnest. Even Fremont backed down—but not all the way. "Ask her," he suggested, his tone plainly indicating what he thought the answer would be. "Ask *her* if she is a victim. Ask her—"

"Your meaning is clear enough," the duke interrupted. He raised his gaze to his daughter. "Katherine. Did Montclair . . . dishonor you?"

Katherine's mind was a jumble of dark nights in nondescript inns, of crackling bedstraw, of whispers and kisses, tobacco and wine. . . . "No," she answered softly.

"You—you understand what he is asking?" the duchess said anxiously. "What he means by 'dishonor'?"

"I do understand. And I say—no."

Madame looked utterly unconvinced. So did General Fremont. But her father was beaming, and Lord Dalrymple's eyes were shining with a holy light. "There!" he declared. "You see, General Fremont, that an Englishwoman's virtue is not so easily relinquished! Tell that to your country's constabulary!"

Fremont was shaking his head in disbelief. "Five weeks she spent with him—*five weeks*—and you expect me to believe—"

"Are you calling my daughter a liar?" the duke demanded, so edgily that the general's dark face went pale.

"I am only *suggesting*," he said, in a more conciliatory fashion, "that she is very young, and was easily led astray."

"She was the victim of a conscienceless kidnapping," Dalrymple declared, "by a man whom you yourself, General, admit is the most sought-after criminal in France. Would you compound the horrors she has endured by ruining her reputation?"

"I never meant—"

"I can't think what *else* you might have meant," the duchess said archly.

"The doormen here at the hotel," Fremont pointed out desperately, "told us she rushed out to him in a rainstorm, in her nightdress, without even shoes on her feet!"

Dalrymple threw up his hands. "Well, there you have it, General! What Englishwoman *ever* would behave that way unless she was afraid for her life?"

"She had opportunity enough to escape from him."

"Escape from him *where*? She doesn't even speak the bloody language!" Dalrymple burst out. "It's not as though he took her from one fine hotel to another! He kept her in—in filthy roadhouses, and then in some godforsaken vineyard, in a hovel with a dirt floor, with no running water, without even a convenience! She is the daughter of the most distinguished duke in England, man! Why in God's name would she put up with such treatment willingly?"

Katherine was listening in utter fascination. It had never once occurred to her, on the long journey back to Paris in the custody of the blue-and-white soldiers, that there would not be hell to pay for what she'd done. Yet here was this earnest young diplomat pleading furiously for her innocence, with her stepmother nodding approval . . . and, by heaven,

General Fremont appeared to be swayed by Dalrymple's out-raged defense. She did not dare look to Madame, though. She was sure enough what emotions she would see *there*.

"It is my understanding," the duchess put in tartly, "that here in France you have done away with distinctions of rank and honor. Let me assure you, sir, that in England, we have *not*. And no daughter of mine, under whatever constraints, no matter *what* the circumstances, would have given her sa-cred honor to a nobody such as Alain Montclair!"

Despite the formidable opposition, Fremont was not will-ing to give in entirely. "With all that said, the fact remains that she may have *unwittingly* learned something of his future plans. Being privy to him for so long a time, it is only natural to assume—"

"You assume too much, General," Lord Dalrymple de-clared. "Perhaps you imagine Lady Devereaux making con-versation with this despicable bounder while she served him tea? Discussing with him current events? News of the world at large? Her innermost thoughts and feelings? Look at her!" He swept his arm toward Katherine, who unconsciously straightened in her seat, settling the skirts of her swansdown gown. "What *possible* subjects of repartee could there be between a young lady such as herself and the miscreant you have described?"

How wine is made. The existence of God. Whether the potage had too much salt. The inequity of a social system based on birth . . .

Yet that system Alain had so scorned, she recognized, was all she had to save her now.

"What *did* you and he talk about?" General Fremont de-manded.

She raised her chin. Her golden ringlets gleamed; sap-phires shone at her ears. "He spoke all the time of the Rev-olution—his admiration of its leveling of the classes."

"And what did you say?"

"I . . . said nothing. What could I reply to such idiocy as that?"

"Spoken as a true duke's daughter," Nanette murmured.

And her father's furrowed brow cleared. Dalrymple was looking at her as though she were the Virgin Mary, that fine and pure. Katherine felt a twinge of conscience—but only a twinge.

If she had learned anything from Alain Montclair—beyond, that is, sorrow and heartbreak—it was this: that one must seize what opportunities came one's way. Hadn't he done exactly that when he'd asked for her pistol in the Bastille? When he'd used her presence in the cart to ease his way out of Paris? When he'd turned her in—how much of the ten thousand pounds, she wondered, had he demanded of Père Bertrand?—for the sake of her parents' reward?

Love was like the peas that stuck to the bottom of the cooking pot—sludge that you scrubbed at and scrubbed at, but that never quite came clean. And faith—faith was a chimera, only there in the darkness, disappearing with first light. She felt as though blinkers had been taken from her eyes. She trained a smile on Lord Dalrymple that was positively dazzling. "I am so glad," she said softly, "that you believe in me."

"The man would be a dastard who did otherwise," he answered solemnly.

General Fremont knew when he was beaten. He rose from his seat, glaring at the duke. "Go on, then. Take her back to England. You are free to leave."

The duchess burst into tears. "Oh, General! We are unspeakably grateful!"

"You are unspeakably *something,* all of you," he retorted, and left them with a click of his heels.

Lord Dalrymple took charge. "I shall arrange for transport first thing in the morning. I'm sure you are all too ready, Your Graces, to leave France behind you."

"Quite right," said the duke. "Must not stay a moment longer than is necessary. Thanks so much, Dalrymple, for your efforts on our behalf. First thing in the morning—how precisely early *is* that?"

Katherine nearly giggled. But seeing Madame's still-tragic expression stifled her. *She is not fooled a bit. . . .*

Dalrymple snapped his heels together as precisely as Fremont had. "Shall we say eleven o'clock, Your Grace?"

"Oh, eleven! Eleven will suit admirably."

"Then I will take my leave. Your Grace. Your Grace." He bowed to the duke and duchess, then approached Katherine. "Lady Devereaux. I only wish I might have spared you . . ."

"You have spared me much," Katherine told him truthfully, and let him kiss her hand.

Twenty-five

"Dinner is served, milady," the butler announced in the drawing-room doorway.

"Thank you, Stoanley. Tell His Grace I'll be there straight-away." The duchess of Marne set down her needlework and rose in a graceful swish of skirts. "Are you coming, Katherine?"

"I'll take the meal here. On a tray."

"I could eat with you," her stepmother offered.

"No. But thank you for offering."

Nanette stood for a moment, contemplating Katherine's blond curls as the girl sat bowed over the cushion cover she was working. She started to speak, then bit her lip and started toward the door. The uneasy truce between her and Katherine of late was far too delicate to withstand overreaching. And Nanette, who had longed for years to win her prickly step-daughter's respect and affection, was determined to take her time.

"I'll have Stoanley bring the tray" was all she said, before starting for the dining room.

The duke was waiting for her there, and had already downed several whiskey-and-sodas, to judge from the flush on his cheeks. She crossed to him and kissed him. "Where is she?" he rumbled in greeting.

"Taking her meal upstairs. Stoanley, see it's sent to her," the duchess told the butler as he slid in her chair.

"Very good, Your Grace."

"Hmph!" said the duke, scowling. "Still ashamed to show her face to me—and so she should be!"

"Richard," Nanette said softly, with a meaningful glance at the servants ringing the room.

"What? What the devil? I'm tired of tiptoeing about, pretending this and that, making excuses for the willful chit! She never gave a moment's thought to how her behavior would reflect on *us*—why should I turn my life upside down on her behalf?"

"That soup smells marvelous, Trent," the duchess noted, nodding at the tureen on the sideboard. "Serve us, won't you?"

The duke leveled a finger at his wife, nearly knocking the ladle from the maid's hand. "And *you* take her side in all this!"

"It isn't taking sides, Richard."

"Well, what the devil do you call it? It's spoiling her, to let her hide away here. If you and she are both so convinced she did nothing shameful, let her hie herself to London and find herself a husband, and relieve me of responsibility for her once and for all!"

"Mmm. Delicious, Trent. My compliments to Cook," the duchess observed, after a sip of the soup.

"Thank you, mum," said the maid, with a nervous bob.

"Where's the bloody wine, Trent?" the duke snapped. "Bring some burgundy!" The maid rushed to do so. It was on the tip of Nanette's tongue to mention that her husband had, by all appearances, already had enough to drink. But she felt for Richard, in his misery and confusion, every bit as much as she did for Katherine. Something had to be done to bring this household back from the brink. Nanette thought longingly of her own childhood home in Cork, of her parents and grandparents and brothers and sisters, and the dogs scrambling for tidbits beneath the table, and the huge bowls of taters and butter and milk, and cheap beer and brown bread, and everyone always, always, talking, shouting, tattling, bickering, but by God, at least sharing it all! Sometimes it seemed that no one in England ever had a real, genuine conversation; they were all too busy keeping those stiff upper lips.

She sipped her soup in silence. Half of Richard's trouble, she knew, was guilt; he was recognizing, belatedly, just how greatly his marriage to her had affected his daughter. Before all this mess with Montclair, he'd always insisted that the ton would come in time to accept Nanette, that she had only to be her lovely, charming self and the dragon-ladies would eventually all be won over—and nothing Nanette had argued could rid him of that conviction. Now, Katherine's head-strong behavior had awakened all his own ingrained reactions to deviance. And he was just beginning to realize that choosing for his second bride an Irish actress with a somewhat careworn reputation had been no less beyond the pale.

Nanette knew little of what the first duchess had been like, other than from the portraits of her that still graced the house. But whatever Nanette might lack in terms of pedigree, she made up for in passion. That passion was what had won the duke's heart. She must cling to that. Somehow, she must make him see that his daughter's unforgivable sins needed to be forgiven. And, more, she must resolve Katherine's future, on which so much of the happiness of the man she loved was pinned.

He hadn't touched his soup, but had downed two glasses of the burgundy when he said suddenly, "She'll be an old maid. No man will have her."

"Darling, how can you say that? She has grown so much, changed so much!"

"She knows it herself. It's why she won't show her face—not even to me, much less to society."

"She needs time, Richard. She's been through such an ordeal—"

He raised his silvery head above the rim of the wineglass, and his eyes were tellingly bright. "You keep on saying that, Nan. 'Give her time.' But who knows how much time I have left? I need to see her settled, dammit! I owe it to her mother. And I want it for myself! Is that so selfish of me?"

Nanette rose from the table, ignoring the startled glances of the servants. She crossed the room to him and knelt at his chair, then pressed her hands to the sides of his face. "We will see her through this, my love. We *will* see her through this. Together."

He turned his head, kissed her fingers. "Oh, Nan. What would I do without you?"

"It has occurred to me," she told him, "that she might not be averse to an outing with her former schoolmates. Something small. Countrified."

"The sort of outing, in other words," the duke said wryly, "she used to so disdain."

Nanette shrugged. "She must start somewhere. If we can find any solace in all of this, Richard, it is that she has discovered her capacity for love."

"She was *abducted*," he began, but without much conviction.

"And, perhaps," the duchess went on smoothly, "that you have discovered her capacity for it as well. It was what you most longed for when you agreed to send her to Mrs. Treadwell's, remember."

His eyes met hers. "So I did," he admitted heavily. "But I never anticipated this."

"Well, you know what we say in Ireland—be wary what you wish for, for it may come true!"

He laughed, just a little. "A country outing. You think you can convince her?"

"I shall do my best. And I'll write to Evelyn and Christiane, to see what on their calendar might prove suitable. Now do eat your soup, my love, before it grows cold." She kissed him swiftly and started to move away. But he caught her and held her, clung to her with sudden force.

"Was it something *I* did, Nan, that made her go with him?" he demanded thickly.

"Oh, Richard. My darling. There is more than enough blame to go around. Don't take on more than your share."

A sennight later, as Katherine sat at the dressing table in her rooms, idly combing out her hair, her stepmother knocked at the door. "Katherine? May I come in?"

"If you like."

Nanette entered, smiling, a little glass of violets in her hands. "I thought you might like these," she explained. "The first from the greenhouses. I know this winter seems endless and dreary, but they are proof—spring will arrive someday!"

Katherine glanced at the flowers without much interest. "They are very pretty. Thank you."

"Do you know what is pretty? No, beyond pretty—beautiful, Katherine. Your hair." Nanette set the vase down on the dressing table and gingerly touched the golden ripples cascading down Katherine's back. "I would sell my soul to have such hair. Would you mind . . . do you think I could brush it? Just this once? And pretend that it is mine, and I'm a fairy princess, and the prince will take one look at me and fall in love?"

Katherine smiled at that, a little. "Go ahead, then."

Nanette picked up the silver-backed brush and made a tentative pass. "When I played Desdemona in London, I wore a wig with such curls. Every time I put it on, I wondered who the unlucky wench was who'd sold such glorious hair, and what had made her do it."

Katherine shrugged. "Craved the money for gin, no doubt."

"Do you think so? I always imagined it quite differently. I pictured her a young bride with a new baby, and her husband killed in Napoleon's wars, and she was desperate for a decent place to live, and because she knew she'd never love anyone again the way that she had loved him, she sold her hair for the sake of their child, and paid her rent for a long, long time."

Katherine's azure eyes met hers in the mirror. "Rather fanciful, don't you think?"

"It could as easily be that as the other," Nanette said blithely. "Besides, a gin-sot's hair would not have had such shine."

That made Katherine giggle. "Have you known a lot of gin-sots, then?"

"Oh, yes. Especially when I first came to London. I was quite penniless, you know. No more to go on than a silly dream to be on the stage." She made another pass with the brush.

"Why would you admire such a shameless profession?"

"Well, it was a step up for me, wasn't it? A brewer's daughter from Cork—anything short of pig herding would have been a step up."

"You've stepped up quite a lot further than that." Katherine's voice held a hint of coolness.

"Oh, I know. Overstepped, in most folks' opinions. Except for my mamma's. She was enraged when I wrote that I was marrying your father. Hasn't written or spoken to me since."

Katherine blinked. "Enraged? Why would she be enraged?"

"She always had it in mind that I would marry Fingal Pherson, that owned the pub around the corner from our house."

"She preferred a publican to a *duke*?"

"Well, of course she did! We all prefer what we're most comfortable with, don't we? That's the great terror of the dragon-ladies of the ton, I think—dealing with unknown quantities. Those whose behavior might not, heaven forfend, be governed by the same set of rules as theirs."

Katherine's eyes had narrowed in the mirror. "But *you* didn't prefer a publican, did you?"

"Fingal was a fool—and a woman-hater. Nothing like a pub for inculcating that. Nothing but men and beer and darts, day in and day out—what would Fingal ever know of what women want and long for?" She paused in her brushing. "Snag here. Might hurt a bit."

"What is it that women want and long for?" Katherine asked guardedly.

"Oh, I'd not dare be so bold as to speak for all women. But I know what it was for me. I wanted a man of passion."

Katherine let out a snort. "And so you married Poppa?"

"I did," said Nanette, not a whit disconcerted. "He's a man of deep beliefs, you know. I saw that more than ever in Russia, where he worked so hard to bring an end to these wretched wars."

"That's not passion," Katherine said dismissively.

"I think it is. That a man with so much wealth, so comfortable a life, should still care about others' suffering—that is passion of the deepest kind."

"The only reason he went to Russia is that you and he had no other place to go. You cannot exactly gad about London, can you? No one respectable will receive him since he married you."

"Is that why you think we stayed at home here?"

"What other reason is there?"

"There was you, Katherine. There always was you."

"Me? You—you abandoned me to Mrs. Treadwell's! You cared nothing about what became of me!"

"I am sorry if you believe that," Nanette said evenly. "Your happiness has always been your father's greatest concern. And because I hold him in such esteem, it has also been mine. It was only after long and deep reflection that we sent you to Mrs. Treadwell's academy. We hoped, you see, that you might . . . make friends."

"Friends?" Katherine sounded aghast.

"Female friends. Confidantes. Intimates. The sort you can tell anything in the world to, and know that they will love you still."

"Mrs. Treadwell's hardly provided that sort of companionship!" But even as she said it, Katherine was remembering, with a twinge of longing, the breakfasts when Alain's gifts would arrive, the shared excitement, the heady feeling of being at the center of attention, Petra's awe, Bess's teasing gibes, Gwen's gentle humor. They *had* been her friends, unworthy though they might be.

Nanette was plying the brush briskly. "When I lived in Cork, my parents sent me to the Academy of the Sacred Heart for my education. I have rarely been so happy as I was there. If you were truly miserable at Mrs. Treadwell's, it is my fault, I suppose. I made the suggestion to your father. I only hoped . . . well. Men come and go in this life, don't they? But woman friends last forever—at least, the right sort do."

Recollections of Mrs. Treadwell's were flooding in on Katherine, piercing her heart. The way the other girls had giggled together at night, after the candles were extinguished. The mirrors shared before country dances, with everyone jockeying for position . . . "It was not all so awful," she said slowly, hesitantly. The fuss over the gloves Alain had sent. The way Bess had danced around the dining room, reading out his poetry . . . "Parts of it were rather fun," she finally confessed.

"I am so relieved to hear you say so! I have been beside myself, worrying that your unhappiness there was what led you to take up with Monsieur Montclair."

"That wasn't it," Katherine admitted, as much to herself as to her stepmother. "That wasn't it at all."

"Well, if that is the case—I might mention I have had a letter from Mrs. Treadwell. She is taking the older girls to her daughter's for a Valentine's Day ball. I thought per-haps—" Nanette hesitated, the brush in midair. "Perhaps you might care to join them."

"No," Katherine said flatly.

"Oh, Katherine. Please. You cannot spend the rest of your life sequestered here! You are causing your father great an-guish. All of his happiness resides in seeing you settled."

"I would be too . . . too . . ." Katherine bowed her head; the word came out as a wisp: "Ashamed."

"Of what? No one here in England knows what went on in France! You may be certain Madame and Mrs. Treadwell have been at the utmost pains—"

"But *I* know, don't I?" Katherine cried despondently. "How am I to behave when a viscount asks me to dance with him? How can I reject him—as I should, by all rights of my birth—when I have—have—" She buried her face in her hands. "Oh, damn him! Damn him for what he has done to me!"

"Katherine." Nanette seized those hands, pried them from her stepdaughter's tearstained face. "You have *nothing* to be ashamed of. A man loved you. You loved him in return—"

"It was not love!" Katherine cried. "It was . . . something dreadful, something animal! Beyond the boundaries of reason—"

"That is what makes me so sure that it *was* love—first love, which is the most desperate of all. But there are other loves, later loves, more settled and reasonable. You must hold to that fact. You must go on from here."

"I don't see how I can," Katherine whispered, her mind a muddle of grapevines and stolen kisses and cooking pots and crackling straw.

Nanette looked down at her. "What will become of you . . . of your father . . . if you do not? Will you have Montclair—this nameless nobody—get the best of you? Will you allow him to ruin your life, when that is so precisely what he set out to do?"

"Oh," Katherine breathed. "It *is* what he was after, wasn't it? To drag me down to his level—"

Nanette had her doubts that had been Montclair's motivation, but she was adept enough at acting to swallow them whole. "I believe it must have been. From what Madame has told me of him, he has not had much exposure to the upper crust. You must have seemed to him as remote and glorious as a star. There always will be those, especially in France, where society is all topsy-turvy, who feel that by degrading others they can lift themselves up."

She watched Katherine's face in the mirror, saw the way her emotions were warring—the regret over what she had done, and the bittersweet memory of it—and she wished, not for the first time, that she might have met Alain Montclair. He had to be a most extraordinary character, really, to have coaxed such outrageous behavior out of this girl.

"You are likely right," Katherine said, with a wisp of a sigh. "Yet he never gave any sign he felt himself my inferior at all . . . or that he felt anything but sorry for me."

"Sorry for *you*?" the duchess said in astonishment. "Whatever for?"

"Oh, for not knowing how to kill a chicken. Have you ever killed a chicken, Nanette?"

"More times than I care to count."

The girl smiled crookedly. "You and he would have made a better match. I was quite hopeless, really. But I tried to learn. I truly did try."

It was the most she had ever spoken about what she had been through. Nanette held her breath, wondering if more would be forthcoming, if the extraordinary honesty would continue. Should she press her? Ask more?

"But the fact is," Katherine went on dreamily, "I was under such a misapprehension. I thought his father owned the château, you see. That I was only playing Cinderella for a little while. And that turned out to be . . . not so."

"I . . . I see."

In the mirror, Katherine's wistful face tilted up to her. "You do see, don't you? Because you have been on the stage. You always told me I should pretend. And you can pretend to be anyone, do anything, so long as you know it's not forever. That someday it will all change."

"When did you realize . . . that he wasn't what he had pretended to be?"

"When he sold me," the girl whispered. "When he sold me to the priest for Poppa's ransom. When I knew the money meant more to him than all that we had shared."

"Oh, my poor Katherine." Nanette instinctively put her arms around her stepdaughter—then recollected herself, and started hurriedly to withdraw. But to her amazement, Katherine would not let her; she clung to her, dissolving into sobs, burying her face against Nanette's fichu.

"I never would have forsaken *him!*" she cried in anguish. "I would have followed him to the ends of the earth—I already had! What more could he have asked of me?"

Very hesitantly, Nanette reached to smooth those remarkable golden curls with her fingertips. "There, there," she whispered. "There, there, my pet. It will be all right. Everything will be all right. You'll see."

"It *won't* be," the girl cried, but Nanette was pleased to hear righteous anger in her tone. "It won't be, because I have made an utter fool of myself, and I have shamed Poppa, and now no man in the world is ever going to wish to marry me!"

"Katherine, how can you believe that? You may say what you please about Montclair, but you are a better person—a better woman—for having known him!"

"Better?" Katherine lifted her tear-stricken gaze in astonishment. "Whatever can you mean?"

"Well, for one thing, you have learned that other females aren't necessarily the enemy," Nanette said shrewdly.

"Oh, you're quite right there!" Katherine declared, rubbing her eyes with vigor. "Men are the enemy! Men such as he!"

Nanette smiled. "No, no. That isn't what I meant. It is more that . . . that other women can be rather handy to have about. To cry with. To share with. To laugh with, sometimes—"

"I don't think," Katherine declared, "that I shall ever laugh again."

"Oh yes you will," Nanette said knowingly. "And someday you will laugh about Alain Montclair."

"Never!"

"About how you ran away from your school to a foreign country for the sake of this man whom you knew nothing about—"

"God, don't remind me!"

"And helped him to escape from the most heinous prison in all Europe—"

"I must have been insane."

"And followed him to the countryside, where you learned to kill chickens—"

"*And* pluck them—and butcher them," Katherine noted with a shudder. "And stomped grapes with my skirts hitched up!"

Nanette gaped. "You stomped grapes?"

"Barefoot! To make the next vintage of Nuits-Saint-Georges!"

"Jesus in heaven. Don't *ever* tell your father that!"

They looked at one another. And Nanette would never afterward be able to say who broke first. She only knew that suddenly they were giggling helplessly, their arms entwined, their foreheads pressed together, tears of mirth streaming down their cheeks.

Katherine *was* the first to draw away, to dab at her eyes with her sleeve. "Nay, I won't tell him. But I don't know how I will ever see that vintage served without wanting to laugh!"

"Nor I, now," the duchess said wryly. "But do you know, I think I will urge the duke to lay in a great store of the '13, and have it served often."

"Why?" Katherine asked in surprise.

Her stepmother reached again, less gingerly, to smooth down her curls. "For the delight," she said simply, "of the secret we'll share."

Twenty-six

"*I have had* the most encouraging letter from the duchess of Marne," the countess d'Oliveri informed Mrs. Treadwell as they sat together in the headmistress's parlor. "She writes that Katherine has every intention of joining the upper-form girls on their visit to your daughter's for Valentine's Day."

"Do you think that wise?" Mrs. Treadwell asked anxiously. "Granted, so far we have managed to contain the damage, as it were. But Vanessa, as you know, has invited quite a number of military officers. Any number of them will surely be aware that. . . . well, that *something* went on in France."

"Speaking of military officers, what do you know about Lord Dalrymple?" Madame inquired airily, plucking at a pulled thread in her skirts.

"Lord Clayton Dalrymple? Why, he is an exceedingly fine catch! Heir to a dukedom, lovely manners, considered handsome . . . why do you ask?"

"He showed great kindness to Katherine in Paris. Indeed, if not for him, I think she might have been imprisoned."

Mrs. Treadwell shuddered. Then she perked up. "You believe he harbors a tendresse for her?"

"I think he might."

Mrs. Treadwell's blue eyes were glowing. "But that would be wonderful! Perfect! Only—do you have any reason for supposing she cares for *him*?"

"I think," Madame said carefully, "she can be brought to. It is inconceivable that she could become enamored of any man and not inform him of her past; she is far too proud for that. But Lord Dalrymple is already acquainted with the salient facts. And despite that, he was her stalwart supporter at our interview with General Fremont in Paris."

Mrs. Treadwell considered this for a long moment. Then she met Madame's gaze straight on. "Christiane. Whatever else might be said of me, I am not the sort to pass off tainted goods as pure, if you follow my drift. Lord Dalrymple comes from an estimable family."

"As does Katherine."

"Dash it all, you know what I mean! If she . . . had relations with that murderer—"

"Lord Dalrymple is twenty-eight years old. Do you suppose him a virgin?"

"It is different for men, and you know it!"

"I rather thought we had agreed when we founded this academy that it should not necessarily be so."

"If Montclair had been someone of consequence, instead of a common criminal—"

This was one of the rare moments when the countess showed impatience with her old friend. "If Lord Dalrymple had slept with a score of Fleet Street harlots, would it be counted against him in the marriage mart?"

"Likely not."

"Then if Katherine—and I am *not* saying she did—slept with *one* man who by all accounts is an extraordinary charmer, why should you hold it against her?"

"Because," Mrs. Treadwell began forcefully, and then faltered. "Because . . . because, dash it all, a girl must be more careful of her reputation than a man! The fact is, this missy absconded to a foreign nation, aided and abetted a felon's escape from prison, and then went off to spend a month's idyll with him in the countryside! In a dirt-floored hovel!"

The countess shot her a sidelong look. "Makes you wonder, doesn't it, what Montclair might have had to offer?"

"Well . . ." Then Mrs. Treadwell recollected herself. "It certainly wasn't honorable!"

Madame took a sip of sherry, hiding her smile. "That, in the end, is for Katherine to decide. But I am delighted that she is strong enough, after her ordeal, to make a public appearance, and even more delighted that it is to be at Vanessa's, since you can arrange for Lord Dalrymple to be there."

"It seems a dreadful trick to play on the man," Mrs. Treadwell said dubiously.

"If you had witnessed his spirited defense of her virtue in Paris, you would not say that."

"Are you telling me he actually believes she wasn't in love with Montclair?"

"I would not presume to know Lord Dalrymple's mind. But I am fairly certain that even if he thinks she *was* in love with Montclair, he is assured enough of his own worth to trust he can make her forget him."

Mrs. Treadwell's pale eyes were yearning. "If only we might salvage some sort of happy ending from this dreadful morass . . ."

"See that Dalrymple is at Vanessa's," Christiane counseled sagely. "I venture you will see your dearest wishes granted. In fact, I will wager you five pounds on it!"

Twenty-seven

Mrs. Treadwell's daughter Vanessa, the countess of Yarlborough, was in her element. Two hundred guests were expected for the evening—just the sort of occasion that brought out the best in her. She darted about the ballroom, issuing directives regarding the placement of tables and chairs and potted palms, in an ecstasy of excitement. Her mother, meanwhile, was attempting ineffectually to keep her two grandsons from skidding across the highly polished floor.

"And the candelabra a bit more to the left," Vanessa was saying, as a harassed majordomo adjusted the lighting. "Is there a *spot* on that cloth?" Her eldest son escaped from his grandmother's clutches to mount a frontal assault on his mamma. "No, Peter!" Vanessa cried in horror. "Not in this dress! Mother, can't you *control* them?"

"Can't *you*?" Mrs. Treadwell muttered under her breath.

A carriage came rumbling up the drive. "Oh, dear Lord," Vanessa declared, "there is nothing I hate so much as early arrivals." She clapped her hands for the boys' nanny, who was sampling the salmon hors d'oeuvres. "Piers! Take these ruffians upstairs at once!"

"Very good, mum." The nanny collared the boys with far more force than Mrs. Treadwell felt necessary. But she held her tongue, observing through the windows that the precipitious visitor was in uniform, and had a handsome yellow mustache.

"Is that Lord Dalrymple?" she asked of Vanessa, who gave a careless glance.

"God, so it is. Trust a military man to hold to the hours on an invitation. Anyone else would know that half past eight means half past nine. Would you mind greeting him, Mamma? I simply *must* do something about my hair."

"I'd be delighted," said Mrs. Treadwell, and made her way to the entrance hall as Vanessa escaped up the stairs.

Lord Dalrymple gave his hat to the butler, then bowed low, seeing his hostess's mother coming forward. "Mrs. Treadwell. What an honor to be invited here by your daughter. I do hope we are to have the pleasure this evening of the company of your students."

"La, Lord Dalrymple! Surely a man of the world such as yourself is beyond the company of schoolgirls!" Mrs. Treadwell said breathlessly.

"It has always been my belief," Lord Dalrymple noted very gravely, "that when a man is in search of a wife, he does well to seek one younger than himself."

As if on cue, Gwen and Bess came tripping down the staircase. "I declare," Mrs. Treadwell said with a matronly giggle, "here are two of my charges now! Miss Carstairs, may I present Lord Dalrymple?"

"Charmed, I'm sure," Gwen said, offering her hand.

"And Miss Boggs." Bess offered her hand as well. But the gestures went unheeded; Lord Dalrymple's gaze was fixed on another figure that had started to descend.

"Lady Devereaux." His deep voice echoed in the silence. "What unspeakable pleasure to see you again."

Bess had drawn back her hand. "Hmph," she muttered to Gwen. "I might as well be wall-covering. As usual."

"Hush," Gwen said sharply. She, too, was watching Katherine, who was wearing a stunning white swansdown gown she had bought, she'd told them, in Paris. The haughty duke's daughter had paused on the stairs, seemingly reconsidering whether she would come down at all.

"Lord Dalrymple," Katherine whispered, her gloved hands clutched together tightly. "I did not expect to see you here."

"His Excellency the ambassador was kind enough to relinquish my services for a time."

"That was very good of him." Still Katherine stood poised halfway down, gloved fingers clenching and unclenching.

"I have been hoping, ever since the last time we met," Lord Dalrymple said with a winning smile, "that you might do me the great honor of dancing with me again, as we did in Paris."

"If *that's* what she was doing in Paris," Bess hissed to Gwen, "I hardly see why everyone is tiptoeing about!"

"Would you hush?" Gwen hissed back, her dark eyes on Katherine, who suddenly did not look one bit haughty or proud. She appeared . . . abjectly ashamed.

Katherine's gaze flew to Mrs. Treadwell. "I . . . I am sorry," she said softly. "I know you mean the best. But I simply *cannot*—" She turned to flee.

"Lady Devereaux!" Lord Dalrymple took the stairs at a bound, catching her hand. She tried to shake him off, but he held on tight as he spoke to her, so softly that Bess, who was straining her ears, could not hear. Katherine averted her face. Again he whispered, gently coaxing. She murmured back, color slowly flooding her cheekbones. And then, astonishingly, Lord Dalrymple said *something* that made her laugh— not her old laugh of disdain, but a rich ripple, like wind blowing over still water. It was a laugh no one at the academy had ever heard before from her, and it made Mrs. Treadwell and the girls stare.

"That's better," declared Lord Dalrymple, tucking Katherine's arm into his and leading her down the staircase. "Now do come along. I've offended our hostess immeasurably by showing up on time, but I was very much afraid that if I didn't, you would try some such foolishness as hiding in your rooms. And you are far too lovely, Lady Devereaux, to stay hidden away."

Her cheeks still becomingly flushed, Katherine went with him willingly if nervously, sweeping past Gwen and Bess in a rustle of swansdown. Mrs. Treadwell was beaming; she followed in the couple's wake like a proud mother hen.

Bess looked after the small procession, shaking her head. "I swear," she muttered in fury. "Only Katherine could come out of such a mess smelling like roses—and with the handsomest man in England paying court to her!"

"I hope he can help her find happiness," Gwen said quietly.

Bess whirled on her. "As for *you*, you are too good for words! *Don't* tell me you're not envious!"

"It's rather odd," Gwen mused, watching Lord Dalrymple escort their former classmate into the ballroom, "but I'm not sure I am."

Lord Dalrymple was exquisitely attentive, Katherine found, anticipating her tangled emotions, taking care to see to her every need. She had only to fan herself for him to suggest they sit for a spell; once, when she tentatively started to say she was thirsty, he held a finger up and left her, returning with a cup of punch. She drank the sugary stuff down. It had none of the subtlety of French wine, but neither did it evoke a flood of memories.

She was drowning in memories these days. Sunlight made her think of that day on the riverbank, and the bright-spangled water she'd crashed through to find him. Clouds put her in mind of the rain that had pattered on the cottage roof. The soft silk of her gowns reminded her of his black hair, and the way his queue had always unworked itself when they made . . .

Love. But they had not made love—at least, he had not. Oh, God, would she never stop thinking of him? Resolutely she turned to Lord Dalrymple, sought to concentrate on what he was saying. "Of course, no one knows for certain," he told her in his deep, reassuring voice. "But it seems only a matter of time now before the Corsican is defeated once and for all." His hand found hers, squeezed it. "Peace will be a welcome relief, don't you agree?"

Peace. An unimaginable concept. She forced herself to look at her companion, truly look at him. His blue eyes were more pale than Alain's, but at least they were honest. He was tall, suave, polished. He was the heir to a dukedom.

And when he touched her hand, she felt nothing—only deadness. *Damn you to hell, Alain.*

Vanessa's rout was now in full swing; fashionably turned-out guests filled the vast, gilded ballroom. Dalrymple caught sight of someone he knew. "There is Lord Bannister. I did not expect to see him here. He served for a time with me at the embassy in Paris."

Katherine hung back. "*Must* we greet him?"

Dalrymple glanced down at her, those blue eyes kind. "Lady Devereaux, anyone who has been in France these past few months can only sympathize with your . . . travails. They all know of Montclair."

"That is what I am afraid of."

His mouth, broad and generous, tugged upward beneath his mustache. "I meant—they know his reputation. His crimes."

"Then they must know of mine."

"Your only crime," he told her, "was in being in the wrong place at the wrong time. You are an innocent bystander, swept into disaster against her will."

Where was my will when I put my mouth to his manhood? Her blush was blossoming again.

"Lord Dalrymple!" Lord Bannister was making his way to them across the room. He was a stout, red-faced man with a chestful of military honors. "What a pleasure, my dear boy! What a distinct pleasure!"

"Lord Bannister," Dalrymple said politely, "permit me to present Lady Devereaux."

Katherine was watching closely, to see if His Lordship would betray what he must know of her. But he smiled quite enchantingly, and bent to kiss her hand. "The pleasure is all mine."

"Lord Bannister. Sir." For the life of her, Katherine could think of no more to say. Fortunately, Lord Dalrymple jumped into the breach, asking after mutual acquaintances. After some few minutes of conversation, Bannister announced himself in need of refreshment and, with a courteous bow, headed off to the wine tables.

"There," Dalrymple murmured, "that was not so bad, was it?"

"He was most . . . gentlemanly."

Dalrymple turned to her. "What else did you expect? I

assure you, those in possession of the facts about your abductor are precisely those most likely to sympathize with you. As for the rest of these folk—" He waved a hand at the glittering assembly. "They know nothing of what went on. And I swear to you, on my *life,* that they never shall."

"If only I could believe that," Katherine said wistfully.

Those eyes that had seemed so pale were burning with intensity. "I said—I swear it on my life."

"I don't see . . ." Katherine began hesitantly. Then she stopped.

"Don't you?" he whispered.

Katherine's head was beginning to spin. "Do you think . . . we might—"

"Get some air." She was taken aback again at how he had divined her thoughts. "I think it would be wise."

He led her through the French doors to the terrace. After the press of bodies in the ballroom, the February night was shockingly bracing. Katherine could not help shivering. Even as she did, Lord Dalrymple removed his coat and set it over her shoulders. His fingers brushed the nape of her neck, and this time, as he touched her, she felt a small frisson. Though it might have only been the chill . . .

He gestured to the low wall. "Shall we?" She nodded, and he lifted her up, his hands on her waist. When he had set her there, he stood back a pace, staring at her. Self-conscious, Katherine clutched the coat tight at her throat. Above their heads, a billion stars glittered in the night sky. The stones beneath her were cold.

"You are . . . so very beautiful," he whispered.

She could not meet his gaze. "Lord Dalrymple, you have been extraordinarily kind to me. Here, tonight . . . and before. In Paris. When you stood up for me against General Fremont—"

"Fremont is an idiot. A blusterer. The son of a pickle maker. He has no notion what a woman such as you is like."

Katherine looked down at her hands. Her heart was pounding. "Milord. Just the same, there is something you should know. I—"

He put his forefinger to her lips. She was surprised by its warmth. "Hush," he told her. "I don't want to hear it. All I want is for you to be happy. Cherished. To be loved . . . as you deserve."

"But I don't deserve—"

"God, you do!" His finger slid across her cheek; he stroked her hair with his palm. She drew back, staring up at him in the starlight.

He smiled. His hand settled on her shoulder. Their breath made clouds in the night.

He leaned down and kissed her with infinite gentleness, the merest wisp of a kiss.

At the press of his mouth on hers, Katherine was consumed by a maelstrom of emotions: shame, aversion, fear, and, illogically, a thin thread of longing. Was it possible, what he proposed? Could she ever be happy again? Did she deserve to be loved, after all her sins?

Already he had pulled away. "Forgive me," he said. "I should not have done that."

But that hint of promise, that whisper of potential passion, had made a sea change in Katherine. If she could feel, even so faintly, a reflection in his kiss of what had been in Alain's, was there not hope for her after all? She was struck lightheaded by the prospect of a future filled with all she had once dreamed of. A husband. A family. An honorable life.

"You," she began. "You . . ."

"I see you have discovered my secret," he murmured, and brought his hand up once more to her shining hair. "I love you, Katherine. I have from that first time we danced."

"*How* can you love me, when you know—"

"It only makes me love you more. The tribulations you endured . . . your spirit in the face of them . . . Oh, Katherine. I do not mean to rush you. But I have been able to think of nothing but you ever since we parted."

"You were so stalwart. My champion."

"You needed one," he said stoutly.

"I never imagined I would find such a one as you."

He caught up her hand, kissed her fingers. "Is there hope, then, for my suit?"

"I—"

"Katherine Devereaux!" Mrs. Treadwell's voice rang out from the doorway. "It is high time you came back inside, or you will catch your death of cold!"

But Katherine did not feel cold anymore; she felt warm to her toes, to her heart. Lord Dalrymple smiled wryly. "Forgive me, Mrs. Treadwell. You are quite right. I ought not to have kept her out this long."

"No, you ought not," the headmistress scolded. But she was smiling as Lord Dalrymple stole one more quick kiss, then lifted Katherine from the wall. His hands were so sure. . . .

"Supper is being served," Mrs. Treadwell observed, as the wayward pair made their way back through the doors. "Did you think to keep her out there all night, Dalrymple?"

"Oh, I would have if I could," he murmured, his arm caressing Katherine's waist as he took back his coat.

Twenty-eight

"Flowers!" Petra Forrester exclaimed in excitement, seeing Clarisse bear a truly overwhelming arrangement of stately ivory lilies into the dining room of the academy. "Whoever are they for? Why, we haven't had flowers on the mantel since Katherine's secret admirer! And now you come back to visit us, Katherine, and it all begins again!"

"Do stop prattling, Petra," Mrs. Treadwell said sharply, making the girl stare.

"Is there a poem with them?" another of the lower-formers asked. "Perhaps it is the secret admirer again, risen from the dead!"

"No poem," declared Bess, who had gone to the mantel. "Only a card. They're from Lord Dalrymple, Katherine."

Petra let out a sigh. "I suppose every suitor can't be a poet, eh, Katherine?"

Katherine had joined Bess at the mantel, to inhale the sweet, spicy scent of the lilies. "Some things are more important than poetry, Petra."

And Petra was so surprised by not being snapped at that she nodded agreement. "Yes. You are certainly right. Pretty words *are* only pretty words."

Madame was watching Katherine closely. She had had, of course, a full report from Mrs. Treadwell of the goings-on at Vanessa's, and it had done much to soothe her conscience. She was still convinced she should have been more vigilant in Paris—and that she *never* should have taken Katherine to the Bastille. But if the exceedingly eligible Lord Dalrymple was paying Katherine court, her worries were over. The rest of the ton would take its cue from him.

Katherine turned to her, her blue eyes luminous. "Do come

and try the scent of them, Madame. They are lovely, aren't they?"

Madame approached the mantel, giving the girl's hand a quick squeeze. "Exceedingly lovely, my dear."

Lord Dalrymple's courtship proceeded at a more leisurely pace than the secret admirer's whirlwind of gifts and poesy. But Katherine, installed again at Marne House, found relief in its very measuredness; it gave her a chance to keep her head above water this time. Over the Easter holidays, she saw him several times, at a ball given by the Tathams and a hunt party at Vanessa's as well as on a visit he made to her parents' home. He was always the same, marvelously attentive, kind and gentle. But she began to sense, beneath the surface of his brief, sweet kisses, a resolute strength in him. He was giving her time. He was not smothering her. But he meant to have her for his wife. A conversation they had at Marne House made that clear.

It was a crisp, overcast afternoon in late March, with a hint of snow in the air. Nanette had suggested that Katherine show their guest the gardens, and though there was little more in them at this time of year than gray stalks and dry leaves, he agreed to the outing, with just enough of a smile darted at Katherine that she knew he found the notion as silly as she did. They strolled out from the dining room through the French doors and took the brick walk that led down to the folly her father had erected, a sort of Greco-Roman ruin set in a circle of trees. Katherine was well bundled, in a coat of marten fur with a cavernous hood, but Lord Dalrymple wore only his military coat and hat. She thought he must be very cold.

"Not especially scenic just now," Katherine apologized as they approached the artfully tumbled Doric columns and bas-reliefs.

He looked down at her and grinned. "I am enjoying the view."

"I must say, I find it quite absurd for Poppa to have spent

so much money installing a small corner of Athens here in Kent."

"Do you? I think it noble enough. The past has lessons for us all." Katherine winced, and he caught it. "I meant," he elaborated quietly, "the historical past."

"The more recent past as well, in my case," Katherine acknowledged ruefully, running a gloved finger along the sheet of ice that capped a bronze sundial.

Dalrymple turned on the path, standing squarely before her. "Tell me. What have you learned?"

"Oh—" She could not begin to think of what to answer. "I suppose . . . that one's heart is not to be trusted."

"Never say that," he responded, so swiftly and passionately that she was taken aback. "It is my greatest fear, you know. That you will never allow yourself to love again."

She dropped her gaze to the bricks. "How do you know . . . that I loved him?"

"If you hadn't, your behavior would truly have been incomprehensible."

"I made such a *fool* of myself," she murmured.

"Isn't that the purpose of love? To show us, all of us, that we are not so strong and self-sufficient as we imagine ourselves to be?"

She raised wide, startled eyes. "Oh! Sometimes I think that you can read my mind! That is precisely how I felt . . . as though I needed no one. That no one was worthy of me. And now I find quite the opposite to be the case. I am no longer deserving of an honest man's love."

"I am an honest man."

"So you are." She tried to laugh. "I almost wish you weren't. Then I would not feel so sullied in your presence."

"I could attempt dishonesty," he offered. "Embezzle from the treasury. Steal your jewels."

She could not help laughing now. "I do not think that you could pull it off."

"Likely not. But I would try." He reached for her gloved hand, raised it to his lips. "For your sake."

"I cannot comprehend what you might see in me," she whispered.

He looked above her, up into the steel-blue sky. "I love . . . your spirit," he said finally. "I have met so many simpering misses, so many spineless ladies of leisure, happy to sit and gossip and embroider while life passes them by. *You* will never let life pass you by. You are the sort who seizes it boldly, fearlessly. I could never be content with a cipher of a woman. There is great passion in you, Katherine. And the truth is . . . in some Byzantine way, I find myself grateful to Montclair for showing that. For bringing it to the fore."

"Oh, Lord Dalrymple." Katherine was touched to her soul. "What a remarkable thing to say."

"It's God's truth. Let us be plain with one another, my dear. There is much in my own past that it shames me to recall. A diplomat . . . foreign lands, foreign ladies . . ."

"I quite understand," Katherine murmured, coloring.

"I'm not certain you do. Compared to some of *my* youthful foibles, your experience is rather pallid. Not," he added hastily, "that I mean to make light of it. Only to say . . . well. Were you the male partner in what went on, no one would blink an eye. Somehow that hardly seems fair."

"A woman's virtue is her most treasured possession," Katherine responded, quoting Mrs. Caldburn.

"Do you honestly believe that? More than her heart? Her fire and light?"

"Having parted with it, I would gladly be convinced otherwise," she said abjectly.

"Katherine. May I call you Katherine? It matters not—I must call you Katherine now. For this. You are the most exciting, most *vital* creature I have ever known. I am twenty-eight years old, and never once before have I felt anything was lacking from my life, that I would not be most happy to go on from day to day precisely as I have. Not until I met you. Now, suddenly, I find myself impossibly distracted—from my work, from sport, from the very act of breathing at times. Your face, your image, haunts me."

It seemed a fair summation of what she'd known of love

so far. And it seemed so very distant from contentment. She voiced the thought: "What about . . . happiness?"

"Ah." He took her hand again. "The happiness will come when the object of this desperate longing is mine at last." He saw her about to speak, and forestalled her with his fingertip. "But I intend to proceed slowly. I'll not press you. You need time to learn to trust your heart again. Know this, though: That is what I live for. The day you speak this one word to me: Yes."

She very nearly said it then, seeing him standing before her, so tall and manly and appealing. He was right, though. To make the same mistake twice, to speed headlong into love again, would be worse than foolish. It would be unforgivable. Not from the ton's view, but from her own.

"You are very wise, Lord Dalrymple," she told him, and smiled, though a tear was trembling at the edge of one eye.

He saw it fall and caught it on the tip of his finger, his hand caressing her cheek. "Mind you don't forget that, and lose your heart to some other man."

"I . . . I think that I have lost it already."

"God, I pray so." He bent down and touched his mouth to hers. He tasted clean and fresh as snow.

"You truly are my champion, aren't you?" Katherine whispered in wonder.

"I always will be."

"And to think I once believed I never would know love again."

"Oh, Katherine. I intend to shower you—nay, to deluge you, to *storm* you with love until the end of my days."

"Katherine!" The duchess's cry echoed over the frozen ground from the dining-room doors. "Vincent says there is snow on the way! You had best come in!"

"The head groundskeeper," Katherine explained, and giggled. "He has an old war wound that aches when the weather is inclement—or so he claims."

"No one should ignore an aching, ever," Lord Dalrymple said, pressing her hand to his heart for a moment before gallantly leading the way back inside.

Twenty-nine

That spring was, by common agreement, the most lovely in memory. The days were unseasonably balmy and dazzling with sunshine; the nights were cool and rife with breeze. The primroses at Marne House unfurled their velvety heads; the fields surrounding the manse were a golden haze of broom. Hawthorn trees spilled their rich scent like unstoppered perfume flagons, and the rush of the swollen river and streams made a backdrop to the symphony of birdsong that rose in the crystalline skies.

Katherine was happy. Against all odds, she had found happiness again, in Lord Clayton Dalrymple. He called on her each Sunday, making the lengthy drive from London, where he had now been posted, simply for the pleasure of her company. She could not quite believe he was willing to forgo the swirl of city society and its eligible misses for the sake of a walk along country lanes or horseback ride through the pastures with her. Yet Dalrymple insisted it was his greatest joy. When he returned to the city, he sent her gifts, small things, proper things, little tokens that she need feel no shame in acknowledging—a letter opener handled in mother-of-pearl, a volume of Milton, a beautiful lacquer-and-plume pen. And once a week, every Thursday, there were flowers from him on the mantel—always lilies, but each time a different hue.

Her father was impressed. "Seems you have made quite a conquest, Katherine," he boomed at dinner one evening in April, observing the latest delivery—a cloud of gorgeous blossoms of a devastating salmon—decorating the mantelpiece.

"He must be running out of colors, don't you think?" Nanette asked slyly, ladling out sauce.

Katherine laughed, the unaccustomed sweet trill that

warmed her stepmother's heart. "I imagine he is," she acknowledged. "He will have to switch soon to some other
posy."

"Or," her father noted, "buy you a wedding bouquet, and
have done with all this courtship nonsense."

"No need to rush matters along, Richard," the duchess observed quietly.

The duke of Marne sliced into the roast mutton. "Seems
to me if his intentions are honorable—" Katherine gave a
little gasp. Nanette scowled at her husband, who looked up
from the meat in confusion. "What? What did I say?"

"I'm quite certain his intentions are nothing but honorable!" Nanette told him hotly, wondering how in the world
men could be so dense. The last thing Katherine's fragile
sense of self required was an insinuation that Dalrymple, one
of the very few eligible men acquainted with the truth of her
French sojourn, might be leading her on!

Katherine, however, had recovered her composure—and a
touch of her old hauteur. "I'll have you know, Poppa, his
intentions are *sterling*. He has told me I only have to say the
word."

"And you haven't yet?" her father demanded. "Good God,
girl, what are you waiting for? Do you think such chances
come along every day?"

Katherine cast a despairing glance at her stepmother, who
calmly went on buttering her asparagus as she said, "It is
always a grave mistake, Richard, for a man to believe a
woman's heart too easily won."

He stared at her, chewing. "What the hell is that supposed
to mean?"

Nanette's gray gaze slanted toward him mischievously. "A
wise, silver-haired diplomat such as you, love, doesn't know
the error of over-quick capitulation to the enemy?"

"The *enemy*—" His eyes went wide. Then he barked a
laugh. "You are only jesting with me, aren't you?"

"Of course," she told him, with a bedazzling smile.
"Would you slice me just a bit more mutton? The crispy

outside; you know that is what I love best. Next to you, of course."

And Katherine, with her hard-won new knowledge of the ways of the sexes, buried her smile as her father beamed at his wife and dutifully cut her off a choice tidbit, offering it on the point of the knife.

When he had withdrawn to his study for port and a cigar and the London newspapers, she was quick to express her thanks: "Oh, Nanette, I am ever so grateful. I don't know how you managed to turn him off the subject like that—"

"I have generally found that food can distract a man from almost anything," Nanette said with a wink. Then she leaned toward Katherine across the table. "So! Lord Dalrymple has asked you to marry him! Did you never think to share that with me?"

Katherine actually blushed. "I . . . I meant to. But I was waiting until—" The blush intensified, and she finished in a mumble: "Until I had decided whether to say yes."

"Do you love him?" Nanette inquired.

"I'm not at all sure I know what love is anymore."

"I see." The duchess topped off her wineglass with more of the excellent Nuits-Saint-Georges they were drinking, then filled Katherine's as well.

"I mean," Katherine began, then stopped, then began again: "It is so dreadfully confusing! I thought I loved Montclair. I *knew* I loved Montclair! And yet it all turned out to be . . . It is very hard to trust one's heart, when one has been so horribly deceived."

The duchess sipped from her glass. "I quite understand. Let us leave love aside, then, for now. You *like* Dalrymple, don't you?"

"Oh, yes!" Katherine said fervently. "He is the kindest man I ever have known."

"You find him . . . attractive? Appealing? In the physical sense, I mean."

"Gracious sakes, Nanette!"

The duchess smiled. "It is an important point of consideration, you know."

Katherine was toying with her wineglass, her slender fingers running up and down the stem. "It is not at all, Mrs. Caldburn at the academy always said. Mrs. Caldburn said—"

"Mrs. Caldburn is an idiot. When you marry a man, you commit to his bed. If you cannot abide the prospect of that—on the contrary, if it does not make you tingle with excitement—"

"I am quite sure Mamma would never have spoken of such things to me!" Katherine cried, embarrassed.

"Perhaps not," Nanette mused, staring into the rich crimson of her wine. "But she would have done you a disfavor."

Katherine's shoulders came up. "I hardly think it's for the likes of you to judge my mamma!"

"The likes of me." Nanette smiled a little, then took a sip from her glass.

Katherine was embarrassed again. "I did not mean that the way it sounded. You . . . you really have been very good to me. And to Poppa. You *are* good for him; I can see that now. It is just that—" And then the dam burst. "One of the girls at the academy said such horrid, wretched things about you! That you had bedded half the nobility in London! That you only married Poppa for his money!"

"Do you believe that, Katherine?" Nanette asked, her voice still calm and quiet. "Because if you do, you are a fool—and while I've called you many things in my mind these past seven years, that was never among them." Her eyes were bright with intensity. "There are fortunes greater than your father's. There are titles as dignified. I married him for one reason only—because I loved him. And I love him still, despite the fact that, like most men, he can be wrongheaded and thick. It would be a very small sort of woman, I think, who would wed a man for money. I had money of my own. I had no need of his."

"Money of your own?" Katherine asked in amazement.

Her stepmother smiled. "The most valuable thing a woman can ever have. Did you think I worked the world's stages for twenty years for small beer? Granted, it might not match up against your father's fortune. But it would have kept me in silk and baubles through the end of my life—if silk and baubles were all I cared about. On the night your father asked for my hand and I said yes, he cried. He needed me far more than I needed him."

That was a novel thought. And yet, as Katherine reflected on the long stretch of her father's bachelorhood that had followed her mother's death, it seemed plausible. Marne House had not exactly been a haven of joy in those days.

"I don't know what would have become of us without you," she admitted, surprising herself. But she'd surprised Nanette even more; her stepmother's face positively glowed.

"Oh, Katherine. What a—a *generous* thing for you to say. Considering that I am, after all, a brewer's daughter from Cork."

"I imagine your poppa made very fine beer," Katherine said with a giggle. "The Irish equivalent of Nuits-Saint-Georges."

"That he did," Nanette retorted proudly, raising her glass to Katherine's with a smile.

Thirty

It wasn't long before Katherine made another visit to the academy. Against all odds, she found herself anxious to hear what Bess and Gwen, not to mention Mrs. Treadwell and Madame, might have to say about whether she should accept Lord Dalrymple's suit. Nanette had so far refused to counsel either yea or nay; she kept repeating that her stepdaughter must listen to her own heart. While Katherine knew that was true, she wanted to learn what a wider circle of women might think of her beau. And perhaps . . . perhaps she longed, just a little, to be the object of her schoolmates' envy again.

She had written to Lord Dalrymple, of course, to tell him she would not be at home for their accustomed Sunday visit. He wrote back that he was most disappointed, but would bide his time until Sunday next. Katherine read the brief missive, set out in a diplomat's plain, clear hand, with a pang of disappointment. It was highly complimentary and full of regret, but it did not inspire her to tuck it against her heart.

At the academy, Mrs. Treadwell engineered for the upper-form girls to be alone with her and Madame in the dining hall after dinner, and broke out a bottle of her sherry. Gwen and Bess, in great good humor, regaled their former school-mate with tales of their latest failures in the social world: Gwen, it seemed, had accidentally offended a very good-looking viscount by telling him all about her dissection of a fetal pig while they were dancing; Bess reduced Katherine to tears of laughter by relating how one of Mrs. Tattersall's creations had simply disintegrated—first the sleeves, then the neck, then the entire bodice—while an overenthusiastic young officer had waltzed with her at Vanessa's last ball.

"I always said that woman couldn't sew a fit stitch, didn't I?" Katherine demanded, wiping her eyes with her kerchief.

"I wouldn't say that," Bess demurred, with a devilish grin. "The corset, at least, held fast!"

"But what is news with you?" Gwen asked, leaning toward Katherine across the table. "That exceedingly good-looking soldier who squired you about at Vanessa's—have you seen him again?"

"Any number of times," Katherine confessed, then hesitated. "He—he has asked for my hand," she finally said.

"Oh, Katherine, how splendid!" Mrs. Treadwell cried in delight, with a triumphant smile at the countess.

"I am not a bit surprised," Madame declared. "I knew the first time I saw you dance with him, back in Paris, that he'd lost his heart."

"I'm so happy for you, Katherine. When is the wedding to be?" Gwen asked.

Katherine looked down at her sherry. "I . . . haven't yet said yes to him."

"What, are you daft?" Bess said in astonishment. "He is outrageously handsome!"

But Mrs. Treadwell was nodding sagely. "You are wise to bide your time, Katherine. Make him think you hard-won. Still, you must take care you do not give a fish too much line."

"Nonsense, Evelyn," Madame said crisply. "If she loves him, she ought to tell him so."

Katherine colored very becomingly. "I have told him. Though not . . . in so many words."

Bess threw up her hands. "If you love him and he loves you, then what is the sense in dissembling? It hardly seems honest to me."

Katherine's blue eyes clouded over. "You don't understand. Lord Dalrymple knows certain things about me . . . about my sojourn in France. . . ."

"I believe," Mrs. Treadwell interjected tactfully, "what Katherine is trying to say is that she wants to assure Lord Dalrymple that she is not flighty. The sort of girl whose fancies are likely to flit from man to man."

"Exactly," Katherine agreed. "If—and I can scarcely believe it myself—he is willing to marry me, I at least owe him proof of my constancy."

Gwen had been quietly musing. Now she spoke up: "That fellow you went to France for—the secret admirer. Have you ever heard any news of him?"

"No. And I pray I never do." She meant the words as she said them. But deep in her breast, her heart tightened like a wound harp string.

"There was nothing honorable about him at all," Mrs. Treadwell sniffed.

"There must have been," said Bess, not quite willing to join in the general disdain.

"Whatever do you mean?" Katherine asked tentatively.

"Why—he wrote you such extraordinary poetry."

"I daresay he stole it from somebody else," Mrs. Treadwell declared.

"I don't know," Bess said dubiously. "I have read most of the English poets, and I've never run across those verses. Madame, have you?"

Madame paused, her wineglass halfway to her lips, torn between wishing Katherine an assured future and some dregs of loyalty to Alain Montclair, with whom the French authorities had surely caught up by now. "He penned them himself," she said finally, with an image in her mind of that brazen, raven-haired thirteen-year-old boy who'd refused to leave the doorstep of La Maison de Touton. "He told me so."

"If any man wrote me poetry such as that," Bess said wistfully, "I don't think I could ever love another."

"Then you are a fool and a dreamer. Pretty words are only pretty words," Mrs. Treadwell noted, with more vehemence than any of them would have expected.

Bess thought about protesting, but the sudden dreamy expression on Katherine's face made her reconsider. "I'm sure you're right, Mrs. Treadwell," she said, against all her soul's urging. "Deeds matter far more than words."

When Sunday came, Katherine went to services in Hartin with the rest of the girls. It was very tranquil in the cool country chapel, and as she listened to the choir, she found herself remembering the church on the Côte d'Or that she had attended with Alain. She thought of how Père Bertrand had embraced her after her first visit, and Alain's teasing recital of the Hail Mary when they'd returned to the cottage. . . . She must have flushed at the memory, for Gwen leaned toward her in the pew and asked, "Are you unwell? Do you feel faint?"

Katherine shook her head quickly, applying her fan. It would not do at all to dwell in the past. She had to look to the future; nay, decide what her future would be. In the pew ahead of her, Petra Forrester had turned and was staring at her curiously.

Katherine resolutely trained her gaze at the altar, at the figure of the crucified Christ there. By any odds, Alain was dead by now. A bad penny . . . Her heart abruptly constricted as she recalled him standing in the raging rain, calling her name outside the Hotel Luxembourg. *Bring nothing of the past,* he'd said. But that wasn't possible. The past was always hounding at one's heels; the past was what created the present. It had been lunacy to think they might ever make a match.

Her hands were pleating her blue sarcenet gown. Realizing the fact, she reached up to straighten her chip-hat, decorated with a spray of spicy stock from Mrs. Treadwell's gardens. She ought to have stayed at Marne House. She should not have returned to the academy, with all its memories. Their first kiss, there in the courtyard . . . the touch of his hands, as gentle as the night wind . . .

"Stand for the benediction!" Mrs. Treadwell hissed, and Katherine hurried to do so. She was glad when the students filed out of the church, filling the late-spring air with their bright chatter, making winsome eyes at the village men.

Her unsettled mood stayed with her all through luncheon. She was not due to leave the academy until the following morning, but she was so restless that she proposed a ride along the river to Gwen and Bess. Gwen declined, citing a new anatomy textbook she was eager to examine. But Bess was willing. "It will help make up for the extra lemon curd tart I ate," she explained as she and Katherine put on their habits. "I only hope Stains won't lag behind us endlessly."

It was a glorious afternoon, the cobalt sky studded with feathery white clouds, the air ripe with promise. Katherine set out at a wild pace that soon left Bess and Stains far behind. There was a reason for her restlessness. The night before, in her old bed in the suite, she had dreamed of Alain, for the first time in ages. He'd been naked, his long, lean body arched above her, his eyes piercing hers. *I believe,* he had whispered in the dream, *there are souls that are twinned at birth. . . .* He had kissed her then, and pushed inside her. So real was the sensation that she'd awakened with a moan of joy—only to sit up in the darkness, praying that her suitemates had not heard.

She'd found repose elusive after that, one memory leading into another until she came up hard against the recollection of what Alain had told her on the day they left Paris for the Golden Slope, when, seated in the shabby cart in her nightdress and that ridiculous straw hat, she had said, "I look like hell."

No. You do not. At all.

He had seen her caked with mud and drenched with rain. He had told her he loved her when she stood knee-deep in grape juice.

Stop! she'd told herself fiercely. He was dead. Even Père Bertrand's machinations could not have saved him, as determined as Lieutenant Giacauld and General Fremont had been. And even if by some miracle he lived, there was no refuting the fact he had betrayed her, turned her in to the French soldiers to assure his own safety. He was just what Madame had told her so long ago—a blackguard, a scoundrel, a rogue of the first realm.

I believe there are souls that are twinned at birth. . . .

Pretty words! She'd turned over and pounded the pillow flat. Like the poems he had sent . . .

That Bess, who loved words, found so extraordinary. She'd risen from her bed, as quietly as she could, and groped inside a dresser drawer, seeking for the cache of notes he'd sent her, that she'd never retrieved. She could not read them in the dark; she'd simply sat and held them, recalling every line: *Lilies, blue larkspur, love-lies-bleeding, confessing what my heart is needing* . . .

Shaking herself from her reverie, she reined Maja in and waited until Bess had caught up to her. Stains was still lagging far behind. "Bess," she said.

"Yes?"

"Given your choice between a man of action and a man of words, which would you choose?"

"I think the ideal mate is something between the two," her form-mate told her thoughtfully. "Words without deeds are useless. But so are deeds without words."

Katherine looked at her from beneath the brim of her trim bonnet. "You could be a poet yourself, Bess, do you know that?"

Bess blushed, her red hair mussed from the wind. "Do you know what I would most like to be in the world? A playwright. Imagine penning words that would stir an audience's heart!"

"You must be a playwright, then."

"But there aren't any women playwrights."

"I can't see why there shouldn't be. See here. You must come to Marne House and speak to my stepmamma. She knows all about the theater, you know. She might be able to help."

Bess, bouncing up and down atop her roan mount, goggled at her. "I thought you despised your stepmamma. And despised me as well."

Katherine looked straight ahead, down the wide-open road. A rider had appeared in the distance. "I did, once. I was wrong to, though. I . . . I have had a great deal of time to think, these past months. Nanette—that is my stepmamma—says that men come and go in this life, but woman friends are forever."

"Like Mrs. Treadwell and Madame," Bess said instantly.

"Yes." The rider was still coming on, though a great distance away. "I suppose it took being away from you and Gwen to realize that I missed you."

"And Martha?" Bess asked shrewdly.

"Oh, God." Katherine looked stricken. "When I think of what I did to Martha . . . it was unconscionable. Beneath contempt."

"She's with child, you know. She wrote to us. And deliriously happy with Peter."

"I am so glad to hear it!"

"That rider's coming on awfully hard."

They were quite near the spot where Alain had first accosted Katherine on the road. She reined her horse in sharply. "Perhaps it is best we wait for Stains."

"Good heavens, I believe it's Lord Dalrymple!" Bess declared, eyeing the figure in the distance. "What on earth can he be doing here?"

And so it was. He pounded up to them just as Stains rejoined them from the rear. "Well met, Lady Devereaux!" he cried, with a sweep of his hat. "And Miss . . . Miss . . ."

"Boggs," Katherine reminded him. "You have met before. At the countess of Yarlborough's."

"So we have. Pray forgive me." He was breathing hard.

"I must say, I never expected to see you today!" Katherine exclaimed. "You had my letter; I know you did, for you responded."

"I could not let a week go by without seeing you." He looked to Bess and then at Stains. "Would you be so kind as to give us leave to ride a bit ahead?"

Considering his direct appeal, neither Bess nor Stains could do more than nod and say, "Of course, milord." He caught Katherine's reins and led her away from the road, into the fields, his roan so close to her palfrey that their thighs brushed.

She waited for him to say something as they set out toward the river at a good clip. When he did not, she ventured to note, "You appear somewhat winded, Lord Dalrymple."

He glanced over his shoulder at Bess and the stableman,

who were dutifully trailing behind. "I have reason to believe Montclair is back in England," he said then.

Her heart gave a wild lurch. "No," she whispered. "That cannot be."

His blue eyes turned to the pasture before them. "And if he is, I think it exceedingly likely that he intends to seek you out."

"Surely he would not dare!"

"As brazen a soul as he is? I would not put it past him. Not for a minute."

"I will not receive him!" Katherine said somewhat wildly. "I never would receive him!"

Dalrymple looked straight at her. "Are you certain of that?"

"Absolutely! I despise the man!"

"The fact that he may have managed to escape here from France," Dalrymple said intently, "worries me a great deal. He is exceedingly clever. It is clear he knows how to play upon his victims' . . . weaknesses."

"I have no weakness any longer when it comes to Montclair," Katherine declared forcefully. "He is a wastrel and a scoundrel. Were he to come to me in mortal danger, I would turn him away."

"Don't judge him too harshly," Lord Dalrymple said with great leniency. "His dastardliness has redounded to my great benefit. He may be a scoundrel, but as such, he is *premier cru*."

She could not help but laugh. "I cannot *believe* you would be so charitable toward him!"

"Nor can I, as envious of him as I am. I cannot imagine you would ever run barefoot from your hotel room to meet me."

"Don't be so certain of that," she told him softly, blushing.

"God knows I am not half so dashing—"

"You are dashing in your own way," Katherine allowed. "And what is more, you have never urged dishonor on me. To the contrary, you have protected me, and counseled me, and—"

"And loved you," he interrupted, his pale blue gaze intense. "I cannot help but wonder, though, if that is enough to make you forget a man who is so much larger than life."

"The sort of life I long for now is quite different from what I wished for six months past," she told him. Bess and Stains were coming up behind them, and she spoke with more haste. "I was not much suited to peasantry."

"I don't imagine you were. In fact, it frequently makes me smile to imagine you in such straits. Still, you held up well. After what you endured, I believe you could hold up against anything. I say it again: You are the most remarkable woman I ever have known."

Their riding companions were nearly upon them. Katherine twisted in the saddle, giving Bess an imploring glance that made her slow her mount. Who knew her sins as well as this man did? Who ever would excuse her shameless escapade with such amazing grace? This man, this loving and supremely forgiving man, was her salvation. Such an opportunity might never come again.

And if Alain truly was in England? The thought shook her to her core. He had won her over with such ease, once. She could not afford for him to do so again. She needed bolstering. She needed certainty. She had to know that if he appeared beneath her window in a driving rain, nothing he said would make her go out to him. She needed irrevocability.

She looked again into Lord Dalrymple's blue eyes, that were desperate with worry. For her. He *loved* her. He loved her. Deeds mattered more than words.

"Lord Dalrymple," she said softly.

"Clayton."

"Clayton." It came out a whisper. "You told me once . . . I had only to say yes. Do you know what I speak of?"

"Do you imagine I spend my days thinking of anything else?" There was a despair to his voice that made Katherine's heart constrict.

She took a deep breath. "I am saying it now."

"You *are*?" he asked in disbelief. "Do you mean it, Katherine?" And the expression on his face was so tremulous and hopeful that she laughed out loud.

"Yes. There's the word you wanted, isn't it? Yes, Clayton. I *will* marry you."

He caught her to him, nearly pulling her straight out of her saddle. His mouth crushed hers; his hand caressed her cheek. "Oh, Katherine! You never will be sorry. I *swear* it to you."

"I know," she said, returning his kiss.

Stains had drawn abreast of them; he cleared his throat, seeing how they were entwined. "Beggin' yer pardon, Miss Devereaux, but it ain't hardly proper—"

"But it is," she retorted. "We are engaged to be married."

Bess let out a squeal. "Oh, Katherine! Are you, truly?"

"Absolutely," Lord Dalrymple confirmed. "At long last, she said yes."

Thirty-one

The academy reacted with unfettered joy to the announcement of Katherine's betrothal. Any ill will she might have earned in her first years there had been more than offset by the recent change in her manner; the little girls clapped and cheered her, and the older ones congratulated her and Lord Dalrymple with genuine affection. Mrs. Treadwell was beside herself with excitement; Gwen was bubbling over with happiness; Bess was smug in the awareness that the news had been shared with her first, before anyone else. And if Madame seemed a bit less ecstatic than the others, surely it was only in comparison with their giddy glee. "So, you have made your choice, Katherine," she observed, as Cook laid out a hastily prepared feast of cakes and punch.

"I have." Katherine searched the countess's face. "God knows, if anyone has cause to doubt my taste in men, you have. But this time . . ."

"This time, no one could argue with the acceptability of your decision," Madame said decisively.

Katherine blushed. "Oh, I know that is true. But that is not why I made it. I do hope you and Mrs. Treadwell will come to know him better. He is so very, very kind. If not for him, I don't believe I could ever have held my head up again amongst the ton."

"You will certainly be holding it high now!" Mrs. Treadwell burbled irrepressibly. "He is a very great catch!"

Katherine wrinkled her nose in a humorous way the old Katherine never would have. "I really do detest that term. As though Lord Dalrymple were some sort of trout that I had hooked on a line . . ."

The subject of the conversation was working his way free

of a cluster of infatuated ten-year-olds. "What's that, darling? Are you calling me a trout?"

"Only in the nicest possible way." Katherine smiled at him, loving him, loving the headiness of the moment.

"You must tell your parents at once," Mrs. Treadwell noted. "You and Stains could take the curricle and be at Marne House by late tonight."

Lord Dalrymple had reached his intended's side. "I stopped to see the duke and duchess this morning, Mrs. Treadwell. Asking your father's permission and all that," he clarified to Katherine. "A bit old-fashioned, perhaps, but—"

"Oh, I don't think so at *all!*" the headmistress exclaimed. "Merely the proper thing to do!"

"Well, it *is* what I was always taught," Lord Dalrymple acknowleged, his arm fast around Katherine's waist.

"Will the ceremony be at St. Paul's?" Gwen put in.

"If that's what Katherine wants," Lord Dalrymple replied. "What *do* you want by way of a wedding, darling?"

"Oh, the whole of it," Katherine said cheerily. "St. Paul's, the trousseau by Madame Descoux, the invitations engraved by Whittier's, a glorious bouquet—"

He bent to kiss her. "Then you shall have it, my love." The lower-form girls simultaneously let out an envious sigh.

"That sort of wedding," Bess noted, biting into an almond cake that left a sifting of powdered sugar across her bodice, "takes a long time to plan. Two years on average—isn't that what Mrs. Caldburn said, Gwen?"

"Two years..." Katherine contemplated that endless stretch of time, then squared her slim, straight shoulders. "I daresay we can bring it off sooner than that, wouldn't you think, Clayton?"

"We shall have to," he agreed, with another kiss that made the little girls swoon.

"Money has a way of smoothing obstacles," Madame observed, her dark eyes sharp. "And in this match, there is no lack of that."

"Quite right," Mrs. Treadwell agreed. "Why, Vanessa's wedding was accounted extremely stylish—I do not think I flatter myself—and yet we managed the entire matter in less than six months. I would be delighted, naturally, to offer you the benefit of my experience."

"I'm sure we'll profit by it greatly," Katherine replied, even as she added up the time in her mind. Six months. It was not so long to wait. They would be wed in the fall. She would be Lady Dalrymple then . . . and someday, a duchess. "But what about *your* parents, Clayton?" she asked anxiously. "Have you told them as well?"

"I informed them of my *hopes*. I'll write to them directly with the news of their fulfillment." He squeezed her hand. "The happiest letter I have ever had cause to pen."

Later, when the lower-form girls had been sent off to bed, she and Gwen and Bess and Madame and Mrs. Treadwell and Lord Dalrymple shared celebratory glasses of sherry. Then, one after another, the others flitted away, until Katherine and her new fiancé were alone in the parlor. He gave his yellow mustaches a twirl, winked at her, and settled on the settee. "Come and sit by me," he invited.

She glanced to the door. "I'm not sure it is proper—"

"Come, now, Katherine! Would your dragons have left us if they did not intend a bit of spooning to go on?"

"Spooning?" she echoed faintly, taking her place beside him on the velvet cushion. "What is 'spooning'?"

"This," he said, and pressed his mouth to hers. The tickly mustache took some getting used to, but there was no doubting his ardor. Indeed, he went so far, with his arms around her, as to let his hand brush her breast. She stiffened, and he hastily rearranged himself, so that he held her shoulder instead. "I will not rush you," he promised again, breathlessly. "But, oh, Katherine! Six months seems like a lifetime!"

"It does to me as well," she confessed shyly.

Emboldened, he let his palm slide downward again. She caught her breath as his fingers brushed her nipple. Oh, she'd been a fool to think that Alain's caresses were magical! Lord Dalrymple was no less adept at lovemaking. Her flesh was tingling beneath the blue sarcenet; she twined her arms around his neck and returned his kiss, albeit bashfully.

"Oh, Katherine. Oh, my love," he murmured, his tongue tracing the curves of her ear. "If you only knew how I long for you . . ." He slipped his hand lower, to her buttock, and ran his fingers over its sweet bend. He'd lowered his head and was kissing the ripe swell of her breasts above the edge of her gown. When he moved to tug the bodice down, however, Katherine straightened suddenly on the seat.

"Lord Dalrymple." She was so ashamed that she was close to tears. "I . . . I hope that being privy to some knowledge of my dreadful past does not impel you to think me wanton."

He jerked away from her. "For God's sake, Katherine! How can you say such a thing? I was only lost in the moment . . . in your loveliness. Forgive me, I beg you. I never will take such liberties again, not until we are duly wed."

It was, of course, the gentlemanly reply. But it was not what Katherine longed to hear. It was certainly not what Alain Montclair would have said. He would have whispered: *I cannot help myself.* He would have told her: *You were meant for this.*

Dalrymple stood, an awkward bulge in his breeches. "It has been a busy day for you, my dear. Perhaps it's best I take my leave."

"I—" She did not want him to go. She wanted for him to take her, subsume her in a flood tide of emotion, prove to her that she was doing the right thing. But of course, such behavior was unimaginable in a gentleman. "I *am* tired," she admitted, then added quickly, "and ever so happy. I can scarcely credit still that you would love me."

"What man would not love you?" he asked quietly, standing, drinking her in. Then he roused himself. "I'll come and see you at Marne House next Sunday, shall I?"

"I'd like that very much." *What I would most like, however, would be to make love to you, to see if I might at long last be free of him.* . . . "Oh!" she said, as he bent to kiss her again. "I nearly forgot. You never told me what I should do if Montclair comes to me. If he truly is in England, that is."

"Now that I reflect, I do not think it likely he will attempt to see you. If he does, however, send word to me at once. I am your champion, remember?" he said with a winning smile.

"I cannnot believe he would still be alive," Katherine said softly.

"Perhaps my information is wrong," Dalrymple told her, with a comforting squeeze. Then he kissed her. She was seized by a sudden fear—of what, she wasn't certain. "I love you, Clayton," she whispered.

"As I love you, Katherine. Forever," he promised, his hand stroking her cheek before he took his leave.

Thirty-two

Katherine's father was so delighted at the news she had accepted Clayton's suit that he insisted on throwing a grand betrothal ball. Of course, he did no more than declare that he wanted it; Nanette was left to plan the whole affair. She consulted Katherine at every turn, ascertaining her wishes in regard to the menu, the musicians, the decorations, the guest list. "It is your party, after all," she told her stepdaughter. "And the duke says no expense is to be spared."

"I have no idea how one goes about putting on such a grand event," Katherine confessed.

"I cannot believe it. Did not that redoubtable Mrs. Caldburn instruct you on such matters at the academy?"

"Oh, of course she did. But—if I may be frank—most of the girls there are not of the first rank. Not that they aren't marvelous good friends!" Katherine added hastily.

"I saw you had another letter yesterday from Miss Boggs," Nanette observed.

"It made me laugh out loud," Katherine confessed. "I want so much to have her here for the betrothal ball. But right there, you run up against Mrs. Caldburn's instructions."

Nanette arched a brow. "Which are?"

Katherine colored faintly. "That climbers and parvenus are to be excluded from true society affairs."

"Which is Miss Boggs, a climber or a parvenue?"

"Well . . . she is not really a climber. She despises society in general, says it bores her to tears."

"Ah. A parvenue, then."

"No, no. I wouldn't say that, exactly. I mean, to be a parvenue, one must have *arrived*. And she has not done that."

"Then we must strike her from the guest list," Nanette said gravely.

"Oh, no! We could not do that!"

"And why not?"

"Why . . . because she is my friend!"

Nanette beamed at her stepdaughter. "Very well. Miss Boggs stays. And Miss Carstairs?"

"Her credentials are impeccable," Katherine noted swiftly. "Her father is Admiral Carstairs."

"Mad old Admiral Carstairs? I never knew he had a daughter!"

Katherine stiffened slightly. "He doesn't pay the least attention to her. She really is the most astonishing creature. Absolutely enthralled with science and medicine, if you can believe it. On my last visit, she was telling me about her adventures with a fetal piglet."

"A what?"

"An unborn baby pig! That she cut apart and inspected!"

Nanette suppressed a shiver. "I will grant you, it is difficult to comprehend why any lady—"

"But she *is* a lady," Katherine shot back. "Her manners are top-notch! To look at her, one would never guess! And she has been kinder to me than anyone else at the academy. Even when . . . when I was beastly to her."

"Then you would like her on the list as well?"

"I would," Katherine said definitively.

Her stepmother smiled. "Are there any other such renegades from the academy that you would care to include?"

"I would invite Madame, but she wouldn't come." Katherine sighed. "I think it's perfectly dreadful that the ton still holds a grudge against her. From what I hear, she was tricked into meeting some ne'er-do-well years ago at a tavern, in the belief she was eloping with her own true love. He—the ne'er-do-well—told the entire ton he'd had his way with her, and everyone believed him."

"It was a great scandal at the time, I recall," Nanette observed.

"Scandals can fall about the ears of the most innocent!" Katherine insisted. "Look at what happened to me!" Nanette did look at her—a long, hard look that made Katherine blush.

"Very well," Katherine capitulated. "I was not entirely innocent. Still, it is easy enough to understand the temptations that can make a woman fall."

"Perhaps," Nanette tendered, "it would be best to invite her, and let her make her own decision?"

"Yes, quite. Thank you, Nanette. That is the perfect solution. And—one more name to add. Petra Forrester."

"I don't believe I've heard you mention her before."

"She's very young. No more than seventeen, I'd wager. Hopelessly romantic. Just like Bess." Katherine colored. "She looks up to me, I think. And she seems to have romanticized my Paris sojourn out of all proportion. As though it were some great adventure, rather than the sordid interlude it was."

"One can't have that, can one?"

Katherine's clear blue eyes met hers. "No. I don't believe one can." She paused. "Nanette . . . I am doing the right thing in marrying Clayton, am I not?"

"Only you can answer that question. And there is only one way to answer it: Do you love him?"

Katherine looked down at her hands. "Yes. I do love him."

"Then there is nothing more to say, is there?"

"No. Just so. There isn't anything more."

Thirty-three

"Why do you think she asked us, anyway?" Gwen inquired of Bess, folding her best gown inside her trunk, then going to light the candles. Evening had only just fallen, but the day had been clouded and dark.

"We're her friends," Bess replied, laying her brushes in her traveling bag. "I daresay we're the only friends she has."

"And why are we going?"

"Same answer," Bess said shortly.

Gwen's small, heart-shaped face bore an unhappy expression. "It is sure to be very stuffy, isn't it?"

"Well, it *is* Katherine's bethrothal ball."

"I shall be all at odds, as always. I wish I could just stay home. Stay *here,* I mean." But the academy was more like home than Gwen's home had ever been, and Bess knew it.

"We owe it to her to go," she repeated for what must have been the dozenth time. "And to Mrs. Treadwell. Sooner or later, you know, we are going to have to marry, if she's to make this academy a success."

Gwen grimaced, settling a chip-bonnet into its hatbox. "I wish Madame were coming. I adore Mrs. Treadwell, of course. But the countess has . . . a firmer grip on reality, if you know what I mean."

"Oh, I do." Bess surveyed the contents of her trunk and let out a sigh. "I am going to stick out like a sore thumb. As usual. A fat sore thumb."

"Please don't start with that," Gwen begged her. "At least when a young man does ask to dance with you, you are never at a loss for words."

Bess plunked herself down on her bed. "Have you ever thought, Gwen, that there must be a more natural means for young men and women to make each others' acquaintance than at these stiff society affairs?"

"Only every day," Gwen said glumly. "Do you know what would be paradise? A school such as this, but with both boys and girls attending. I might have a chance of catching someone's eye in the classroom—a faint chance, mind you, but a chance."

Bess waved a dismissive hand. "There will never be such schools. Not while the female mind is held in such low estimation." There was a knock at the door to their shared suite, and both girls sang out: "Come in!"

Petra Forrester, her thick brown hair untidy, poked her head in. "I am in such a tangle!" she wailed. "Mrs. Treadwell keeps saying this is my grand opportunity to make my mark on society, and all I can think is, there is a hole in my good chemise!"

Bess, laughing, pulled her into the room. "Join the club, then. We were just bemoaning our misfortune in being invited to Katherine's ball."

"I can understand why she asked you two," Petra said, her hands running through her hair in a way that made clear how it had reached its current state. "But why me? Is she punishing me, do you suppose, for having been cheeky to her in the past?"

"No, no," Gwen assured her. "She likes you, I think. I truly do."

"I wish she'd found some other means of expressing it. A formal ball at a duke's residence—I am not ready for that!"

"Of course you are," Bess soothed her. "You have had two years of lessons in decorum and comportment. You have a gorgeous curtsy. And you are very pretty. When"—Petra's fingers had come up to her head again, and Bess tugged them down—"you are not fretting with your hair!"

"I had a letter from my mamma today," Petra confessed. "Impressing upon me how great an honor the duke and duchess are bestowing on me, and how I must at all times keep in mind how unworthy I am. Hardly the sort of thing to inspire me to confidence, is it?"

"At least they take an interest," Gwen noted, somewhat wistfully.

A scattering of rain against the windowpanes made all three girls glance that way. "Oh, Jesus, my hair will go all to frizz!" Bess moaned, with such drama that her schoolmates laughed. "Mock if you like, but Katherine once said my hair was my best feature!"

"As I recall, she said it was your only good feature," Gwen reminded her thoughtfully, as another clatter of drops burst onto the window.

Petra moved to wind the casement shut. "Your bed will be soaked, Bess, if you don't—" She stopped dead, looking at the sill. "That's peculiar. It isn't even damp. You'd think—" And then she let out a screech as the glass rattled once more.

"What is it?" Gwen and Bess cried in tandem, rushing to her side.

Petra couldn't answer; she only pointed down into the yard, where a shadowy figure was stooping to gather another handful of gravel from the drive.

"It's a *man*," Bess said in wonder. "Why, Gwen, you closemouthed thing, you never even hinted that you—"

"Hush!" Gwen said sharply, staring down from the window. The figure had raised his arm to toss the gravel toward them, but instead staggered backward to slump against the ivy-covered wall.

"Is he drunk?" Petra whispered, wide-eyed.

"I think he is hurt," said Gwen, straining to see through the gloom.

"I'll go and tell Madame," Petra offered, starting toward the door.

"Wait!" Bess commanded, shoulder to shoulder with Gwen. The man's hat had fallen from his head, revealing a shining black queue. "Look at his hair, Gwen. Who does that put you in mind of?"

"Why, I have no idea!"

"The comte de Clairmont," Bess breathed. "That we met at Lady Tatham's ball. Don't you remember?"

"But why would he come here?" Gwen demanded.

"He is Katherine's mystery suitor—I will stake my life on it!"

"The man she went to France for?" Gwen shook her head. "That doesn't make any sense. If he is a count, why would everyone have been tiptoeing around after her great adventure?"

"Because he isn't really a count," Bess hissed at her. "Don't you remember what Katherine said about French titles being notoriously unreliable?"

"But Katherine isn't here," Petra said slowly, moving back from the door.

"He has no way of knowing she is anywhere else, has he? Oh, I'll wager he is something truly dreadful. A highwayman! A vagabond! A—a murderer!"

"I really am going to tell Madame," Petra said nervously.

Bess grabbed her by the arm. "Don't you dare!"

"Why . . . what else would you propose to do?"

"He *is* hurt," Gwen announced definitively, seeing him stagger to his knees, hugging his arm to his chest. "He needs help. Madame can send for Dr. Caplan—"

"Don't be daft," Bess declared. "She's more likely to leave him for dead. You saw how shaken she was—and Mrs. Treadwell, too—after she finally managed to fetch Katherine back to England. They'd hardly have been in such a state if he had been a suitable gentleman, would they?"

"And you think he should be permitted to expire while leaning against our garden wall?"

"No, no! We must help him, of course. But we cannot let Madame and Mrs. Treadwell know."

Gwen cocked her head at her friend. "You truly have been reading too many novels. I suppose next you are going to propose that we smuggle him to Katherine's betrothal ball."

Bess's eyes lit up. "Actually, I was only going to suggest that you tend to his injury. But now that you mention it . . ."

"Do you think that we *could*?" asked Petra, her eyes equally aglow.

"Lord, two of a kind!" Gwen moaned. "Such insanity! If

Madame and Mrs. Treadwell felt this fictitious count was an inappropriate match for Katherine, don't *you* think he is?"

"Madame didn't feel that way entirely," Bess said stoutly. "She defended his poetry, remember. Said he'd written it himself."

"You don't even know it is the same man!" Gwen whispered furiously, gazing down into the yard again.

"But what if it is?" Bess retorted. "Don't you think we at least owe it to Katherine—and him—to hear what he might have to say?"

Gwen glanced at her sharply. "Hoping for some crumbs from that table, are you?"

Bess faced her with equanimity. "Of course not. He is far too fine for the likes of me—whether he is a real count or no."

Petra had come all the way back to the window. "He doesn't look in very good straits, does he?" she whispered nervously. "I really had best fetch Madame."

"Only thinking of Katherine's happiness, I suppose?" Gwen asked Bess, speaking right through Petra.

"Only thinking, as it happens, of that poetry."

Gwen appeared to falter. "I'm no connoisseur of verse. Is . . . is it that fine, Bess, what he wrote her?"

"It is," her friend said firmly.

For another instant, Gwen hesitated. Then she caught up a little leather satchel from beside her bed and started for the doorway. "Petra. Go and make sure the maids are all busy in the kitchens. Engage them in conversation."

"What sort of conversation?"

"How should I know? Complain about tonight's supper."

"Tonight's supper was lovely!"

"Say the roast was leathery," Bess advised. "Cook used to hate it when Katherine told her that. It would start a row with the entire staff."

"As for you, Bess . . ." Gwen began.

"I know. Keep Madame and Mrs. Treadwell in the parlor."

"Exactly."

"But where do you propose to take him?"

"Where else but here?"

"To your own *rooms*?" Petra squealed, enthralled.

"I could take him to yours," Gwen acknowledged, "but Candace and Mariah and Roseanne would surely ask questions, don't you think?"

"I am sorry to be such a ninny," Petra said, crestfallen but brimming with excitement. "I have never engaged in any sort of subterfuge before."

"Neither has Gwen," Bess told her, grinning as she held open the door.

The figure slumped against the wall was so still as Gwen approached him that she was nearly certain he was dead—and, truth to tell, she felt a certain relief at the prospect. But when she reached to find a pulse at his neck, he stirred and grabbed her hand, so that she nearly screamed.

"Katherine," he breathed, clinging tightly to her wrist.

"Of course I am not Katherine," she said shortly. "Katherine isn't here."

He raised his face to her, and in the twilight she could just make out that he was, indeed, the comte de Clairmont. "Not . . . not here?"

"But I can take you to her," Gwen promised rather recklessly, and felt his rigid body relax with relief.

"Thank God. I must see her . . . must explain . . ."

"You must stop talking is what you must do. What has happened to you? How were you injured?"

"Sword wound. Here." He pointed to his chest.

"How long ago?"

"Three days."

Beneath the cloak, his waistcoat was wet with blood. Gwen had a sudden intimation that she was in over her head. A three-day-old sword wound to the chest—it could have gangrened; it could have pierced his lung or his heart. She summoned up strength. "I need to get you inside, sir. I need light to examine you—"

He went rigid again. "I'll tell you nothing—nothing!" he said wildly.

"I don't mean question you, dammit! I mean examine your wound!"

His eyes, swimming slightly, met hers. "To . . . what purpose?" he managed to gasp out.

"It just so happens I am trained in medicine."

At that, he laughed—a tight, strangled laugh, but a laugh all the same. "Oh, Christiane!" he murmured, taking the arm Gwen offered him and staggering to his feet. "What sort of school is this that you created?" Then, leaning heavily on Gwen, he let her help him into the deserted front hall and up the stairs.

Thirty-four

"Well?" Bess demanded, leaning over the ashen-faced man laid across her bed. "How is he?"

"I won't know unless I can *see,*" Gwen noted testily. "Bring more candles here." She was slicing away the blood-soaked waistcoat; the linen shirt beneath was even worse. "God. He has lost a lot of blood."

"Is there something I should fetch?" asked Petra, who was hovering at the opposite side of the room. "Tea?"

The man's mouth parted. "Brandy . . ."

"Not a bad idea," Gwen said briskly. "Get a bottle from the cellar."

"How am I supposed to get a bottle of—"

"Use your imagination!" Petra sidled from the room, mumbling to herself. "Water and toweling, Bess."

Bess hurried to bring them. Gwen dipped a corner of a towel in the basin and used it to swab the blood from the wound. It was above his left nipple, more than two inches wide, but not, she thought, too deep. She took a pincers Dr. Caplan had given her, held them over the candle for a moment to clean them, and then parted the edges of the cut.

Bess made a gagging noise in her throat. "God, how can you bear to—"

"There is catgut on that spool in the bag, and a needle in the silver case. Thread the catgut through the needle. Mind you don't touch it more than you need to."

"What are you going to do?"

"Sew him up," Gwen said grimly.

The man on the bed squirmed abruptly. "I'm not . . . some 'broidery project."

"Quite right. You're a man who is going to bleed to death if I don't tie off that artery."

"Cauterize it," he ordered, licking his lips.

"I can't. I can't abide the smell."

"Just my luck . . . to get a finicky surgeon. Where's that brandy?"

"It should be along any moment. Who put his sword in your chest?"

"A man . . . I cheated at cards."

"My, Katherine does know how to choose them, doesn't she?" Bess said almost cheerily, pulling the gut through the needle's eye.

The man on the bed turned his head to her. "Where is Katherine?"

"At her parents' house."

"I was so sure . . . she would be here."

"You shouldn't talk," Gwen told him. "You must conserve your strength."

"We're to go to see her tomorrow," Bess burbled on. "We are invited to her—ouch!"

Gwen had stepped on her foot. "Time enough for that later. Where's Petra with that brandy?"

"Here I am!" the lower-form girl said breathlessly, coming through the door with a bottle clutched in her hand.

"Latch that behind you," Gwen told her. "Now, Monsieur Clairmont, no screaming, do you hear? We don't want Madame or Mrs. Treadwell coming round." She held the bottle to his mouth, and he took a long, long gulp.

"Madame . . . Christiane . . . she would come to my aid," he murmured, letting his head sag back against Bess's pillow.

"I wouldn't count on it. Not now. Bess, give him something to hold between his teeth." Somewhat hesitantly, Bess proffered him a roll of the toweling. He bit down on it, hard. "Ready?" Gwen asked. He nodded. Bess handed her the needle. Gwen sent up a swift, silent prayer: *Do no harm. . . .*

As the needle pierced him, he went rigid, his eyes wide and staring. But he made no sound.

Gwen's hands were shaking. A live human being, she had just discovered, was quite different from a dead fetal piglet. "Give me some of that brandy as well," she told Petra, who put the bottle to her lips. Gwen swallowed, felt the warm burn steady her. "And more for him." Bess removed the towel, and the comte de Clairmont downed a quarter of the bottle. Then his blue eyes met Gwen's, and he nodded.

"Go on," he whispered.

She gripped the needle and did.

It took most of the rest of the bottle of brandy to sedate the patient, but Gwen finally got his wound sutured to her satisfaction. By then, Petra was slumped in a chair, head down to keep from retching. Bess was terribly pale, but she'd stayed at Gwen's side to the end. The comte de Clairmont drifted in sleep, mumbling now and then, sometimes in French, sometimes in English. Gwen washed the closed wound carefully, washed her hands, and said softly, "Well! That was not so bad."

"It was *amazing*," Bess declared in wonder. "That you could do such a thing! Make a man whole again—"

"That's yet to be seen." Gwen took a deep gulp of what remained of the brandy. "There is always the danger of putrefaction, or of fever. We'll need to keep a close watch on him. But overall, I think I gave Dr. Caplan no reason to be ashamed of me."

Petra had lifted her white face at last. "Keep a close watch on him for how long?"

"Two or three days, I'd say."

"And how are we to do that when we are leaving for Katherine's ball on the morrow?"

Gwen and Bess stared at each another. "Damn," Gwen muttered. "I hadn't thought of that. Well, I won't go along, that's all. I'll stay here—"

"And hide him in the room?" Bess shook her head. "That will never work. You'll have to come out for meals—for classes."

"I could say I was ill."

"And have Madame and the maids drop by every hour or

so with beef tea and rusks? You know how Cook fusses when any of us is sick."

"We could move him into the barn," Petra proposed. "Get him up into the loft."

Gwen frowned. "He'd be sure to catch a fever there; the place is filthy. Not to mention drafty and cold."

"What if we took him to Dr. Caplan? He's discreet, isn't he?" Bess inquired.

"Very. But he's also in London for a meeting of the physicians' society."

"There's nothing for it, then, but to tell Madame," Petra declared.

"We can't do that!" Bess insisted. "He came all this way to see Katherine. And you can be certain Madame isn't about to allow that. You saw how overjoyed she and Mrs. T. were when Katherine's betrothal was announced. They were terrified no man would ever marry her after her French escapade."

"You're quite right," Gwen agreed. "True love is all well and good, but it's hardly on a footing with marrying a duke's heir."

"Shh!" Bess cautioned. The patient on the bed was stirring; she laid a damp cloth across his forehead. He smiled, in his brandy-induced haze, and murmured, "Ah, Katherine! *Merci, chérie.*"

"He certainly is handsome," Petra whispered.

"I'd take him over Lord Dalrymple any day," Bess noted.

"But Katherine has made her choice," Gwen said matter-of-factly.

"Took her a devil of a long time to decide, though," Bess retorted.

"Meaning?"

"Well, she could have been waiting, couldn't she have? Hoping this comte de Clairmont would come for her."

"Which he didn't."

"No, but he has now! There could have been circumstances that prevented him from coming. It could be like

Romeo and Juliet—star-crossed lovers, doomed never to know happiness."

"You are such a hopeless romantic," Gwen said with a sigh. "I suppose you think we really ought to take him along to Katherine's betrothal ball."

"As it happens, I do."

"Don't be ridiculous," Petra put in. "How could we ever manage it?"

"Stick him in the baggage cart. Hide him in a trunk."

Gwen snorted. "Oh, that's just the treatment for a man with a sword wound—jogging twenty or so miles in an open cart, shut up in a trunk. We'd lift the lid at the end to find a corpse on our hands."

Petra shuddered. Bess, however, was insistent: "We could think of some way if we only put our minds to it!"

Gwen began to gather up the bloodied cloths and towels to wash them, as well as the comte's shirt. "Be practical for once in your life, Bess. If he is so madly in love with her, he can go and see her after his wound heals properly."

"But it will be too late!" Bess wailed. "The ball will be over! There will be no turning back!"

"People break betrothals all the time, don't they?" Petra asked hesitantly.

"Not people like Katherine! She can't afford so much as another whiff of scandal."

"Still, it is her decision to make," Gwen insisted.

"And how is she to make it properly if she doesn't even know this man has crawled his way to England to see her, bloodied and wounded, practically dead? If any man ever loved me so well as that, I'd . . . I'd . . ." Tears welled in Bess's green eyes; she swiped at them impatiently. "And if I ever discovered later that my friends had known he'd done so, and hadn't so much as told me, I would never forgive them for so long as I lived!"

The notion of being the eternal object of Katherine Devereaux's wrath was sobering even to Gwen. "Remember what she did to Martha," Petra whispered fearfully.

Gwen recovered herself. "Very well, then. We *shall* tell her, when we arrive at Marne House."

"What if she doesn't believe us?" Petra ventured. "What if she should decide we are only out to spoil her happiness?"

"Precisely," Bess agreed. "And that is why we must take him to her. We must let him make his suit himself. In his own words. Face-to-face."

Gwen considered her closely. "You are so sure that she is still in love with him?"

"Remember those poems he wrote her."

"Petra, what do you say?"

"Well . . ." The younger girl hesitated. "I don't know about the love part. But there *is* what Bess said about Katherine holding a grudge. And he *has* risked his life to come to her. If I were in her boots, I would want to know that."

Gwen rolled her dark eyes. "*Two* hopeless romantic fools."

Bess put her hands on her hips. "Do you mean to tell me if you were in Katherine's position, you would not want to know your true love had come for you at last?"

There was a long pause, while Gwen twisted the towels in her hands. She glanced at the sleeping man on the bed, then at Petra's fearful face, and finally at Bess. "I suppose I would."

"Well, then! It is all settled. He is coming to Marne House with us," Bess pronounced happily.

"All that's left," Gwen said, a lot more dubiously, "is to figure out how."

Thirty-five

"Egyptian measles?" Mrs. Treadwell echoed with alarm, staring at Bess's scarlet-pocked face across the breakfast table.

"I'm positive of the diagnosis," Gwen assured her. "Dr. Caplan and I had a lengthy discussion of the condition just before he left for London. I have my notes," she added helpfully, patting a copybook by her plate.

"But where in the world would Bess have contracted such a disease? She's never been to Egypt!"

"Napoleon's soldiers brought it back with them from Africa, and it has since been spreading slowly throughout Europe, Dr. Caplan says. The good news is, there is very little risk of contagion once the marks appear."

"Good news indeed," Madame observed from the end of the table, where she was buttering her toast. "Are there other symptoms we should be aware of?"

"I had a sudden dreadful headache as I got ready for bed last night," Bess told her. "And I slept rather fitfully."

"I did hear quite a bit of moving about from upstairs," Mrs. Treadwell said worriedly. "I merely thought you were packing. You ought to have sent for me! And Cook would have brewed up beef tea."

"Dr. Caplan says the preferred course of treatment is to fast," Gwen informed her, with a sharp glance at her suitemate, whose mouth was open for a slice of bacon. Bess set it down again, reluctantly.

"But what dreadful timing!" Mrs. Treadwell declared. "What about Katherine's betrothal ball?"

"Oh, there's no reason why she should miss that. The pockmarks last for less than twelve hours. It is really a most innocuous disease—though the spots are alarming."

"Quite," said Madame, crunching toast between her teeth.

"But what if you or I or Petra should unwittingly pass the disease on to others? Or, worse, come down with such spots ourselves?"

"Ah," said Gwen, referring to her notebook. "I've taken care of that. Dr. Caplan gave me instructions on how to prepare a tincture that ensures the condition will not spread. As soon as I observed Bess's symptoms this morning, I made up enough of it for everyone here."

"How very thoughtful," said Madame.

"Indeed it is!" Mrs. Treadwell cried. "As many times as I have said your studies with the good doctor are . . . well, be that as it may, I am grateful for them now!"

Gwen reached into her reticule and drew out a corked bottle filled with a dark-brown liquid. "One teaspoon each is the dose," she said brightly.

Mrs. Treadwell clapped her hands for the students' attention—not that anyone in the room was doing anything but listening avidly. "Girls! If you will each hold out your spoon, Miss Carstairs will be coming around to give you a dose of medication to prevent an outbreak of the . . . the . . ."

"Egyptian measles," Madame prompted.

"Yes, yes. Egyptian measles. So unless you want to wake up looking like poor Miss Boggs one of these mornings, do drink up!"

Gwen made her way around the tables. The younger girls sniffed the medicine suspiciously. Petra Forrester was the first to actually swallow the concoction. "Not bad at all," she assured the others. "Tastes rather like treacle."

"Why, so it does!" Phyllis Roderick declared, licking her lips in the wake of her dose.

Gwen approached Madame with the bottle. "Your teaspoon?" she prompted.

"I was exposed to Egyptian measles long ago, in Florence," the countess noted calmly. "Surely Dr. Caplan told you that once you have suffered through a bout, you are thereafter immune."

"I . . . I believe he did mention it. But I should have to consult my notes," Gwen said warily.

"Well, I for one am very grateful to you, Gwen," Mrs. Treadwell declared, swallowing her dose. "It *is* very like treacle, isn't it? And you are quite sure Bess can attend Katherine's ball?"

"Absolutely certain." Gwen paused, filling her own teaspoon.

"I agree, Evelyn, that the risk of contamination is absolutely nil," the countess put in, with a sharp glance at Gwen.

"There is one thing more," Gwen noted, not quite meeting Madame's dark gaze.

"What's that?" Mrs. Treadwell demanded.

"Well . . . because it can take several hours for the tincture to take effect, to be absolutely *certain* we are safe, it would be best if Bess traveled to Katherine's in a separate carriage."

"That should not be difficult to arrange," the headmistress said. "We can simply take the second carriage instead of the baggage cart."

"Just what I was thinking," Gwen agreed.

"My very big trunk can ride inside the carriage," Petra Forrester piped up.

Gwen shot her an alarmed look, and Bess choked on a sip of tea.

"I only mean," Petra said nervously, "it is so very big, my trunk. I doubt it would fit comfortably atop a carriage. As opposed to in a baggage cart, I mean. Because it is so very big."

"Comfortably?" Madame echoed, her brows arched.

"Is that the wrong word?" Petra babbled. "No doubt it is the wrong word. I am so extremely wrought up at the prospect of my first formal ball, I swear to heaven, I can barely think!"

"Obviously," Bess muttered.

"I believe," Gwen said between her teeth, "we can rely on Stains and the other hands to arrange the baggage suitably."

"Yes. Yes. Of course we can," Petra murmured, sinking down in her seat.

"Now, Petra." Mrs. Treadwell beamed at her. "After all your lessons here, I am quite sure you will make a grand success at Marne House. You have never given us any reason to doubt your readiness for society. Has she, Christiane?"

Gwen and Bess looked to the countess anxiously. "Not until this moment," Madame observed softly, staring at the spots on Bess's face.

"Hideous, I know," Bess murmured. "But Gwen has promised me they won't leave scars."

"Oh, I'm quite sure not," the countess noted, those dark eyes agleam. "On you, at any rate."

Petra, duly ordered to keep her mouth *shut,* hovered nervously as Stains and a groomsman hefted her trunk up from the floor of Gwen and Bess's room and started toward the door. "Do be—" she started to say, but Gwen withered her with a glare.

"That goes in Miss Boggs's carriage, Stains," she said shortly.

"Very good, miss," he grunted, wincing at its weight.

"Perhaps I'd best follow," Petra murmured, "just to make certain—"

"Stay here!" Bess hissed, hurrying to shut the door behind the men. "And do stop fretting, or you will give the entire game away!"

"Madame knows something is up," Gwen noted distractedly, stuffing her own trunk with odd items of clothing. In the excitement, she had completely forgotten to finish packing.

"But she hasn't stopped us," Bess reminded her.

"I am only waiting for the other shoe to drop." The door opened then, to reveal the countess. "And here it is!"

"I do hope I am not interrupting," Madame said, taking in the trio of guilt-faced girls—Bess's aspect made more suspicious by her wealth of spots, which had begun to smudge slightly.

"Not at all!" Petra assured her, moving blindly backward and stumbling over Gwen's open trunk.

"Petra, don't be such a nimwit," Bess pleaded, with a meaningful glance.

"I'm so very sorry. Do forgive me. I am simply overwhelmed by the prospect of this ball." And Petra sat down hard on the bed, her hands clenched in her lap.

"That you are up to something, all of you, is not exactly news," the countess mused, crossing the room, going to the window that let onto the yards. Stains's voice could be heard as he remonstrated with the groomsman; then there was a sudden loud thump. Petra let out a squeal.

"Up to something?" Bess said faintly. "Us?"

"What it might be, however," Madame went on, "I must say, I haven't any idea." And she wheeled on Gwen. "Egyptian measles?"

"You said you had suffered through a bout yourself," Gwen retorted calmly.

"In my youth. One is prone to so many such maladies in youth. Recklessness, I believe, is the ultimate cause."

"Dr. Caplan would disagree with you on that."

Madame turned back from the window to peer into Gwen's trunk. "You haven't packed your unmentionables."

"I thought it looked rather sparse." Gwen calmly went to the wardrobe, scooped up an armload of underthings, and laid them in.

"Heaven knows I am not one to squelch youthful rowdiness," Madame observed. "You've left out your good shoes as well."

"So I have. Perhaps, Madame, you ought to go over the contents of Bess's and Petra's trunks as well as mine." Petra gasped at this audacious suggestion. But the countess merely laughed.

"I am very much afraid of what I might find. Heed me, though, girls. Your headmistress and I have a great deal invested in this school. We believe in it to the depths of our souls. We have tried our best to impart to you our values—what we believe matters most in this world, if not in the next."

"And you have done a fine job of it," Bess said fervently.

"As to that, time will tell. I would only say—you are responsible for your own reputations. Whatever game you are playing, mind you do not let it diminish those of the other students here." Petra was visibly shaken at her words. And even Bess had turned pale beneath her flurry of spots.

Gwen, however, remained utterly calm. "You may assure yourself, Madame, in going to Katherine's, we fully intend to uphold the principles that you and Mrs. Treadwell have worked so hard to impart to us."

For an instant, a smile flickered across the countess's lovely face. Then she pulled it straight. "Perhaps that is exactly what I am afraid of."

Stains and the groomsman had appeared again in the doorway. "Aught else?" Stains asked wearily, rubbing soreness from his hands. "That last lot was fearful heavy."

"I . . . I wasn't sure what to wear. So I packed everything I own," Petra said in expiation.

Stains's ancient face softened. "Aye, well, 'tain't often a girl goes to her first ball, then, is it? I reckon my back will recover soon enough."

"Whether the academy does," Madame murmured, as Gwen snapped her trunk shut and latched it, "remains to be seen."

"As I live and breathe," Mrs. Treadwell declared in wonder as she dismounted from the carriage on the drive of Marne House. "You were correct in your diagnosis, Gwen. See how all the spots on our poor Bess are gone!"

Gwen stepped down as well and glanced at Bess, whose face was perfectly pockless but bore the look of having very recently been well rubbed. "I'm not a bit surprised. I do hope, Bess, your ride was not too lonely."

"Not at all," Bess declared, fluffing up her skirts, smiling at the good-looking footman who had handed her down. "I found the time passed quickly."

"More than I can say," muttered Petra.

"My," Mrs. Treadwell said, turning to look up at the splendid outline of Katherine's ancestral home. "Do you know, I'd quite forgotten how imposing this place is." The girls followed her lead, staring at the magnificent Elizabethan hall. Bess gulped, Petra blanched, and even Gwen felt a twinge of apprehension. But just then the front doors flew open, and Katherine came dashing out, radiant and smiling, her arms spread wide.

"Oh, you are here at last!" she cried, hurrying to embrace Mrs. Treadwell. "It seems forever since I've seen you. Gwen, you look so lovely!" Gwen gingerly returned her hug. "And Bess—why, I adore what you've done with your hair. It is your best feature; I have always said so. And Petra." Petra, quaking only slightly, allowed herself to be enveloped in Katherine's slim white arms. "I have missed you all so!" the duke's daughter declared, shepherding them toward the doors. "You must tell me all the gossip. Is Madame well? How is Cook, and Clarisse? Is old Stains still hanging on?"

"Well enough, thank ye, miss," said the man in question, who'd been driving the first carriage.

Quite to everyone's astonishment, Katherine laughed and embraced him, too, kissing his leathery cheek. "Silly thing, I was only teasing! Do you think I shall ever forget that you were riding with me when I finally consented to Lord Dalrymple's suit? It was a moment I will treasure always."

Gwen and Bess exchanged somewhat nervous glances. "Is Lord Dalrymple here?" Gwen asked tentatively.

"Not until later. Business in the City," Katherine said airily, tucking an arm through Mrs. Treadwell's. "But come in, come in! I don't believe you've ever met my stepmother, girls."

Bess had frozen as the duchess of Marne appeared in the doorway. "Welcome, all of you," Nanette said in her thrilling voice. "Welcome and well met at Marne House. Mrs. Treadwell, it is a pleasure."

"Oh! You are as beautiful as my father always said," Bess whispered, gazing at the former actress with wide eyes.

"He must have seen me in my youth, then," Nanette replied, blue eyes twinkling. "Now, let me guess. I know you are Miss Boggs, because Katherine has told me over and over again how much she envies your hair." She contemplated the remaining girls. "You are Miss Carstairs," she told Gwen, offering her hand. "There is much of your father in you, isn't there? But rather more of your mother."

"You knew my mother?" Gwen said in surprise.

"Knew her and loved her, as anyone would have. She would be infinitely proud of you today, if all that Katherine tells me of your talents is to be believed."

"I'm sure Katherine exaggerates," Gwen said, blushing.

"On the positive side? I doubt that," the duchess said, with a sly smile.

The girls of the academy held their breath, expecting an explosion from Katherine. But she just laughed gaily and replied, "Oh, Nanette! I have turned over a new leaf; you know that!"

"So you have, darling. And you, my dear, must be Miss Forrester."

"De-de-delighted to make your acquaintance, Your Grace," Petra stammered, bobbing a curtsy.

"As I am to have yours. Sirs!" She clapped her hands at the array of footmen. "See the baggage is brought to the young ladies' rooms instantly. They must be weary and eager to refresh after so long a ride. Mrs. Treadwell, it is unspeakably good of you to have come so long a way for our little celebration."

"Oh, I would not have missed it for the world," the head-mistress said quite honestly, as they all moved indoors.

"Did you hear that? She actually called Katherine 'darling'!" Bess whispered to Gwen in wonder as they trailed after Mrs. Treadwell and the nobility.

"And Katherine didn't so much as wince," Gwen murmured back. "I am beginning to wish I hadn't let you two romantic fools talk me into what you did!"

It took some time to shake off Katherine and Mrs. Treadwell and the duchess; everyone was in such ebullient high spirits that Gwen was contemplating painting Egyptian measles on her own face lest the poor comte de Clairmont suffocate in his trunk. But at long last their hostess announced that she and Katherine had to dress for the ball; they withdrew, and Mrs. Treadwell followed. In their wake, the three girls stood for a moment amidst the splendor of their quarters—marble floors, mural-painted walls, broad leaded windows—before Bess made a dive for Petra's trunk. "He was perfectly hale when I closed this on him. And you did make airholes for him, Gwen," she whispered, fumbling with the catches and flinging the lid open. "A mite pale, as you can imagine. I did everything you instructed me to, though. Changed his dressing twice, and bathed the wound in tincture of mercury—"

"Beggin' yer pardon, ladies," said a pretty Irish-inflected voice from the doorway.

Bess slammed the lid shut again.

"I am Moira," the girl in the doorway informed them, "and I am to be ye maid."

"We don't need a maid!" Petra declared fearfully.

Moira appeared perplexed. "Don't need a maid, miss? But who is to unpack ye trunks?"

"We—we do that ourselves," Bess told her. "Mrs. Treadwell insists upon it."

"But it was she who sent me here."

"It was a test," Gwen said promptly. "To see if we would capitulate and turn lazy. But I assure you, our instructions are to unpack for ourselves."

Moira shrugged. "As ye please, of course. But perhaps I could draw a bath? Bring some tea or coffee? Wine?"

"Nothing, thank you," Bess said brightly.

"Such lovely hair ye have, miss! I would consider it an honor to dress it for ye for this evening!"

Bess hesitated, flattered. But even as she did, Gwen spoke up again: "Thank you, Moira, but you will find us most self-sufficient. Is that not right, Bess?" There was a pause. "Let me remind you, Bess," Gwen muttered, "that this was all your—"

"Yes, yes! Quite self-sufficient." The words sounded as

though they had been dragged out, but at least Bess had said them.

Moira shrugged again. "And ye, miss?" she applied to Petra.

Petra's gaze was riveted on her trunk. "What's that?"

"I merely asked if ye need any assistance in dressin' for dinner."

"Oh! Oh, no, thank you. But thank you very kindly."

Moira gave a shrug and went out, closing the door with a click. All three girls dove for the trunk.

Bess flung the lid up. "Oh, God, if he is dead—" The figure lying within, against considerable padding, was ungodly pale. But Gwen checked his pulse against the side of his throat and nodded in relief.

"Still alive. I daresay he could use a drink, though."

"I brought a flask of brandy," Petra offered.

Gwen and Bess both goggled at her.

"My mamma always carries one when she travels," Petra explained, withdrawing it from her reticule. "In case of emergencies, she says."

"God knows this is one of those." Gwen took the flask and held it to the comte's full-lipped mouth. The moment the liquor seeped into him, he roused from his sleep. Finding himself lying inside a trunk, with three anxious young faces peering down at him, he stretched his cramped limbs and grimaced.

"I am certain I ought to recall how I have arrived at this pass—"

"Ssh!" Gwen said curtly. "You are inside enemy lines."

The comte sat up slightly, taking in the elegant surroundings. "I am? The last I recall, I was at the academy."

"We had to bring you here to see Katherine," Bess explained. "This is her house. Or castle, rather."

"You brought me to her? Oh, *mon Dieu!* You have my eternal thanks!" The comte reached to grasp Bess's hands as she leaned over the trunk.

"Yes, well." She glanced at Gwen and Petra, saw no

chance of help from them, and swallowed. "I hope that we have done the right thing."

He smiled—a smile that, even in his weakened condition, made their hearts quicken. "But of course you have! I only must see her again, I tell you. I must explain to her why I left as I did, and all will be well!"

Petra unobtrusively took a small nip from the flask of brandy. Bess sighed and scratched her head. It was left to Gwen to explain: "There is something you should know, monsieur. We have come to Katherine's house for a ball."

He nodded. "Yes, yes, of course! So as soon as I can explain—"

"A ball to celebrate her betrothal. To another man," Bess finally mustered, gulping. "Lord Clayton Dalrymple."

"Lord Dalrymple?" The comte appeared bewildered. "But how can this be?"

"Well, you *were* gone a rather long time from the scene," Gwen noted.

"I had no choice! I was on the run, doing my best to evade enemy forces!"

"There, you see!" Bess cried triumphantly. "I told you!"

The comte was waving a hand. "It is a misunderstanding, no more. Once I tell Katherine all that happened—"

"Yes, yes. You must do that immediately," Bess urged him.

He started to struggle to his feet. "Where can I find her?"

The door to the suite opened once more. Gwen forced the lid of the trunk down right over the comte's head. Mrs. Treadwell looked in: "What's this about your sending the maid away, girls?"

There was the merest flutter from inside the trunk. Bess promptly sat on it. "She . . . she is sure to be so busy, what with all the other guests," Gwen stammered. "And we are all *used* to doing for ourselves, so we thought . . ."

Mrs. Treadwell beamed at them. "Why, how considerate of you! You make me very proud. Now, don't lollygag! The ball begins at nine. That leaves you only three hours."

"We'll be ready," Bess promised, giving a hearty *thump*

to the lid of the trunk, which was threatening to rise beneath her.

Mrs. Treadwell nodded, then paused to sniff the air. "Is that brandy I smell?"

"My . . . my new cologne," Petra said hurriedly. "Rather pungent, isn't it? I believe it must have turned in the bottle. I'll be sure to wash it off."

"See that you do, please!" The headmistress gave a cheery wave and went out again.

"Get off of there!" Gwen hissed at Bess, who sprang to her feet and tugged at the lid. The comte rose up, blinking.

"If someone would just be so kind as to explain what is going on," he began.

"It's rather complicated," Gwen said breathlessly, just as Bess chipped in:

"No one else knows you are here but us, you see, and—"

And Petra, on the same beat, declared, "Well, it was Bess's idea to start with, but then—"

"Whoa! Whoa!" The comte put up a hand. "One at a time, if you will!"

The girls looked at one another. "It *was* your idea, Bess," Gwen reiterated. "You explain it."

"Very well, I will." There was a pause. "How . . . how do you feel, sir?"

"Rather light-headed, in truth."

"More brandy," Petra counseled, offering him the flask. He took quite a long swallow from it, while Gwen nudged Bess, mouthing: *Go on!*

"It's . . . it's this way," Bess began nervously. "You see, while you were away, in the time she did not hear from you, Katherine became the object of another man's affections. Lord Dalrymple. He asked her to marry him. It took her forever to agree, even though he is considered quite the catch."

"Quite the . . ."

"Excellent husband material," Gwen noted helpfully.

"Why?" asked the comte.

"He is the son of a duke," Bess explained.

"Give him his due," Petra urged her schoolmate. "He is also very handsome. And rich."

Gwen had pursed her mouth. "I don't believe that's what mattered to Katherine. I honestly don't. But Lord Dalrymple was posted in Paris at the time when Katherine . . . well, when whatever went on there in France between you and her went on. We don't know all the facts, but we've gathered from Mrs. Treadwell and Madame—that's the countess d'Oliveri—that it was quite scandalous."

The comte's brow had blackened. "Scandalous? True love, the love that Katherine and I have for one another, *scandalous*?"

"This *is* England, after all," Petra noted.

The comte made a *harrumph.*

"The point," Gwen hurried on, "is that Lord Dalrymple knows about all that, yet is willing to offer her everything a girl could want: respectability, a fine old name, a fortune."

"*That* is what English girls want out of life?" the comte demanded in outrage.

"It's not what *I* want," Bess said promptly. "But then, I'm not the daughter of a duke."

The comte had recovered from his shock. "It matters not," he announced grandly, waving a hand. "I have been absent from her for too long a time; that is all. When I see her— *when* can I see her?"

Again the girls exchanged glances. "Would you excuse us for a moment, monsieur?" Gwen said, and drew the other two back toward a window. "This was all your idea, Bess!" she hissed then, with a glance over her shoulder at the comte. "What do we do now?"

"We need romantic surroundings," Bess said hopefully. "Someplace glorious, for their reunion." All three of them looked through the window to the gardens.

"There!" Petra said, pointing to a lovely little Greco-Roman ruin that crowned the top of a hill, not too far distant from the house.

"Perfect," Bess breathed. "At sunset. If we hurry, it can

be at sunset. But how are we to get him there? We can hardly have the servants haul my trunk all that way!"

"Monsieur," said Gwen. "Do you feel up to a small excursion out of doors?"

"If it means seeing Katherine again," he declared thrillingly, pushing back his wild black hair, "I would walk to the ends of the earth."

Bess let out a swooning sigh.

"One of us should go with him, though," Gwen muttered. "That is quite a long haul for a man with a sword wound who's been cooped up in a trunk all day."

"It had better be you," Petra noted, "in case there is some health emergency."

"And Petra and I will fetch Katherine, and lead her out there." Bess sighed, overwhelmed by anticipation. "Oh, Petra, let's go and get her."

"Give us a healthy start," Gwen advised. "Bring her out there in half an hour."

"A quarter-hour," Bess quibbled. "Or they'll miss the sunset."

The comte had clambered awkwardly out of the trunk. "I wish to see her now," he announced, wincing a little at the pain of his injury.

"Fifteen minutes," Bess promised. "Can you get him out of here without being seen, Gwen?"

"Of course I can," Gwen hissed. "The question is, can you get Katherine to follow you out to that folly on the night of her betrothal ball?"

"Leave it to us." Arm in arm, Bess and Petra started for the door. Bess opened it, peered outside, then nodded back at Gwen. "The coast is clear!"

"Come, monsieur." Gwen offered her arm to the comte; his limbs were rubbery, and she was still concerned her stitches might not hold. "Petra! Leave me the brandy!"

"Oh. Quite right." Petra tossed her the flask.

"How do you feel, monsieur?" Gwen asked anxiously.

"Are you jesting? I would endure anything for my Katherine," he declared, and strode boldly, if somewhat unsteadily, out into the corridor.

Thirty-six

"*What sort of* surprise?" Katherine asked again, as Bess and Petra, each holding tight to one of her arms, steered her through the French doors that led onto the terrace.

"If we told you, it would not be a surprise, would it?" Petra said, and giggled nervously.

Katherine glanced back worriedly at the manor. "Nanette is going to be quite wroth if I am late to the ball. Not to mention what my father will say. He has been grumbling the whole day long about how much this affair is to cost him."

"This will only take a few minutes," Bess assured her, scanning the grounds, hoping desperately that Gwen had managed to steer the comte into place.

"And isn't the cool air refreshing?" Petra added gaily, earning a congratulatory glance from Bess.

"Well, I must admit, it's been quite deadly having the maids fuss over me for the past two hours," Katherine noted. "What is the sense of having friends come to visit if I am to be sequestered away in interminable grooming?"

"I take it that Lord Dalrymple has arrived?"

"Oh, yes. Half an hour ago."

"And all is well between you?" Bess inquired, with perhaps too much anxiousness.

Katherine shot her a quick glance. "Why should it not be?"

"No reason," Bess said hurriedly.

"I imagine Bess is only thinking how frayed her nerves would be in such circumstances," Petra put in, earning another approving look from her friend.

But Katherine was on edge. "We are all going to be late. I really do think we had best leave your surprise for the morrow, and—"

"Tomorrow will be too late." Bess, steering her down the

path through the gardens, realized how desperate that sounded and tried to regroup. "That is . . . we wanted you to have this before the official announcement. While we are all still friends."

"We will always be friends." Katherine sounded bewildered. "My betrothal won't make a whit of difference in that. Except that I shall be better placed to aid all of you in securing husbands of your own."

Petra stumbled a bit on the gravel path. "Good Lord. I hadn't thought of that."

"Of what?" Katherine inquired.

This time, Bess's glance at Petra was frankly warning. "Of . . . of a husband of my own!" the younger girl quickly stammered.

Katherine looked at her. "Are you jesting? You've thought of naught else ever since you came to the academy, just like every other girl there. Except, perhaps, Gwen. Where is Gwen, anyway?"

"There!" Bess pointed with relief at the folly. Gwen was waving broadly from in front of the tumbled columns.

"This really is most irregular," Katherine noted, with another anxious peek over her shoulder. "Nanette won't be happy with me at all."

"What is more important—the happiness of others, or your own happiness?" Bess demanded suddenly.

"Why—I think the ultimate end is to merge the two," Katherine answered, plucking a burr from the skirts of her elegant blue-and-white-striped gown as they brushed past a stand of thistles. "I must have these paths properly cleared; I can't imagine what Poppa is thinking of, to let them fall into such a state. Do you know, he—"

"You must go on alone from here," Bess said suddenly. They were nearly to the folly.

"I must what?" Katherine's brow clouded with suspicion. "I do hope, Bess, this isn't one of your juvenile tricks. I won't appreciate showing up for the ball drenched in syrup, or covered with whitewash."

"It is nothing like that," Bess assured her, watching from

the corner of her eye as Gwen flitted away from the folly into the surrounding woods. "All you must do to see your surprise is walk down the path. We'll wait here."

Curiosity had gotten the better of Katherine. "Just walk on down the path?"

"Mm-hmm," Bess promised, with a quick glance at the sky. It was all she could have hoped for—night falling fast in the east, with a few faint stars showing, while the western horizon was just starting to run to crimson and gold.

With a final bemused shrug, Katherine acquiesced, stepping along the gravel in her dainty kid boots. "How far must I go?" she asked, pausing to look back.

"That is entirely up to you!" Petra declared, with a giggle.

Katherine eyed her askance, then laughed, too, and turned back toward the folly, whose artfully disarrayed ruins were gleaming bone-white in the slanting sunlight. "Very well, I shall go on!" And she stepped into the shadow of the temple's walls.

"Katherine."

Alain had held his tongue as long as he could, watching her come toward him, seeing her again after such an eternity. But he could stay silent no more; he ached to touch her, embrace her as he had through those nights on the Côte d'Or. "Oh, *ma chère* Katherine—"

She had frozen at the sound of his voice. "No," she whispered.

"Yes," he breathed, stepping forth from the niche where he'd been hidden.

Katherine looked wildly back along the path for Bess and Petra, but they had vanished. "What are you doing here?" she demanded.

"I have come for you at last," he said simply, with great dignity.

An immeasurable commotion had seized Katherine's heart. She fought to conquer it, to maintain control of her senses. "Now?" she said, and heard her voice squeak into incoherence. She tried again: "After all this time?"

"No one regrets the delay more than I do," Alain said, smiling, reaching for her hands.

She snatched them back. "How dare you come here? How dare you show your face to me again? After you betrayed me, sold me out to those soldiers—"

"I had no choice, Katherine," he said patiently, calmly. "When you told me that man had accosted you at the river, I had no other choice. From the way you described him— the hooked nose, the thinness—I knew it had to be Giacauld. *He* put me in the Bastille."

"And so you left without me!"

"Katherine, consider! I knew no harm would come to you—your father is too grand a man for that. And Père Bertrand would make certain. But if they had taken me—"

"You would have gone back to the Bastille."

"They would not have bothered with that. They would have killed me at once."

"For what? For murdering Mimi Boulé and the man with the mustache?" she asked coldly.

"Still harping on that?"

"I do beg your pardon. It may all be quite casual to you, but in my circle, murder is abhorrent."

"What have they done to you, Katherine?" he asked suddenly.

"What has *who* done to me?"

"I don't know." He sounded hurt, perplexed. "What have they said to you about me?"

"They didn't need to say more than the truth—that you are dishonest and murderous and—and—and—"

"A bad penny?" he whispered.

"A bad sovereign is more like it."

He laughed then. "*Dieu merci,* they have not conquered you entirely." The laugh made his wound constrict; he bent over suddenly, clutching his chest.

"What is wrong?" Katherine demanded.

"Nothing. Nothing at all, now that you are here."

But she had glimpsed the bandages through the throat of his shirt. "Are you hurt?"

"Only a bit. Your friend Miss Carstairs dressed it for me." He straightened slowly.

"My *friend*—I am not at all sure anymore who my friends might be."

"I am your friend. Your best, your truest friend. Always. Forever."

He was as handsome as ever, leaning up against the blanched column that reflected all the colors of the brilliant sunset sky. She had forgotten what a fine-looking man he was—the way his upper lip curled when he smiled, the brilliance of his blue eyes. He still had the beard she had loved so in France. He reached again for her hand, pressed it to his heart. "God, how I have ached for you."

Again she glanced nervously over her shoulder. "You ought not to have come."

"Not come for you? How could I not, when we are—"

"Don't you say it!"

"Two halves of a whole. Twinned souls."

He was grinning at her, teasing, but she felt her heart reach out to him in agreement. "You don't understand!" she said desperately, even as he caressed her fingers, touched his mouth to their tips. "I have put all of that—all that went on between us—behind me. I have found a man—"

That upper lip curled, though not in a smile. "A *sort* of a man—"

"I'll not hear you speak against him! An honorable man, with more to offer me than danger and disgrace!"

"A duke's son."

"And what if he is?" she demanded. "There is no shame in that!"

He paused, stock-still, her fingers still at his mouth. "No, *chérie*. But there is shame in denying what you know in your heart. You love me."

"I am marrying him," Katherine said stubbornly. "The betrothal ball is tonight. I will marry him, and we will live happily ever after—"

"Have you slept with him?" he asked quietly, infuriatingly.

She yanked her hand from his. "That is no business of yours!"

He reached out and put his hand to her hip, caressing its curve beneath the demure striped gown. She stood as still as one of the tumbled statues. "Does he touch you this way?" His hand moved upward, to her waist, and then higher still, smoothing the curve beneath her right breast. "When he touches you, what do you feel?" His voice was a satin whisper, intimate as his caress. Just before his fingers found the bud of her nipple, she jerked away.

"How dare you?" she hissed, ignoring the way the dying sun's rays illuminated his eyes, put touches of fire to his hair. "You abrogated any right to such questions when you abandoned me."

"I could never abandon you, Katherine. I might leave you, but you would not be abandoned. Can the stars abandon the night? Can the ocean abandon the shore?"

"Pretty words," she sneered. "Deeds are what matter. I am wiser now than when you deluded me into running away after you with your cheap whoremonger's tricks."

He drew back, affronted. "Is that what you call my lovemaking? *Our* lovemaking? All that we shared together?"

Her heart was fighting madly to deny it. But she clung to reason, answered him firmly: "Yes."

He half turned, warring with himself. *If she is settled. If she is happy* . . . He was in uncharted waters; what duty did a man such as himself owe to her? The honorable move, surely, was to leave her, put a brave face on it and walk away with his head held high. But how did one walk away from the only thing that made life worthwhile, that had sustained him through the long months of running, the sole image that had given him hope, a reason to go on?

It dawned on him, faintly, that this was precisely what she thought he'd done when he'd left her at the Côte d'Or.

"Katherine." His voice was a croak. "When I told Père Bertrand who you were . . . told him to come and fetch you . . ."

"Ten thousand English pounds," she said coldly.

"God, you think I did it for the *money*? I did it to keep you safe from harm! Giacauld is a bastard, an unreasoning bastard! If he had come for us in the cottage—if there had been a fight—if you had been in the way—"

The words burst from her in a fury: "You ought to have asked me! You ought to have let me decide for myself! I would have run away with you! Endured anything. Followed you . . . anywhere."

"But you will not, now."

"No." Her chest was heaving; she took a deep breath. "It is too late. Too much has come between us. I could never believe in you again. Not as I did then."

He nodded a little, considering. "And you mistrust my words. Not to mention my intentions. So there is nothing I can say—"

"Nothing."

"*Eh bien.* It is ended," he said resignedly.

"I am sorry . . . that you went to so much trouble," she whispered in apology. "Coming all this way, I mean—"

"It does not matter." He squared his shoulders, tossed his mussed blue-black queue. She could not help but admire the blithe insouciance of the motion, caught as she was in a maelstrom of misery. "A farewell kiss?"

"I . . ."

"What harm can it do?" His smile blazed at her.

"Very well." She bent forward a bit, puckered for a peck.

His mouth closed on hers. His arms encircled her, pulled her toward him, into the heat of his embrace. He tasted of brandy, of gunpowder and mystery, of life in all its mad grandeur. His tongue pushed at her mouth, and her lips parted even as she tried to withdraw. God, how had she lived without this? His hands were at her breasts, tugging down her bodice. She fought against the flood of wildfire his touch threatened to unleash even as his mouth found her breast and claimed it. Tentatively she let her fingers come to rest on his hair, remembering how those blue-black waves had looked, hundreds of nights ago, against a white pillow in a French country inn.

"You want me still," he whispered, pausing to stare at her, his eyes bright in the dying light. "You know that you do. Oh, Katherine, come away with me! Come with me now—"

"Where would we go?" she breathed.

"Anywhere!" He was laughing, his head thrown back. "Africa! China! The New World! It is ours, all of it. Ours to claim."

"How would we live?"

"As we have lived before. Day to day. Hand to mouth. But together. As man and wife, Katherine! Just as we had planned. I will show you such wonders—"

"No," she said.

He drew back a little, and the sun slipped from his eyes, sank below the horizon. "We do not have to marry, of course, if you do not wish, but—"

"No." Her voice was stronger. "I mean, Alain, I'll not come with you."

"But . . . *chérie!* You love me!"

"Aye, I do. More's the rue. But there is more to life than . . . than cards and wine and playing at love. There are responsibilities. The duty I owe to my father—"

He'd staggered on his feet, was staring down at her. "You owe him no *duty*."

"You are wrong! That is the trouble with you! We don't exist alone together in a bed somewhere. We have a place in the world—both of us do, much as you try to deny it. There is more going on about us than you seem willing to acknowledge. There is a war, there is my family, there are my friends—"

"I adore your friends! Miss Carstairs saved my life with her stitchery!"

"And how often would I see my friends after you dragged me off to China?"

He was glaring at her, flummoxed. "What difference does that make? You and I, Katherine! You and I are what matters!"

"What about the future?" she cried, desperate to make him

understand. "A home, children, everything I long for! Some sort of . . . settledness. To know what is to be tomorrow, and the day after tomorrow, and the day after—can you offer me that?"

"Perhaps not now," he said swiftly. "But someday, someday, surely, yes!"

"I cannot wait for someday!" she said in anguish. "I cannot make the same mistake twice. There are people who have placed their trust in me. Who believe in me. Mrs. Treadwell. My stepmother. Madame."

"Dalrymple." The name was a snarl.

"He has been unspeakably kind to me! He does not deserve that I should treat him so shabbily."

He straightened abruptly, letting go of her hands. "And what do I deserve?"

Her tears spilled over. "I don't know."

"But you know this—I don't deserve you, eh? Not the precious English princess." His voice was so cold that she shivered.

"I am not a princess."

"You may as well be."

He was breathing hard, in short, angry spurts. Darkness was crowding in around them. Katherine wished she knew how far off her schoolmates had gone. She crossed her hands over her bared breasts.

"I could *take* you with me," he said, his voice low and threatening. "I could make you see reason."

"You could take me with you. But you would not change my mind. And I would run at my first chance."

He stood silent for a long, long moment. Then the words burst out of him, furious: "Does it signify *nothing* to you that I love you?"

"I never will forget you, Alain."

He turned from her bitterly. "Go to him, then. Go to your duke's son, and wed him. Bear him a passel of babies. Know every morning when you wake what the day will bring. And the next day! And the next! I thought more of you."

"Then you mistook me," she said quietly. "I am not what you thought me to be."

He whirled back. "But you *are*. If only I knew how to make you *see* it—"

She shook her head sadly. "We had our moment, Alain. Our . . . wildness. The desperation of youth. But I have grown up now. You should as well." And she pulled her skewed bodice up, covering her breasts.

"If I . . ." he began, then stopped, as if teetering on the edge of a cliff.

Katherine laughed then, a little, through tears that were still falling. "Became respectable, Alain? Traded in your devil's ways? Became a proper gentleman? There's a wish to be wished. But we both know it never will happen."

"For you, I could try."

"It is too late, I fear."

There was a commotion somewhere in the distance. "Katherine!" It was Nanette's voice, sailing over the gardens. "Katherine, are you there? The guests are arriving!"

"I am coming!" she called back. Still she stood, looking at her lover in the shadowy dusk. Dear God, he *was* a handsome man. She fought down an urge to touch his face just once more, to let her fingers slide over the plane of his cheek.

"You will regret this," he said shortly, harshly.

"Perhaps," she acknowledged.

"In the dead of night. And when you lie beneath him. When you bear him the children that should have been *mine*—"

"I would have regrets whatever my choice," Katherine told him bravely. "But I will have fewer, I think, this way."

"Because I am not a rich man."

"Because we are too different."

"Because he is a duke's son. And you are a duke's daughter."

"I cannot change what I am," she whispered.

"You are wrong in that. People change all the time. You lack only the will."

"No. *You* are wrong. And you will never change, Alain."

She faltered. "I would not want you to, in truth. But I cannot spend my life with you. It is . . . too much to ask of the likes of me. I am not your soul's twin."

She feared he would be angry. But he only scuffed the gravel on the path with his boot. "If you believe that, there is nothing more to say."

"But there is. I—must thank you. For what you did show me of that wide world. You taught me so much."

He had recovered his insouciance—she could not know at what cost. "Little good it has done me, eh? One more kiss, then? For parting?"

She could not help but laugh. "I don't think so, Alain."

He shrugged. "*Eh bien.* Then it is only adieu."

"Adieu," she whispered. "God go with you."

"And bide with you, *chérie.*"

"Katherine!" Nanette's voice, increasingly vexed, floated out from the house. "The orchestra is tuned! The guests are all wondering! And Lord Dalrymple—"

"I really must go now," Katherine said apologetically, turning back to him. But he was already gone; the folly lay empty and bare in the twilight. For a moment, bereft, ungrounded, she contemplated calling out to him, drawing him back. She felt as though some great, puissant force had vanished from her world. He could not be beyond the reach of her voice. She had only to cry out the words—"Wait! I will go with you!"—and he would return, take her with him, into the vast maw of the unknown. . . .

"Katherine?"

She whirled about and saw Gwen standing awkwardly beside a fallen pillar, pleating her skirts in her hands. "I did not listen. I did not hear what went on," her friend assured her, and then seemed to crumple. "Oh, God, forgive us! We meant well, we honestly did! We thought that you loved him!"

"I did," Katherine told her, and heard her own voice as though from a long way off. "I did love him. But that was long ago. Thank you for healing him, though. And for bringing him here to me. It is good . . . that we had the chance to say farewell. I would have wondered, otherwise, what had become of him."

Bess and Petra straggled up as well. Bess's face was tear-stained, and Petra was shaking. "I don't know how you could be so strong, Katherine," the lower-form girl whispered in wonder. "To send him away . . . when he loves you so desperately . . ."

Katherine put an arm around her shoulder and gave it a squeeze. "I made a fool of myself over him once. I like to think even I am wise enough not to make the same mistake twice."

"Katherine!" the duchess wailed hopelessly from the terrace.

"Coming, Nanette!" Katherine called almost gaily, then smiled at the trio of stricken faces surrounding her. "There's no harm done," she assured them. "I cannot blame you for believing I might choose him over Clayton; Alain has always been exceedingly charming. But the truth, when you come down to it, is that he *is* a bad penny. If my escapade in France taught me anything, it was that a girl must look out for herself in this world."

Thirty-seven

"*Who in the* world are Lord and Lady Mintzer?" Katherine inquired, pausing in her perusal of the wedding guest list Lord Dalrymple had handed her.

"He is with the Home Office."

"And who is she?"

"His wife."

Katherine's mouth curved in a smile. "No—I mean, is she accepted?"

Lord Clayton Dalrymple stretched his legs on the settee in the drawing room of Marne House. "How the devil should I know? And what does it matter?"

Katherine shrugged, her quill hovering over the list. "I only thought . . . considering your standing, your family's standing—"

"Christ, you sound like some medieval maiden. Lord Mintzer has the regent's ear. That ought to make him acceptable enough."

Katherine put down the quill and scratched her forehead. "It is only that there are so very many names on this list you have made." She tallied them quickly. "Three hundred at least! I was hoping to winnow it down a bit, so that the wedding doesn't turn into a rout. There aren't nearly so many on Nanette's list."

"That's not exactly surprising, is it?"

Her eyelids flickered, almost imperceptibly. "What do you mean by that?"

"If you are talking acceptability, surely there's more risk of offense from your family's side."

Katherine was tempted to protest. But she did not want to quarrel with him, especially not when he was, by any standard, in the right. "That makes four hundred and fifty guests altogether," she noted worriedly.

"Your poppa should be able to afford it. You're not inviting those ragtag girls from the academy, are you?"

"What, Gwen and Bess and Petra? Why wouldn't I? They are my friends!"

"You'd do well to look for new friends. More stylish ones." He took a long sip of brandy.

Katherine nibbled her lip. "I know they are not *soignée*, exactly—"

"Don't speak French. I won't have it."

She laughed. "You must be jesting!"

"I spent too much time fighting Napoleon to jest about that."

"The war is over, Clayton," she reminded him. "Napoleon is shut up on Elba." All of England had rejoiced at the news of the Emperor's defeat in April, none more so than he.

"Yes, and it's a new world. Diplomats such as myself must have a care to their futures. That is why Lord Mintzer stays on the list."

Katherine rested her chin on her hand, staring at him. "What do you see as your future, Clayton? As our future?"

He smiled at her, arms crossed behind his head as he relaxed on the settee. "I don't see any reason why I shouldn't be prime minister someday."

"That would make you happy?"

"Very happy."

"I hadn't known that." But it did, she thought privately, explain the scope of his list. More than half the names were those of strangers, men and women she'd never even heard of. "You haven't included Lord Bannister," she noted.

"What's that to you?"

"He . . . was so kind to me at the countess of Yarlborough's ball. And you served with him in France."

"I think it best we escape the circle of those who know what you did in France."

Her cheeks flamed. He was perfectly correct, of course.

He was always perfectly correct. "Except for Madame and Mrs. Treadwell," she noted.

"Mrs. Treadwell may attend, if you like. But not the countess d'Oliveri. I'll not have her there."

"In heaven's name, why not?"

He gave her a withering glance. "Her name is synonymous with scandal."

"Through no fault of her own!" Katherine said heatedly. "That was all a million years ago!"

"The ton has a long memory."

"She came to fetch me in Paris! She—she saved my life!"

"She took you to the Bastille to see Montclair and started all the horror. Drop her."

Katherine sat up straighter. "I won't. I won't be married without her there. I owe her too great a debt. And so do you, though you may not know it."

"What do you mean by that?"

"She has been your staunchest supporter! When Mrs. Treadwell and the other girls . . ." Katherine realized where she was headed, and swallowed.

He'd suddenly leaned forward, his pale eyes sharp. "When Mrs. Treadwell and the girls *what,* Katherine?"

She waved what she hoped was a negligent hand. "Nothing. You know how silly girls are. They thought Montclair was highly romantic."

"A kidnapper romantic? A murderer *romantic*?"

"They read too many novels," she said in excuse.

"I hadn't realized that sort of rubbish was on the academy curriculum."

"Of course it's not," she retorted. "Madame bemoaned it all the time."

"Then where did they get the novels?"

Katherine giggled. "From Mrs. Treadwell. She has a great store of them."

He pulled out a cigar, sliced the end with ruthless efficiency, and lit it. "I wonder more and more how your father could have consigned you into such creatures' care."

"The academy provides as fine an education for young

ladies as any school in England," Katherine said stoutly. "It places a great deal of emphasis upon social propriety."

Lord Dalrymple released a puff of pungent smoke into the air. "Stick to the linens and foodstuffs, my dear, and let me worry about the guest list. I know what I am doing."

Katherine was on the verge of saying more on the subject—she hated it when he was patronizing. But if she pressed him, she knew, he'd only manage to turn the conversation back to her adventure in France, to point out that when it came to respectability, she had long since ceded any authority. She set the list aside. "Very well, then. The menu. Have you any suggestions for the wedding dinner?"

"Good, plain English food. None of those damned French sauces that ruin the stomach. Roast venison. Duck. A haunch of beef."

She noted these down. "No sauce at all? It will be a shabby board we set."

"A good thick gravy with the beef."

"We may as well be hosting Poppa's squires," she mumbled mutinously.

"What's that?"

"Nothing. What wines would you prefer?"

"I liked the red your father served last night. What one was that?"

"Nuits-Saint-Georges," she whispered, and felt the grapes between her toes.

"Frog wine, eh? Never mind, then."

"Clayton, for heaven's sake! The French make the only decent wines on the planet!"

"That's not true. What about sherry? Port? Madeira?"

"Those aren't dinner wines!"

"I like 'em. Serve them instead."

She pushed her notebook aside. "You're being childish, you know. The war is over. The blockades have ended. We will look extremely unfashionable if we serve sherry with dinner!"

He released more smoke. "Let's have ale, then. Good, plain English ale."

"God! Like a pair of country crofters!" She shuddered at the idea.

He grinned at her, a few last wisps curling from beneath his mustache. "You're a bit of a snob, aren't you, Katherine Devereaux?"

"I was brought up always to remember my station in life," she said hotly.

"Ah. Yes. That's what you were thinking of, I suppose, when you slipped that pistol to Montclair."

He had done it again. She lowered her gaze, her cheeks flaming. But then he surprised her, laying his cigar aside and coming to the desk, tilting her chin up and kissing her gently, sweetly. "I can't help it," he told her, "if I am still jealous of him."

"There's no cause for you to be."

"Apparently there is. For his sake, you were willing to toss away the ton's regard and run off to the ends of the earth. For mine, you won't serve sherry with supper."

She laughed a little. "I see what you mean. But, Clayton dearest, you must know, my recognition of the . . . the blemishes in my past make it even more vital that my current conduct be beyond reproach at all times. In every way."

He ran his finger down her cheek, and she felt a small shimmer of excitement. They had been betrothed for three months now, and he had yet to venture beyond chaste kisses. Of course, considering the way she had accused him of thinking her of easy virtue that one time he *had* sought to touch her breasts, she had no right to blame him. Still, she wished sometimes that he would try again. Those words Alain had spoken to her out at the folly still rang in her ears: *Have you slept with him?* There was no reason to expect that Clayton would be any less . . . ardent than Alain. Or was there? The first time she'd been alone with Alain, he'd had his hands up her skirts within minutes. She wished, she really wished, she had the nerve to initiate further intimacies with Clayton. Perhaps he was just waiting for her invitation. But what if he simply thought her wanton instead?

Nothing ventured, nothing gained. Holding her breath, she

put her hand up to cover his as it caressed her cheek, smiling into his eyes, and then drew his hand lower, along the line of her jaw to her throat. To her great relief, he leaned in for another kiss, a bit more lingering than the last. As his mouth pressed hers, she guided his fingers lower still, toward the curve of her breasts above the bodice of her gown. His breath quickened; she felt a surge of relief. If he would only touch her! If she could only know—had it been Alain, or had it simply been that he was a man?

"Tease," he murmured, nibbling at her earlobe. "You are a terrible tease, aren't you?" He let his fingers delve into the shadowy vee between her breasts, fumbling amidst the forest of muslin and linen and stays. He brushed her nipple, and a flash of white heat surged up from her belly. She was aching for love; she wanted it so desperately. Boldly she put her hand to his breeches, caressed the sudden bulge there.

He drew away with a gasp. "My God. What whore's tricks did he teach you?"

"It isn't about him!" she cried, craven, humiliated. "It isn't him I want, Clayton! I chose you!"

"It is up to the man to do the leading," he said tersely. "And for the woman to submit."

"I know that. I know that!" She started to cry; she had never in her life felt more miserable. All she longed for was for him to kiss her as if he could not bear the waiting, to touch her as though his life depended on it. *The way Alain had. . . .*

His stern face softened as he gazed down at her. He reached into his breast pocket, took out his handkerchief, wiped her tears away. "Never mind, then," he said softly. "It isn't your fault, is it? I shall teach you all over again. We will erase the past."

She nodded, sniffling. "Thank you. I am so very sorry. I did not mean to be . . ." What? Forward? Usurping of his privilege as a man? Alain had loved it when she'd touched him; he hadn't thought it presumptuous. Dammit, she had to stop thinking of him!

"You'd best go dress for dinner, hadn't you?" he told her.

"Your father told me Lord Pettigrew is coming with his wife. I am anxious to further my acquaintance with him. He is in quite tight with the regent."

"Yes," she whispered, rising from her chair. "I'll go and dress."

In her room, though, she dismissed her maid, stripped naked, and lay atop her bed, letting her own fingers rove over her breasts and belly, eyes clenched shut as she sought a release for the dreadful tension that coiled inside her, climaxing in bitten-back sighs as she pictured Alain's face.

Thirty-eight

"It's come!" Nanette proclaimed, her eyes bright with anticipation as she led Katherine, who was still panting from an afternoon ride, into her bedchamber. "All the way from Paris!"

"I should wash," Katherine protested, pulling off her cap, smoothing her tangled hair. "I am bathed in sweat; I must smell to heaven."

"How can you bear to wait?" Nanette demanded. "Inge, bring her some water, so she can lave down." Inge, Nanette's redheaded County Cork maid, hurried to fetch the pitcher and basin. Katherine dutifully splashed water on her face, took off her riding jacket and sleeves, and ran a soaked cloth over her arms and breasts. The package atop Nanette's bedstead was imposing, the size of a small trunk. "Do open it," Nanette pleaded, practically dancing with anticipation, "and try it on. If Madame Villeneuve has made any error, we have only two months in which to see it undone!"

Katherine laughed at her stepmother's agitation. "We could have a dozen wedding gowns made in that time."

"But not by her! There won't be days enough to pack it off to France and have it back again."

Inge brought a knife, and Katherine sliced through the cording. The box was sturdy leather, embossed with Madame Villeneuve's name. "No wonder it cost so much," Katherine noted dryly.

"What did you expect her to send it in—a diplomatic pouch? Go on and open it!"

Katherine dutifully unfastened the brass clasps and raised the lid. Inside was a nest of white tissue. She pulled the first layer out, then another, and another. "Like a Chinese box," she said, raising another handful. Nanette let out her breath in a sigh that was matched by Inge:

"Ohhhh!"

Katherine stared down at the ice-blue satin, embroidered all over with silver fleurs-de-lis and seed pearls. She reached down and lifted up the dress by the shoulders. It cascaded from the trunk in wave after wave of gloriousness. "Look at the sleeves," Inge breathed, eyeing the lace-encrusted cuffs, where the fabric was brought to dainty points, each crowned with a larger pearl.

"Look at that bodice!" Nanette countered, laughing as Katherine held the gown against her chest. "They are very naughty in Paris these days!"

Katherine glanced back into the trunk. "What is that?" Yards more of the satin still lay inside.

"Yer train, miss," Inge told her, gathering it up and showing her how it attached to the back of the gown.

"It will take me five years to turn about at the altar." But the ice-blue splendor raised her spirits; how could it not? The cloth alone was the most beautiful she'd ever seen.

"And the veil," Nanette noted, pulling that forth as well. "Look how she has worked the headpiece, Inge! Have you ever seen anything so clever?"

"Never," the maid avowed, eyeing the clouds of fluffy tulle sewn to a cap of blue trimmed in glittering stones.

"For paste, they're awfully bright," Katherine said, touching one of the gems.

"They aren't paste at all; they are your mother's diamonds. I had them sent to Madame Villeneuve by way of your father's courier," Nanette confessed.

Katherine looked at her, amazed. "You ought not to have gone to the trouble—not to mention the expense!"

"Your mamma wore them when she was married," Nanette replied blithely. "I thought it only right you should wear them as well."

Katherine, touched, kissed her stepmother's cheek. "Thank you. But I still say—"

"Try it on! Try it on!" Inge urged, as delirious as her

mistress, undoing Katherine's bodice and stays.

Katherine laughed and let them fuss over her.

"It needs pressin'," Inge noted fretfully. "I'll see to it myself, miss, if you like. Don't trust no other iron on such stuff as this."

"I'd be honored, Inge." She stepped out of her riding skirts, then stared down at her boots. "Not exactly the preferred footwear to go with such a gown, but—" She held her breath and lifted her arms as Inge gathered the acres of satin and raised them over her head. The skirts fell over her face with a smooth swoosh.

"Don't look yet," Nanette ordered. "Close your eyes until we have it fastened up." Katherine complied, though it took the two of them some time to work the elaborate pins and hooks and buttons into place. Then their busy hands withdrew, and there was a long moment of silence.

"May I open now?" Katherine asked.

"Aye," Nanette said uncertainly.

Katherine raised her lids and gazed across the room at Nanette's pier glass. She understood the reason for the silence instantly.

"I cannot comprehend it," Nanette murmured. "I took your measurements myself—you recall, Inge, for you helped me!"

"Damned bloody Frogs," Inge muttered. "Can't read plain numbers, clear enough."

The gown was too big. It gaped about the bodice, swam at Katherine's waist where it ought to have been snug—even the elaborate sleeves hung loose and floppy. Nanette pawed through the tissue. "Here, now, look, here's a plain copy of the measurements we sent. Bodice thirty-four inches, waist twenty—that's right, isn't it, Inge?"

"As I recall it."

"Fetch the tape, Inge. For either the gown is wrong or the numbers are wrong, and I cannot see how either can be. Not when we were so careful!"

"Have it off again, then," Inge said darkly. Nanette helped Katherine crawl out of the mountain of satin, then laid the gown on the bed. Inge, frowning, put the measuring tape around the waist. "Twenty exactly," she read off, nonplussed. "Now, how can that be?"

"Measure Katherine."

The maid did so. "Ach, that explains it," she announced, straightening up. "Gone down to eighteen inches, she has."

"And the bodice—what of that?"

Inge whipped the tape around Katherine's chest. "Thirty-*two!*"

"I cannot understand it!" Nanette fretted. "But now I look at you, pet, you are thin as a rail. What's happened to your bosom, then?"

"I don't know."

"She hasn't been eatin' of late," Inge put in.

"How would you know such a thing, Inge?" Katherine demanded.

"Susan that waits at table mentioned it to me."

"*I* hadn't noticed," Nanette countered.

"Mayhap not, but so Susan did tell me. Peckin' at meals like a bird, young mistress is, she said, and never touchin' the sweets."

"Have you been off your appetite, Katherine?" Nanette said accusingly.

"I haven't realized it, if I have." But now that she considered, she couldn't recall the last time she had been truly hungry. Food bored her, as so many things seemed to nowadays.

"Is anything troubling you?" Nanette asked, far more gently.

Katherine flushed, not knowing what to say. *That I have ruined my chances for happiness.* That Clayton was only marrying her for her position. That when their wedding night finally came, she would be as disappointed as she had been in his ardor so far . . . But how could she voice such qualms to anyone, even Nanette?

"Inge, leave us," Nanette ordered suddenly, tossing the armload of blue satin back into the trunk. The maid quickly did so. Nanette pulled Katherine down onto the bed beside her. "What is all this about?"

"All what?" Katherine asked, playing for time.

"A girl doesn't wither away for no reason! Is something making you unhappy?" Katherine said nothing. "Is Lord Dalrymple making you unhappy?"

Katherine winced. "Of course not. He is as kind to me as ever."

"Kind," her stepmother echoed, frowning. " 'Kind' isn't what a bride looks for, is it? Does he kiss you?"

"You have seen him kiss me."

Nanette cast her a scathing look. "You know what I mean. Does he kiss you as you want to be kissed?"

"He . . . tried once. But I stopped him."

"Why?"

"I did not want him to think me a wanton." Katherine nibbled her lip. "It was kissing Alain Montclair that started all this mess, for once he started in on me, I scarcely had the will to stop him! I was afraid that with Clayton, the same would happen. And that then he would lose his good opinion of me."

"Men," Nanette said scornfully. "A girl is damned if she does and damned if she doesn't. La, they are impossible creatures. But surely he has tried again!" Katherine shook her head cravenly. "And you would like him to?"

"I would like—I would like to be certain—" She stopped, not able to put her vague longings into words. But Nanette seemed to intuit what she meant, for she sat back and sighed.

"I dearly wish, pet, I could tell you lovemaking is the same one man to the other."

"It's not, then?"

"Nay. The difference can be night and day. Some men won't let you into their hearts—they're the cold ones, that do it for their own satisfaction and never have a care to yours. And some—not many, mind you, but some—take such concern with your feelings—'Does this suit you?' 'Does this pain you?'—that you wish like the devil they'd just get on with it. There's precious few get it right."

Katherine didn't even stop to think how ludicrous the conversation was—that without her stepmother's wealth of experience, which Martha Westin had thrown up at her so many months ago, the two of them could never have discussed this. "Alain—he was one of the few," she whispered. "At least, I think he was. Unless it was just the *act*—do you know what I am saying?"

"The act's not so grand when not done right that you'd be mistaken," Nanette told her wryly.

"Clayton could be one of the few as well, couldn't he?"

"Of course he could."

"But what if he's not?"

"Ah, pet, that's the shame in it all. If you'd stayed a virgin until you were wed, you'd never know the difference, would you? But now you will. Men have the better of us there as well."

"How so?"

"It doesn't matter to them nearly as much. Just the release is all. That's why a man will take a drunken, pockmarked whore in the dark and rouse up afterward without regret." Then her lovely face brightened. "But you can teach him what pleases you!"

"I don't think so," Katherine murmured, more miserable than ever. "When last he visited, he kissed me and stroked me, and I . . ." Her face was burning, but she pressed on; this was too important not to. "I touched him. There. Just—a touch. Alain had always liked that."

Nanette's lips pursed. "And Lord Dalrymple?"

"He said Alain had taught me whore's tricks." Katherine's lip trembled. "And he said—he said—he'd teach me over again!"

"Mm. That's not so good, I'm thinking."

Katherine hesitated, longing to go on confessing, yet constrained by her shame. "Afterward, I . . ." But that, she could not speak.

"Pleasured yourself?" Nanette said promptly.

Katherine's gaze flew toward her. "How did you know?"

"Do you imagine you're the only woman ever did? Why, I have friends say 'tis the only satisfaction they've ever known!" Katherine giggled behind her hand, and Nanette joined in for a moment, then sobered. " 'Tis lonesome, though, compared to coupling with a man you love." She sighed. "So. What are we to do?" She turned to gaze straight at Katherine. "If you want to withdraw, even now . . . it is late, I grant you. But I'd take your side in it."

"It would kill Poppa."

"Your poppa can withstand a tad more scandal, I reckon." And she winked. "Or I can bring him round to."

"It's a good thing you never taught me *your* tricks." Then Katherine realized how that sounded. "Oh, dear God! I didn't mean—"

But Nanette was laughing. "I still could teach you, if you'd like!"

"You are so good to me, after I was so—so *horrid* to you for so long," Katherine said in wonder.

"Why shouldn't I be? Your happiness is the largest part of the happiness of the man I love. I'm not altogether altruistic."

"Not the largest part, surely."

"Oh, I think so."

Again Katherine paused. "Do you remember the night of the betrothal ball?" she asked finally.

Nanette scratched her head. "Betrothal ball? Nay, I cannot say I recall it. Unless you mean that monstrous huge affair that cost the household three thousand pounds. Would that be the occasion you mean?"

"Don't tease. There's something I didn't tell you. My friends—Gwen and Bess and Petra—they brought me a gift that night."

"Did they, now? How nice. And what was it?"

"Alain Montclair."

That startled Nanette. "Whatever do you mean?"

"Just what I say. He'd come to the academy to fetch me— wounded badly. A sword wound in his chest. Gwen tended it for him, and they—don't ask me how—smuggled him inside Petra's trunk and brought him here, without Mrs. Tread-well ever knowing. They had him out in the folly when they took me there. I saw him. I spoke to him."

"Did you now? And what did you tell him?"

"I sent him away."

"Because you no longer loved him?"

That sleek gold head shook faintly, side to side. "He knows that I love him."

Nanette reached out and tilted Katherine's chin up. "Then why?"

"Because he is a bad penny! Because he has no prospects! Because he is a—a murderer and a rogue. What sort of life could I ever have with him?"

"And what did he say to you?"

"That I would think of him . . . dream of him . . . every time Clayton came to me. And when I bore the babies that ought to have been his."

"Oh, he's the very devil!"

"Exactly!" Katherine cried, tears streaming down her cheeks.

"Or else he loves you madly."

"Don't *say* that! What would *you* have done in my place?"

"I don't know," Nanette admitted. "How can I know?"

"I *hate* being a woman!" Katherine announced, in another burst of sobs.

"Oh, pet. Sweet pet." Nanette cradled her in her arms. "I know. I know."

She let Katherine cry it out, which took a good long while. But at last the flood subsided; Katherine sniffed, and Nanette offered a handkerchief. "I said dreadful things to him," Katherine confessed. "Really quite dreadful things. But all the same, it was not fair of him to come just when I was so happy with Clayton!"

Nanette patted her shoulder. "No. No, it wasn't. I do hope, though, you weren't cross with your friends."

Katherine blew her nose roundly. "How could I be? They meant well, as I said. They all thought for certain I would run away with him again. They read those novels of Mrs. Treadwell's—" She broke off, remembering what Clayton had said about that.

"There's a fair space between what's writ in books and

what goes on in life," Nanette observed. "More's the pity. Still, my offer stands. If you've a mind to renege on your marriage to Lord Dalrymple, I'll be behind you."

Katherine's eyes as she raised them had a haunted look. "How can I do that? How can I go on the marriage mart pretending to be something I'm not? At least Clayton knows the truth. And he has forgiven me. He is better than I deserve."

"You made a mistake," Nanette said gently. "A simple mistake. It's not worth spending the rest of your life paying penance for it."

But Katherine, remembering the splendor of those stolen weeks, the sensation of Alain's rod thrusting inside her, her cries as she'd welcomed him, shook her head. "My behavior was inexcusable. And yet Clayton is willing to excuse it. I owe everything to him."

Nanette seemed on the verge of arguing. Hurriedly, Katherine rose from the bed, with forced cheerfulness. "So the quandary, I suppose, is what to do about the gown. Should I stuff myself with marzipan and almond milk until it fits me, do you think, or can we take it in?"

"We can make it fit you. The real question is, will Lord Dalrymple fit you?"

Katherine drew a deep breath, staring into the future. "I'm sure he will, in the end."

Thirty-nine

Katherine's betrothal to the very proper heir to the very proper duke went a long way toward warming the ton to her stepmother, and for that, she was glad. The family found itself invited to a whirlwind of concerts and suppers and receptions and balls—so many, in fact, that they removed to the duke's town house in London, so as not to have to journey up from Kent. Katherine could not help but be caught up in the excitement. She had a passel of new gowns and wraps and shoes, and Clayton had given her the most absolutely stunning yellow diamond ring—Nanette said it must be three carats, at least—to wear on her left hand. And her father looked so proud as he escorted her and Nanette from affair to affair! It was worth the wrench of forgetting Alain, she assured herself, to see the duke out and about in society again.

There was a bad moment once, at Lady Montague's, when she bumped into Martha Westin on her husband Peter's arm. Katherine flushed scarlet and froze as she recalled the beastly trick she had played on her schoolmate by sending that anonymous letter. She and Martha stood and stared at one another for a moment. Then Katherine curtsied, very low.

"Martha," she said haltingly. "I am so very sorry that I tried to come between you and your husband with such dreadful, wicked lies. It was very wrong of me."

"So it was *you*," Peter began in outrage.

But Martha hushed him quickly, as gracious as could be. "What's past is past, Katherine," she said, kissing her cheek. "There was no harm done in the end, was there? Let's speak of it no more." She went on to inquire after Bess and Gwen, exclaiming to her husband about how much she missed all her friends from the academy, and urging Katherine to come and visit them at their home as soon as she could. Katherine managed to stammer that she would be delighted to, but all she could think was how dreadful it would have been had Martha's bid to kill herself succeeded. She looked radiant; it was clear she and Peter were a perfect fit.

Katherine kept thinking about that "fit." Did she and Clayton fit together so well? Everyone spoke of what a handsome couple they made. He was very good at dancing, and he had a way of carrying himself, from his diplomatic service no doubt, that was very distinguished. Sometimes, at balls, she would look about at the older couples and wonder which of them she and Clayton might come to resemble in a few years. Would they be like Mrs. Treadwell's daughter Vanessa and her husband the earl, who scarcely passed a word to one another through an entire evening and gaily waltzed with other partners? Or would they prove more like Lord and Lady Latimer, who could not, it seemed, bear to be parted from one another for the length of one dance? She wished she knew. When she mentioned this to Nanette, her stepmother assured her that love, once found, was easy to keep alive.

But still Katherine wondered. There were times when she thought she saw Clayton look at her with a sort of forced patience, as though he were hobbled by her already. And he had not, still, progressed past a good-night kiss.

She wished so much that she had Gwen and Bess to talk to. Nanette was marvelous, of course, but Katherine didn't like to discuss her qualms with her; it made her stepmother look so worried and pale. So she forged on as the thousands of details of the wedding-to-be slowly solidified into reality—the guest list set, the menu chosen, the florist's orders given, St. Paul's engaged for the third Saturday in September, the invitations engraved and addressed. She no longer thought of calling off the wedding. There was so much to attend to that she hardly had time to think at all.

She was grateful, then, when a quiet evening of cards was arranged at Admiral Preston's late in August. Clayton escorted her, and he was unaccustomedly solicitous as they set out in the curricle from her father's town house, tucking a rug over her lap against the slight damp in the air. She felt at peace. She was wearing her favorite violet-sprigged muslin, and a new jacket of the most alluring periwinkle-colored silk that closed with frogs at the front. Her hair had gone up perfectly beneath the charming violet-trimmed leghorn hat. As Clayton whipped his team out onto Holborn Road, he actually put an arm around her. "You look splendid tonight," he whispered, his fingertips caressing her shoulder. Katherine colored with pleasure. He did have his moments. Perhaps tonight, on the drive home, he would kiss her passionately.

Just then, someone hailed them from a passing carriage. Annoyed at the interruption of their intimate moment, Katherine glanced at the passenger who had called. He was familiar to her somehow.

"Dalrymple! I say, Dalrymple, it is good to see you!" A stout man, florid-faced, with a ready smile . . .

Clayton had by courtesy reined in. "Lord Bannister. A pleasure to come across you as well," he responded, but his arm had tightened on Katherine's shoulder, and his voice sounded odd. "What brings you to London?"

"You must know that! 'Tis the matter of Montclair's citation! I must say, I hope the secretary won't give me trouble over it, not when the man proved so uncommon valuable to our cause. Is that charming creature you accompany Lady Devereaux?"

"It is. You'll excuse us, I know, Lord Bannister, if we drive on. We're late to an engagement." And Clayton urged the horses on.

"I did hope," Bannister called after them as they started off, "that I might count on your support for that citation! I'm quite sure that . . ." But the rest of his words were lost on the wind.

Katherine sat stock-still, her hands in her lap, a sudden chill in her heart.

"Well!" Clayton said. "I do hope you'll remember not to overbid this evening, my dear; you have a terrible tendency to do so. I don't mind losing, but I hate to do so when the cards are in our hands."

"What did he mean—the citation for Montclair?"

"Did he say Montclair? I daresay he mistook himself; he means Lord Montgomery, who is up for some honor from the regent."

"He distinctly said Montclair. And he asked for your help," Katherine said doggedly.

"And I tell you, he meant Montgomery."

She looked him straight in the eye. "He said Montclair."

There was a moment's pause. Then he sighed. "I'd hoped you wouldn't have to learn of it. I did not want to drag up bad memories. Not when we are on the verge of such great happiness together, you and I."

"Learn of what?" She didn't give an inch.

He waved his hand. "Bannister has got some bee in his bonnet about seeing Montclair honored for his service in the war."

"*What* service in the war?"

"It's all nonsense, Katherine. It's—"

"*What service in the war?*"

She thought for a moment that he wouldn't answer. But he did, finally, though the words seemed dragged from him. "His service as a spy." Katherine gaped at him. He laughed and nodded. "I know. It's perfectly absurd. But to give the man his due, he was of some negligible aid in identifying military targets and plotting their movements. All for cold cash, of course. He was selling out his own countryman in giving us Napoleon, for God's sake. Nothing lower than that."

"*He* gave you Napoleon?"

"That's a gross exaggeration, I assure you. He—"

"My God, Clayton. Why did you never tell me this before?"

He looked straight ahead, his mouth taut beneath his mustache. "Because it doesn't change a thing. And if you don't see that, you are as blockheaded as Bannister. Montclair is still a cheat and a thief and a murderer. A murderer, believe me! There is proof of that!"

Katherine's heart was heaving so, she thought her chest would explode. "He was working for England?"

"Who knows who he was working for? A renegade such as he—"

"But England paid him? To spy?"

"Some few trifling sums. You must understand, war brings out the scum of the earth in search of their own profit."

But Katherine was remembering how bitterly Giacauld had spoken of Alain. "That was why the French wanted to capture him so badly. Not because of Mimi Boulé. Not because he had escaped from the Bastille. Because he was a spy!"

His face was stern in profile. "I'll not have you making him over into some sort of hero, by God! He did what he did from the basest of motives—for gold, so he could go on gambling and wenching and living a dissolute's life. And Bannister is daft if he thinks I'll ever join his petition. For what he did to you alone, Montclair deserves the guillotine. I'd pull the cord myself."

What a confused flood of emotions was tumbling through Katherine! That Alain had been a spy—it explained everything! His anxiousness to leave the fair after the man with the yellow mustaches was murdered. His reluctance to explain what had happened with Mimi Boulé. What he'd said when she'd pointed out that he'd promised never to lie to her: *That does not mean I might not keep certain things hidden.* Yet she could understand, and readily enough, why Clayton had withheld the information from her. It was too much like some romantic novel come to life. She remembered now that strange moment when she and Madame had gone to see Alain in the Bastille, how he had asked if the ambassador had sent her. "The English ambassador?" Madame had answered, amused. "Why should he?" But there had been a reason, one he'd never breathed a word to her about.

She was furious with him for not entrusting his secret to her. She was furious with herself, for having scorned him as an idler and sent him away from Marne House as coldly as she had. But why, *why,* hadn't he told her? Had he thought he couldn't trust her?

She knew the answer, though—or at least knew what he would say if she could somehow ask him. It had been fun for her own protection. If she had known what she knew now when General Fremont had questioned her in the hotel in Paris, would she have been able to lie, straight-faced, without a qualm? Or would she have given herself away with a look or a word, and wound up in the Bastille—or worse—despite who her father was?

God, no wonder he had left her as he did.

But when he'd come to Marne House, there at the folly— surely he might have told her then. When everything, her future, his, depended on it, could he not have confessed? Why hadn't he?

Because he hadn't wanted it to matter, a niggling voice whispered. *Because he wanted you to love him as he was, with no guarantees.*

Tears were trickling down her face. Clayton glanced at her and cursed beneath his breath. "Pull yourself together, for God's sake," he said sharply. "We are almost at the admiral's. And that bounder isn't worth your tears."

Katherine squared her shoulders, composing herself. "Forgive me, Clayton. It just comes as such a shock to me. I do wish you had told me before." Before, say, the betrothal ball. But it was too late now. . . .

His head whipped toward her. "Why?"

"It merely . . . explains many things." He'd reined in at the admiral's. She drew a deep breath as a footman came to take the horses. Clayton leaped down, then reached for her. His hands were surprisingly gentle on her waist.

"Katherine," he murmured, so that the servant would not hear. "I'm sure you think me a jealous fool. But it is so hard at times . . . when I know that you and he . . ." He swung her down, his face bright red.

Touched, she felt the anger drain from her, and stood on her tiptoes to kiss his cheek. "I understand," she told him, and pressed the tangle of her emotions into check, deep within her breast. "We'll speak no more of it. It makes no difference, as you say. But see here. If you are holding a very good hand tonight, will you give me a signal? Kick me beneath the table? Or wink at me? So I will know I may safely overbid?"

He laughed, his arm tight around her as the admiral's butler opened the door to them. Katherine laughed with him, and in the drawing room upstairs, the admiral and his other guests looked to one another knowingly and smiled. "That will be Lord Dalrymple and Lady Devereaux," Mrs. Prestin declared with satisfaction, and Mrs. Fallowforth nodded:

"Oh, those two are ever so gay!"

Forty

Katherine had meant the words as she said them to Clayton—
It makes no difference. And for the space of that evening,
while the ladies chattered to her excitedly about the wedding,
and the men teased Clayton about his good fortune in his
choice of bride, and Clayton beamed at her and was as solicitous as could be even when she badly botched the bidding, they were true. In such company, while she was the
object of the women's envy and the men's admiration, it was
easy to agree with what Clayton had said: that Alain's motives were base, that he was only out for profit, that a man
who would sell out his own country was a dastard and worse.

It was only when he'd left her at home, after kissing her
good night—with, she noted, more fervor than usual, and a
very tentative caress of her bosom that started her heart
pounding—that her doubts resurfaced. Nanette came into her
rooms to ask about the evening—she and the duke had been
to the opera—and Katherine longed to tell her what she had
learned. Before she did, though—

"Do you happen to know Lord Bannister?" she asked in-
nocently, as she brushed out her hair.

Nanette, perched on the bed across the room, nodded.
"Aye. Used to know him quite well, years ago. Surely he
wasn't at the admiral's tonight!"

"Why do you say that?"

"Well—he's an odd bird, Bannister. Good-hearted, mind
you. The sort who always thinks the best of everyone."

"Is he, now."

"Some folk think that makes him a ninny."

"And what do you think?"

Nanette smoothed her skirts down. "He was always very
kind to me. He squired me about a bit after he'd seen me in

A Midsummer Night's Dream. What struck me most was that he hadn't any patience with gossip. He said he liked to take his own measure of a soul, without the ton weighing in. I found that admirable, as you can imagine. And he was such a gentleman! Treated me like a true lady. Aye, I liked him well." Her eyes met Katherine's in the mirror. "And no, I didn't have him to bed. He never once took liberties."

"But you stopped seeing him."

"I met your father just then. Why do you ask about him?"

"Would he think it strange, do you suppose, if you and I called on him?"

Nanette was plainly perplexed. "What, after all these years? Why would I do such a thing?"

"Because I need to speak to him."

"To Lord Bannister? Whatever for?"

"I can't tell you. Not yet."

Nanette couldn't help laughing. "What a creature of mystery you can be sometimes, Katherine!"

"I am sorry. It's just something peculiar I heard about tonight, that he has knowledge of. I would not ask if it weren't important."

"Hmm. I suppose I *could* call. Though it's not such a good idea for you to accompany me, frankly. He does have a reputation for quirkiness. Perhaps if you were to give the question you would ask him to me . . ."

"No," Katherine said quickly. "I need to ask him myself. Face-to-face."

"And am I ever to discover what this is all about?" Nanette teased.

"That depends entirely," Katherine told her, "on what Lord Bannister has to say to me."

Nanette was plainly intrigued by Katherine's hints, for the very next morning they paid a call on Lord Bannister together. His house was in Bloomsbury—"Hardly the nicest section of town," Nanette noted, "and doesn't it need paint!" The door was answered by a burly butler in a mismatched livery, who took their card and withdrew. "I forgot to mention—His Lordship never cared a whit for fashion, either," Nanette murmured, as they waited in a front hall adorned with a hodgepodge of stuffed animal heads and Oriental carpets and dusty umbrella jars.

A moment later, His Lordship himself appeared, unwigged, in a dressing robe. "Nanette!" he cried, clearly tickled. "How exceedingly kind of you to call on me! My, you look as lovely as ever."

Nanette smiled as he kissed her hand. "Are you acquainted with my stepdaughter, Lady Devereaux, milord?"

"I had the pleasure once of being introduced. At the countess of Yarlborough's, wasn't it, m'dear?" the old man asked Katherine. "I must have been invited there by a mistake, you know. I'm not thought much of by that crowd."

"My fiancé, Lord Dalrymple, speaks of you most highly, milord," Katherine lied unabashedly.

Bannister's dark gaze fixed on hers. "Oh, I doubt that. But you are kind to say so, anyway. Come in, come in! Will you have tea, Nanette? I beg your pardon; I must call you Your Grace, mustn't I, now? How is your husband?"

"Very well, thank you. And tea would be lovely."

"Godshaw!" Lord Bannister shouted to the butler. "Rustle up some tea—and see you scrub out the pot first. And any cakes we have lying about that aren't too stale!" Godshaw grunted and disappeared into the bowels of the house, while their host led them through a doorway into a front parlor whose decor was even more peculiar than the front hall's had been.

"Best brush it off a bit," Lord Bannister cautioned, as Nanette prepared to lower herself onto a settee. "I've not much company these days." Katherine watched, mildly intrigued, as her stepmother dutifully gave the cushion a whack and it let forth a brief cloud of dust. She herself took a plain wooden chair.

"I always did enjoy your company, Joshua," the duchess said with a laugh. "And was surprised when others didn't."

"Aye, well, being plainspoken don't get a man ahead in

this world, so I've learned." Their host plunked onto a worn seat, reaching for his pipe. He lit it, drew in, let out a puff, and then belatedly asked, "Mind, do you?"

"I see—or smell, rather—that you are still being supplied with that cut-rate Turkish tobacco," Nanette said, a twinkle in her eye.

He laughed. "That's why I always liked you, m'dear! Not one to mince words, are you? But I'll take my Turkish, and the world be damned." It was, Katherine thought, a sentiment to be admired.

Lord Bannister might be peculiar, but he wasn't stupid; his next utterance showed it. "And to what, pray tell, might I owe the honor of this visit from you, Your Grace, after— good God, how many years has it been?"

"Seven or eight, I suppose," Nanette said calmly. "But you would have to apply to my daughter for the cause. We came at her request."

"Did you, now?" Those keen eyes raked over Katherine. "I've yet to congratulate you on your betrothal, m'dear. Read about it in the *Gazette,* of course. And it's on the tongues of all the ton—not that many of them have much to do with me anymore. Can't say I mind, frankly. Bunch of idiots, if you ask me. A bit more backbone to the lads they're bringing up nowadays, and we'd have put Bonaparte down years ago."

"But he is safely shut away on Elba now, milord, isn't he?" Katherine inquired.

"There's no 'safe' where that one's concerned—not until he's in his grave."

"Come now, Joshua!" the duchess chided. "Surely you are overcautious. He had his moment in the sun, but all that has passed."

The admiral shrugged, pulling at his pipe. "Time will tell. But if you asked me to lay money on it, I'd say we'd yet to hear the last of him."

The butler, Godshaw, backed into the parlor then with a tray bearing an exceedingly tarnished tea set and a plate of moldy-looking biscuits. He set the tray down at his master's hand, and the admiral cast a dubious glance at the plate. "May as well take those away," he directed. "You like yours with just lemon, Nanette, I believe?"

"So I do. Fancy your remembering, after all this time."

"And you, Lady Devereaux?"

"Two sugars, please. And . . . please, do call me Katherine."

He grinned at her. "Two sugars, then. And I shall." He handed them the cups—badly chipped, both of them—poured his own, took a sip, and winced. "Gad. I have two witnesses, Godshaw, that I instructed you to scrub out the pot."

"And so I did," the servant countered in a rumble.

"With what—rhubarb? Never mind, then. Go along and run next door to Mrs. Minnefer's, why don't you, and beg a few cakes?"

"Please, Joshua, don't have him go on our account," Nanette urged.

"Why shouldn't he? I pay his wages; let him earn them!" Godshaw went out, scowling, and a moment later, they heard the slamming of a door from somewhere in the rear of the house. "Good," the admiral declared. "The man's a dreadful snoop. Let's down to it, then. Since I haven't seen you in years, Nanette, and there have been only two times in my life, Katherine, when I've spoken to you, I must assume your visit concerns Alain Montclair."

"What?" Nanette cried, startled, her gaze flying to her stepdaughter.

Katherine nibbled her lip. "I suppose, Nanette, I should explain. Last evening, on our way to Admiral Prestin's, Lord Dalrymple and I encountered Lord Bannister in his rig. We stopped to speak, and he asked Clayton's help in a petition he is putting to the regent." She looked across to the old lord. "Could you tell me more about that?"

"Easy enough to do. I've put Montclair up for a valor citation. And a nominal stipend. A hundred pounds a year for life."

"Valor? How so?" Nanette demanded, dumbfounded.

"On account of his services to the regent in the late war."

"His services to . . ."

"He was a spy," Katherine explained.

"And a highly valuable one!" His Lordship put in. "It was his prolonged agitation amongst the French that led to the army riots and the defection of Marshal Marmont. The regent could not have had a more adept advocate."

"Are you telling me Montclair was in English employ?" Nanette asked dazedly, and actually sipped some of the awful tea.

"That's a bald way of putting it," Lord Bannister declared, setting his own cup aside and taking up his pipe. "I prefer to think that we were providing him with the means"—he rubbed his thumb and forefinger together—"to keep body and soul together while he made his arguments on behalf of liberty. He's frightfully keen on liberty. So it's not so much that he was working for the regent as that he was allowing the regent to aid him in his work."

Nanette blinked. "I'm not sure I see the distinction."

But Katherine knew Alain would. "What I think His Lordship means is that Ala—that Montclair would have said he was working only for the French."

"Precisely!" Lord Bannister said, beaming. "But the end result is that his travails aided England. And he deserves recognition—and recompense—for that."

"Katherine, did you know of this?" Nanette demanded.

"Not a bit. I heard him talk often enough against the emperor. I knew he hated the generals for the freedoms they had stolen from his people. But I took it as talk, and no more."

"That's what made him so good," His Lordship said approvingly. "That idler façade. The drinking and gambling and wen—and general carrying-on."

"Did your father know of his efforts, do you suppose?" Nanette asked Katherine.

"Oh, I doubt that," Lord Bannister put in. "Only the Home Office knew. And it was kept close to the chest even there. That's what's so damnably unfair. The man worked his tail off to see Napoleon defeated. But because he was so accomplished at what he did, no one will ever know. Unless"—and here he brightened—"I can convince the regent and the Parliament to recognize his contributions."

Katherine recalled how Clayton had belittled Alain's motives and efforts. "Somehow I don't think you will manage that."

"Perhaps not." The old man knocked out his pipe. "But I feel obligated to try. Valor's not so common anymore that it should be allowed to go unnoticed, don't you agree?"

Nanette's lovely face was troubled. "Katherine. What does this mean to you? Why did you ask that we come here?"

Katherine wasn't certain herself. "I simply wanted to hear . . ." But that wasn't quite true. "I thought . . ." She was grateful when Godshaw, the butler, banged back in just then, bearing a plate of jam cakes, which he set down at his master's side with a bit of a sniff.

"Thank you, Godshaw," His Lordship said mildly. "You may go." He offered the plate to his guests in turn. Nanette shook her head, but Katherine reached eagerly for one of the cakes and took a huge bite, chewing while she thought of what she would say.

But as she was still swallowing the last bits, Lord Bannister spoke up for her: "I imagine, Nanette, she simply wanted some confirmation that she wasn't a complete and utter ninny." Both women stared at him, and he barked a laugh. "Well, I would, in her place! Lost her heart and her . . . whatever else to a fellow like that—who wouldn't be gladdened to discover he wasn't such a blackguard after all?"

"Yes," Katherine whispered gratefully, dusting crumbs from her skirts. "Yes, that's exactly it."

"Not," the old lord said shrewdly, "that it makes any difference now. Not when you are all cozy and settled and as good as wed to Dalrymple."

"But," Nanette began, and then bit her tongue.

"And no one seems to know where Montclair is, even now, when he could readily come forward. Gambling debts still keep him lying low, no doubt."

"No doubt," Katherine agreed. "But if you don't know where he is, Lord Bannister, what's the sense in your petition? Or in that stipend, if you could not even get the money to him?"

"Why, it's the principle of the thing, my dear! There aren't nearly enough folk anymore who are willing to stand on principle, if you ask me. The man did his service to the regent, even if his methods were sometimes unsavory. And he ought to be recognized for that."

Katherine leaned forward on her chair. "Who are his parents, do you know?"

"Of course I do. The former comte and comtesse de Montclair. They owned a huge château on the Côte d'Or—it is where Nuits-Saint-Georges is made. But when the Revolution came, they were turned out in favor of their overseer. Despite that, they were dedicated followers of Napoleon, for a time. Joseph lost two sons in the Egyptian campaign, I believe."

"Joseph?" Katherine echoed faintly, picturing Veronique's tall husband in his hut lined with books.

"Aye, aye. Terrible tragedy for both him and Veronique."

Katherine pondered this while Nanette deftly turned the subject, engaging the old lord in conversation about mutual friends, most of whom seemed to be dead. She was startled from her reverie when her stepmother set her cup aside and stood up. "It's been lovely seeing you again, Joshua," she declared warmly, "but we must be on our way."

"Of course, of course. Wedding to plan and all that. Well, life belongs to the young, doesn't it, m'dear?" he asked Katherine, who nodded faintly. "I wish you every happiness. Good man, Dalrymple. Steady. Very steady indeed. Do come by again soon, Nanette. If you let it go another eight years, I may well be dead!"

Nanette laughed and went to kiss his leathery cheek. "I will come by, Joshua. But don't you be such a stranger to society! I know any number of widowed matrons who would love the chance to tidy up your drawing room."

Lord Bannister shuddered. "God deliver me from widows,

now and always. I've managed to avoid letting any woman get her hooks into me for sixty-eight years, and I intend to keep it that way."

"Then you mustn't complain that you are shunned by the ton," Nanette teased, "since it is mostly made up of widows!"

"Godshaw and I do well enough by each other, thank you. Katherine, so kind of you to call on an old man."

"It is I who owe you thanks," she told him, and also kissed his cheek. Then she and Nanette took their leave, as he sat in his dusty chair.

Back in the carriage, Nanette looked thunderous. "I'm sorry," Katherine whispered, fearful of her anger. "I ought to have explained the purpose of our call. But I—"

"Oh, I'm not fierce at you, pet, not at all! It's Lord Dalrymple, that knew all this and never breathed a word to your father or me!"

"He *is* still a scoundrel," Katherine pointed out. "Clayton was quite right; nothing can change that."

"Such news would have gone a long way toward soothing your poppa back in France."

"But Clayton couldn't admit he knew Alain was a spy in front of Fremont, could he?"

"No. I suppose not. A word in private, though, to the duke or me . . ." She looked sidelong at Katherine. "You cannot convince me such silence was admirable behavior. What has Lord Dalrymple to say for himself?"

"What he always says when these matters come up. That he is tortured by the thought of me and Alain together." The duchess's lips drew up tightly. "He says it quite movingly!" Katherine hurried to add. "Is it not good that he can admit to his jealousy? Think of his position! Think of all that he has done for me!"

Nanette looked as though she would speak, then shook her head and said nothing. Katherine leaned back against the carriage seat, feeling weary and drained—but somehow, also, exhilarated by Lord Bannister's news. Alain was a hero. The world might never learn of it; the English might never admit it. God wot, Clayton never would. But she had the knowledge now, to hold in her heart like a small, bright pearl. Her judgment had not been so awry.

The knowledge was power. She felt it seeping through her, radiating all the way to her fingers and toes. She straightened on the seat; her bowed head came up, and her shoulders, and her chin, so that Nanette eyed her curiously. "What are you thinking, pet?"

"That I'll not be so meek and apologetic the next time Clayton tells me that I overbid at whist—not when the fault's more his than mine!" Katherine declared, eyes flashing with something of her former hauteur.

Forty-one

"The wedding menu," Katherine announced, holding a sheet of parchment out to Clayton as he lounged, puffing a cigar, in the town house parlor.

"Good, good! Glad to see you've been putting your mind to—" He broke off, eyeing the list. "Foie gras sautéed with shallots in sauce Bercy . . . endive braised in champagne . . . poitrine de faisan—what the devil is poitrine de faisan?"

"Breast of pheasant," she answered calmly. "In a sauce of mushrooms with tarragon and wine. You had it here last night at supper, and praised it extravagantly."

"Dammit, Katherine, did we not agree to serve plain English food, without these frivolous French fillips?"

"No. We did not agree. You ordered that it should be so. You may recall, I argued quite strenuously that your menu choices would make us a laughingstock amongst the ton."

"And so you have defied me." He looked at her, his eyes slightly narrowed.

"I have given the matter a great deal of thought, and have come to the conclusion that your opinion is wrong."

"My opinion is—" For a moment, he was speechless. Then he regathered his thoughts, with an indulgent smile. "An opinion cannot be wrong, my dear. An opinion is just that— an opinion. You knew my *wishes,* then. Yet it seems you've disregarded them."

"I have wishes as well. I see no reason why yours should take precedence in all things. Especially not in something as inconsequential as this."

He tapped off the lengthening ash on his cigar. "I see. Are you intending any further changes to the wedding plans we have discussed?"

"I have. You expressed the wish that I carry lilies. I will have roses."

"May I inquire why?"

"Because I prefer roses to lilies."

"You know that my mother carried lilies at her wedding."

"Yes. You have mentioned that."

"Custom means naught to you? You care nothing for tradition?"

"Nanette carried roses at her wedding. I would honor that tradition instead."

"Over that of my family."

"Yes."

He cocked his head at her. "An actress's preference over that of a duchess?"

She wanted to slap him, but she stopped in time. "She is a duchess as well."

"The whole world knows what she is."

"Why must you be so hateful toward her?"

"She is a pernicious influence on you."

Katherine laughed. It seemed to unnerve him a little, and that made her glad. "Say what you like about her; I will carry roses."

"What has gotten into you, Katherine?" He sounded so bewildered that she softened.

"You told me once—do you not recall it?—that you had no use for simpering misses. That you admired—that you loved—my spirit."

"And so I do. But not when you use it to usurp my authority!"

"I see. So I am to be spirited, but only as it suits you."

"The man is the head of the family. It says so plainly in St. Paul. 'Wives, submit unto your husbands . . .' Why, in our vows, you will promise to obey me! Or do you intend to counteract that as well?" His handsome face bore a hint of amused indulgence; he gave the end of his mustache a twirl.

"What is a husband's duty unto his wife, pray tell?"

"To honor her and love her," he answered promptly.

She leaned in close to him, bending down. Her bodice was cut low, and the vantage point afforded him a plain look at the firm mounds of her breasts. He drew back in surprise. "And do you honor me?" she asked.

"Certainly I do!"

"So long as you honor me, I will happily obey you."

He nodded uneasily. "Then we should get on very well, don't you think?"

"I think we are getting on better every day," she told him, and plucked the menu from his hand. "This suits you, then, the meal?"

"I—"

"And the roses?"

"Mother will be most—"

"And the roses?"

He stared into her eyes, which were lit by a strange, unfamiliar flame. "I don't see why it should make such a difference to you. It is only one flower for another."

"Then why should it make a difference to *you*?"

After a moment, he shrugged, conceding. "As you will."

Katherine bent down again, but this time to kiss him. "Thank you, Clayton."

He was seized by an abrupt, nigh-overwhelming desire to draw her into his lap. Almost as though she sensed it, she caressed his cheek—and then pulled away, turning to the door. "I must go and have the order sent to the florist."

"Mother always uses Farringer and Bauer." Aware of a sudden bulge in his breeches, he sought to cover it by crossing his legs.

"Yes. I know. Nanette much prefers Minham's." She blew him a kiss from her fingertips. He watched her go out, her silk skirts swirling in her wake, and swallowed, reaching for the snifter of brandy beside his chair.

With the wedding but a week away, a small caravan arrived at the duke of Marne's town house from Mrs. Treadwell's, bearing the beaming headmistress, Bess and Gwen and Petra. . . .

"Where is Madame?" Katherine asked, glancing inside the carriage.

"She declined to come," Mrs. Treadwell replied.

"But I especially requested—"

"My dear Katherine. And she was so very touched that you did. But you must understand, simply willing the ton's opinion away does not make it disappear. The countess is aware, even if you are not, that her presence at your wedding would occasion an unspeakable stir."

"We tried," Bess murmured to Katherine in apology.

"This is to be your shining hour," Mrs. Treadwell decreed, flush with happiness. "It is best to let nothing detract from that, don't you think?"

"Mrs. Treadwell!" Nanette had appeared to greet the new arrivals. "We are so glad you are here. Come in, come in! Not too tiresome a journey up from Kent, I trust?"

"Oh, no, it went exceedingly quickly. Journeys always do, I've found, when there is such grand satisfaction at their end. Come along, girls! And we have gifts for you, Katherine!"

"None so upsetting as our last present to you," Petra whispered, which made Katherine laugh.

"You look glorious, as always," Bess allowed, as Katherine led them into the front hall. "I had fond hopes you might have broken out in hives, or at least have broken a fingernail."

Katherine laughed again and hugged her. "I have missed you all so!"

Gwen was eyeing her intently. "You *do* look well, Katherine. More than well. You look . . . at peace with yourself."

"Your friend is quite a philosopher, isn't she?" Nanette asked gaily.

"A physician, rather," Bess corrected her.

"Don't be foolish, Bess! Women can't be physicians," Mrs. Treadwell said, with a hint of worry constricting her brows.

"Well, I am quite contented, both in body and mind,"

Katherine declared, "so whether Gwen is a philosopher or a physician is a moot question."

Mrs. Treadwell let the girls go on ahead, drawing Nanette aside. "There haven't been any . . . apparitions? Ghosts from the past?" she murmured tentatively.

"No."

"Oh, thank heaven!" The headmistress fanned herself emphatically. "I am ever so relieved. Christiane and I have been beside ourselves with worry that *he* might turn up again. He is, you know, a bad penny."

Nanette shook her head, smiling a little as the girls' bright laughter rang through the house. "I had my fears as well. For a time there, it seemed Lord Dalrymple was determined to rule her with an iron hand. But Katherine appears to have found her own way through it all. He is absolutely besotted with her nowadays; everyone remarks on it."

"Then all's well that ends well."

"Yes. It certainly seems so."

"God be praised," Mrs. Treadwell said heartily. "Do you suppose I might trouble you for just a wee bit of sherry? The road was dreadfully dusty."

"And rocky as well," Nanette murmured, sending the butler for two glasses straightaway.

That night, after a celebratory dinner at Gaillard's and then a stirring performance of *Othello* at Covent Garden, the misses of Mrs. Treadwell's assembled in their nightgowns in the room Gwen and Bess and Petra were sharing. Bess was still greatly affected by the play: "So very tragic," she sniffled, leaning into Gwen's shoulder as they sat side by side on the huge bed.

"So very stupid, rather," Gwen countered, pushing her away. "If Othello and Desdemona had but been honest with each other, not even Iago could have come between them."

"The costumes were lovely, didn't you think?" Petra asked, starry-eyed.

Katherine giggled. "Nanette told me the outfit Desdemona

wore for her death scene was the exact same gown she herself played the part in, a dozen or more years ago!"

"I would have loved to see her do it," Bess said eagerly. "She has such joie de vivre, your stepmamma. She had me absolutely in stitches at dinner, teasing the waiter as she did. 'And is the roast beef succulent?' " she mimicked the countess's beguiling Irish accent.

Gwen laughed with her. "The poor lad was so taken with her, he could scarcely stammer an answer!"

"She did look lovely tonight, didn't she?" Katherine said fondly.

Gwen gave her a sideward glance. "You seem to have turned a corner in your relations with her."

"She is my best and truest friend—when I haven't the three of you about to bedevil me."

Petra flounced down on a pillow. "Well, we are here for a week, and in that time we expect to bedevil you enough to last your marriage's first year!"

"Lord Dalrymple hadn't much to say tonight," Bess mused, plucking at a corner of the coverlet.

"He doesn't approve of you three," Katherine confided. "He believes you are a bad influence on me."

Petra was indignant. "How dare he say such a thing!"

"I imagine it is because I told him you urged me to rebuff his suit and go on pining for Montclair."

"No wonder, then," Gwen put in. "What would make you tell him that?"

Katherine paused, then brushed back a golden ringlet. "He was being beastly at the time. He can be perfectly beastly. But he is less so now than before."

"What made him change?" Bess asked eagerly. "Just in the unlikely event I ever have a suitor, either beastly or unbeastly."

"The change was in me," Katherine said slowly. "For such a long time, I had felt . . . beholden to him, for rescuing me in Paris. For standing up for me. My disgrace was so complete that I felt utterly unworthy. And so I . . . I let him push me about a bit. Oh, not physically!" she assured Petra, who had recoiled. "Only in terms of our behavior with one another. And then I learned—something."

"What?" the other three demanded in unison.

"You won't believe it," Katherine said softly.

"Of course we will!" Bess protested.

"Well . . . it was about Montclair. I found out, through rather circuitous circumstances, that he wasn't the ne'er-do-well murderous cad that everyone had been assuring me he was."

"What was he, then?" asked Petra, wide-eyed.

"An English spy."

Bess drew in her breath. Petra clutched her heart. Only Gwen looked skeptical: "Montclair an English spy? I find that rather hard to swallow."

"Lord Dalrymple admitted it to me himself. He was working for the English all through the war—well, not so much for the English as for what he saw best for the French, which *wasn't* Napoleon. What's more, I discovered that Montclair's lineage is perfectly respectable. He really is—was—a comte. His parents owned a grand château on the Côte d'Or before the Revolution. They were turned out of their home in favor of their overseer when French society went all topsy-turvy."

"Think of that!" Petra breathed.

Gwen, again, was the Doubting Thomas. "I can't see how learning such stuff about Montclair—even if it is true— would have changed your relations with Lord Dalrymple."

"Can't you? You have so little imagination sometimes, Gwen!" Bess said indignantly. "If Montclair truly was a comte, not to mention a spy, not to mention unspeakably handsome and dashing, then it's not so incomprehensible that Katherine fell as she did for him!"

"There's naught wrong with my imagination," Gwen retorted. "Running off to France after a man you hardly know, and frightening us and Mrs. T. and the countess half to death—not to mention her parents—can hardly be excused by the fact the fellow is of noble birth! And spies—" She made a face. "They're the lowest form of life."

"Not if their work is in the service of some great cause!" Bess said angrily.

"The difference," Katherine interjected, "was not in my feelings toward Montclair so much as in how I saw myself." She paused, trying to think how to phrase it. "I know you all used to bemoan my pride as my worst sin. But my pride had been so completely crushed! I hadn't the backbone to stand up for myself in anything. And Clayton—Lord Dalrymple—took advantage of that. He was trying to *rule* me. And I was so cowed that I didn't object to it. Once I had learned the truth about Montclair, I had the courage to—be strong. To speak out. Not to merely let myself be led about like a stupid cow."

"I can't imagine the change has pleased Lord Dalrymple," Petra said worriedly.

"Oddly enough, I think he was relieved. We are on a much more equal footing now. Oh, like all men, he *thought* he wanted a complacent, obedient, mindless wife. But what man truly would, when it comes to that?"

"Lots of 'em," Gwen said promptly.

"I'm not so sure," said Bess, scratching her nose. "As I understand it, Madame and Mrs. T.'s purpose in founding the academy was to achieve just such an equal footing. They believe men will be happier and more contented when their wives can think and do for themselves—and the wives will be, too."

"Exactly," Katherine declared, azure eyes aglow. "It must be a dreadful trial for a man always to have to boss his wife about! And Clayton, I am pleased to say, has come to realize that."

"It sounds as though you have achieved a true meeting of minds with him," Petra said with approval.

"I believe we have. We discuss, we each voice our opinions, and then we decide, together, what we will do." Katherine smiled benignly.

"And so you discussed the fact that we are bad influences on you?" Gwen asked, with mischief on her small face.

Katherine would not be flustered. "He gave me his opinion, certainly. I gave him mine. And then I . . . ignored his."

"Where is the equality in that?" Petra wondered, looking perplexed.

"Don't be a simpleton," said Bess, who was grinning. "It's a perfectly marvelous template for marriage!"

"I think so as well," Katherine declared, flouncing onto the bed to envelop all three of her classmates in a hug.

Forty-two

The final days leading up to her marriage were so filled with a swirl of receptions and balls that Katherine had scant chance for more such tête-à-têtes with her old classmates. Still, she took great pleasure in their enjoyment of the social buzz. Not even Clayton could argue with their deportment, and though it could not honestly be said that either Bess or Gwen made a conquest, Petra managed to attract the attention of a very well-to-do viscount, which gratified Mrs. Treadwell no end.

Katherine was very much at peace. For reasons she did not entirely understand, Clayton had turned so passionate in his behavior toward her that it was hard for her at times—when they were discreetly left alone in the town house drawing room, after the guests had gone on to bed—to withstand his advances. "I love you so, my darling," he would murmur, pressing close to her on the settee, his hands caressing her bodice or thigh. His mustache would tickle her neck as he pressed kiss after kiss there; he seemed on fire for her. She responded more freely than she would have done in the past; she returned his kisses, though she never had the nerve to touch him intimately.

And she held him off from the prize she felt sure he would readily have taken, even in so unsuitable a venue as her parents' drawing room. "Only a few nights more to wait," she would murmur to him as he stroked her breasts, his thumb playing at her nipples.

"God, I cannot bear it!" But he did, as did she. She was so relieved by his newfound ardor that she did not dare risk giving in to it at this point, lest the shadows of the past intrude on their happiness. She comforted herself with the thought of what such delicious tension would lead to on their

wedding night, when they were at last free of Alain Montclair's ghost and could begin life together, pristine and new.

Mrs. Treadwell was deliriously happy for her. Gwen and
Bess and Petra, if they still harbored any doubts, concealed
them admirably. The duke reveled in his role as father to the
bride of the season. Only in Nanette's eyes did Katherine
occasionally glimpse uncertainty.

It appeared, very clearly, at a fête thrown by Lord and
Lady Wormuth for the engaged couple, when Lord Bannister
turned up among the invitees. "His Lordship insisted," their
hostess murmured to the duchess, within Katherine's hearing.
"Quite an embarrassment, so far as I'm concerned. The old
dolt's not got half his flags to the wind." Which may have
been why Katherine so greatly enjoyed the next moment,
when Nanette called across the ballroom:

"Joshua! How splendid it is to see you out and about!"

Lord Bannister, in a somewhat stained frock coat, waved
at her above the crowd and came plunging toward them.
"Nanette, m'dear!"

"I . . . was not aware that you were acquainted with His
Lordship," Lady Wormuth stammered.

Katherine kissed the old man soundly, whispering into his
ear: "How fares your petition?"

"Badly, I'm afraid. Very badly indeed. The Home Office
seems to have decided that Montclair is too great a blackguard to ever be redeemed."

"Well, we know better, don't we?" Katherine murmured
to him, squeezing his hand. From across the room, where he
was chatting with the foreign secretary, Lord Dalrymple
glared. But the next moment, Katherine was swept away by
a bevy of chattering misses; she could only give Lord Bannister a rueful glance and a shrug of her shoulder before they
carried her off on a wave of eager questions and laughter.
He responded with a wink.

Later that night, they went on to the Rushingtons' for a
late supper, and then to the Singleys' for cards. Somewhere
in all the excited movement, Katherine wondered briefly
whether she and Clayton were getting along so well because

they scarcely ever saw each other anymore except across crowded rooms. She was reminded of how she had contemplated what sort of married couple they would become—inseparable, or more like ships in passing—and was forced to conclude the latter was more likely. Clayton gravitated toward the politically connected, and though Katherine did her best to follow their conversations, she found them convoluted and dull. The gossip of the ladies was hardly more scintillating, but at least there, she occasionally had something to add. To her surprise, she found herself at times taking the side of an "unsuitable" suitor in the general debate. "A blackguard isn't always a blackguard when you get to know him," she observed once to the very proper Mrs. Trustlebury, who instantly retorted:

"How on earth could you say such a thing, Lady Devereaux?"

Katherine caught Mrs. Treadwell's alarmed glance, but chose to ignore it. "Because I've found it to be true," she said simply. Gwen jumped into the conversation just then, uncharacteristically commenting on Mrs. Trustlebury's sleeves, which were of some newfangled and, to Katherine's eye, monstrous cut. But Gwen admired them at length and even secured the name of Mrs. Trustlebury's mantua maker, until the awkward moment was forgotten in a flurry of talk about fashion's likely turns in the season to come.

She thought less often of Alain in those last days, partly because she was so terribly busy and partly because of Clayton's new ardor for her. When something did remind her of him—a glimpse of blue-black hair against a coat, a word of French dropped into conversation, or simply the way the sun slanted through the trees in these days of late summer, as it had on their journey to the Côte d'Or—the memories had a dreamlike quality, so far-off and distant, as though she had read them in a book long ago. Who was that reckless girl who had slipped him her pistol in the Bastille? Had plunged into a river in a frenzy to save him? Had lain with him on a crackly straw bed, covered only with a careworn blanket? Had laughed with him, and cried when she feared he had left her, and made love to him without restraint? Surely not Lady Katherine Devereaux, heiress to the duke of Marne, betrothed of the heir to the duke of Sutherland, cosseted and coddled belle of the ton. And yet it *had* been her, impossible though it now seemed.

On the evening before the wedding, Lord Dalrymple headed off with a company of male friends for a final bacchanal—one that, he assured her, kissing her tenderly and sweetly, would involve nothing more risqué than gambling and drinking. "And I'd far rather be with you," he whispered, his tongue caressing her earlobe. "But it is de rigueur, I'm afraid."

"I know. Behave yourself, though!" she scolded. "I would not have you bleary and red-eyed when you speak your vows."

"I shall be in bed before you are, I daresay. You and your schoolmates will be up the entire night, whispering and giggling—"

"I won't allow that, you may be certain!" Nanette announced from her seat, where she was putting a last touch of embroidery to the wedding gloves.

"I am glad to hear it." Clayton kissed Katherine again. "Until tomorrow, then."

"Until tomorrow," she whispered, feeling him press up against her. How had she ever thought him lacking in passion? His mouth was urgent beneath the brush of mustache; his arms were encircling her so tightly she could scarcely breathe.

"Enough of that, then," Nanette said with mock sternness. "Go on to your whiskey and cigars!"

He left them with obvious reluctance, and a final kiss for Katherine. "Tomorrow night," he told her, "my dreams will come true."

Katherine hoped with all her heart that it would be so.

Forty-three

"Rain on your wedding day is lucky," Mrs. Treadwell observed at breakfast, as a steady downpour pounded against the shutters. "Everyone knows that."

"It's quite true," Nanette confirmed, as the maids brought in sirloin and poached eggs and toast. "It rained on *my* wedding day."

"Do you feel nervous, Katherine?" Petra inquired shyly. "I certainly would."

How did she feel? Katherine wondered. "Excited, rather, I'll venture," Bess said with a sly wink, "considering the way Lord Dalrymple cannot keep his hands off you."

"There's more to marriage than that, young ladies," Mrs. Treadwell announced. "A great deal more, Your Grace, wouldn't you say?"

Nanette, thus appealed to, cocked her head. "I *suppose* there is. . . ." That made all the girls giggle and Mrs. Treadwell blush.

Gwen kindly sought to change the subject. "Where will you be breakfasting tomorrow, then, Katherine?"

"We're to head for the Lake District. Clayton's family has a house on Lake Windermere. It's very lovely, very tranquil, he says."

"Sounds the perfect spot to begin a family," Bess put in.

"For heaven's sake, Bess!" Mrs. Treadwell remonstrated.

"What? I daresay before the year is out, we'll be back to London for a christening."

"Are you looking forward to having children, Katherine?" Petra asked breathlessly.

Go to your duke's son, and wed him. Bear him a passel of babies. Know every morning when you wake what the day will bring. And the next day! And the next!

"Of course I am," Katherine said firmly, shaking off that voice. She took up her fork, meaning to try the sirloin, but the meat on her plate had left a puddle of blood. She stared at it, feeling faintly queasy.

"Stick to the toast, pet," Nanette advised.

"I believe I will."

When breakfast was finished, she bathed and then dressed, with a myriad of hands to help her. Gwen and Bess and Petra were in high spirits, and Mrs. Treadwell sniffed away tears as Nanette settled the veil over Katherine's curls. "You look so very lovely!" she cried, dabbing her eyes with her kerchief. "Oh, I do wish—"

"That Madame could be here," Bess finished for her. "We all do, Katherine. She is so very, very proud of you."

"Is she?" Katherine eyed her reflection in the looking glass. Who was this girl—this woman—clad in ice-blue satin, veiled and trained, gloved and coiffed, in the very pink of fashion? Had she ever really trod grapes with her bare toes?

"Of course she is," Mrs. Treadwell assured her, fluttering with the folds of the veil. "We all are."

Katherine's gaze met Nanette's in the mirror. Her stepmother gave a reassuring nod: "So we are."

Katherine nodded as well, resolutely. "Where is my bouquet?"

Petra bustled toward the long florist's box. "Here you are. And aren't they perfectly exquisite? I do love lilies."

Katherine's chin came up. "Lilies? There must be some mistake! I was supposed to have roses—just as you did, Nanette!"

But the bouquet Petra lifted from its cocoon of tissue was indisputably of lilies—great, gorgeous white ones that filled the room with their heady scent. "Is that a card?" Bess asked, glimpsing pale lavender paper among the stems.

Katherine reached for it, read it. *Forgive me, my love,* it said. *Lilies suit you better. You must trust me in this, as in so many things. C.*

"It seems my groom has tricked me," she said slowly, contemplating the mass of waxy blossoms.

"Oh, not a trick, surely," Mrs. Treadwell demurred.

Nanette's brow was furrowed—but only for a moment. "I think he's quite right. Roses are so ordinary," she said then.

"Her mystery suitor didn't seem to think so," Petra piped up. "They were the first flowers he ever sent her, don't you recall? 'Roses, blue larkspur, love-lies-bleeding . . .' "

There was a moment's silence. Then, "It is only one flower for another," Gwen said reasonably.

"Exactly," Katherine agreed, her voice dark.

A knock sounded at the door to the chamber. "Coaches are here, m'ladies!"

"What, already?" Mrs. Treadwell exclaimed. "They cannot be! It is only—"

"Half past ten," Nanette confirmed, with a sudden swift glance at her stepdaughter. "Exactly on time. Everything is proceeding according to plan."

"Must be Lord Dalrymple's military training," Bess said gaily. "Feel free to keep him waiting, though, Katherine. No sense in setting bad precedents."

For one wild instant, Katherine was tempted to keep him waiting forever. She eyed the lilies Petra extended to her, and her head swam with their thick, close scent. She swayed a little on her feet.

"Catch her—she is fainting!" Mrs. Treadwell cried. "I knew she should have had more than toast!"

Gwen and Bess had clutched her elbows. Katherine closed her eyes as Mrs. Treadwell waved hartshorn under her nose. "Butterflies are quite to be expected, aren't they?" Petra asked anxiously, gone pale. "Mrs. Caldburn always said—"

The way his black hair had fanned against the pillow at the inn, that first night, when he had feigned sleep.

In our vows, you will promise to obey me! Or do you intend to counteract that as well?

You want me still. How his eyes had shone in the dying light! *You know that you do. Oh, Katherine, come away with me! Come with me now—*

*I don't see why it should make such a difference to you.
It is only one flower for another.*

We are—

Don't you say it!

Two halves of a whole. Twinned souls.

The room was swimming. Katherine leaned into Gwen and
Bess, willing her heart to steadiness. How could it be that
something she had thought she wanted more than anything
else in the world should frighten her so now? "I love him,"
she whispered, the ache inside her close to overwhelming.

"Of course you do!" Mrs. Treadwell said brightly. But
Bess and Gwen had averted their faces, and Petra was trembling.

Katherine looked again at her headmistress. She thought
of her father, and of the long line of coaches even now drawing up to St. Paul's. She turned to Nanette, but her stepmother was bent over, gathering up the yards of train.

"Time to be going, Katherine," she said, her voice so calm
and assured that they all came to their senses.

"Yes. Yes, of course," Katherine murmured, catching her
skirts in her hands.

"Don't you want a final turn at the looking glass?" Bess
asked teasingly, steering her toward it.

Katherine ducked her head, dodging the image there,
afraid of what she might see. "No. I am ready." She took a
breath, took another, then took the lilies from Petra. "Shall
we be on our way?"

The rain had died down to a smattering by the time Katherine's carriage and that carrying her schoolmates pulled into
the churchyard. They rushed in through a side door, with the
footmen hurrying and dodging to keep umbrellas over their
heads. The small antechamber was chilly and damp; Katherine rubbed her satin sleeves, trying to keep warm. Mrs.
Treadwell leveled an appraising glance at her, then reached
into her reticule. "A touch of brandy?" she asked, holding
forth a flask.

"Why, Mrs. Treadwell!" Bess exclaimed in feigned shock. "Before luncheon?"

But Katherine reached for it gratefully. "Easy," Nanette cautioned, as she tipped it back. "You aren't used to spirits."

Oh, Katherine thought, *but I am. I live with them each night.* The burn of the brandy brought her to a sort of resolution, however. She had come this far. Clayton was a fine man; everyone said so. They would be happy enough.

"Lady Devereaux?" The acolyte, small, black-robed, peeked in at the doorway.

Katherine squared her shoulders. "Is it time, then?" He nodded. Through the door, she heard the swell of the organ. Handel; Clayton had wanted Handel. She hadn't had any opinion in that, so she had acquiesced.

Mrs. Treadwell reached to make a final adjustment to the bride's bodice. Nanette took Katherine's face in her hands and kissed her on each cheek. "Good-bye," she said.

"You needn't make it sound so final!" Katherine said bravely, clutching the lilies' stems.

"Oh, but your entire life is about to change!" Petra bubbled, her eyes wide and shining.

Bess hugged Katherine once, tightly. Gwen did as well. "What else could you do?" the dark-haired girl murmured, so softly no one else could hear.

What indeed? Her father was waiting beside the acolyte, to walk her up the aisle. Katherine gave him a bright smile. "I've never seen you look so beautiful, Katherine," he said hoarsely, and offered her his arm.

Mrs. Treadwell and the girls scurried out ahead of them; Nanette, who was Katherine's matron of honor, followed in their wake. Above the organ's stately chords, there was a flutter, a flurry of anticipation from the guests, like the clapping of hundreds of doves' wings.

The duke curled his fingers over Katherine's hand. "I am so proud of you," he told her, and led her out into the vestibule.

The red-carpeted aisle seemed a thousand miles long; the vaulted ceiling, a thousand miles high. Katherine felt as insignificant as a mote of dust amidst the grandeur. Far, far ahead, she could see Clayton waiting for her, tall and straight in his military uniform. The faces of the guests were a blur of smiles; sighs ascended as she passed.

The Christ on the cross above the altar had blue-black hair.

After ages, aeons, they reached Clayton's side. Incense hung in the air; the flames on the candles were high and flickering. The priest was speaking now: "Dearly beloved . . . in the sight of God . . . who gives this woman to be married?" The duke bowed a little, relinquishing her hand with a benevolent smile. Clayton's yellow diamond sparkled there. She looked down at it, took comfort in its permanent glitter. She felt steadier now, with the solid splendor of stone all around her, with the timeworn words of the priest. Everything was just as she had always imagined. Clutching the host of lilies, she stole a glance at Clayton. There was admiration in his eyes.

"If there be any man here," the priest said, the words a little rushed, perfunctory, "who knows of any impediment to the joining of this man and this woman—"

"I know of an impediment," a voice said suddenly.

The priest, on an accustomed roll, kept going: "Let him speak now, or hold his peace."

"An impediment exists," that voice insisted, over an abrupt babble of outrage from the congregation. Katherine stood staring up at the martyred Christ, unable, unwilling, to acknowledge what had just soared into her heart.

Clayton felt no such compunction; he let go her hand and put his fist to his sword. "What the devil," he growled.

The priest was looking dumbfounded. "An impediment?" he managed to squeak out.

"Aye," said that deep, French-inflected voice. "A prior betrothal of the lady."

Clayton's head whipped to Katherine so quickly that his mustache quivered. "A *betrothal*?" he said—nay, shouted at her. "A *betrothal*? You agreed to marry him?"

"I . . ." Katherine gave up the fight, gave in to the enormous chasm yawning at her silk-clad toes. "I suppose I did."

"Under duress!" Clayton bellowed. "For fear of your life!"

For fear of her life . . . Katherine turned then, looking to Petra and Bess and Gwen. Had they—but their mouths were hanging open; their eyes were enormous with astonishment. And Mrs. Treadwell never . . . She let her gaze move further, sought him out among the crowd. He was standing in the midst of the aisle, coatless, his white shirt unbuttoned at the throat. Laughter threatened to overtake her; she quelled it quickly as she saw that his blue eyes had uncertainty in them still. "No," she confessed. "Under no duress."

The priest cleared his throat. "A prior betrothal . . . confirmed by both parties . . . I'm very much afraid . . ."

Clayton yanked Katherine's arm, pulling her back to face the crucified Christ. "By God," he hissed, "this is your last chance, Katherine. Renounce him. Renounce him now."

She tried to turn to Alain, caught only a glimpse of Bess shaking her head frantically, and Gwen and Petra standing petrified, and Mrs. Treadwell swooning down into a pew. Somehow, she found her voice. "I do renounce him," she said firmly, the words ringing in the hush.

Beside her, Nanette let out her tight-held breath.

"Katherine! How can you!" Alain shouted to her.

"That's my girl," Clayton said complacently, patting her hand as he clasped it in his.

"Why? *Why*?" Alain Montclair demanded, coming forward, boot heels clicking on the stones.

And Clayton let her turn at last. "Because," she said to that solitary figure in the aisle, "I am not worthy of you."

Clayton drew away from her, repulsed. "*You* are not worthy?"

But Alain was grinning, striding toward her. "Ah, *chérie*. You must never say that."

"It is true!" she insisted, as Clayton stared at her in dismay. "You are so much my better—"

The hubbub in the church had risen to an uproar. "Not *worthy*?" women were echoing. "Her better?" the men were barking. "Who the devil is he, anyway?" "Never saw him before in my life!" In the sea of faces, Katherine saw, quite clearly, Lord Bannister, who was nodding emphatically.

Clayton had recovered himself; he grabbed for her, thrust her behind him. "I'd strongly suggest you remove yourself, sir!" he roared at Alain, brandishing his sword.

Alain had raised his shoulders in a shrug, Katherine saw as she peeked around Clayton. "Do you barbarous English take your brides by force still?" he asked, with his rogue's smile.

"Not one more step!"

Alain clucked at the sword pointed toward him. "Against an unarmed man, milord?"

"Don't think that will stop me!" Clayton roared.

Alain spread his hands in a gesture of reconciliation. "*Eh bien,* suppose we leave it up to the lady?"

"We will do no such thing!" Clayton whirled on the priest. "Go on. Go on and speak the service, dammit!"

"M-milord, I cannot! If they are already promised in the sight of God—"

"That blackguard knows no God!"

Alain laughed, and Katherine's heart buckled at the sound. "Ah, but I do, now. Katherine?"

Clayton's fist over hers was like iron. "Don't you listen to his poison! A man without honor, without reputation—what sort of life would you have?"

"It never will be dull, *chérie,*" Alain promised, making Petra giggle from her pew.

Katherine hesitated, raising her eyes to the vaulted ceiling so high above her. It was lofty, aye, but it was still a ceiling. A limit. An end. Whereas with Alain . . .

Gently she reached down, disengaging Clayton's clenched hand from hers. "I'm sorry," she told him. "I truly am sorry. I tried. But it seems I am a bad penny too." She dropped the lilies where she stood, tugged the veil from her hair and let it drift to the floor. Then she unfastened the pearls she wore at her ears, and the necklace that matched them, and slid the yellow diamond from her finger. They fell with a dull clatter. The congregation let out a collective gasp.

Alain's blue eyes were shining. "Bring nothing with you,"

he said, holding out his hand to her. "Nothing of the past."

She knew better than that now, though. "Poppa," she said, looking to where the duke stood, ashen-faced, in the front pew. "Poppa, forgive me. I love him. What else can I do?" The duke of Marne opened his mouth to speak, but she ran to him and hugged him before he could. "And I love you too. Forever, Poppa. Be happy for me. I am so happy. Please."

"I—"

"God go with you, Katherine," Nanette said quietly, kissing her brow. And the duke's arms, that had encircled his daughter as though to hold her there, opened slowly to let her go.

"Hip-hip-hooray!" old Lord Bannister shouted with glee.

That started a general ruckus. Gwen and Bess and Petra pressed into the aisle toward Katherine to embrace her. The guests were craning to see, chattering, gesturing, exclaiming. Alain waited silently, smiling, until she had made her adieus. Then he swept her up, train and all, and kissed her, so soundly that her schoolmates sighed and more than one matron had to fan herself wildly. In that kiss Katherine tasted the future, limitless and boundless, and she threw her arms around his neck and returned it just as passionately.

He carried her all the way down the long aisle to the doors. She did not once look back.

Forty-four

They rode toward Dover in a soft autumn rain that streaked Katherine's fine skirts and plastered her curls to her head. She cared nothing for it; his arms were around her, and she leaned against his chest. He had a cloak in his saddlebag that he drew about them. "Typical of you not to wear it into the church," she muttered, "so you would at least be decently clad."

"I thought the shirtsleeves more dramatic. Don't you agree?"

"You were very dramatic. And for once, your timing was apt."

"I'll have you know I was more than two hours early. I had to skulk about the churchyard in the rain until the opportune moment. Is it any wonder I looked a sight?"

She laughed. "Who sent for you?"

"I never will lie to you, Katherine. But I may not always tell the entire truth."

"Was it Lord Bannister?"

"No."

"You know he thinks you a grand hero. He wants to settle an English pension on you, have you decorated by the regent."

She felt him shudder. "Dotty old man."

"Was it Bess? Gwen? It could not have been Petra—"

"Stop guessing," he said, and kissed her ear. "Then I won't have to lie. Where would you like to stop for the night?"

"Oh, am I to be in charge of our itinerary?"

"That much of it, at least."

"Where *are* we going?"

"I haven't decided yet."

"Would you do me a favor?"

"Anything."

"Would you cut away this damnable train?"

He obliged, with a knife he pulled from his belt. Ten yards of spangled French satin tumbled down into the roadside mud. "That will make some early rising farmwife exceedingly glad," he observed.

"You are such a commoner at heart. Why did you never tell me that Veronique and Joseph were your parents?"

"You never asked."

"Do they know that you came here after me?"

"I told Veronique. I am counting on her to bring my father around."

She laughed again, tasting the sweet rain. "Odd. I am counting on Nanette for the same thing."

They had rounded a hill. The Kentish countryside stretched out before them, dun-brown and sodden. Across a stretch of empty fields, Katherine glimpsed a small hut, the sort her father's shepherds used on summer nights while they watched the flocks. "There," she said, pointing. "Let's stop there."

"Oh, no. An inn. Someplace where we can get you warm and dry, have a hot meal—"

"If you are the man I think you are, Alain Montclair, you have bread and cheese in these saddlebags. Well?"

He paused, then admitted: "I do. And a very fine *saucisse*. I also have a bottle of Nuits-Saint-Georges."

"And a corkscrew?"

"And a corkscrew."

"That settles it, then." She grabbed the reins and steered their mount away from the road.

"I did think a bed, at least," Alain murmured, as the horse's hooves plunged into the mud.

She turned to him accusingly. "Do you know how long it has been since I have lain with you?"

"Three hundred and forty-four nights."

The precision of the answer brought her close to tears.

The hut was empty, of course, at this time of year. But there was a mound of straw in one corner, not too matted, and the dirt floor was dry. He spread his cloak across the straw, brought out the bread and cheese and sausage, uncorked the wine, and handed her the bottle. "A toast," he proposed, and then stopped, his breath catching.

Katherine stared at him, clutching the wine. "What is it?" He looked so different suddenly, so unlike the cocksure man who had swept her away from her groom in front of all the ton. His azure eyes were shaded gray, and his smile had vanished, replaced by a strange, grave uncertainty.

"What have I done to you, Katherine?" he whispered brokenly. "Have I done wrong by you? I have so little to offer—"

"You have everything I need," she told him fiercely, and set the wine aside to kiss him, pushing him into the straw. "I was nothing without you."

"He—"

"Never loved me. Never *knew* me. Not the way you do." She pressed against him in her soaked finery. "Twinned souls," she whispered, and he laughed.

"So. You admit it at last."

"I do. It is one of the great mysteries of the universe. But there you have it. We are halves of one whole. There never could be anyone else for me."

He raised himself up on the straw to kiss her mouth, sweetly, tenderly. "Nor for me. Marry me, Katherine."

"We are wed already. We have been since time began."

He stared straight into her eyes as he pulled the sleeves of her wedding gown away. She felt his manhood surge to hardness at her thigh, and the sensation was devastating. She put her hand to him there, and he groaned with pleasure, pressing against her eager fingertips. Katherine sighed with relief. "What?" he demanded, drawing away.

She pulled him back. "Never you mind. Get me out of this gown."

He complied, coping admirably with the complicated hooks and buttons. "Have you ever undressed a bride before?" she could not resist asking.

"Never. But I am enjoying it immensely." He released her stays, put his mouth to her breast with wild eagerness. She arched against him, mad with longing, and could hear the pounding of his heart.

"Where have you been all this time?" she whispered.

"After you sent me away, you mean?" He was rolling her stockings down.

"I am sorry for that," she said abjectly, then remembered, with a flash of spirit: "But why did you not tell me then that you were spying for England?"

He paused, his hands caught in a web of silk. "I never was a spy for England," he said with firm dignity. "I was a spy *against* Napoleon. There is a difference. And I did not tell you because you would not have believed it."

"Of course I would have!"

"You would not. You would have thought I was making up tall tales."

Would she have? Probably. But it did not matter anymore. Not now. She nodded at him as he held the stocking halfway down her calf. "Are you going to get on with that?"

"I don't know. Are you going to interrupt me with more questions?" She shook her head, wet curls swinging. "Very well, then. I will." And he did.

She knelt then, clad in only her drawers, and unbuttoned his shirt, drawing it over his head while he aimed kisses at her breasts through the linen, making her laugh. He unfastened his belt himself, and his breeches, as she kissed the side of his neck. The wound on his chest had healed over in a smooth, raised welt; she traced it with her tongue. "Wait, wait," he murmured, yanking the breeches off. But his frantic haste dissipated as he looked down at her in the dim light; he simply sat, naked, and stared, for so long that she ducked her head, arms crossed in front of her.

"Nanette says I am grown too thin," she said, biting her lip.

"Languishing for me, were you?"

"I believe I was." She hoped he would not laugh.

He didn't, of course. He reached to pull her arms away, ran his fingers slowly downward from her shoulders, over her breasts to her waist. "No one has ever languished for me before," he whispered, then followed his hands with his mouth, kissing her with impossible gentleness. As his lips brushed her nipple, Katherine shivered. He drew the cloak around them with one hand as the other tugged at the string to her drawers. The bow slid free, and he pushed the linen— so carefully embroidered, with so different a life in mind— over her belly, her thighs, her knees. He let his fingers play through the tight curls that capped her mound of Venus, kissed her there, slid a hand behind her buttocks as his mouth came up to claim hers. His manhood was rock-hard against her. He kissed her nipple, took it in his mouth, rolled it with his tongue, pulled at the taut bud.

Katherine felt the stirrings of that long-lost fire in her loins, wondered how she had ever thought anything she felt for Clayton had compared to it. Then she pushed him out of her mind—or he was pushed away, rather, by Alain's caresses, as winsome as the autumn rain.

"Oh," she whispered as his fingers reached down again and stroked her thighs, as he rose onto his knees and kissed her breasts with wild longing. "Oh, Alain, I *have* missed you!"

He did laugh then, but it came out a strangled groan; she had wrapped her hand around his manhood, was guiding it toward her. Guiding it . . .

"Home," he grunted, as that thick shaft pierced her, sank into her, as he buried himself in her warm, wet sheath. "Oh, we are home at last!" And it was true; she knew it even as she tightened her knees at his waist, drawing him closer, deeper, as far as forever. Home was here; home was wherever she was, so long as she was with him. The ceiling of the hut, not so high as his shoulder, was as distant as the measureless stars.

He began to move inside her, up and then down again, in a strong, sure cadence. She opened herself to him, clinging to him, sighs mounting as he quickened his pace. He looked into her eyes and smiled. Then he laughed, abandoning himself to the sensation of her flesh enclosing his, her hips following his, her arms encircling him, their mouths together, their hearts pounding, their souls, their twinned souls, rejoined in this miraculous way. Again and again he thrust into her, plunged inside her. It was everything she had remembered in those long, lonely nights of remembering—it was that, and more. For there were no barriers between them now; they were both laid clean and whole and bare. He gave, and she gave, and there was no separating their pleasure, just as there were no ears but theirs to hear their wild, breathless cries.

"I. Love. You," he told her, matching each word to a hard, swift thrust.

"Oh, Alain. Alain—"

"Forever. Forever. Forever." He could not hold out much longer; he was near to bursting.

"Alain! Oh, Alain! Oh, God!" She was dangling from the verge of a cliff, hanging on by sheer will, wanting to prolong the moment, wanting him to come with her, wanting him to go first, wanting—

"Ohhhh," he groaned, with a final thrust that sent his seed spurting.

"Oh!" Katherine answered—screamed—as he emptied himself into her, as the ecstasy shimmered through her in tremulous waves. She grabbed at him, holding him tighter while his manhood pulsed, convulsed with flares of fire. They shuddered against one another, trying desperately to catch their breath. He surfaced first, flinging back his midnight hair that had worked loose of its queue.

"To think of all that passion wasted on an English duke's son," he said, an eyebrow cocked.

Katherine lay with her eyes closed. "I never . . . went so far with him."

"Of course you didn't. How would you dare to, after you'd had me?"

Her eyes flew open. "Oh! You are the most conceited—"

"With good reason," he said complacently, reaching for the Nuits-Saint-Georges.

"With good reason," she confessed, and he handed her the bottle first, with that grin.

"Hungry?" he asked then.

"Ravenous."

He fed her slices of sausage and cheese and bread from the tip of his knife, until she could eat no more. Then he devoured the remains, every crumb, while she curled contentedly beneath his cloak, watching him eat and drink. "We shall have a scant breakfast," she observed.

"It is a long time till breakfast," he said, and caught her in his arms again.

When he had made love to her once more, thoroughly, with languid leisure, she fell asleep inside the curl of his arms. Alain waited until he was sure she would not waken, then settled her on the straw and went to his saddlebag. He took out ink and quill and paper, lit a candle, and penned a note in his neat, square hand:

21 September
Her Grace, the duchess of Marne
Marne House, Kent

Ma Chère Duchess:
 Ten thousand—nay, ten million—thanks for your timely message. We have spent the night, at Katherine's instigation, in a crofter's hut along the through road. It does not seem to have caused your daughter to regret her choice. Please convey my apologies to His Grace for the unseemly disruption of this afternoon's ceremonies. Assure him as best you can that I will take care of her. I treasure her more than I do my life. When we are settled—wherever we may settle, if indeed we settle—we look forward to welcoming you both to our home.

He turned to look at Katherine, asleep in the candlelight. Her gold hair lay in long, bright curls against the blanket; her rosebud lips, bruised a bit from their passion, were parted in a smile. He smiled, too, recalling what he had told Christiane once about his distaste for English misses. He must write to Christiane as well to thank her, and to Mrs. Treadwell. But not tonight.

There was a little wine still left in the bottle. He reached for it, tipped it toward Katherine and then toward the heavens in a silent toast. He could taste her toes in its heady savor. The notion made him smile.

She stirred in her sleep, one long white arm stretching above her head and then falling to the straw beside her, reaching for him. He hurried to conclude his letter, before she should wake.

My life has been something less than honorable until now, he wrote, chewing on his lip, wondering how to put down in words what he felt in his soul. *But what you have committed into my care is a gift so precious, it takes the breath from my chest. I will not fail you, or her. I swear it to you, by the stars in my Katherine's eyes.*

"Alain?" She sat up in the tangle of his cloak, wide awake and frightened. "Alain, where—" Then she saw him, and the tension went out of her, visibly. "I was so afraid," she whispered. "Afraid . . . that it was only a dream."

He scrawled his name, folded the letter swiftly, tucked it into his bag. "It *is* a dream," he told her, and pinched out the candle, slipping back beside her on the straw, taking her in his arms, kissing her forehead. "A dream come true."

"It is, isn't it?" she said happily. "There were so many nights that I dreamed of you. Did you dream of me?"

"Every moment. Waking and sleeping," he told her fiercely, and she laughed. "What? What is it?" he demanded, his head at her breast.

She stroked his silken hair. "When I . . . when I would go to balls and such with Clayton, I would look at the couples around us and wonder—what sort will we wind up to be, after we are married? And I never could envision an answer. Now I know why."

"Why?"

"Because I never saw him in my future. Only you. Always you." She raised herself up on her elbows in the darkness. "Oh, we are blessed, aren't we, Alain My Dear Heart?"

"Beyond measure. Beyond reason, Katherine," he told her, and kissed her again.